Teach Me to Fly

TANISHA HEADLEY

PLAYLIST

Panic Room - Au/Ra
Hi-Lo (Hollow) - Bishop Briggs
River - Bishop Briggs
Tears of Gold - Faouzia
Trampoline - SHAED
Joke's On You - Charlotte Lawrence
Walls Could Talk - Halsey
Savage - Bahari
Dark Side - Bishop Briggs
Nightmare - Halsey
Monsters - Ruelle
White Flag - Bishop Briggs
Soldier - Tommee Profitt, Fleurie
Overwhelmed - Royal & the Serpent
Queen - Loren Gray
I'm a Mess - Bebe Rexha
Born Without a Heart - Faouzia
Sweet Little Lies - bülow
Good in Goodbye - Madison Beer
Assassin - Au/Ra

Devil Devil - MILCK
Black Sea - Natasha Blume
Dance in the Dark - Au/Ra
Devil I Know - Allie X
Princesses Don't Cry - CARYS
Afterlife - Hailee Steinfeld
Yes & No - XYLØ
911 - Ellise
This Mountain - Faouzia
Middle Finger - Bohnes

CONTENT WARNINGS

This book contains sensitive subject matter that may be distressing for some readers. Themes include: sexual assault, non-consensual and dubious consent scenarios, self-harm, suicidal ideation, suicide attempts, depression, emotional trauma, and parental neglect.

This story is a fictional exploration of pain, survival, intimacy, and healing. It reflects my personal interpretation and lived experience with mental health, trauma, and neglect. Every journey is unique—this one is raw, imperfect, and honest in the ways I know how to tell it.

Please remember that while reading, it's okay to pause, step away, or choose not to continue. Your mental and emotional safety always comes first.

If you or someone you know is struggling, you are not alone and you matter.

Canada: Talk Suicide Canada — Call or Text 988 (available 24/7)
https://talksuicide.ca

USA: Suicide & Crisis Lifeline — Call or Text 988 (available 24/7)
https://988lifeline.org

Samaritans (UK & Ireland) — Call 116 123 (Free, 24/7)
Website: https://www.samaritans.org

If you're outside Canada, the U.S., or the U.K., you can find local crisis lines through
Find a Helpline (by Lifeline International):
https://findahelpline.com

**Some details of the professional ballet world have been altered for your reading enjoyment.**

To the ones who flinch from touch,
You did not deserve what happened.
You did not cause it.
You were never meant to carry that blame.
Not then.
Not now.
Not ever.

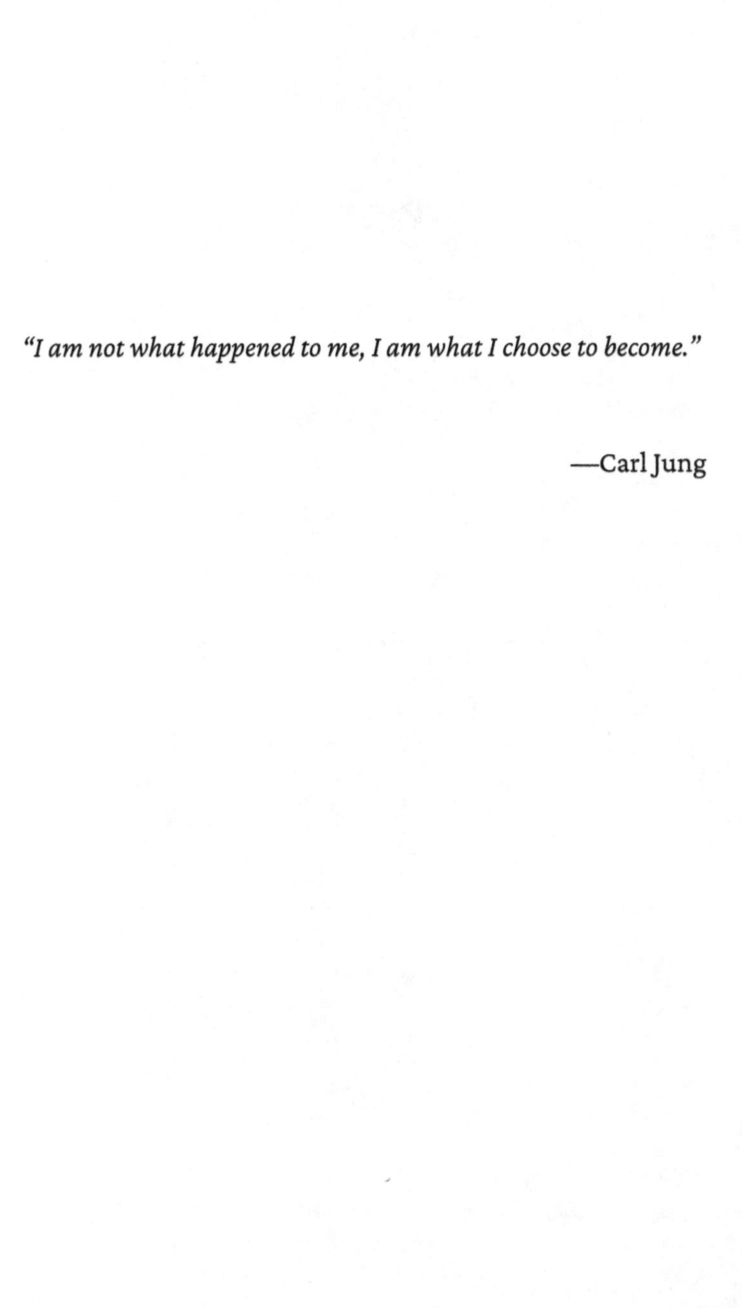

"I am not what happened to me, I am what I choose to become."

—Carl Jung

CHAPTER 1

ANGELIQUE

The New York sun melts against the horizon as long, golden orange rays beam through the tall windows of Studio Three at the Big Apple Ballet Company. Dust motes dance in the light while I stand at the centre of the floor, sweat clinging to my spine under my black leotard.

We should've called it hours ago but my dance partner, Alec, insisted we stay after hours. He said we needed to run the lifts again, and he's not wrong. We fucked up almost every single one during group rehearsal today. We were out of sync and clashing every chance we got, which is highly unusual for us. And with opening night just around the corner, it's not something we can afford to ignore.

Alec is attractive—dark, tousled hair, light brown eyes, and a jawline sculpted for Hollywood. But he's arrogant, and distastefully cocky. He's the type of guy who thinks talent and his parents' money make him untouchable, and I've never liked him for it.

"Okay, Alec," I say breathlessly, hands braced on my

1

hips. "Let's get our shit together and hit this one clean. I want to go home."

He nods, just as winded, but I notice something flicker in his eyes as he stares at me. A shift, or more like a crack in his mask, but I brush off the wariness that creeps into my subconscious, and that's my first mistake.

We move into position again and he lifts me—hands finding my waist as I rise, arching backward across his shoulder, my arms extended in perfect swanlike form. I prepare for the descent, the controlled slide down his body to the ground, but his hand moves. Sliding down, fast and firm, over the curve of my ass and slipping between my thighs. He cups me through my tights, bold and obscene.

I gasp, startled, as my body locks in midair. My spine jerks in on itself, trying to recoil until Alec finally releases me and I fall, the impact knocking the wind from my lungs as I hit the floor hard, my hip slamming against the wood, pain exploding from the impact.

"What the fuck was that?" I scream, looking up at him, pissed and humiliated.

He stalks toward me in two quick strides before he's on top of me, shoving me flat on my stomach and forcing my face against the floor. The wood is cold against my cheek and the pressure of his palm on my skull is almost unbearable. My limbs scramble, flailing for leverage, but he's too strong.

"Alec, stop. What are you doing?" I ask, my voice shaking and desperate sounding.

"Shut up," he spits. "I'm sick of you always calling out orders in front of everyone as if you run shit."

His hand trails down my back, fingers grazing the arch of my spine before going lower.

"No," I beg as my voice cracks and tears blur my vision. "Please don't do this."

But he's already pulling at my leotard, fingers curling into the seam between the fabric and my tights. He yanks hard, ripping it down, and the sound of the tear echoes in the studio.

"You think just because your mom's the director that makes you untouchable?" he sneers, dragging his fingers through the torn gap in my leotard. "You're just a spoiled little brat who needs to be put in her place."

A scream tears from my throat, jagged and strangled, but it doesn't even sound like me anymore. He rips through my tights and underwear next with a vicious yank, the sound of tearing fabric drowned only by the shuffle of his own clothes. A second later, I hear the unmistakable crinkle of a plastic wrapper and instantly know it's a condom.

My heart hammers in my chest as I try to crawl away from him, but he's too strong as he pins my wrists, and his knee digs into my thigh as he presses the head of his cock against my entrance.

"No—please—" I gasp, but the word barely escapes my lips before he shoves himself inside me.

A white-hot pain rips through me, like fire, like being split in two. I scream again, but it's swallowed by his palm as it clamps over my mouth. My eyes lock on the mirror in front of us, unable to breathe, as I see my face twisted in horror.

Is this real? Is this actually happening to me?

He thrusts, hard and fast, each time worse than the last, like he's trying to destroy something inside me. The friction is unbearable and my vision swims as I clench my teeth, trying to anchor myself, my fingers clawing at the wooden floor as I try not to fall apart. I want to disappear, to vanish into the air, into the mirror, into the light outside of the windows. I want to be anywhere but here.

It doesn't last long and when he finishes, he pulls out and yanks the condom off quickly, holding it up like some twisted trophy.

"You'll never be able to prove it was me if you try to tell anyone." He sneers, breathless, tucking himself back into his tights with that same sickening ease.

He glances down at me, spent and shattered. "See you tomorrow, pigeon," he mutters, a smug little smirk curling his lips.

Then he turns, the condom still dangling from his hand, and walks out of the studio, leaving the door wide open behind him.

I don't move for several minutes. I can't. So, I stay on my stomach, exposed and shaking, my cheek still pressed to the same floor I danced on only moments ago. My body aches in places I didn't even know could hurt and when I reach down and touch between my legs, I'm not at all surprised to find that my fingers come away stained red.

I stare at the blood, gutted. I didn't think *this* would be how I lost my virginity—violated on a cold studio floor, with no choice, no love, no tenderness. Only fear, and pain. I'd always thought my first time would be... something else. Maybe not perfect, but real. Chosen. Something I'd remember because I wanted to. Instead, this is what I get. Blood and silence and shame.

Slowly, I curl into myself, my arms wrapped tight around my body, trying to hold in the pieces of who I used to be. And I cry until there's nothing left inside me except numb, hollow silence.

When I can finally stand, I limp toward my duffel bag, my muscles screaming with every step. I shakily peel off what's left of my leotard and tights and use them to wipe the blood from my thighs before tugging on my sweatpants. The softness of the fabric against my torn skin feels like a mockery.

Before I leave, I catch my reflection in the mirror again, but the girl staring back at me isn't the same person she was only hours ago. The guilt hits me like a truck, shame seeping into my bloodstream.

"I let this happen," I whisper, voice barely audible. "I let myself get raped."

I cry again, silent, broken sobs that only I hear.

I DON'T GO TO REHEARSALS THE NEXT DAY, OR THE DAY AFTER. Instead, I stay curled up in bed, limbs sore, stomach twisting every time I close my eyes and see his face. It takes four days before my absence is escalated to the company director, who happens to be my mother. She summons me to the company with a clipped email. No warmth or concern, just a demand that I meet her in her office at three this afternoon.

When I step into the building, I'm drowning in the baggiest sweatpants I own and an oversized T-shirt that hangs off me like a curtain, swallowing every curve of the body that no longer feels like mine. A black baseball cap shadows most of my face, concealing the hollow, sleepless bruises beneath my eyes.

I keep my head down, praying that no one looks too closely. But I can't shake the suffocating paranoia that everyone's watching. That somehow, they all know what happened, and they're silently judging.

I hold my breath the entire walk through the halls,

flinching every time I hear footsteps behind me, terrified that it's Alec. That he'll corner me again, touch me again, break me all over again as if it's possible to break any more than I already have.

When I reach my mother's office, I knock softly, my knuckles barely making a sound.

"Come in," she calls, distractedly.

My mother, Analise Sinclair, is seated behind her massive oak desk, manicured fingers flying across her keyboard, the rhythmic clicking the only sound in the room. Her long blonde hair is pulled into a high ponytail, so tight it tugs at the edges of her already botoxed face, not a single strand out of place. Her skin is pale, porcelain-like, a stark contrast to my tanned brown complexion—one of the many reminders that I belonged more to my father than to her.

When I step into her office, her green eyes lift and scan me, taking in the baseball cap, the baggy clothes, the hunched posture. But then she returns to typing, like none of it matters.

"Take a seat," she says, chin jutting toward the chair across from her like I'm just another staff member she's too busy and annoyed to deal with.

I move stiffly across the room on trembling legs, and lower myself into the seat, wincing when my body touches the cushion, still tender. I sit upright, rigid, hands folded tightly in my lap as I try to breathe past the pain. She finishes her typing with an aggressive tap of the Enter key, then turns to me with a tight-lipped frown.

"Care to explain why our principal dancer has been skipping her rehearsals?" No *hello* or *is everything okay?*

"This production is crucial, Angelique," she continues before I can reply. "Your understudy has had to fill in for your parts, and frankly, she can't compare. The board's been breathing down my neck to make sure everything runs flawlessly. You disappearing? It's put me in a tough position."

I stare at her. The woman who used to kiss the bruises on my knees once upon a time and tell me I was born to dance. The one who, as a child, I believed would burn the world down to protect me. But all I see now is the director. The brand. The mask she wears for the company that's consumed her since she divorced my dad ten years ago and moved here. Whatever warmth existed in her eyes back then is long gone.

"Something happened," I manage, my voice quiet and raspy. It feels like the first time I've spoken since that night.

Because it is.

She stiffens, pausing mid-scroll. "Elaborate."

"Alec." I almost vomit at the sound of his name coming from my mouth.

Her eyes narrow and there's a long pause before she speaks again. "Did you two fuck?"

I blink. "What?"

"Are you pregnant?" she asks, folding her arms across her chest, jaw clenched, tone ice-cold.

The breath leaves my lungs in a gust. "No, mom...he raped me," I whisper. "He...he held me down and—" The words die on my tongue, caught in the barbed wire of shame and agony. My throat burns and I feel like I'm choking on the words.

Silence stretches between us, thick and suffocating. I fidget with my fingers while I wait for her to erupt. For her face to twist with outrage on my behalf, and for her arms to open as her voice trembles with horror. I wait for the mother I thought I knew, but when she finally speaks, it's like she's picking her words from a crisis PR handbook.

"Angelique...do you understand what you're saying?" she asks, as if I'm delusional. "Alec is one of our senior dancers. His parents donate hundreds of thousands to the company every year. If this story gets out—if the press gets wind of it—it won't just be him they come for. It'll be the company. It'll be you. Do you want the world to know that you've been raped?"

A sharp ache slices through my chest, sudden and deep, as if something inside me has cracked clean in two.

That would be my heart.

"I don't give a fuck about the press," I say, my voice rising. "Or what the world thinks."

She exhales sharply through her nose, composed even in disgust. "We can't be reckless about this, okay? We need to protect what we've built. Think about your future, and your name. You don't need something as shameful as this following you around for the rest of your life."

The bile rises in my throat, burning the back of my mouth as I stare at her, stunned.

"Shameful?" I repeat. "Am I the one that did something wrong?"

She doesn't answer, but I can tell by her expression that I'm beginning to get on her nerves.

"Are you...are you asking me to keep this quiet?" My voice breaks at the idea. "You want me...to protect him? To protect some sort of company image?"

"I want you to be smart," she snaps. "Think about the bigger picture. You're a dancer, Angelique. You've trained your entire life to get into a company as prestigious as this and become a principal dancer. Are you willing to throw it all away over one misunderstanding?"

"Misunderstanding?" I whisper.

She falters, just for a moment, then pivots, eyes darting toward her schedule. "Take some time away. Maybe it's best if you go back to England for a while. Stay with the Harrington's. You've always said you loved it there," she says, returning to her typing. "I'll find a way to give you a respectable exit from the company."

Her words land like a blow to the chest. That's it. No rage, no tears, no *I believe you*. And it's in that moment—sitting in her cold, sterile office, aching in every part of my body—that I know she doesn't believe me. Or worse...she does, and she just doesn't care.

"You're letting me go? But what about the production?" I ask, feeling my hands go cold from the lack of oxygen. It's hard to breathe when your heart feels like it's ripping out of your chest.

"We'll make do with your understudy," she says with a shrug.

I keep staring at her, waiting for something to shift. For a sign of the woman who used to braid my hair and sneak me hot chocolate before rehearsals. But there's nothing behind her eyes except cold calculation and ambition.

And that's the moment it all breaks. Everything. My faith, my trust, and the last tiny piece of love I held for her. Without a word, I rise and walk out of her office, my footsteps echoing in the quiet halls, and I don't look back as I push my way out the front doors.

By the time I'm in a cab and heading to my small apartment, the numbness in me cracks. My heart is shattered, my body bruised, and my soul? It feels scraped raw. I make a silent promise to myself in that moment that I'm never dancing professionally again.

CHAPTER 2

ANGELIQUE

ONE MONTH LATER

When I step out of the arrivals terminal at Heathrow, the sun has dipped low enough to create long shadows that stretch across the tarmac. Lavender clouds stain the sky, tinged with burnt orange, and the air smells faintly like jet fuel and impending rain.

Almost immediately, I spot my best friend, Lando. He leans against his sleek black Audi like a cover model. Gold-rimmed sunglasses perch on his head despite the fading light, and his loosely knotted designer scarf flutters just enough to make it seem intentional.

He wears tailored linen pants and a form-fitting beige sweater that somehow looks both impossibly cozy and undeniably couture. His blond curls are tied back in a half-bun, and his entire posture oozes a casual glamor I've never been able to pull off.

He waves excitedly the moment he sees me, then breaks into a jog, but the second he gets close enough to get a good look at me, his smile falters and he comes to a full stop.

"Jesus, bestie," he whispers, stepping forward, his

voice cracking with concern. "You look like roadkill. Beautiful, slightly tragic roadkill, but roadkill nonetheless."

I try to laugh, but it comes out broken. Thankfully, he doesn't push for an actual smile. He just reaches out and wraps me in his arms, but the second he touches me, I flinch, and he freezes.

"Sorry," I murmur, shrinking away from his touch. "I... I'm just..."

"It's okay," he says quietly, pulling back and taking my suitcase from my hand. "I'll follow your lead."

It takes everything I have not to break apart right then and there. The softness in his voice nearly undoes me, but I nod, biting the inside of my cheek until I taste blood, and follow him to his car.

"Thanks again for buying my ticket to come here," I say as we get into the car. "I would've bought it myself, but I haven't been working for a few weeks, and I guess I never expected New York to eat up my years of savings within a single month."

"You don't have to thank me," he says. "You know I'd do anything for you."

I swallow past the lump in my throat. "I promise as soon as I get my shit together, I'll get my own place and pay you ba—"

"Don't be ridiculous, Angelique," he interrupts, shooting me a look. "You can stay for as long as you'd like, you know that my family adores you. And you are not paying me back."

After a pause, he gently adds, "But I hope at some point you'll tell me what really happened. I didn't even know you left The Big Apple Ballet until I saw the company's post thanking you for your 'years of contribution.'" He lifts a brow. "What the hell does that even mean? You were their star."

My throat tightens again, but this time for a different reason. I look out the window, unsure how to answer. I'm grateful when he doesn't press further, letting out a soft sigh.

We start the drive in silence, except for the radio playing mellow indie music while the world blurs past my window. The further we get from London, the more my shoulders drop, as if the air in the city was too heavy to breathe properly, as if every inch further from New York brings back a sense of safety.

I've always preferred the countryside over the city. Out here, in the open stretch of land leading to Marlow, I feel the ache of tiredness settle deep into my bones. Lando glances at me every so often, his knuckles tight on the steering wheel. I know he wants to ask what happened, and I can feel the questions pushing at his teeth, but he waits.

"Do you remember this road?" he asks, as we pass a curve in the road lined with tall sycamores that lean like they're listening in.

I nod. "Yeah, my dad used to let me ride in the front seat when we'd come back from the city. He always said the curves make it more fun."

Lando hums. "I remember. He used to call them 'the ballerina bends' and always said they reminded him of you."

The ache that rushes up my throat is sharp and immediate. I stare straight ahead, blinking fast, the weight of his memory pressing into my chest like a knife. I remember sitting in the front seat, balanced on the edge of the armrest, arms stretched out like wings. My dad would laugh and tell me to hold on or I'd fly right out the window.

He never once told me to sit properly or to be careful. He always wanted me to feel free.

When ballet started consuming my life, he was the one who grounded me, and after rehearsals, regardless of if I did well or not, he'd drive me to the little ice cream shop on Main and let me get the biggest cone they had. He'd always joked that ice cream had special powers and that maybe I'd grow wings if I ate enough of it. My dad never cared if I was the best, not the way my mom does. He only cared that I was happy.

I always thought I'd have more time, more drives, more laughter, more ice cream trips. Maybe I would have appreciated all those moments more if I'd known that one morning he'd be there—standing in the kitchen, humming under his breath while making coffee—and then by nightfall, he'd be gone.

A major heart attack, the doctors had said. *Quick and mostly painless.* As if that was supposed to be some kind of mercy. But it hadn't felt merciful. Instead, it had felt like the ground had cracked open and swallowed me whole. Like the entire world had gone deaf to the sound of my heart breaking.

I stopped dancing after he died, because for months I couldn't even look at my pointe shoes without feeling like a fraud. Moving forward felt like a betrayal, and I didn't know how to exist without him rooting for me, without him believing in me even when I didn't believe in myself.

Despite that, life moved on, and the seasons shifted. My mom flew me to New York City shortly after his funeral, and after months of pressuring me to join the company she worked at, The Big Apple Ballet, I started dancing again. But every plié and every pirouette felt hollow in a way I couldn't fix.

My mom didn't comfort me while I mourned his death, she just threw herself deeper into her career instead. Sometimes I wonder if she had been relieved to have one less soft thing in the world to slow her down after the divorce, and there I was uprooting her new life with my softness. With my feelings.

I press my forehead lightly to the cool window glass as we drive on in silence until we finally reach the edge of Marlow. The town hasn't changed much; red brick buildings with ivy-covered facades, little shops with hand-painted signs, the quiet, postcard charm of a place that seems suspended in time. My childhood lives in these streets—in every tree-lined path, and in every cobblestone crack.

By the time we pull up the long gravel driveway of the Harrington estate, the sky is tinted navy, and the air has cooled into evening. The main house looms ahead, ivy creeping along the white stone. To the right, tucked behind a low hedge and a cluster of peony bushes, is the guesthouse. Smaller, yes, but still cozy and beautiful.

Lando parks and turns to me with that same quiet, worried look that he's been wearing since he picked me up.

"Are you okay?" he asks, voice low. "You got quiet on me there."

I manage a nod, though it feels like a lie. "I'm fine."

He doesn't press. Instead, popping the trunk and retrieving my suitcase for me.

The guesthouse is almost exactly as I remember. Same open concept living room with soft, worn couches and white curtains that billow slightly with the breeze. The same gallery wall of framed ballet photos that Lando's mother insisted on hanging before she abandoned his family.

One of them is of me and him, age thirteen, mid-lift during a summer recital. My smile was wide and bright, causing an intense sadness to flood in at the sight of that version of me, forcing me to look away. Lando notices and quietly flips the frames around.

"I thought you might want to stay in the guesthouse instead of in the main house since you have more privacy here."

"Thank you," I whisper.

I don't know how to tell him I'm terrified of being alone in the quiet, but more terrified of not having the option.

"I had the staff prep some chamomile tea before we arrived," he says, trying hard to sound casual. "It's on the counter with honey, because you're a honey girl, not a sugar baby."

I want to smile, and the effort is there, but it doesn't quite land. Thankfully, he doesn't seem to mind. I drop my bag next to the suitcase by the entryway. My body is screaming for a hot bath or shower, for rest, for time to rewind and undo everything that's happened. I drag myself to the kitchen, hands trembling as I wrap them around the mug set out for me.

He doesn't ask me anything, not right away, he just moves through the kitchen like we both belong here.

"Do you want to talk?" he finally asks, leaning against the kitchen island. His voice is soft, careful. "Because I can be the *talk it out* bestie or the *let's drink wine and watch trash TV in our pyjamas* bestie. I'm adaptable."

I shake my head, lowering the mug. "I don't even know where to start."

He nods like he understands, but the crease in his brow deepens. "Alright, well, for the record, I'm here. Okay? You're not alone."

The weight of those words nearly buckles my knees. A breath shudders out of my chest, and I nod, swallowing the rising lump in my throat.

"Thanks, Lando."

"Don't thank me yet. I'm moving into full mother-hen mode. I've already stocked the pantry with all your comfort foods, and yes, I bought three different kinds of chocolate and six kinds of tea because I didn't know which version of your post-breakdown personality was going to show up."

Despite everything, a soft laugh escapes me. It's small, barely there, but it's real. He brightens at the sound, gently taking the mug from my hands.

"I also stocked the fridge with all your favourites, and there are bath salts in the bathroom. I even got those gross jellybeans you used to obsess over as a kid."

I laugh again, a choked little sound that surprises both of us. "You mean the vomit-flavoured ones?" I groan, half-laughing, half-crying.

"Truly, you were a disgusting child." He grins, and for a second, the past feels like a place I can still visit. "Come on. Let's get you settled in. Your room is made up, and I even fluffed the pillows."

"Did you spray them with lavender mist like you used to?"

"Of course I did."

I let him guide me down the short hallway to the primary bedroom, where a queen-sized bed, warm lighting, and an absurd number of pillows wait for me. He sets the tea on the nightstand and dims the lights.

"Go run a bath, I'll drink my tea while I wait. And if you want to cry, scream, or throw something fragile, we have excellent insurance on this place." He says it with a wink, but there's tenderness beneath the joke.

I catch a glimpse of myself in the mirror as I pad into the bathroom across the hall minutes later, and my reflection startles me. I look haunted; the clothes hanging off my thinning body, and my eyes are ringed with shadows. I barely recognize myself.

But maybe that's the point. Maybe the girl who left New York died somewhere in that studio, and the one who arrived in Marlow is all that's left. And if that's true... I have no idea who she is yet.

THE BATH IS HOT ENOUGH TO STING WHEN I SINK IN, A SHARP BITE that used to come from something far more destructive. I don't burn myself with lighters anymore, but sometimes I still chase the ache. The smell of the eucalyptus bath salts fills the air while I let the water scald the day off my skin, watching the surface ripple with each trembling breath. My legs float to the top, golden-brown and tense, the muscles wiry from running on fumes.

On the edge of the tub, beside the untouched bottles of shampoo and body wash that Lando must've set out for me, sits a razor, still wrapped and clean. My gaze catches on it and won't let go.

I used to cut after my dad died. It was the only way I could feel anything that made sense, and the pain was mine, at least. It was predictable and something that I could control, but I stopped when I joined The Big Apple Ballet, when dancing gave me something else to ache for again.

But now, after the last few weeks that I've had, the urge is back. The idea of feeling that kind of pain, of choosing it on my own terms, terrifies me. But what terrifies me more is how much I want to. Just to make it stop, to get a breath in without my lungs catching fire, to remind myself I'm still here. That he didn't take *everything*.

❧

AFTER THE BATH, I MUST'VE LAID MY HEAD ON THE PILLOW AND drifted off, because I jolt awake an hour later—screaming. It tears out of me, violent and guttural, like my lungs are rejecting the memory before my brain can even process it. My body jerks upright, drenched in sweat, sheets twisted around my legs like restraints. My throat burns from the sound clawing its way out, part sob, part scream.

The door slams open seconds later, and I flinch violently, scrambling backward until my spine hits the headboard. Lando stumbles in, wide-eyed and barefoot, wielding the TV remote like a weapon. His sweater twists off one shoulder, hair sticking up like he passed out on the couch. He looks half-crazed with panic.

"Angelique!" he shouts, eyes sweeping the room. "What the hell happened? Are you okay?"

His eyes dart around like someone might step out from behind the curtains, but when he sees that we're alone and it's just me, sobbing into the duvet and shaking uncontrollably, he drops the remote with a thud and rushes over, instinctively reaching for me.

"Hey, hey. It's okay, you're safe. It was just—"

"No!" I shriek, my voice thick from the tears.

I curl in on myself, arms shooting out in a defensive push before I even register what I'm doing. He stumbles back and freezes, mid-step, hands raised like I've pulled a knife on him.

"I'm not going to touch you, love." he says gently, lowering his voice. "You're safe with me. I promise."

The silence that follows is thick and ragged as my breath wheezes in and out of me like my lungs forgot how to work. I pull the duvet higher, burying my face, trying to force my mind back into the present, to remember that I'm in a bedroom miles away from Alec and that it's over; I survived.

"I'm sorry," I whisper after a long, shaking pause. "God, Lando, I'm so sorry."

Lando lowers himself into a crouch beside the bed, slow and careful as his eyes search mine, soft with worry.

"Don't apologize for having a nightmare," he says.

I wipe my face with the sleeve of my robe, the cotton soft against my skin, but I can still feel the ghost of Alec's hands, even though they're long gone. Lando takes a deep breath, then sits down on the edge of the bed with his hands clasped together, elbows on his knees. He draws in a breath, heavy with exhaustion.

"Alright," he says. "I wanted to put this off until you felt ready, but we need to talk. I need to know exactly what I'm dealing with."

I hesitate, but something about the way he says it, free from judgement and with genuine concern, makes it feel possible. So, I tell him everything.

He listens, his jaw tightening as I speak, and his hands curling into fists, but he never interrupts. When I reach the part about my mom, he looks like he might throw up on my behalf.

"Your mother," he mutters, voice trembling with fury. "I always knew she was cold-hearted, but this..." He shakes his head, eyes wild. "She knows and all she did was tell you to come here like it's some fucking holiday?"

I nod. "She wants to protect the company, I guess. And the money his family donates."

"She should want to protect you," he snarls.

Lando shoots to his feet, the mattress lurching from the shift in weight, and begins to pace in tight circles. His fingers tangle in his curls like he wants to rip the rage out of his scalp.

"I'm flying to New York," he says, firmly. "I'm going to strangle that bastard, and your mother, too."

A little unhinged, Lando, but it's warranted, I think to myself.

A sudden buzz cuts through the air, startling him. He groans as he fishes his phone out of his pocket and looks at the glowing screen.

"Shit, I forgot about the party."

He answers, tone clipped. "Yeah? What? No, I'm not dressed yet, because—" his eyes flicker back to mine, softening a little. "Look, I might skip. Just tell them to go easy on the champagne and not to break anything."

He hangs up with a sigh and sits back down beside me, the fight draining from his posture, guilt tugging at the corners of his mouth.

"I planned a thing," he admits. "A house party. Before I knew you were coming. I completely forgot to cancel it."

"Is anyone I know going to be there?"

"Max, Willow, and Alfie." He pauses. "You remember them, right?"

I groan softly, burying my face in the duvet again. "Tell them I'm dead."

"Consider it done," he says dramatically. "Or grievously maimed. Or mysteriously vanished into the Thames River."

Now there's an idea.

"You don't have to stay," I say after a beat. "I mean it.

Go. Have your party. I just want to sleep. That's all I've wanted for weeks."

Lando hesitates. "You sure?"

I nod. "Don't worry about me. I'll lock the door and I'll be fine."

He stands, leans over, and presses a soft kiss to the top of my head. It's the gentlest thing I've felt in years.

"I'll be back in the morning then," he says, voice warm with care. "With croissants, and possibly the blood of my enemies, depending on how drunk Alfie gets me."

"Croissants first," I whisper. "Blood second."

He grins, one of his genuine, Lando-smiles that lights up his whole damn face. "Deal."

And then he's gone, the front door clicking shut behind him. I lay there in the dark, the echo of my nightmare still humming under my skin, but it doesn't feel quite so suffocating now that my best friend knows. For the first time since it happened, I feel a thread of safety wrapping around me—thin and tentative, but real. It's not much, but it's something.

CHAPTER 3

ANGELIQUE

Thirty minutes.

That's how long I lie in bed, eyes wide open, staring at the ceiling as if it holds the secret to sleep. *News flash, it doesn't.*

My mind is a wrecking ball, slamming again and again into everything I'm trying not to think about. I need to knock myself out, and what better way to do that than exhaust my social battery? Exhaustion has always been a better lullaby for me than peace and quiet.

With a groan, I shove the covers off and drag my suitcase onto the bed, digging through it until I find something halfway decent—black boyfriend jeans, a cropped grey tank top, my old black leather jacket, and sneakers.

It's not completely baggy—more fitted than what I've been wearing these past few weeks—but the pants and jacket will keep my shape hidden enough where I won't feel so exposed. Small steps. That's all I can manage right now.

I pull the tank top over my head, then reach for my jacket, and that's when I see them. Two thin, raw lines

22

slashing across the soft brown skin just beneath my wrist bone. They aren't deep—it was too difficult to cut deep using a shaving razor—just fresh enough to sting when the fabric brushes over them. Shame twists sharply in my chest, carving through the numbness.

I hadn't planned to do it, it just happened. The bath had been too quiet, the silence too heavy and my mind too loud. I needed something to cut through the suffocating weight pressing me down, and it had worked—for a little. Long enough to sleep, at least, until that nightmare had dragged me under again.

Guilt pushes its way up my throat like bile, so I yank the sleeves of my jacket down over my wrists, turning away from the mirror. I can't stand the way my reflection looks back at me, hollowed out and frayed at the edges.

At the vanity, I quickly dab on concealer, then a sweep of blush, trying to fake some life into my face without looking at myself long. It's not perfect, the shadows under my eyes still bleeding through, but it's enough to pass if nobody looks too closely, and I don't let anyone get that close anymore, anyway.

Outside, the night air is shockingly cool. It smells like wet earth and new blossoms, fresh and damp. The gravel crunches under my sneakers as I make my way down the path toward the main house. Every sound feels too loud in the darkness, and every shift of the shadows prickles at the back of my neck. I hate the dark and how it makes me feel on edge now, but I keep walking.

The music from the party is loud enough to rattle the ground, the low thump of the bass punching the air. I step into a cloud of cigarette smoke and laughter as I squeeze past a group of guys clutching red solo cups outside the front door. One of them gives me a slow, lazy once-over and I look away fast, heart thudding.

It's chaos inside. Bodies packed together, writhing, laughing, and singing off-key. A sea of sound and movement, and my gut twists tight. Coming here was a mistake, a terrible one. I keep my head down, weaving through the crowd, dodging elbows and drinks that slosh dangerously close to my clothes. Every brush of a stranger's hand makes my skin crawl, a tightness settling in my throat.

Why the hell did I think I could handle this?

Thankfully, I spot Lando moments later. He's leaning against the kitchen counter, flirting with a guy who looks like an underwear model. His curls bounce as he laughs, his entire face lit up with that effortless, mischievous energy he's always had.

When he spots me, his eyes widen, and he practically shoves Hot Underwear Model Guy aside without a second thought.

"You came!" he shrieks, barreling toward me and grabbing my wrist to drag me into the kitchen.

Before I can get a word out, he's already pouring something fizzy into a red cup.

"I don't really—" I start.

"Shhh," he grins. "It's champagne. We're celebrating!"

I raise a brow. "Celebrating what?"

"Your return to Marlow, babe," he says, clinking his cup against mine.

A genuine laugh escapes me, a little shaky, but real. The bubbles fizz across my tongue, sweet and sharp. For a while, I let him steer me through the crowd, introducing me to faces I haven't seen in years. Every time my drink gets low, Lando tops it up without saying a word, keeping it filled with that golden, dangerous effervescence. I'm not drunk—just loose enough for the edges to blur, for the warmth in my chest to spread to my cheeks.

"Sinclair," a familiar voice says from behind me. "Is that really you?"

I turn and come face to face with Max, Willow, and Alfie —people I used to know. Once upon a time, they were my closest friends, but after my dad died, they slowly drifted away. I quickly learned that grief makes people uncomfortable, even the ones who swore they'd always be there. I wasn't mad at them for it, I understood, but I never reached out to them again, either.

They move in for hugs with awkward smiles and uncertain eyes, but my body stiffens, panic tightening every muscle. Without missing a beat, Lando slides smoothly between me and them, pulling them into his own bear hug instead. I mouth a thank you and he winks at me, like it's the easiest thing in the world to protect me.

After a while, the noise grows louder, and the walls begin to feel closer as the crush of bodies becomes too much. The champagne has settled warm in my veins, and the slight buzz that once felt manageable now has my head swimming a little too much. I'm smiling too easily, swaying on my feet, and the air inside suddenly feels too thick to breathe, almost unsafe.

I slip away without telling anyone, and wander through the house, passing the sunroom where Lando and I used to build forts out of couch cushions and blankets. The library where I fell asleep reading Wuthering Heights for the hundredth time, losing entire afternoons inside battered paperbacks, and the back hallway where we used to race in our socks, crashing into walls, laughing until we couldn't breathe. Our fathers were best friends, so I spent almost every long weekend and summer break growing up here.

I keep walking until I find the side door that opens into the gardens and take a step outside, the cool air a welcome relief now. The gardens are even more beautiful than I remember—rows of moonlit flowers, soft paths winding through neatly trimmed hedges, the scent of lavender, honeysuckle, and wet grass thick in the air. Out here, the music is muffled, just a dull thump under the stars.

I walk without direction, past the bench that Lando and I used to fight over, deeper into the winding paths. A breeze lifts my dark curls from my shoulders as I walk and I close my eyes for just a second, breathing in the stillness, and slam straight into something solid.

I stagger back, my breath catching in my throat as I instinctively swing my arms out to steady myself just as someone's hand shoots out, gripping my upper arm, every nerve ending exploding from the contact.

"Careful," a low voice murmurs, and goosebumps creep up my arms at the sound so achingly familiar.

I look up and freeze, my eyes landing on Lando's older brother, Reign. He towers over me, and it feels like the world stops for a second, like the champagne buzzing in my blood and the music thumping from the house have both been sucked into a vacuum. Gone. Replaced by the sound of my pulse, deafening in my ears.

He's a few inches taller than I remember, his frame lean and sculpted like the powerful dancer he is but also stronger and more dangerous now than it was when we were younger.

The moon carves his features in silver—sharp cheek-bones, an angular jaw, and a mouth that looks like it rarely smiles. His hair is so pale it's almost white, tousled like he's been running his hands through it. And his eyes—God, his eyes. Icy, electric blue, pin me in place, unreadable but intense enough to make the air around us shift.

The summer before my dad passed away, when I turned seventeen and Reign turned eighteen, we'd explored our unsaid feelings in secret. In front of Lando, he'd tug my ponytail or push me into their pool, just to make it seem like he didn't like me. But in the afternoons, we'd sneak off into the gardens together and make out next to the peonies, his hands learning the curves of my body, our breaths mingling.

Now he's looking at me as if he doesn't remember who I am. But why would he? We never spoke again after I left.

"Are you lost?" he asks, before pointing over my head. "The party is back that way."

His voice is deeper than I remember, rougher too. It wraps around me like velvet and smoke, and I jerk my arm out of his grasp without thinking. His touch had ignited something in me that I haven't felt since I left Marlow. A spark of heat tangled together in a single heartbeat with the fear and awareness I now hold.

What a paradox.

"Sorry," I manage, breathless. "I didn't see you there."

"You weren't looking." His tone is distant and cool as he watches me.

"You've changed," I blurt, then immediately curse myself for sounding like an idiot, feeling heat rise to my cheeks under his gaze.

Thank God it's dark out, because if it wasn't, this would be ten times more mortifying. Somehow, despite the years, the distance, and everything that's happened in my life, some part of me still cares far too much about what Reign thinks of me.

His mouth lifts into the ghost of a smile. "So have you,

Angel." His eyes burn a path down my body and back up, his electric blues finding my eyes once more.

So, he does remember me.

He's never called me Angelique, always shortening my name down to Angel, like I'm some saint. We stand in the gardens, silence stretching between us, but the air feels charged. Being this close to Reign feels like standing too close to a fire, feeling the pull of the heat even when you know you might get burned.

"I didn't mean to bump into—"

He shakes his head before I can finish. "It's fine."

I take a moment to really look at him and realize he's wearing standard rehearsal gear—black joggers, fitted shirt, and a duffle bag slung over his shoulder.

"Late-night rehearsal?" I ask, folding my arms across my chest and shifting on the balls of my feet. I feel awkward and stupidly exposed.

He nods but doesn't elaborate.

Alrighty, time for an exit.

"Well... it was nice seeing you aga—"

"Are you staying at the guesthouse?"

I pause, surprised. "Yeah," I say. "Just for a bit."

"And then back to New York?"

I guess Lando never filled him in on my arrival.

"No, actually," I say slowly, carefully picking my words. "I'm back in Marlow. For good."

His brows raise subtly. "Won't your company need you?"

I shake my head and force out an awkward chuckle. "No, I..." I swallow. "I guess I quit."

His brows furrow as he slowly slides his hands into his pockets. He studies my face, as if he sees right through me. I look away and wait for him to say what's on his mind.

But all he says is, "Welcome home, Angel."

He steps around me; the faint brush of his shoulder causing an explosion of electrical currents to run up and down my arm. I stand there beneath the stars, the scent of his cologne, musk and mint, clinging to the night air. And my hands won't stop shaking.

THE NEXT MORNING, I WAKE TO SUNLIGHT AND A STIFF ACHE IN MY neck. I blink up at the ceiling, disoriented, then glance around and freeze. I'm on the couch with a throw blanket tangled around my legs, and the TV is on but muted.

I push myself upright slowly, heart thudding, trying to make sense of it. I don't remember coming out here. I remember saying goodnight to Lando before walking back to the guest house, and I remember brushing my teeth, pulling on the oversized shirt I slept in, and crawling under the duvet. I even remember the way the mattress dipped beneath me and the way I curled into the pillow, still slightly tipsy.

I frown as I try to piece together the gap in my memory, but before I can trace it back far enough, there's a knock at the door, or rather, a rhythmic, theatrical pounding that sounds like someone's using their forehead instead of their hand. I sigh and drag myself up, blanket still half-clinging to one ankle, my mind still stuck on how the hell I ended up here.

I crack the door open and find Lando looking like absolute hell in an oversized hoodie, plaid pyjama pants, and designer sunglasses comically large for his face. He's holding a paper bag in one hand and a takeaway tray with two coffees in the other, like some bedraggled saint of hangover survival.

"I come bearing croissants," he croaks, slipping inside dramatically. "Also regret, and potentially liver failure."

I step aside to let him pass, biting down a smile. "You look like you got run over by your own party."

"I did." He drops the bag on the kitchen counter like it weighs a thousand pounds. "Twice."

He slouches onto the barstool, setting down the coffees with a groan. I grab one of the cups from the tray and hand it to him, raising an eyebrow.

"Did you sleep at all?"

"Define sleep," he says, wincing at the light as he peels off his sunglasses.

His eyes are bloodshot, and his mascara is smudged just enough to give him the tragic air of a rockstar mid-bender.

"More like passed out face-first on the sofa with an empty bag of kettle chips for a pillow."

"And yet you still remembered the croissants," I say appreciatively, digging into the bag.

"I'm a mess, darling, not a monster."

He takes a long sip from his coffee as a comfortable silence settles between us. I pull apart my croissant, my thoughts drifting back to last night's run-in with Reign.

"I know that look," Lando says, dragging me back to the present. "Spill it, love. What's on your mind?"

I shrug, keeping my eyes on the flaky mess in front of me. "I ran into your brother last night," I say, trying to sound casual before taking a bite.

He groans dramatically. "Ugh. Was he a total buzzkill?"

A small laugh slips out before I shake my head. "Not exactly. I think he was just getting back from a late-night rehearsal."

I reach for my coffee, grateful for something to hide behind, and take a sip.

"He likes to use the estate studio at night," Lando says, then tilts his head to the side. "But the real mystery is why you're being so coy right now."

I glance up to find him watching me, eyes narrowed with that knowing, teasing smile. His painted nails tap out a slow rhythm on the counter, and I know I'm caught. Leave it to Lando to see through me without even trying.

"I'm not being coy," I say defensively, my voice higher pitched than I intend.

Lando bites his lip, trying to hold it together, but the laugh escapes anyway. "Don't tell me you still want to get in my brother's pants."

"Lando!" I shriek, scandalized but also laughing as I shove his arm.

"I knew it!" he shouts before immediately wincing as he clutches his head with a groan. I bite back a smile when he slumps forward dramatically.

"Angelique Sinclair," he mumbles into the countertop, pointing in my direction with all the gravitas of a hungover oracle. "I swear to God, if you're still pining after my emotionally lacking brother, I'm staging an intervention. You could do better blindfolded."

I roll my eyes. "Relax, I only brought him up because he seemed surprised to see me. You didn't tell him I was coming?"

Lando waves a lazy hand without lifting his head. "I barely see the guy. If my father didn't tell him you were coming, then yeah, he probably was surprised."

"He's still avoiding you?"

"Like the plague," he mutters, finally peeling his cheek

off the counter. "But I'm not special. He barely talks to anyone these days."

I trace the rim of my coffee cup with a fingertip, quiet for a moment. "That sounds lonely."

"Oh no. Don't even go there," he says, glaring at me.

"Go where?"

He points at me accusingly. "You've always had a savior complex. But he's not some sad, abandoned puppy you can rescue. He's a fully grown man with a brooding problem and a perfectly functioning phone. He can deal with his own damn loneliness."

I know Lando has a point, but there was a time when Reign was different. He used to laugh more, and let people in. But ever since their mom walked out, something in him changed. Almost like he decided it was safer not to need anyone at all. And I guess I've always wondered if anyone's ever tried to pull him out of it.

"Please," I scoff, weakly. "I've got more than enough of my own mess to fix."

Lando arches a brow, unconvinced.

"I'm serious," I insist.

"Sure," he mutters, before letting his head fall back to the counter with a dramatic thud.

I let the silence linger for a few minutes, my fingers curling around the warmth of my coffee cup. The words sit heavy on my tongue before I force them out. "Can you show me the way to the studio? I can't remember how to get there."

Lando peers up at me, brow arched like he's trying to read between the lines. "Thinking about coming out of retirement already?" he asks slowly.

I shake my head instantly, the thought alone too loaded

to entertain. "No," I say, too quickly. "I was thinking maybe it'd be nice to dance again. Just for me."

I keep my eyes on the rim of my cup, tracing it with the tip of my finger. "No rehearsals, and no corrections. Just movement, without expectation and no one telling me what it's supposed to mean or look like."

There's a pause, and I finally look up to find Lando watching me with that same look he gets when he's about to say something profound and inappropriate in equal measure. But instead, he nods and slides off the stool with a groan, rubbing a hand down his face as if remembering the hangover all over again. He crosses the kitchen and nudges my shoulder gently with his own.

"Come on then," he murmurs. "I'll show you."

I follow him, heart already fluttering at the thought of stepping back into a space I swore I'd never return to. But this time, it'll be different. This time, I'm not dancing for anyone but myself.

CHAPTER 4

REIGN

TWO WEEKS LATER

The leaves crunch beneath our shoes noisily as my father and I walk the winding path through the west gardens. The estate is quiet this morning, still damp from last night's rain. Sunlight filters through the heavy clouds, forming a pale glow over the clipped hedges and wild roses that climb the stone walls.

He's talking about renovations again—budgets, community outreach, expansion plans for the Fall. His voice, once a guiding force in my life, now drifts somewhere just above my thoughts, grazing the surface but never quite sinking in.

"We need new flooring in Studio B," he says. "And the east wing's heating is still unreliable. If we want guest artists to stay through winter, we can't have them dancing in scarves."

I nod absently, scanning the tangled rows of roses. "Noted." But my mind is elsewhere.

For the last few years, he's been slowly passing the torch—handing me control of the family ballet company, Imperium, piece by piece, like I'm being trained for something I never agreed to want. It's all written in his will, of course. When he's gone, the company is mine, and I'm not blind to what Imperium means—not just to him, but to our family, to the dancers that work there, to the art. It's the company that built our family name. The legacy he's spent a lifetime perfecting. The crown jewel of British ballet.

And sure, I could do it. I could lead the company, help choreograph productions and manage the board. I know how things work. I've danced every principal role, endured the politics, learned how to make a room bend without ever raising my voice. But the truth is, I don't know if this is what I want, because this company exists for one thing, and one thing only. Dance.

And while dancing is something I've mastered out of necessity, expectation, and obligation, music is the only thing that ever felt like mine. Late nights at the piano, alone in the studio, letting the weight of the world bleed out of my fingers—that's where I come alive. That's the only place I'm not haunted by the shadows of who I'm supposed to be.

But there's no space for music in a place built on the bones of ballet. No room for me—not the real me, anyway. Just the version of myself everyone sees on stage. The mask and the myth. And if I stay, if I take it all on, I can't help but feel like I'll be carving off the part of myself that matters most. Burying it beneath expectations. Sacrificing it at the altar of duty.

My father glances at me as we round the corner of the hedge-lined path, still talking about bringing in new talent for the spring showcase. Does he notice how quiet I've gone? Probably not. Or maybe he does, and he's just pretending not to—just like I'm pretending not to always feel the weight of all this pressing down on my spine.

"Reign, Imperium can't stay in stasis. We need to

adapt." I know he's right. I just don't think I'm the right person to lead it. "We can build new studios, hire better instructors, bring in more international talent, but without something special—something unforgettable—we're just another company."

I stop walking and he does too, sensing the shift in me.

"You want a performance that changes lives," I say.

He nods. "One that reminds people why they fell in love with ballet in the first place."

My father keeps talking, but his voice cuts off suddenly at the sound of soft piano notes floating through the open window of the studio. I slow my steps and arch a brow, already turning toward the sound.

"Someone's in the studio," I murmur.

He follows me without a word, both of us straining to hear. The music crescendos and I unmistakably recognize it as Tchaikovsky. I step off the path, walking toward the half-closed doors, careful not to make a sound.

Inside, Angelique moves across the floor fluidly. Her long hair is pulled back in a loose, messy bun, dark curls escaping to cling to her damp neck and cheeks. She's in a black leotard and a sheer wrap skirt the colour of ash, the fabric fluttering around her thighs with every movement. She rises effortlessly onto the tips of her pointe shoes, her lines flawless, her control devastating.

Every extension, and every tilt of her head carries a kind of grief that's almost too intimate to witness. I shouldn't be watching, not like this. Not when it feels like I'm intruding on a moment she didn't intend to share. But I can't look away.

The way she dances has always taken my breath away. Watching her dance was one of the things I missed most after she moved away. It's what I've always envisioned when I play the piano, her moving across the floor to my compositions. My way of remembering the girl who left with a piece of my heart.

My father finally joins me at the threshold, his breath catching the moment he sees her, and then he exhales, reverent.

"She's dancing Swan Lake," he says quietly, like he needs to say it aloud to believe it.

I don't take my eyes off her as I nod in agreement. "Odette," I whisper, confirming what we both already know.

There's a long silence before he murmurs, more to himself than to me, "I think she might be the answer we've been looking for."

I don't respond, because I know he's right. Watching her dance does something to me—something I can't quite name. Her dancing is more than technical brilliance, more than physical control or artistry. There's something raw and honest in the way she moves, like she's telling a story without saying a single word, and somehow, I understand all of it.

It's the kind of performance that makes you stop breathing, just so you don't miss a second. And it's not even a performance because she's not trying to impress anyone. She doesn't know she's being watched, and that's what makes it feel even more real.

I feel something shift in me, in what I thought I knew about this career, about this company, and about what dance could be. This—*she*—makes it feel worth it again. Not the legacy, not the business, not the stage lights or accolades. Just someone dancing like it's the only way they know how to survive, and suddenly, I want to be a part of that. Not for the company, not for my father, but for myself.

Before I can stop him, my father steps forward and pushes the studio doors open. The loud creak of the hinges breaks the quiet.

"Well done!" he says, clapping his hands with a flourish as he strides forward.

Angelique startles and stumbles to her feet, her cheeks flushed. I follow behind him reluctantly, muttering a curse under my breath as I step inside, dragging my expression back into my neutral and detached mask.

"That was excellent, my dear," my father beams, stopping a few feet from her, his arms spread wide as if he's just witnessed a miracle.

Angelique shifts uncomfortably, brushing a loose curl behind her ear. Her eyes skim my face—quick and cautiously—then back to him.

"You are certainly your father's daughter," he says, and I see that quick, unmistakable pang of pain that crosses her face at the mention of her dad. Her posture tightens, the line of her shoulders closing inward like a door being quietly shut. "He would've been so proud," my father adds, softer now.

Her father, Elijah Sinclair, was like a second dad to me. He was my father's best friend, and the reason I was able to see Angelique as often as I did. They would stay in the guesthouse every summer, until he died.

She nods, but the smile she gives him is tight around the edges. "It's nice to see you again, Charlie." His face warms at the familiarity of her voice.

"Lando mentioned you were staying in our guesthouse," he says, folding his arms as if settling in for a proper chat. "I'm sorry I haven't had a moment to pop by and say hello."

"No, please," Angelique says quickly. "You've no reason to apologize. I've been keeping to myself."

I stay silent, watching the two of them with a strange sense of displacement. Like I'm the third wheel in this conversation.

My father glances back at the barre where her sweatshirt drapes across the rail. "That piece," he starts, tilting his head like he's pondering something he already knows the answer to. "Was that Swan Lake?"

Angelique's lips twitch, just slightly. "It was," she says, brushing her palms down the sides of her legs. "It's the solo piece I was rehearsing at The Big Apple Ballet Company, before I quit."

I shift where I stand, suddenly hyper-aware of the way her voice shakes around that name. The Big Apple Ballet is a company we all used to revere, one that she left without fanfare, apparently.

"Ah, yes. The Big Apple." My father nods, considering her with those assessing eyes. "Why'd you leave?"

Her gaze drops to the floor, and for a second she seems to shrink into herself. Not visibly, though. She does it in a way most people wouldn't notice, but I see it, and it makes me curious.

What's going through her head right now? What memory did she just fall into?

"I had... different values," she says at last, the words evasive, but loaded.

A beat passes between us while my father watches her for a moment longer. He surprises the hell out of me by doing the one thing I thought he never would.

"Well," he says, straightening up. "How would you feel about joining Imperium?"

Her head jerks up, startled.

"To dance Swan Lake, with Reign," he adds.

My chest goes tight.

What the fuck?

She blinks. "Excuse me?"

"We've been searching for something special. Something transformative." He smiles. "I saw it in you today, Angelique. The grace, the hunger, the pain. You'd be the perfect Swan Queen."

She looks at me then, briefly, like the suggestion physically touched her, and she's not sure how to react. Her eyes shine with hope, fear, and maybe disbelief. And I know her well enough to know she's calculating the cost.

Angelique exhales, slow and steady. "That's... kind of you to offer, Charlie," she says carefully. "But I don't dance anymore. I quit when I left The Big Apple."

My father chuckles, brushing the air like her words were a joke. "Is that so? Because from where I'm standing, you were dancing just now—and beautifully, might I add. That was a performance people would pay good money to see."

She stiffens suddenly, her arms pressing closer to her body, her chin tilting down like she's trying to disappear. And still, he keeps going.

"You know," he says lightly, strolling a few steps deeper into the room. "Since you're staying at our guesthouse, it would be a real gift to the company, to the town of Marlow, and to our family if you'd considered it. Just a short run, nothing overwhelming."

My jaw tightens. Of course he'd twist it like that—wrap an offer in something that sounds generous but lands like a debt. It shouldn't surprise me. It's textbook Charlie Harrington—polite, persuasive, and perfectly timed to make someone feel like saying no would be selfish. And Angelique... she's too polite to push back, and he knows it.

Her eyes flash, barely, and then the panic sets in. Subtle, like a tremor in the earth before the ground gives way.

"I... suppose I could consider it," she mumbles.

That's not a yes, not really, but it's enough for him.

"Brilliant," he beams, already halfway out the door like everything is confirmed. "Reign will work out the details with you. I want this production to be extraordinary—and the two of you, together..." He claps a hand to my shoulder as he passes. "Brilliant." And then he's gone.

The silence he leaves in his wake is stifling. Angelique is staring at the floor, lips parted as if she's still trying to understand what just happened.

"You should've said no," I mutter, then turn and walk out before she can answer.

Because the truth is, I want nothing more than to dance with her. To lose myself in her movement, and to find meaning in the shapes our bodies make onstage. But only if it's hers to give. Only if she's dancing for herself. And what I saw just now—that wasn't a choice. That was cornering a bird already too broken to fly. And I'm not going to be the one who cages her.

CHAPTER 5

ANGELIQUE

"You said *what*?!"

Lando's voice echoes across the guesthouse, practically shaking the French press in his hands. I wince, tugging the sleeves of my sweater over my palms as I sit curled in the armchair, trying—and failing—not to feel like a total idiot.

"I didn't know what to say," I mutter, staring into my coffee like it might have the answer. "I panicked."

"Angelique." Lando plants both hands on the kitchen counter and leans forward. "My father ambushed you in the studio and asked you to star in Swan Lake and you just... agreed? No questions asked?"

I groan and press my fingers to my temples. "I didn't *agree* agree."

He blinks. "What is '*didn't* agree *agree*' supposed to mean?"

"It means I didn't *want* to say yes, but I didn't exactly say no either. It all happened so fast and—God—he made it sound like I owed it to him just for staying in his guesthouse."

Lando rolls his eyes. "Classic Charlie Harrington. Emotional manipulation but make it classy."

"I should've said no."

"Damn right you should have."

"I froze, okay?" I look up at him, voice cracking. "Even Reign looked surprised."

Lando softens, moving toward me with a sigh. "I'm sorry, love. That wasn't fair. To you or Reign."

My throat tightens. "Yeah, well ... Reign wasn't exactly thrilled that I agreed."

"Oh no. What'd he say?"

I force out a bitter laugh. "*'You should've said no'*, and then he left."

"Oof." Lando winces. "That's ... very Reign of him."

I nod slowly, sinking back into the chair. My legs feel heavy, like all that unspoken tension is dragging me down. "Now I'll be dancing with a partner that doesn't even want to do this."

"Well," Lando sighs, plopping down on the armrest beside me and nudging my shoulder with his. "Maybe it's time we figure out what *you* want. Screw my dad's schemes, and screw Reign's broody dramatics. What do *you* want?"

I go quiet because that's what I've been trying to figure out since moving back to Marlow, isn't it? I used to want everything. The spotlight, a future...a stage to make magic on. But now? All I want is to feel whole again, to breathe without guilt, and to dance for myself.

"I don't know yet," I whisper. "But I think... maybe this is how I'll find out?"

Lando shifts beside me, his knee bouncing slightly, which only happens when he's holding something back.

"What?" I ask.

He hesitates, then exhales through his nose. "If you're

going to do this… I mean *really* do this—Swan Lake, with Reign—you need to put your whole damn soul into it."

I blink at him. "Gee, thanks for the pep talk?"

"I'm serious." His tone sharpens. He leans forward, elbows on his knees, eyes locked on mine. "Reign isn't easy to dance with. He's intense, demanding, and ruthless when it comes to the work. You've seen what he's like on stage—he gives everything. And he expects the same in return."

"I know how he dances," I say, bristling. "We grew up watching each other dance."

"Watching each other is different from being partnered with him." His voice softens, but the warning stays. "He's broken dancers almost every single time he's done a pas de deux. He pushes hard, and if you go in half-present, trying to protect yourself, or trying not to feel too much—he'll break you too."

My chest tightens. "You think I can't handle doing this?"

"I think you can." He places a hand over mine. "But only if you're doing it because you want to. Not because Charlie cornered you and not because you think you owe anyone something. You've already survived too much to be torn down by someone else's version of perfection."

I stare at our hands, his rings cold against my skin. "What if I fall apart in front of everyone?" I whisper.

Lando squeezes my hand. "Then you fall, and I'll be right there, hauling your ass off the floor and feeding you chocolate ice cream until you're human again."

I laugh, watery and weak.

"But if you give it your all," he continues. "You might not fall; You might fly."

I close my eyes, breathing in the weight of his words as my chest tightens. It's not just what he said, it's how he said it. The same cadence, the same softness that made those words feel like a promise instead of a risk. My father used to say that to me before every big performance, every leap into something terrifying and new. '*You might not fall; You might fly*'. It was his way of telling me I was braver than I believed, stronger than I felt.

Hearing Lando say it now, with everything cracked wide open between me and the life I left behind, it unravels me a little. Like a thread pulled loose. It's a reminder of who I used to be, of the man I loved more than anything, and of how far I've fallen since he died.

I swallow hard and open my eyes, blinking fast to chase the burn behind them.

"Don't say things like that," I whisper, not trusting my voice. "It makes it harder to pretend I've let it all go."

Lando's expression softens, and he reaches over, gently squeezing my hand. "Maybe you don't have to let it go. Maybe you just need to find your own way back to it."

Even though I want to fight him on it and pretend I can keep one foot in and one foot out—keep dancing without really committing to it again—I know deep down that he's right. That kind of half-heartedness won't survive on an actual stage, especially not partnered with someone like Reign.

If I do this, I need to let the dance take me. All the way in, no matter how much it scares me. Because anything less... and I really will fall. And the worst part? I'm not sure I'd be able to get back up again this time.

"I just..." I sigh, sinking deeper into the chair. "I wish I could dance with you instead."

Lando doesn't respond at first. His fingers go still over the edge of his mug and his jaw works, like he's trying to decide if it's worth saying what's on his mind.

"Yeah," he murmurs. "Me too."

I look over at him, startled by the quiet ache in his voice. He gives me a soft, crooked smile, but it doesn't reach his eyes.

"You've always been my favourite partner," I admit. "You made everything feel easy and safe."

Lando lets out a dry laugh. "Yeah, well..." He leans back, stretching out his legs with a sigh. "Doesn't matter much when your own father won't even consider casting you in a lead role because he thinks your queerness makes it impossible for you to connect with a woman."

My stomach drops. "What? I didn't know he..." My words die off.

"He never says it outright." Lando waves a hand. "He just conveniently forgets I exist when it's time to cast Prince Whatever in whatever classic they're putting on, and says things like, *'You're a strong corps dancer, Lando,'* or *'Leave the leads to the ones who understand the story.'*"

I reach over and take his hand again, threading my fingers through his.

"But you do understand the story," I say, fierce now. "More than half the straight guys in tights I've danced with ever did."

He chuckles, but there's no joy in it. "I can't help who I love, darling. But to him, that makes me less than. Like I'm incapable of portraying desire, or longing, or heartbreak unless it's aimed at a man. As if art must match real life exactly for it to be real."

"That's bullshit."

He looks at me, his gaze heavy. "Try telling him that."

"I will."

We sit like that for a moment, hands clasped. Then he bumps my shoulder gently with his again. "Hey."

"Yeah?"

"If you really are stuck dancing with my emotionally inept brother," he smirks, "just remember who taught you how to nail a perfect arabesque."

I smile, for real this time. "You."

"Damn right." He grins. "Now go be brilliant, and if Reign gives you a hard time, tell me so I can key his car."

I laugh, leaning my head on his shoulder. For a second, the world feels almost right again.

THE ESTATE STUDIO IS FILLED WITH GOLDEN LIGHT THIS MORNING, and the windows are foggy from my heavy breathing. I sit on the floor with my legs outstretched, folding into a deep stretch, breathing through the satisfying pull in my hamstrings. My heartbeat is just beginning to settle from my warm-up, a quiet pulse in my ears, when I hear something behind me. I jolt upright, nearly slipping on the smooth floor, my head snapping toward the sound.

Reign is standing in the doorway, leaning against the frame with his arms crossed. His dark shirt clings to his body in a way that feels offensive this early in the morning, and his blond hair, slightly damp, curls at the nape of his neck. He looks like sin personified, and I hate how easily that thought comes to me.

God, why is he so attractive?

I swallow hard, dragging my eyes away before I do something reckless. Like stare longer. Or drool.

"Ready to talk business?" he asks, voice low and steady.

I nod, trying not to look as flustered as I feel. He pushes himself off the wall and strolls over to the piano in the corner, lowering himself onto the bench.

"You'll be dancing both Odette and Odile," he says matter-of-factly.

My brow furrows. "Why isn't there another dancer for Odile?"

He lifts a brow like the answer is obvious. "Because I want you to do both."

The air shifts, and suddenly the studio doesn't feel as warm as it did a moment ago. My pulse stutters, and I try to cover it with a casual toss of my hair over my shoulder.

So, this is what Lando meant.

I narrow my eyes. "To be honest, I didn't think you wanted me dancing at all."

"What are you talking about?"

"Yesterday," I say pointedly. "You told me I should've said no to your father."

His brow lifts higher, the corner of his mouth twitching. "I did."

"So, what is this? Did he guilt trip you too?"

"No," he says simply. "I do want to dance with you."

The words knock the breath out of me. I blink, heat creeping up my neck as I silently curse whatever part of me still reacts to him like this.

"But," he adds, "I also want to make sure you're doing it because you want to. Not because my father put on the charm and pressured you into it."

I look away, trying to will the blush off my face, but it's already too late.

"You could've said no," he says quietly. "I wouldn't have held it against you."

"I should have," I admit, my voice lower now. "I quit dancing."

"And yet here you are," he murmurs, gaze locking with mine again.

I exhale slowly, eyes dropping to my hands as I fidget with the hem of my top. "I want to see if it's different here," I say. "If Imperium can be something The Big Apple never was."

His brow furrows, but he doesn't interrupt.

"I want to know if I can be the kind of dancer I used to dream about being before life got all twisted."

He's quiet for a beat, and when I finally look up, his eyes are soft.

"You might be surprised," he says. "Imperium has a way of giving people room to become who they really are."

"But Reign..." I start, choosing my words carefully. "I don't think I can dance Odile. That role is—" I stop myself before I say too much. "It's just not in me."

"Yes, it is," he replies without hesitation. "You just haven't realized it yet."

I don't know whether to be flattered or terrified.

He leans forward, forearms resting on his knees. "We'll run rehearsals at Imperium during the day, like any other company. And we can put in extra time after hours until you feel like you've mastered your version of Odile."

My stomach drops. "After hours?" I ask, and I hate how my voice shakes.

His head tilts, just slightly, eyes scanning my face with quiet focus.

"As in, just us two?" I ask again.

"If you'd prefer someone else present," he says slowly, "we can make that happen. If that makes you more comfortable."

"That'd be great," I say, but the words trip over themselves in their hurry to get out, and I instantly regret how desperate they sound.

He nods once but says nothing as his eyes continue

studying me, like he's cataloguing every buried fear I'm trying so hard to keep hidden. I shift, finishing my stretch and folding my legs in front of me, palms flat against the floor for something to ground me.

"What about our understudies?" I ask, mostly to fill the silence.

He raises a brow. "Are you planning to break a leg or something?"

I don't smile. "I want Lando to be yours."

Reign stills, his brow knitting as he blinks once. "Lando?"

I nod.

"Does he even want to dance the part?"

"He does," I say firmly, meeting his eyes.

He runs a hand through his hair, visibly thrown by the suggestion. "I thought he didn't enjoy leading roles."

"He's never been given the chance to find out if he does."

Reign studies me for a long moment, before he finally nods. "Alright. He can be my understudy."

Relief rushes through me like a sudden breeze, momentary but real.

"But we'll hold auditions at Imperium for your understudy," he adds.

I nod again, then wrap my arms around my knees, pulling them to my chest. The room feels colder now, and the weight of what I've just agreed to settles deep into my bones.

"We start Monday," he says, standing up and making his way toward the door.

"Wait," I call out.

He pauses, turning just enough to glance over his shoulder at me.

I sit up straighter. "We haven't talked about how much I'll be paid."

A small smirk tugs at the corner of his mouth—infuriating and undeniably attractive. "I was wondering when you'd ask," he says. "I'll have a hiring agreement emailed over by the end of the night."

I narrow my eyes slightly. "Do you even have my email?"

He begins walking again, his voice casual as it floats back to me. "I'll text you for it later."

I blink. "You have my number?"

He doesn't answer, and he's gone before I can ask again, leaving nothing but the faint scent of his cologne behind. I stare at the empty doorway, my heart thudding annoyingly loud in my chest.

~

UNKNOWN NUMBER:

What's your email address?

ME:

Who is this?

UNKNOWN NUMBER:

Tall.

Blond.

Handsome.

Probably has opinions about your fouettés.

ME:

Reign?

UNKNOWN NUMBER:

I always knew you thought I was handsome.

My cheeks burn as I add his number to my phone.

ME:

Don't flatter yourself, Harrington. What do you want?

REIGN OF TERROR:

Your email…unless you'd rather I drop the contract off in person.

My heart pounds violently as I picture him turning up at my doorstep this late at night, but instead of scaring me, it turns me on, and *that* scares me.

REIGN OF TERROR:

ME:

You're ridiculous.

REIGN OF TERROR:

That's not a no.

I roll my eyes and send him my email address.

ME:

How did you get my number, anyway?

REIGN OF TERROR:

It's a secret.

ME:

Do you always go around 'secretly' collecting numbers?

REIGN OF TERROR:

Just yours.

I fall back onto my bed, holding my phone above my face with the world's goofiest smile. Reign Harrington, texting like a menace and somehow making it... cute? Who knew he still had this side to him.

REIGN OF TERROR:

Agreement is on the way.

Check your inbox.

I switch to my inbox and find his email at the top.

Offer – Imperium Ballet

I click the email, scrolling through the attached agreement, and when I see the pay, I drop my phone straight onto my face.

"Ow," I groan, clutching my nose as the sting radiates between my eyes.

I blindly fumble around the bed, feeling for my phone and pulling the screen back up again to make sure I'm not seeing things. There are so many zeros. I reread the contract header. Then scroll. And scroll again.

ME:

Is this amount of compensation even legal?

REIGN OF TERROR:

Sweet dreams. 😊

CHAPTER 6

ANGELIQUE

The weekend slips by faster than I expect, and I spend most of the time doing barre work in the studio and stretching at the guesthouse, while Lando flits around the living room in silk robes and sunglasses, offering iced coffee like it's holy water. But no amount of prep could've made today easier, because the day I've been dreading has finally arrived.

Imperium Ballet stands like a fortress in front of me with its tall columns, vast windows, and a grand set of stairs that sweep toward the entrance. The building is made up of white stone, weathered with time but still pristine, and the Harrington crest is etched into the stone above the double doors. It looks more like an elite art museum than a dance company, but maybe that's what Charlie was going for when he built the place.

Lando parks out front, sunglasses sliding down his nose as he shoots me a grin. "Ready for your first day?"

"Not even remotely," I mutter, but I still follow him up the stairs.

Inside, Imperium feels like a different world. Cool

marble underfoot, high ceilings that echo with laughter and the rustle of warmups, pointe shoes tapping softly against tile. The halls are already busy with dancers spilling out of studios, chatting, stretching, and sipping from steel water bottles.

Lando leads the way, practically gliding, his dance bag slung effortlessly over one shoulder. He cuts through the crowd like a celebrity, which, to be fair, he sort of is here. We reach a small circle of familiar faces by the lockers.

Alfie is halfway through an aggressive hamstring stretch and moaning like he's dying, Max leans against the wall, sipping cold brew and watching Alfie, unimpressed, and Willow's sitting on the floor in a split, arms propped on her knee like it's effortless. They all light up when they see me.

"Look who finally came to play," Alfie grins.

"Took you long enough," Willow adds, reaching up for a quick hand squeeze.

I smile, my nerves easing just a bit as I crouch down beside them.

"She's back," Lando declares, dropping his bag dramatically. "And I come bearing new introductions."

He gestures toward a trio I don't recognize—two girls and a guy, all lounging nearby.

"This is Quinn, Alfie's long-suffering boyfriend," Lando says, motioning to the guy with pink buzzed hair and a septum ring. He gives me a little salute.

"And that's Sora and Jules, Willow and Max's partners."

Sora, in oversized sweats and flawless eyeliner, smiles and waves, while Jules, with her ginger curls and quiet energy, offers a soft "*hey*".

"Angelique," I say, offering a small wave. "Nice to meet you."

"She's the infamous one," Alfie says, nudging Quinn. "The one I told you about who dipped from Big Apple."

"Big Apple can suck it," Willow mutters, then turns back to her stretch.

I laugh under my breath, and for a second, everything feels almost normal. Like I've always been here. The plan was always to join Imperium, but when my father died before my eighteenth birthday, I had no choice but to move to America under my mother's care. And when I finally turned the legal age to return, I'd already landed a principal position at Big Apple, so it made little sense to come back.

We head to Studio B together; the group falling into a comfortable rhythm. The floor is cool as I claim a spot near the back, sitting down and stretching while the others talk about Swan Lake.

"I heard auditions are next week."

"I bet Reign already picked Wendy as his partner."

Wendy?

"I doubt he'll be in this one. He hasn't danced a production in almost a year."

I keep quiet, folding into a forward bend, palms flat on the floor. No one knows the lead roles are already taken, and I'm not about to be the one to tell them. Suddenly, the atmosphere shifts and the murmurs die down as Reign walks in, dressed in black. His shirt is fitted, his sleeves pushed up, and on his arm is a girl.

She's petite, with sharp cheekbones and smooth, luminous skin. Her long, inky hair is pulled into a slick high ponytail that swishes with every step. She wears a blood-red leotard, and a soft ballet wrap tied neatly at her waist, her legs in pristine white tights.

I notice how her hand rests on his arm, and how she smiles while she speaks to him. Something tightens in my chest. Of course he has a girlfriend now. I mean, he always could've had anyone he wanted, so why did I think he was single?

Maybe because I never dated anyone in the time that I've been gone.

Maybe because a part of me had hoped he'd do the same, even if he was the one that ghosted me.

Lando leans in and whispers out the side of his mouth, "You're staring."

I look away quickly, pretending I'm fascinated by the way my foot looks in a flexed stretch, my neck burning. "I was not."

"You so were," he whispers, like the smug little chaos fairy he is.

I keep my head down and reach for the barre, pretending the pressure building in my chest is from my calf muscles, not whatever the hell that just was. Forcing my focus back to my stretches, I press into a deep lunge, trying to shake off the static under my skin. But I can still feel his presence in the air surrounding me.

Curiosity wins out after a few minutes, and I look up one more time. Reign is on the other side of the room, one leg up on the barre, leaning into a stretch with intense, effortless control, but he's not focused on his posture, or on Wendy. He's looking at me. Dead-on. Eyes locked. My breath catches—a small, sharp inhale that feels like an internal scream. He doesn't look away, so I do, my gaze snapping back to the floor, my heart thrumming behind my ribs.

The studio doors open seconds later, and I nearly sigh in relief as a woman walks in, tall and willowy, with long honey-brown hair cascading down her back and green eyes that scan the room warmly. She wears beige wide-legged trousers and a fitted black sleeveless top, moving with the grace of someone who doesn't need to prove she belongs here because everyone already knows.

And rightfully so, she was Imperium's biggest success. A prima ballerina that went big, travelled the world guest starring at various companies that paid exorbitant amounts of money to Imperium to borrow her. And once she retired as a dancer, Charlie offered her an instructor position.

She claps once, drawing the room to attention. "For any newcomers," she says, her voice calm but confident, "welcome to Imperium. My name is Layla, and I'll be your techniques instructor."

Her gaze finds me in the crowd and softens as she gives me a small, encouraging smile and I nod back with a small smile of my own, but my insides are still tangled.

Layla begins the warm-up moments later, the energy in the room shifting as everyone removes their sweats and ties their hair into buns. Dancers silently fall into formation, heads bowed, bodies alert. There's a hunger here that hums beneath the surface.

Layla walks us through a brutal series of pliés, tendus, dégagés, and battements. Her voice is calm, but her expectations are anything but. She corrects angles, demanding sharper articulation, and never lets a single bent wrist or lazy port de bras slip past her gaze. My muscles scream in protest halfway through, but I grit my teeth and push deeper, harder.

When she calls for adagios at the centre, I feel the shift in the air as everyone's postures straighten. This is where the actual competition begins. We move through a round, each combination testing my balance, control, and artistry. My legs and arms burn, but I keep going, sweat trickling down my spine until she finally signals the end of the session.

But before anyone can scramble for their towels or water bottles, she lifts a hand. "Before you all disappear, I have a few announcements regarding our upcoming production."

Everyone freezes and Layla smiles. "If you haven't already heard, we'll be staging Swan Lake." There's a collective murmur, excitement rippling across the room.

"As many of you know, Swan Lake is a technically demanding and emotionally layered ballet, therefore we've already begun casting for principal roles, and I'm thrilled to be the one sharing some of those decisions today."

The room stills as Layla turns to Reign. "Congratulations to Reign Harrington, who will dance the role of Prince Siegfried."

Applause breaks out, mixed with a few whispers of shock about him returning to the stage.

"And his understudy," Layla continues, "will be Lando Harrington."

Lando stiffens beside me for a beat, his eyes finding mine instantly, and when I smile softly the floodgates burst and it's even better than I could've ever imagined.

"Holy shit, Lando!" Alfie crows, grabbing his shoulders.

Max pulls him into a hug and Willow squeals, squeezing his arm while the rest of the group laughs and congratulates him with cheers and shoulder pats.

When he glances down at me, his eyes are wide and glassy with disbelief. "Is this real?"

I nod. "One step closer to being cast as Prince Whatever."

His lips tremble in response as he blows me a kiss, and I

laugh before turning back to Layla. She waits a beat for the room to settle, then continues.

"And Angelique Sinclair," she says, scanning the crowd, "will dance the dual roles of Odette and Odile."

It feels like time slows as the room falls into a hush.

"Excuse me?" a sharp voice cuts through the silence.

I turn to see Reign's maybe-girlfriend step forward, arms crossed, and fury etched into her every feature. "Who the hell is *Angelique*?" She says my name like it's diseased.

Layla gestures toward me. "Wendy, Angelique. Angelique, Wendy."

Heat flares across my face as every head swivels in my direction. I hold still under the weight of their stares, my grip on the barre tightening. Wendy zeroes in on me like a predator and I internally groan at the fact that I've somehow made an enemy on my first day, and of course it's Reign's girlfriend, of all people.

"The customary response, Wendy," Layla says coolly, "would be to congratulate your fellow dancer."

Wendy whips around to glare at Layla, then turns to Reign with betrayal in her eyes when he doesn't respond, choosing to ignore her altogether. She grabs her bag and storms out of the room without another word.

"Looks like Wendy's not thrilled someone else gets to dance with her boy toy," Willow murmurs beside me.

Layla continues, as though none of it happened. "Angelique's understudy hasn't been selected yet. So, if you're interested, let me know, and I'll sign you up for the upcoming audition."

There's a faint buzz in the air as dancers disperse, conversations picking back up. Before leaving the studio, I risk a quick glance at Reign and his eyes find mine, but this time I don't look away until he does.

~

THE SUN PEEKS THROUGH A PATCH OF CLOUDS, LIGHTING UP THE white stone steps outside of Imperium. It's finally lunch break, and the steps are already crowded with dancers lounging in the sun, peeling off their warmup gear, and eating from Tupperware or takeout containers. It's rare to get a sunny day like today in Marlow.

I sit on the third step from the bottom with Lando next to me, one hand shading his eyes as he squints up at the sky, studying the cloud shapes. Willow plops down cross-legged in front of us, her lunch balanced neatly on her lap, and Max and Alfie lean against the nearest column with overpriced smoothies. Their partners stayed behind to speak with Layla about other available roles in Swan Lake, too eager to pass up a chance to impress her.

"I still can't believe it," Lando, who's positively glowing, says for what must be the tenth time, picking at the corner of his sandwich wrap like he needs to touch something to ground himself. "Understudy to the prince."

"You earned it," I say, bumping his knee with mine. "Every bit of it."

Willow raises her iced coffee in salute. "And Angelique is just over here casually snatching both leads."

"Odette and Odile," Max adds with a dramatic bow. "All hail our new swan queen."

Alfie whistles low. "Did you see Wendy's face? The girl looked like she was about to breathe fire."

"Alfie," Lando warns, half-laughing, half-scolding.

"What?" Alfie grins. "I'm just saying. That was some top-tier dramatics."

We all laugh, and for a moment, it's easy to get swept up in the energy, the camaraderie, the weird comfort of being seen and not judged. The minute I became a principal dancer in New York, the other dancers kept their distance, gossiping behind my back and sometimes in front of me. They all thought I had got there with the help of my mom.

But something itches at the edge of my mind, and before I can second-guess it, I ask, "So... how long have Reign and Wendy been dating?"

The conversation stutters and Willow blinks at me. "Who said they're dating?"

I try to keep my voice light. "I don't know. They came in together and she was hanging on him, so I just assumed."

"They're not," Willow says, shaking her head. "They've been cast opposite each other a lot in the past. There's chemistry, sure. But it's not like... sexual...at least not for Reign from what I've seen."

"They probably do fuck though," Alfie mutters around his straw.

Lando smacks his arm. "Alfie, shut up." Then he turns to me with a wince. "Ignore him. He has the emotional depth of a teaspoon."

"Wait a minute," Willow says slowly, her voice curling with disbelief. "Do you have a thing for Reign?"

My head snaps up. "What? No. Absolutely not."

"Ouuu, the blush is blushing," Alfie teases, pointing a straw-stirrer in my direction before putting it back in his mouth, biting down on it as he grins.

"I do not—he's not—Reign isn't..." I throw up a hand. "He's no one to me."

"Is that so?" a deep voice says from behind me.

The silence that follows is too sudden and I feel my stomach drop as I realize who that voice belongs to. I twist slowly in my spot, and sure enough, there he is, standing a few feet behind me, hands in his pockets, his icy blue eyes locked on mine.

My face explodes with heat and my skin prickles with awareness, mortification flooding through me in waves. As serious as he looks, I catch the faintest twitch of his cheek —a half smile that sends my stomach into free fall.

"Holy shit," Alfie whispers to the others behind me. "Is he smiling? Like... actually smiling?"

He falls silent again as Reign lifts his chin, breaking eye contact with me long enough to look at Lando and give him a short, respectful nod.

"I just came by to congratulate you on landing my understudy," he says, as if he wasn't the one who decided.

Lando straightens in his seat, his face lighting up before he quickly clears his throat, voice a little deeper than usual. "Thanks."

Reign nods again, then looks back at me. "I'm leaving early today," he pauses. "See you both at home."

Home.

He says it like it belongs to me too and something inside me stirs, wild and electric. Reign walks down the rest of the stairs and toward his parked car. Once he's out of earshot, it's like the group finally takes a breath of air.

"I know I'm taken," Alfie says, slowly, "but holy shit, your brother is so hot, Lando."

Willow snorts into her drink and Max leans in slightly, brow raised. "He was giving Angelique *fuck me* eyes."

Lando groans in disgust, but I barely register it because my heart is still pounding, my skin buzzing, and I can't stop hearing his voice in my head.

See you both at home.

CHAPTER 7

ANGELIQUE

"I'm so embarrassed," I groan, tugging the drawstrings of my hoodie until the fabric bunches around my face like a makeshift mask. Slumping into the passenger seat of Lando's Audi, I curl toward the window, wishing I could disappear into the doorframe.

My first day at Imperium is over—a miracle in itself—but all I can think about is the lunch break. More specifically, Reign, and the stupid, humiliating thing I said, and the look on his face after. It's been hours, but the mortification still clings to my skin like sweat. I said he was nothing to me, as if we hadn't been teetering on the precipice of love before I moved away. What was going through his mind after he heard me?

Lando chuckles, his voice light as he shifts the car into reverse and backs out of the lot. "Babe, it's been hours. Reign probably doesn't even remember."

"I wish I could forget," I mumble, letting my head thump gently against the cool glass.

As we drive up the estate driveway moments later, I nearly grab the wheel and turn us right back around after I spot Reign sitting just outside the guesthouse, a cigarette burning between his fingers, one elbow resting on his knee.

He looks up locking eyes with me, and I make a strangled noise, something between a gasp and a whimper, before dropping to the floor of the car.

"Oh my God. Turn around," I beg, panicking. "Turn around."

Lando snorts. "I hate to break it to you, but he definitely saw you."

"Take me back to the airport."

He laughs like I'm kidding, but I'm not. "And where would you even go?"

"I don't know. Canada, maybe?" I peek up at him from behind my hands, face burning.

Lando barks out a laugh. "And do what? Hide in an igloo?"

"I'll live in the forest, befriend the wildlife, build a cottage, be one with the trees."

"Okay, Snow White," he deadpans. "Except instead of dwarves, you'll have bears."

"Better than facing your brother."

Lando parks the car and steps out, circling around to open my door. "Alright, princess. Time to face the big bad wolf."

I step out with reluctance, still wrapped in my hoodie. "That's Red Riding Hood, not Snow White," I correct, but my breath is siphoned right out of my lungs when I come face to face with Reign.

He raises a brow while looking between Lando and me. "Sounds like I interrupted an intriguing conversation."

He brings the cigarette to his lips, taking one last pull before dropping it to the ground and putting it out with his boot.

"When did you start smoking?" Lando asks, his brows knitted together.

Reign shrugs. "Does it matter?"

"I guess not," Lando says, but his face says differently.

Reign turns to look at me and my face burns hotter as I hold his gaze, noticing the subtle way one corner of his mouth tips up in an amused smirk. I feel my nipples pebble under the soft cotton of my hoodie, and I thank six a.m. me for deciding to wear a hoodie today.

Oh, for fucks sake, Angelique. Start moving!

I give him a nervous smile. "I'll, um...get going."

I slip past him, trying not to brush his arm, but I can feel his eyes on my back as I walk down the path to the guesthouse, and when I look back, both him and Lando are following me. He's watching me with that same smirk, but Lando is watching him with a confused expression.

They're just walking you to the house, I think to myself, facing forward again. *Stop overthinking it.*

I dig through my bag for the key as I reach the front door, but before I can fish it out, a large hand reaches around me. Reign turns the knob and pushes the door open.

"I thought I locked it," I murmur, stepping inside with a frown.

"You did," he says casually, following me in.

Lando halts in the doorway, his voice snapping. "Okay. What the hell is going on here?"

Reign walks to the kitchen, calm as ever, and pours himself a glass of water. "I moved in."

My heart skips. "What?"

All the blood rushes from my body, my fingers beginning to tingle as I whip my head toward the second bedroom. I speed walk to the door and swing it open only to find that his belongings are in fact there.

He's not lying.

"Reign," Lando says, his tone a warning as he turns away from my shocked expression to glare at his brother. "What are you playing at?"

Reign chugs the rest of his glass before placing it in the sink, bracing his hands on the counter and lifting his gaze to me as I stand dumbfounded in the hall, staring back at him.

"It was part of the hiring agreement," he says, turning to look at Lando. "Angelique agreed to have me live in the guesthouse with her during this production."

Lando whips his head to me with a shocked and confused expression. I raise my hands, taking a step back. "No, I didn't," I say, my voice small.

Reign clears his throat, and pulls out his phone, beginning to read. "Clause Seven; Angelique Sinclair gives Reign Herrington permission to live in The Harrington Guesthouse with her for the duration of The Swan Lake production."

Before my brain even registers what I'm doing, I rush across the hall and snatch his phone right out of his hand and scan the screen.

There it is. Clause Seven.

As I continue scrolling down the length of the agreement, I find my signature. I must have been so distracted by the outrageous salary that I didn't even read the whole thing properly. I pass the phone back to him with shaking hands.

"I don't think I can do that," I say out loud, panic rising like bile.

"You've already agreed to it," Reign says, coolly.

Lando looks pissed as he stares at Reign. "What exactly

is the end goal here then?" he spits. "Are you trying to get laid?"

The room goes silent, and I can feel the anger humming off Reign as he straightens slowly.

"My end goal, brother," his voice sounds barely controlled, "is none of your business."

Lando doesn't back down. "Tricking her into a room-mate clause isn't the way we do things at Imperium, Reign."

I close my eyes and rub at the ache between my brows. This conversation is getting out of hand, and I don't want to be in the middle of it if they decide to physically fight here, like they used to when we were kids.

"It's fine—" I start to say.

"No, Angelique. It's not fine." Lando cuts me off, turning red as he glares at Reign. "He manipulated you into another one of his games."

"Lando." I step between them, grabbing Lando's arms to redirect his attention back to me. "I'll be fine."

Do I know that for sure? No. But the look of guilt on Lando's face means I need to at least pretend that I do.

"I promised you a safe place," he whispers, his face crumpling.

"Am I suddenly a danger to her?" Reign snaps, offence drenched in his tone as he crosses his arms.

I ignore him, keeping my focus on Lando. "If anything happens, I'll call you right away."

Reign exhales sharply, pushing past us and shoving his boots on. "I'm not here to hurt you, Angel."

I see a flash of hurt in his expression before it vanishes, and his cold mask falls back in place. Guilt gnaws at my gut as he steps outside and lights another cigarette.

"Maybe you should come stay in the main house instead?" Lando suggests quietly.

I shake my head because I know Reign would only end up following me back there, anyway. There's a reason he wants to live here with me, I just don't know what it is yet.

"Don't worry about me. I'll be fine," I give him a small smile and he tries but fails to return it.

"Call me right away if anything that you're not comfortable with happens," he says, finally.

I nod in agreement, and he looks at me one last time before walking out the front door. He says nothing to Reign as he passes him and when he's gone, I join Reign outside. He stays quiet while he smokes, staring straight ahead at the sinking sun just over the trees in the distance.

I let out a sigh, shoving my hands into my hoodie pocket before coming to stand beside him.

"I didn't mean to imply you'd hurt me," I say after a beat.

He doesn't reply, instead taking another pull of his cigarette, and I don't say anything right away either. Because the truth is... he did hurt me. When I left for New York, he disappeared from my life like I never mattered. One day we were talking, sharing music, whispering secrets and then the next, it was like I didn't exist. No goodbye or explanation. He just ghosted me.

And for a long time, I told myself I understood, that maybe I hadn't meant as much to him as he'd meant to me. I convinced myself it was easier for him to let go this way, but it still gutted me. I don't say any of that now, though. I'm not sure I know how.

I take another deep breath and turn to face him. "But, if you're going to be living here with me, then we need rules."

He turns his head and finally looks at me—those blue

eyes sending a tingle through my body—exhaling the smoke out the side of his mouth.

"Rules?" He asks, his tone curious.

I nod. "So that we're both as comfortable as possible with this arrangement."

His lip twitches and he turns his body to face me now, leaning his shoulder against a support beam. "I'm listening."

"Okay, well for starters, we're not allowed in each other's rooms." The last thing I want is to be haunted by the idea of him walking into my room while I'm asleep.

"Deal," he says with a lazy smirk. "If you think you can manage that."

I frown. "What's that supposed to mean?"

He laughs to himself but says nothing, so I roll my eyes and continue.

"Also, if you're going to invite your girlfriend over, let me know beforehand so that I can leave," I say, looking away now and feigning nonchalance as my cheeks warm. "The last thing I want is to hear anything I shouldn't or have her try to rip my head off in the place that I sleep."

He raises an eyebrow. "Girlfriend?"

"Wendy," I clarify.

"She is not my girlfriend."

"Okay, fine. Fuck buddy," I throw my hands up in exasperation. "Whatever."

"She's not my fuck buddy, either," he says, meeting my eyes. "But I get your point."

"Well then, the rule applies to whoever *is* your girlfriend or fuck buddy now.

He takes a long drag, studying me, then exhales slowly. "Same goes for you, then."

I blink. "What?"

"No boyfriend or fuck buddy," he says, observing me.

"I don't have either," I say, slowly.

I don't miss the twitch of his lip again and the playful glint in his eyes. "Noted."

My cheeks warm and I look away again.

"Any other rules?" he asks after a beat, tossing his cigarette to the ground and putting it out with his boot.

"If I think of more, I'll let you know."

"Okay," he says, before turning and walking back into the house.

DETANGLING MY CURLS TAKES NEARLY AN HOUR. THEY'RE ALWAYS the most tangled after a day of dancing but once detangled I always think I look my prettiest. Each tug of the brush causes my fresh cuts to sting when I bend my wrist, but I power through and when I'm finally done, I feel a little more human.

I throw on an oversized T-shirt and poke my head out of my bedroom to see if I can hear Reign. When I hear the water from the shower beating down in the bathroom across the hall, I tiptoe out of my room all the way to the kitchen and grab myself a glass of water for the night.

What I don't expect is for the bathroom door to swing open on my way back, and for Reign to step out into the hall with his bare, damp, chest and a towel loosely hanging off his waist, steam rolling behind him like a movie scene.

I freeze, like a deer caught in headlights, my jaw dropping open as I stare at him. My face grows so hot, and I'm positive I'll combust any second. Water droplets trail down the ridges of his abs, and my entire body short-circuits.

I realize he can clearly see me checking him out, and my

eyes snap up to his, but what I see sends my heart into a panic. His eyes are dragging a path down my body—devouring me—and that's when I remember that I'm only dressed in an oversized T-shirt.

Without a word I bolt back to my room, water from my glass sloshing all over the floor, and slam the door behind me, pressing my back against it as I take calming breaths, my heart beating out of my chest. My glass of water is now only a quartered filled when prior to my big escape it was filled almost to the rim.

Great.

I place the glass on my nightstand and crawl into bed, but minutes later, my phone dings and I slowly reach for it on my nightstand only to find a text lighting up the screen.

REIGN OF TERROR:

For the record, I didn't mind you looking.

CHAPTER 8
REIGN

My first night at the guesthouse with Angelique was... revealing. Not in the way you'd think—though, to be fair, Angelique in that oversized T-shirt came damn close. I always figured she was the type to wear matching pyjama sets. Button-down silk with little piping details and probably monogrammed. Maybe because she's best friends with Lando, and that man wouldn't be caught dead in anything less than coordinated sleepwear, but that's not what I saw last night.

She crossed the hallway barefoot; curls still damp and frizzing slightly from her shower, the hem of her T-shirt grazing the tops of her thighs like it didn't know it was flirting with indecency. The fabric clung to her just enough to make me wonder what it would look like tangled in my hands. Her skin was flushed from the heat, her eyes wide when she saw me bare-chested, water still dripping down my skin, towel hanging low.

The look in her eyes—like she didn't know whether to run or step closer—lit something in me I thought I'd buried years ago. It satisfied a darker part of me, the part that wants her to remember what it feels like to want me. The part that wonders if she ever stopped.

I lay awake most of the night replaying it, imagining that look again, trying to talk myself out of wanting to provoke it; out of craving it. Wondering if I should start walking through the halls shirtless just to see if I can break her composure again and see if the idea of me still lives under her skin the way she still lives under mine.

It's not about feelings. I don't do those, not anymore. But deep down, I know that's a lie, because before she left for New York, Angelique and I weren't just friends. For that one, impossible summer, we were something else. Something secret and urgent and entirely too real. I wasn't supposed to fall for her, but I did, or at least I was about to. And just when it felt like I'd finally found something solid to hold on to again, she was gone.

She'd reached out after she left, and at first it was constant, like she needed to keep a tether between us. But then it faded, turning into every few days, then once a week, then once a month, until eventually it stopped. But that wasn't on her, that was on me, because I never answered. Not once.

I knew that if I heard her voice again, I'd tell her everything I wasn't supposed to feel. That I missed her, and that I wanted her to come back. I was afraid she'd never look at me the same way again if she stayed out there long enough. But I knew if I said any of that, she would have come back for me, and I couldn't let that happen.

She had a real shot at everything she'd worked for, and I didn't want to be the thing that made her hesitate. I didn't want her to resent me for it one day. So, I made the choice for both of us, and I let her go. I let her believe I didn't care, and now, somehow, she's back. Not the girl I remember, though, she's harder around the edges now, more timid, and a lot quieter.

She left the house early this morning, probably thinking she could avoid the tension, or avoid me. But we both know she can't. Not here and not at Imperium. Not when the past still lingers in the space between us, and not when I still ache with every step she takes away from me.

LAYLA PACES THE STUDIO, CORRECTING THE ARMS AND POSTURE OF other dancers before she claps her hands and announces she wants everyone to partner up. Wendy latches onto my arm immediately, her claws digging in like she owns a piece of me, and Angelique gravitates to Lando.

No surprise there.

"Let's have our leads partnered together for this one," Layla calls, gesturing toward me and Angelique.

Wendy releases my arm with a huff, storming toward Lando like she's ready to rip Angelique's hair out on the way.

As Angelique steps toward me, I lean in and murmur, "Early morning today?"

"I didn't sleep all that well," she replies, and I catch the slight tremor in her voice.

"Are you cold?" I ask, frowning as I notice her hands are shaking too.

"No," she answers too quickly.

Layla claps her hands again, looking at Angelique and me. "Front and centre, please."

We make our way to the front of the room, Angelique keeping her eyes pointed downward the whole way.

Is this just rehearsal nerves?

I watch as her gaze lifts slowly, and she locks eyes with Lando through the mirror. He's staring back at her, his brows tight and arms crossed over his chest. His attention doesn't waver, not even when Wendy talks to him.

What am I missing?

"Alright, let's start with some basic partnering moves."

Angelique slips one of her hands in mine, her back facing me, but when I reach for her waist with my other hand, her body jerks beneath my fingers

"You okay?" I murmur, barely moving my lips.

She doesn't answer, instead lifting her chin and staring at her own reflection in the mirror, but her expression is terrified. I try to ignore it as we move through sequences, but I can feel her resisting me and, by the look on Layla's face, she's noticed it too.

"Do you two want to try a lift?" Layla asks, approaching with her arms crossed.

"No," Angelique answers.

What the hell?

Is she mad at me for what happened last night? No, there's no way she's bringing that into the studio, not when she knows Layla is watching her.

Layla studies her but doesn't argue, instead calling for a break and waiting for the others to disperse into smaller groups to stretch or chat while sipping water from their bottles. She comes closer to where Angelique and I stand, hand on her hip.

"Is everything alright with you two?"

Angelique struggles to keep eye contact with Layla as she nods. "I'm just not ready to do lifts yet."

A principal dancer from The Big Apple Ballet not ready to do a simple lift? Or is it that she's not ready to do a lift with me?

Layla's expression shifts because she's not buying it

either. "We need to work on lifts today. I get that you two are new partners, but nerves won't help you come performance day. I'll schedule a session with the new Chemistry Coordinator for later today."

Angelique opens her mouth to object, but I cut in before she can speak.

"That's a great idea," I say, voice clipped. "Please schedule it."

Angelique looks up at me with wide wounded eyes, but I force myself to look away pretending not to notice.

"Great," Layla says, her expression calm. "He'll meet you both in Studio A."

CHAPTER 9

REIGN

Studio A is the biggest studio in the building, with vaulted ceilings, mirrored walls, and a polished floor that shines like glass. It smells like your typical dance studio; sweat and bleach.

Waiting inside is a man who looks like he walked straight out of a cliché ballet movie. Round in the middle, balding on top, and dressed in snug black slacks and a charcoal turtleneck that clings to his stomach like it's trying to escape. His eyebrows are thick and stern, and his energy is deadly calm. He's one of my father's most recent hires, a world-renowned Dance Chemistry Coordinator from Russia.

"Ah," he says, clapping as we enter. "Reign Harrington and Angelique Sinclair. Finally." His voice is rich with a thick Russian accent.

"I am Dmitri Volkov. You will call me Mister Volkov. Not *sir*, not *coach*, not *man who ruins dreams*. Just Mister Volkov." He smiles, but it doesn't reach his eyes.

Of course my father would hire someone that speaks in riddles and theatrical declarations like some tyrant God of ballet, forged in vodka and contempt. I nod once and Angelique offers a quiet *"Good morning"*, her voice swallowed by the size of the room.

We move to the edge of the studio, and she sits beside me, slipping out of her warm-up booties and hoodie. I start my stretches, letting muscle memory take over, while Angelique rolls out her ankles. Her hands move slower than usual when she slides her pointe shoe onto her feet, a constant tremble in her fingers as she fumbles with the ribbon. She's struggling, but she isn't asking for help, even when she notices me watching.

"So stubborn," I mutter under my breath as I slowly lower myself into a crouch in front of her.

I don't wait for permission as I take the ribbon, my fingers brushing against hers. I hear her breath hitch at the contact, and she freezes, shifting something in me. It's subtle, but I feel it—like my entire body tunes into her silence, every nerve suddenly aware of the space between us, and how little of it there is. I force myself not to look up, focusing on the ribbon instead.

Her ankle feels smaller in my hands than I expect—delicate, but deceptively strong. I work the ribbon into a knot with ease, my movements steady and careful, but my chest is tight, and my pulse is annoyingly loud in my ears. She still hasn't breathed, and neither have I.

"You're shaking," I say, if only to take the attention off myself.

"I'm fine," she answers quickly.

I finish the knot and look up, willing my eyes not to linger on her lips. Her eyes meet mine, holding my gaze, and I can see the fear behind them.

"Don't lie to me," I say, quietly.

When she doesn't respond, I let go of her ankle and

return to stretching, acting like I don't care, even though she's consuming my thoughts.

Minutes later, Volkov claps his hands together. "We begin. Solo first." His gaze cuts to me. "Prince Siegfried. Show me who you are."

I rise without hesitation and step forward into the centre of the studio, getting into position. The pianist plays behind me, soft and steady, and with the first note, I let everything else fall away as I move.

The choreography runs through my blood like it's second nature. My body follows the music, sharp lines and clean turns, and I don't allow myself to falter—not here. Not with Angelique watching, and definitely not with Volkov dissecting every angle. When I land the last position, I hold it as Volkov steps into the centre of the room, arms folded, his eyes locked on mine.

"Technique..." he starts, lifting a hand to kiss his fingertips, "Perfect. Like watching swan eat caviar."

I arch a brow at the comparison but stay quiet. Instead, I glance toward Angelique for just a moment, surprised to find that she's already staring back at me.

"But," Volkov continues, voice shifting into something sharper, "you dance like robot with heartbreak setting turned off."

He throws up both hands and starts pacing.

"Where is love? Where is desperation? Prince Siegfried is not just noble man—he is romantic, he is tortured, he is *alive*."

Volkov turns sharply, jabbing a finger at me like he's accusing me of a crime. "When he sees Odette, it should split him in two. Audience must believe he would burn down kingdom for her. That he would throw himself into lake. That he cannot breathe without her."

My jaw tightens, but I keep my mouth shut because I know there's no point in arguing with a man like him.

"Right now?" He shrugs with exaggerated disdain. "I see man doing beautiful moves, not man in love. And ballet without love?" He scoffs. "Is gym class."

He turns away, sighing dramatically. "We fix this, eventually. Hopefully in this lifetime."

I walk to the corner of the studio and grab my water bottle, keeping my movements even and unbothered. Like his words did nothing for me. But they did, of course they did. It's always the same critique, in different shapes. Too cold. Too closed. Too controlled.

No one ever says it directly, but the truth is clear—they want more than perfection. They want pain. They want me to feel something when I dance. But letting myself feel is what cracked me open once before and left me bleeding with no one to notice.

I twist the cap off the bottle and drink slowly, ignoring the heat creeping up the back of my neck. When I was a kid, I didn't know how to hide, and I hadn't learned the cruel parts of life yet. Back then, I laughed sometimes, and I let people get close. I think there was even a time I believed in safety, and things not falling apart. Until everything did.

Home turned to static, and my mother left without a backward glance, like we were just a chapter she skipped. I learned, fast, that silence was safer than hope and shutting down hurt less than being left open and waiting for another blow. I became this unreachable machine. So, Volkov's not wrong, he's just telling me something I already know.

"Enough," he barks. "Angelique. Your turn."

She wipes her palms on her thighs and rises, but I see the tension tucked in the corners of her posture. She danced a solo at the estate studio, but the way she steps into position now, it's like she's heading into battle instead.

When the music starts, she moves fluidly, but it's not right. She's desperately trying to disappear into Odette, but I can see her fighting her own body, like her limbs are too heavy. Her arms droop, and her extensions waver. When she eventually slips on a turn and stumbles, the piano cuts out with a discordant stop.

Volkov exhales like he's been wounded. "I said Odette," he mutters, pinching the bridge of his nose, "not dying swan from children's recital. Again."

Angelique glances toward me and I look away, stretching one leg out, and draping an arm over my knee.

Am I making her nervous? Or did she develop some sort of stage fright and that's why she left New York?

The questions cloud my mind as Angelique takes her mark again, drawing in a deep breath. Volkov paces in the corner, muttering something under his breath, but I tune him out as I focus on her again because I can feel something shift in the air as she closes her eyes. It's not something you can name, but I feel it, like the hush before a storm.

And then she moves, differently this time. She doesn't force the steps; it's almost like she surrenders to them. Her sorrow bleeds through the lines of her body, her extensions aching with grief, not just technique. Her arms aren't arms anymore, they're wings, and she's transformed into Odette. There's something achingly honest and beautiful about it.

This is the Angelique that the world needs to see.

By the time she hits her final position, I'm not stretching anymore. I don't even remember standing. My arms hang loosely at my sides while I stare at her, my pulse high in my throat. For a second, I forget this is a rehearsal. I forget Volkov is here. And I forget myself.

Volkov claps once, the sharp crack snapping me out of my trance. He's dabbing at his eyes with a ridiculous handkerchief like the dramatist he is.

"Brava," he breathes. "A swan I believe. You will make beautiful Odette." Then he waves a hand like he's bored again. "Break time. Go hydrate or cry in bathroom. I don't care."

Angelique slips out without a word, vanishing down the hallway. I watch the door long after she's gone, choosing not to follow right away because I need a moment to understand why her dance cracked something in me. It was like being punched in the gut by everything I've been trying to forget. The way she used to look at me, the way she left me, and the way I let her.

Wanting her like that again is dangerous, and I already know how that story would end if I let her back in; she'd just leave me again. So, I won't let myself get tangled up in her, because it's safer not to feel when you're the one always left behind.

When she doesn't return after a few minutes, I make my way into the hall. I don't even think about where I'm going, but I end up outside the lady's bathroom, leaning against the wall with my arms crossed, one leg bent as I wait for her.

The door swings open minutes later, and as predicted, Angelique steps out, hair slightly mussed, cheeks flushed, skin damp. She pauses when she sees me, her eyes widening slightly.

"Everything okay?" I ask, for what feels like the tenth time today.

She nods, brushing water from her cheeks with the back of her hand. "I just needed a minute."

I hum, noncommittal, and glance away, about to let her

go, then stop myself. "You were good in there," I say flatly. "Better than I expected."

She blinks. "Is that a compliment?"

I press my tongue to the inside of my cheek. "Don't let it go to your head, Sinclair," I mutter. "You did what you were supposed to do."

She exhales, half a laugh. "And here I thought you stopped noticing me."

"I notice everything." That lands heavier than I intend.

Her eyes search mine, like she wants to say something but is thinking better of it. I push off the wall, ready to leave, but I hesitate again.

"Whatever you tapped into...don't lose it."

She swallows hard, her expression fragile. "You make it sound like it's easy."

"I know it's not," I say, quieter now. "But you make people feel something when you dance like that, and that's exactly what Imperium needs."

It's what I need.

She glances down at the ground and says—so soft I almost miss it—"Maybe you should try tapping into that too."

That stops me cold, and I let out a short, surprised laugh that startles even me. I stare at her like I'm seeing her for the first time, like I'm not sure what to do with this new version of her, but I like it. The younger Angelique would never have the courage in her to say something like that to me.

She looks up, cheeks flushed. "I didn't mean—"

"No," I cut in, still half-smirking, half-stunned. "You did."

I step back slowly, eyes still locked on hers. "Careful,

Angel," I murmur, voice dropping. "That almost sounded like you still care."

Then I turn and walk away, back down the hall toward the studio. But every step feels heavier now, like she's branded something into my chest just by standing there and daring to speak the truth. I don't know what just happened, but I know it's just the beginning.

BACK IN THE STUDIO, VOLKOV CLAPS HIS HANDS. "BREAK IS OVER. Enough water. Time to dance like you care." He shoots me a pointed look before waving his hand between me and Angelique. "Pas de deux. Act Two. Start from the lift."

From the corner of my eye, I see Angelique freeze beside me. Her breath hitches and her spine locks straight.

"The lift?" she whispers, more to herself than anyone.

There it is again, her fear of a lift. Lifts should be muscle memory by now, so I don't understand what has her so spooked.

Does she think I'll drop her?

I step into position without speaking, waiting for her to join me. Her eyes search mine like she's weighing something invisible, but then she crosses the floor, each step looking like it takes extreme amounts of effort.

When I hold out my hand, she places hers in mine, but there's a tremor in her fingers again. Her touch is light, barely there, but I can still feel her hesitation all the way up my arm. Her body stays rigid, muscles coiled like they're bracing for impact, and she looks away, jaw set like she's trying to keep herself from falling apart.

I know I could ask Volkov to skip the lift today, but something about how terrified she is intrigues me, and I need to understand it. Not to push her past a line she isn't ready for, but because whatever she's carrying, it's heavier than the choreography, and if I don't figure out what it is she's fighting so hard to hide, it could tear the whole production apart before we even begin.

It might even tear her apart.

"Ready?" I ask, and she nods, avoiding eye contact in our reflection.

The music begins, and we move, or at least we try to. Angelique's timing is off from the first count, and her extensions falter, the lines of her body not quite holding, as though she's dancing underwater. Her breaths come unevenly—too fast, then held too long—disrupting the natural rhythm as if she's trying to match the music while fighting her own body. She's worse here than she was in Layla's class earlier.

I ease my hand to her arm, trying to guide her into the first sequence with just enough pressure to ground her, but she jerks at the contact, flinching so sharply I feel it down to my bones. I stop for half a second, uncertain, but she doesn't. She barrels forward, like momentum is the only thing holding her upright. Still, I can feel the tremble in her frame, the way she's barely keeping it together.

What the hell is going on with her?

When it's time for the lift, I attempt to place my hands on her waist, but her whole body stiffens, recoiling before I can even touch her. Her eyes snap to mine in the mirror and for the briefest moment, I see it—real, naked panic. Not nerves or stage fright. This is deeper and more feral.

She turns on her heel and bolts across the studio without a word. Her pointe shoes slapping against the floor in harsh, uneven thuds. Silence crashes down around us as the pianist stops playing. No one breathes. Not even me.

Angelique is halfway across the room, both hands gripping the barre like it's the only thing tethering her to earth. Her chest rises and falls in shallow bursts, like she's unraveling right in front of us, and I don't know how to fix it.

Volkov stares, baffled. "What in hell was that? Is rehearsal or horror movie?"

She tries to speak but can't get the words out. After a few breathless seconds, she swallows and chokes out an "I'm so sorry."

Volkov throws his arms in the air. "No, no. I do not understand. You dance Odette like Swan Queen reborn, and now? Now you run like scared kitten?"

He paces a few feet, muttering under his breath in Russian, then turns back to her. "This is pas de deux. Not solo. You must trust partner." He jabs a finger in my direction. "You must trust him."

Trust.

The word clangs around in my skull like an echo. I know exactly what kind of damage breaks that kind of thing. I've lived it. Is that what this is about? She doesn't trust me?

But why should she after I abandoned her like it was nothing?

Angelique won't meet anyone's gaze. Not mine, and not Volkov's. She stares at the floor instead, as if it might swallow her whole, as if she wants it to. Her cheeks burn with shame, and I can see how hard she's trying not to fall apart in front of us, her eyes glistening.

Volkov scoffs. "Again. From the lift. This time, do not run."

"No." The word leaves my mouth before I can think, sharp enough to cut through the tension in the room.

Volkov turns slowly. "What do you mean, '*no*'?"

"She's not ready," I say, calmly. "You're pushing too hard."

"She must be ready. We do not have luxury of delay."

"We'll figure it out," I reply, my tone final. "But not like this."

Volkov stares at me like he's deciding whether to fight me or knight me. The man's too dramatic for either. Eventually, he makes a disgusted sound and throws his hands in the air.

"We have prima ballerina who does not like to be touched. How you dance pas de deux like this? With force field?" He throws a glance toward the pianist. "Fine. Princess needs more time. Five minutes. Then we try again."

He stalks off, muttering curses in Russian, but I stay exactly where I am and glance toward Angelique. She's still clinging to the barre like she might collapse, but she's breathing slower now, just barely. And I know—whatever this is, whatever made her panic like that—it's not something a five-minute break will fix.

Her hands are still wrapped tight around the barre, knuckles white against the wood, as I approach, careful not to get too close.

"I didn't mean to ruin rehearsal," she whispers.

"You didn't," I reply, leaning my hip against the barre.

She glances at me, and I watch as her eyes search mine for judgment. I see shame in her eyes, or fear of being seen too clearly, but I see enough, and what I feel in response is something akin to a shield pulling tight around her.

"I'm sorry," she breathes. "I don't think I can do the lift today."

I glance toward Volkov, who's now striding away from

the pianist and toward the studio doors, ranting to someone in Russian on his cellphone.

I turn back to her, voice low. "Is it because you don't trust me?"

She freezes. "I..." Her throat works, but the words get stuck, and she meets my gaze, her eyes apologetic.

"You were scared," I say, trying to prompt her to share something. *Anything.*

The silence that follows is thick enough to drown in, but I don't give up.

"Does this have anything to do with why you left New York?" The second the words leave my lips, I know I guessed right. Her face blanches, shoulders stiffening.

Got it.

"Alright. We'll go at your pace." I say quietly, holding my hands up.

She exhales, barely audible. "Thank you."

I nod and step back, giving her more space than she needs. "Let's run our solos again, then."

She nods without looking at me, and we separate like magnets, losing their pull, drifting to our own sides of the studio without another word.

But I watch her while I warm up, aware of every shift in her weight, every time she stumbles and corrects herself before anyone can notice. She's trying so hard to bury whatever feelings or memories are coming up for her, but her eyes find mine sometimes, like she knows I'm still there, watching.

The studio door creaks open moments later, and the bitter stench of cigarette smoke rolls in before Volkov does.

He clears his throat loudly. "Enough lovers drama for today. Odette is weak and sentimental. We try Odile now. Thirty-two fouettés."

Angelique blinks, still catching her breath from every-thing that just happened. "Already?"

He waves a dismissive hand through the air. "You fall like Odette, maybe you rise like Odile."

My eyes jump to Angelique, who looks taken aback. Her expression shutters, then hardens as she lifts her chin. I raise a brow at her, trying to gauge how far she'll let herself be pushed today before she breaks.

Volkov's finger slices the air in her direction. "Odile is seduction and trickery. Black swan in white feathers. Can you do this, or do I send you back to Zumba class?"

Her throat works as she swallows. "I can do it."

But I hear the lie in her voice, the way her words shake with doubt as she says them. If she could only turn that fear into anger, turn it into something dangerous instead of something that keeps her small, she'd make a lethal Odile, and I want to be the one that helps her find that edge.

Volkov doesn't understand. He wants art born from cruelty, but I know hers will come from survival, and if she learns how to wield that... God help anyone who stands in her way.

Volkov smirks, turning to signal the pianist. "Good. Impress me."

The piano kicks in again, fast and electric and she moves immediately, throwing herself into the role. Her arms cut cleanly through the air, surprising me, her move-ments unrelenting. This is what she needs to channel when she's Odile, because power suits her.

She looks dangerous, and it makes me want things I shouldn't, because within seconds I'm hard. I shift my weight and subtly adjust the waistband of my sweats, praying no one notices. Her body spirals in tight, controlled fury. Thirty-two turns. Not a stumble, or a break. She lands the final one with precision, arms closing at her sides, chest rising and falling in ragged rhythm.

"Beautiful," Volkov murmurs, his expression just as surprised as my own.

Angelique straightens, shoulders trembling. Her face is flushed, her skin shining with sweat, and I can see how much that took out of her. Volkov circles her slowly, rubbing his chin like he's searching for the flaw.

"But now…" His tone shifts. "We test real Odile. The seduction. Prince is fool, but not blind. Odile must make him love her. Trick him. Tempt him."

He turns and points to me. "Prince, come. Odile, seduce him."

Angelique freezes. "What?"

"It is character," he says with exaggerated patience. "You are not inviting him to dinner. You are seducing. The stakes are life or death. Show me how you lie with your body. Make him want you."

"With my…body?" Her eyes dart to mine, wide and startled.

I keep my face neutral, but inside, something clenches. Not because of the request, but because of how cornered she looks, like a rabbit in a snare.

"I—I can't just—"

Volkov groans, rolling his eyes. "Are you virgin?"

And just like that, whatever I was feeling a moment ago dies, because now I'm pissed.

What the fuck?

Angelique's body tenses. "What?"

"You move like you do not know touch," he says, shrugging. "No man has ever wanted you? No one has ever—?"

Heat rises in my chest, and I clench my jaw to keep from losing it. It's not just inappropriate—it's cruel. She's already standing on trembling legs, doing everything she can to hold it together. This isn't direction, it's humiliation.

I watch her flinch, her shoulders tightening, and something ugly sparks in me—protective and furious. He doesn't get to do that, not to her, and definitely not while I'm standing in the same room.

"Alright." I step forward, putting myself between them to shield her. "That's enough."

Volkov blinks at me, as if just remembering I'm still here.

"She just danced thirty-two fouettés," I continue, my jaw like stone. "Maybe it's time you shut the fuck up."

"It's discipline," he says, eyes narrowing.

I can tell he's offended by my words, but I guess it pays to be the heir of the company he works for.

"No," I say, steady. "It's harassment."

I stare him down, daring him to push it further. One more word. One more little dig, and I won't just use my voice next time. But Volkov, for all his bravado, knows not to push me further. He sighs like we've both offended his artistic soul and flings his hands in the air.

"We are done for today," he announces. "This..." he gestures vaguely between Angelique and me. "This is not connection. This is strangers on subway, not lovers on stage."

Volkov rounds on me. "You must fix this. You are lead. You are prince. Make her trust you. Make her love you. Make audience believe." He jabs the air again. "Right now, you dance like man checking mailbox. I need passion. Heartbreak. Devotion! You have face like funeral. Give me fire, Reign."

He steps closer, pointing a finger straight at my chest. "Just now, you had fire. Defending her. I want that in your dancing. That heat, that edge. You threaten like man who would kill for love—so dance like it."

I bite down hard, hands flexing at my sides, but I stay silent. I shouldn't have let that much emotion show. She's not mine, and she never was, but try telling that to the part of me that would burn the whole fucking world just to stop her from hurting. I dig my nails into my palm while I lock that part of myself down before it costs me everything, before she costs me everything.

Then he swivels back to Angelique. "And you..." He sighs, pinching the bridge of his nose before waving his hand like she's an unsolvable equation. "Drop the fear, it stinks. You want to be Odile? Then stop acting like girl in corner at school dance. Call me when ready to dance like real partners."

Her cheeks flame but Volkov doesn't wait for either of us to reply. He slings his bag over his shoulder and storms out, muttering under his breath before the door slams behind him. I cross my arms, eyes pinned to the floor, trying to sort through everything I want to say and everything I know I probably shouldn't. Then I exhale and look up.

"He's right."

Her head snaps toward me.

"Not the virgin bit. That was bullshit." I pause. "But the rest of it... he's not wrong. We can't pull this off unless we trust each other," I say, keeping my tone calm, measured.

She nods, slow and uncertain, like she's bracing herself.

I study her a beat longer, then say, "It looks like if we want Volkov to work with us, we'll have to start off by practicing without him until we're ready."

Her brows lift. "Like... alone?"

I nod. "If it feels like too much, then we can bring our

understudies," I offer. "Just until you're more comfortable around me."

"Okay," she breathes, her eyes lowered.

"I'll meet you at the estate studio tonight, around eight," I say, grabbing my belongings from the corner and making my way out of the studio.

"No," she calls out, stopping me in my tracks.

I turn to look at her with a lifted brow. "Let's do it tomorrow morning instead," she says. "I don't rehearse at night."

I don't tell her I don't do early mornings, instead I nod and turn to leave.

I'M RIPPED OUT OF MY SLEEP BY THE SOUND OF ANGELIQUE screaming at the top of her lungs. With a speed I didn't know I had, I grab my pocketknife from my nightstand and run down the hall, bursting into her room. But I find her all alone, her sheets tangled around her as she whimpers in her sleep, tears streaking down her face.

"Angel?" I whisper, frowning as I watch her.

"Please..." she whimpers, still asleep. "Please stop, Alec."

Alec? As in her dance partner in New York?

Instead of waking her, I back out of her room slowly, mindful that I've just broken one of the rules she set and close the door behind me. Standing in the hallway, listening to her whimpering behind the door, a piece of my heart fractures.

I clench the knife tighter in my hand, my knuckles burning white. I don't know the full story, but from how she's begging him to stop, I know that if I ever see him, I'll slit his fucking throat.

I turn and press my back to the wall, my chest heaving as I fight the urge to go back in and wake her up just to hold her and tell her she's safe. I sit on the floor outside her door, knife still in hand, and I wait until the whimpers stop. Then I close my eyes and lean my head back against the wall.

"I've got you, Angel," I whisper into the dark. "Even if you don't know it yet."

CHAPTER 10

REIGN

The next morning, while I sit at the kitchen island and wait for Angelique to come out of her bedroom, I take to the internet to try to find out more about Alec. It doesn't take long for me to discover that he goes through female partners like they're disposable— smiling on opening night, gone by season's end.

I'm not one to judge. I'm no better, but I can't stop thinking about Angelique's voice last night, begging him to stop.

Stop what, exactly?

My jaw tightens as I keep reading. According to a dated but detailed Wiki entry, every single one of his partners quit ballet altogether after dancing with him. It's a pattern that doesn't sit right as I recall Angelique saying she quit dancing, too.

What did he do to her?

I lock my phone at the soft creak of her bedroom door opening, placing it back in my pocket as I bring my coffee mug to my mouth. She walks out of her room dressed in rehearsal gear and makes her way down the hall. Her curls are bunched into a messy bun atop her head and the dark circles under her eyes tell me the rest of her night must have been just as restless as mine.

"Morning," she murmurs, yawning as she passes me without so much as a glance.

"Morning," I reply, watching her pour herself a cup of the coffee I made earlier. "Sleep okay?"

She hesitates, taking a sip before setting her mug down. "Yeah, how about you?"

I consider her for a moment. Should I pretend like nothing happened? Or should I bring it up and see if she opens up to me? I stand and walk over to the sink.

"I was," I say lightly, rinsing my empty cup and placing it in the sink. "Until I heard you scream and figured someone must have broken in to kill you." I raise an eyebrow, attempting for humour to soften the delivery. "Then I stayed up the rest of the night wondering if I was next."

She spins to face me, eyes wide with alarm. "I screamed?"

"Loud enough to wake the dead," I confirm with a nod. "Do you do that often?"

She swallows hard, gaze falling to the floor. "Sometimes," she says quietly. "But I usually wake myself up before it gets bad."

I face her and lean my hip against the counter, crossing my arms over my chest.

"I thought I heard you say the name Alec at one point," I say, testing the waters.

She takes a shaky step back as soon as his name leaves my lips, her hip hitting the side of the counter. She has the same look of panic on her face that she had yesterday when we almost tried the lift.

"I was starting to wonder if you'd broken one of our rules and brought a guy over." When she doesn't say anything, I keep going. "He was your partner at the Big Apple, right? Were you two dati—"

"I decided on another rule," she says quickly, voice trembling. "No more asking about anything to do with New York."

She turns on her heel and walks out the front door, leaving her steaming coffee behind on the counter, and I know then and there that whatever happened in New York was bad. I stay frozen for a beat, staring at the door she left open, long enough to let in the morning chill before I pick up her mug and walk it to the sink.

Her reaction said more than any answer could have. Whatever Alec did, it's something that buried itself inside her and stayed there like rot. My mind won't stop building its own narrative, stacking possibilities of what he could have done.

Did he hurt her during rehearsal? Like drop her during a lift?

My grip tightens on the ceramic as I try to breathe through the rising anger and keep from letting the storm inside of me spill out, but then I picture her flinching away from me in the studio, and lying in bed, twisted in the sheets, crying, begging him to stop.

Did he force her to do something she didn't want to?

I see it—and I feel it. The violence of it; the violation—and I know that in that moment Alec took a piece of her she'll never get back. Something inside me snaps as I close my eyes and clench my jaw so tight my teeth ache. I slam the mug into the sink harder than I intend, hearing the sharp crack of ceramic on porcelain followed by a shatter.

Glass fragments burst in every direction like shrapnel

while I stand there, chest heaving, my hands braced on either side of the basin, staring down at the broken pieces. If I find out Alec laid a hand on her—if he's the reason she's like this—God help him if I ever see his fucking face.

~

I FIND ANGELIQUE AT THE ESTATE STUDIO TEN MINUTES LATER. She's already stretching at the barre when I walk in, her posture tense. She doesn't see me yet, so I say nothing, choosing to watch for a moment instead.

Her energy used to be so loud when we were younger, and I remember watching her curiously back then, too. I couldn't understand how someone could light up a room the way she had. I'd always been jealous of Lando for having someone like that in his life, someone to brighten up the dark days.

But she's different now, more guarded. Grief did that to her when her dad died. I remember how empty she looked afterward, like the light had been siphoned out and no one noticed except me. Losing him hollowed her out in ways I think only I fully understood.

She still looks empty inside now, but I don't think it really has anything to do with her dad, and all to do with why she moved back to Marlow. What would happen if she ever trusted me enough to let me in again and tell me what happened in New York? But what if she tells me something horrible? What then? Do I fly to New York? Beat the shit out of the person who hurt her?

Yes, I growl in my head.

But even I can admit that'd be an overstep on my end. She's not my friend, and she sure as hell isn't mine. Not anymore. Yet I can't help but feel protective of her, curious even. But curiosity can turn cruel when you don't have the heart to follow through.

I don't believe in love, not the way people talk about it, like it's some kind of salvation. Not since I've learned that love is just another word for leaving. For breaking things that don't deserve to be broken. I've lived under the philosophy that people always leave. No matter how tightly you hold them, they find the door eventually. Because love is a temporary, fleeting feeling.

And Angelique? She already looks like she's barely holding herself together. The last thing she needs is someone like me getting too close, because if she ever lets me in again, I don't know that I'll be able to give her anything real, and I sure as hell don't want to be the one who ruins her any more than she already is.

I watch her closely, noticing how she avoids looking at the mirrored wall, avoids looking at herself. If she had glanced that way, just once, she would have seen me already.

"There you are," I say, pretending not to notice when she startles. "Wasn't sure you'd still come."

She stands up straighter and wipes her hands before tugging her sleeves lower.

"Yeah, well. The show must go on, right?" She looks around the studio, her eyes softening. "I never had time to say it last time we were in here, but this place hasn't changed much."

I shrug. "I didn't want it to."

This building is the only part of the estate untouched by my father's endless renovations. Either he forgot it existed when he laid out the floor plans for the construction crew, or he didn't care enough to gut it like everything else.

It still feels like my mom in here. She used to teach

private lessons, long before the rest of the house turned cold. I miss her, as stupid as that sounds, and this studio is the only thing she didn't take with her, the only part of her that I have left.

Angelique moves toward the barre, trailing her fingers along the worn wood, and when she turns back to face me, I take my time looking at her. She's beautiful. She's always been beautiful, but now it's different, older. There's a softness in her that calls to something brutal in me. I want to touch her, wreck her, just to see if she'd let me put her back together again. That thought alone should scare me, but it doesn't. It excites me.

I make my way to the piano in the corner of the room, flip the lid open, and let my fingers fall over the keys. A few scattered notes ring out, steadying me. Music has always made more sense than people. It doesn't lie, and it doesn't leave. It just exists—pure and exact, the way I wish life worked.

"I thought we'd start with the lakeside scene in Act Two," I say, pulling out my phone and connecting it to the Bluetooth speakers.

She nods, moving to stand in fourth position, but I can tell she's trying her hardest to look brave. I hit play and set the phone down on the piano before turning to face her.

"Already warmed up?"

Angelique nods again, so I step toward her. She doesn't run, but I see how her body braces for my touch in the way her spine subtly stiffens and how her shoulders lift just a fraction too high. She inhales and holds it like she's waiting for me to hurt her, and it pisses me off how automatic that reaction is; like it's muscle memory; like being touched means pain to her now.

What the fuck happened to you, Angel?

"We'll take it slow," I whisper. "No lifts unless you want to try them."

She gives another small nod, still avoiding my gaze.

I step behind her, hands hovering just off her hips. "You ready?"

She exhales. "As I'll ever be."

The first few steps feel mechanical. Her body knows the motions — the sweep of her arms, the angle of her chin — but there's no emotion in it, no connection. It's like she's trying to keep herself out of her own skin and disappear mid-performance. Maybe telling her she said his name was a bad idea after all.

"I can feel you thinking," I murmur as we turn, my palm grazing the small of her back. "Stop it."

"I'm not thinking," she lies.

I catch her waist more firmly this time, anchoring her. "Yes, you are." She stiffens but doesn't pull away.

"The audience won't need perfection," I say. "But they'll expect honesty in our dancing."

The music swells as I guide her into a slow pivot that lands her back against my chest. I don't move, choosing to let her stay there and feel the steady rise and fall of my breath. I should step back, but I don't. I like her close.

She smells like lilies, her curls brushing against my jaw as the heat of her body bleeds through the cotton of her top.

Her voice is small. "What if I don't know how to show that in my dancing anymore?"

"Then we learn how," I pause, "together."

I ease her into the next set of steps, slower than the tempo. I want her to feel safe in the movement, not pressured by it. When my hand glides over her rib cage to catch her underarm, I feel the shiver that ripples through her, but she still doesn't flinch or step away.

Progress.

We reach the part of the duet where the lift would begin and I stop, letting my hands fall away as I step back.

"Do you want to try it?" I ask, already knowing the answer, but asking anyway.

She hesitates and I watch her throat work as she swallows. "I... not today."

If she were anyone else, I'd already have them in the air, whether they were ready or not. I've done it before; tossed dancers higher than they could handle and let the chips fall where they may. But I want her trust more than I want her in the air, and that pisses me off because the part of me that craves control, that wants to own every inch of her skin and breath and movement, hates being gentle.

I nod. "Okay."

When we're done rehearsing, I reach for the door and hold it open for Angelique. She slips past me, and I follow her out into the early morning light, the studio door swinging shut behind us with a soft click.

We walk side by side toward the guesthouse, the silence between us more comfortable than it was earlier. It's not tense, or awkward, just quiet in that way two people can be when they're tired.

I look over to her as we walk, noticing how her hair's falling out of the bun, a few strands clinging to the side of her neck. She's flushed, cheeks still pink, her top sticking to her back in places. She's beautiful—frustratingly so—and the worst part is, I don't think she even knows it.

I shouldn't be thinking about her like this, but fuck, a part of me doesn't care. I want to claim her as mine again, but I grit my teeth against it. That would only end up with us both feeling broken all over again.

"You did good in there."

She glances over, skeptical. "I didn't finish the scene a single time."

"Still," I shrug. "You tried, and that counts."

She's quiet for a moment, brows pinching slightly. "Thanks for not pushing, but you don't have to be so nice to me."

I nod, not sure what else to say. I never know what to do with gratitude—especially when it's directed at me. She pulls ahead slightly, and I let my gaze linger on the curve of her waist, the way her leggings hug her hips. It's a problem, how aware I am of her.

We're just a few paces from the guesthouse when I slow my steps. "I've been thinking maybe we could bring Lando in for the next few sessions. Just to help you get more comfortable with lifts before we try again?"

She pauses, just slightly, then turns to face me. "I'd like that." I catch her almost-smile. It's the first trace of the girl I remember, the one who used to laugh too loud and dream big.

We reach the guesthouse and stop walking. I watch as she lingers in front of the door, fingertips trailing across the wood, her chest rising and falling a little too fast. My gaze dips—just for a second—and I have to lock my jaw to keep from thinking about what it would feel like to touch her again. I almost reach for her just to feel her warmth under my hands, but I don't. Because if I touch her now, I won't stop, and she deserves softness, not the hunger clawing at my ribs.

"Thanks," she says softly, her eyes lowered. "For... making it feel safe."

That shouldn't be something she has to thank me for. It should be a given, not a gift. The fact that it isn't makes my stomach twist. My fists clench at my sides, the need to touch her eclipsed by the deeper need to protect her from every hand that ever made her feel unsafe in a space that was supposed to be hers.

"Good morning," Lando shouts in the distance. I look over my shoulder and see him making his way over.

"Bring him to tomorrow's session," I say, voice low, already backing away.

Because if I stay a second longer, I might not be able to keep this rage from spilling out of me for a second time this morning. I turn and head toward my car, jaw clenched, fists in my pockets, not daring to glance back at her.

CHAPTER 11

ANGELIQUE

"What was that about?" Lando's voice cuts through the silence as he joins me outside the guesthouse. We both watch as Reign climbs into his burgundy Porsche, the engine growling to life before he peels away down the gravel path.

"I honestly do not know," I mutter, pushing open the guesthouse door.

Lando trails behind me, closing the door with a soft click. "Did you two just get back from a morning rehearsal?"

"Yeah, and he wants you to join us tomorrow."

He looks at me, dumbfounded. "Me? Reign wants me there?"

I nod, biting back a smirk.

He stares at me, utterly bewildered. "Well damn. I guess I've officially been promoted to third wheel."

I laugh, swatting his arm, and he grins in return. I cross to the kitchen and reach for my water bottle, twisting off the lid, but as I go to fill it at the sink, I notice that resting on a folded paper towel by the basin are the shattered pieces of the mug I'd filled with coffee earlier. I stare at it wondering what the hell happened after I left.

"Ready to get to work?" Lando asks, oblivious.

"Yeah," I say quickly, screwing the lid back on and tossing the bottle into my duffel. "Let's go."

"So," Lando says as he backs out of the driveway, trying—and failing—to look casual. "How was your first night with Reign?"

I groan, burying my face in my hands. "Do you want the shirtless and dripping wet version, or the part where he heard me having a nightmare?"

Lando nearly chokes on his breath. "Wait—what?"

"Yup." I rub at my temples. "I can't believe I didn't wake up from this one. Who knows how long I was screaming for?"

"Uh, no. Absolutely not. You don't just drop *'shirtless and dripping wet'* like that and then skip ahead. Back it up, because I need context. Now."

I let out a tired laugh and lean my head against the window. "I was getting a glass of water and thought the coast was clear. Then—BAM—the bathroom door swings, and out walks Reign, shirtless, dripping wet, steam and everything, and of course his towel was barely hanging on."

Lando blinks at the road. "Oh my God," he whispers, scandalized. "Continue."

I shoot him a look. "That's basically it. I froze, he stared, I panicked and ran, water went everywhere."

He chokes on a laugh. "And what, he just let you escape?"

I roll my eyes. "No. He texted me five minutes later saying, and I quote, *'For the record, I didn't mind you looking.'*"

Lando cackles so hard the car swerves to the left. "I knew he'd enjoy the attention. He's such a menace."

When we pull up to Imperium, it begins to rain. We grab our bags and make it inside just in time for Techniques, but Reign isn't here, and neither is Wendy.

I try to focus, but Layla corrects me more than once, and every time she touches my arms or angles my hips, I flinch —not from pain, but from getting caught being distracted. My thoughts won't stop spiraling.

It's still pouring when our lunch break rolls around. "Looks like we can't go out on the steps today," Willow says somberly as we watch the downpour from one of the hallway windows.

"What about the auditorium?" Alfie offers.

Max shakes his head. "When I walked past there earlier, it looked like they were preparing the space for something."

Four pairs of wide eyes turn to me.

"What?" I touch my face self-consciously.

"It's got to be auditions for your understudy," Willow whispers.

"Come on," Lando grabs my wrist, his excitement barely contained, "we're going to spy."

SEVERAL MINUTES LATER, I'M HIDDEN AWAY IN THE SHADOWS OF the back rows inside the auditorium, along with the others. Willow was right about auditions for my understudy being today. I spot Reign seated near the front along with Volkov, Layla, and one other person I haven't met yet.

"Who's that?" I whisper to Lando, nodding at the stranger.

His eyes light up. "Terry Baker. The hottest choreographer in the country. Probably the world. Total genius but a bit of a sadist."

He's tall, with a buzzed head and inked arms. He looks like he could break someone in half and still choreograph a masterpiece while doing it. Attractive, sure—but the kind of attractive that's almost terrifying. More intimidating than Reign, even.

"Why's Reign up there but not Angelique?" Max murmurs, unzipping a sandwich.

"Volkov probably wants to see the chemistry between Reign and the candidates," Alfie replies, taking a bite out of a liquorice stick.

Lando frowns. "Reign didn't tell you about this?" I shake my head, my stomach knotting.

The music starts and we watch dancer after dancer perform pieces from both Odette and Odile. In the end, it comes down to Wendy and another girl I've never met. I watch as Volkov leans in and whispers something into Reign's ear, and moments later, Reign stands up and strides onto the stage.

"Here we go," Lando mutters.

He begins a pas de deux with the girl I don't recognize, but he moves fast, so much faster than she's able to keep up with and I hold my breath as I watch her struggle before crashing onto her ankle at a horrible angle. She screams out in pain, and it reverberates around the auditorium, sending a shiver down my spine.

"That's what I meant when I said he breaks his partners," Lando murmurs, eyes fixed on the girl as she's helped offstage. "You keep up, or he leaves you behind."

But Reign hasn't been like that with me. He's been gentle. Why is he a different person here?

It's Wendy's turn now, and she's started with Odile. I

watch her enter the stage, fierce, her eyes never leaving Reign, and when he joins her, the energy between them crackles.

"Wow," I whisper as I watch them, something close to envy twisting in my chest.

This feels like I'm intruding on something personal. I can't help but think this is exactly what Volkov wants from me, and I know for a fact I don't have it in me to pull this off. Ever.

"They should just split the role. Let her have Odile," I whisper, more to myself.

"Angelique Denise Sinclair, I never want to hear those words come out of your mouth ever again," Lando hisses, twisting to look at me.

I wince. "Gross, I haven't heard my full name said like that in years."

"I'm serious. Don't compare yourself to Wendy."

"How can I not?" I whisper. "She's literally auditioning for my role."

He goes quiet, and we watch as Wendy finishes the adage with Reign. She's brilliant and passionate enough to mask the complete lack of emotion in him. I'm not at all surprised to find not only Volkov standing and clapping at the end, but Layla and Terry as well.

"If only Angelique danced like this," Volkov says, his voice bouncing around the room.

My stomach drops and humiliation floods through every ounce of my body as I feel the stares of my friends turn to me, but I refuse to look at them as I hold my breath.

"That is the seducing I talk about," Volkov continues, gesturing to Wendy. "Maybe she should be Swan Queen."

His words land like a slap and without a second

thought, I stand and quietly make my way up the auditorium stairs, toward the back exit doors. I'm too humiliated to sit here and listen to Volkov point out that I'm not the right fit for this role.

"Angelique is my partner," Reign says, his voice firm. "If she doesn't dance, then neither do I."

I freeze, my hands hovering on the door handle as I look over my shoulder. He's still standing on the stage, but his eyes are on me now.

How the hell did he even see me from that far away?

My heart pounds viscously as I hold his gaze, his words ricocheting in my head.

"What?" Wendy demands. "The whole point of an understudy is so that you can still perform without her."

Reign drags his eyes from mine and looks down at Wendy, bored. "Like I said, if Angelique doesn't dance, then neither will I. You can dance with my understudy if that happens."

Wendy's jaw drops as she watches him jump off the stage, rage written all over her face.

"Who's that?" Terry asks from below.

I look down at where he and the instructors are seated and see that he's facing me now, watching Reign stalk up the stairs toward me.

"That is Angelique Sinclair," Layla replies, glaring at Volkov. "Our Swan Queen."

"Is that so?" Terry grins. "I'd like to meet with you both in an hour."

Reign nods and turns back to me. "Let's go." He takes my hand without hesitation, Willow squealing excitedly a few rows down, and walks out of the auditorium, gently tugging me along.

We catch the attention of nearly half the company on our way down the hall and up flights of stairs, each person looking at our joined hands in shock.

"Where are we going?" I ask, trying to pull my hand free, but Reign only tightens his grip and stays quiet.

A few minutes later, we step onto the rooftop and into a glass-domed greenhouse. Of all the things to find on the rooftop of a ballet company, a greenhouse would have been at the bottom of my list.

"Wow," I breathe, staring at the lush chaos of greenery around me.

Reign finally releases my hand and crosses to the far end, lighting a cigarette in the open doorway. I watch the smoke curl into the rain outside as I stay quiet, waiting for him to speak first.

"I'm sorry you had to hear that," he finally says, staring at me over his shoulder before looking back out at the pouring rain, taking another pull.

I take slow steps until I'm leaning on the frame opposite him. "It's not like what Volkov said isn't true," I say, my voice quiet.

Reign growls in frustration, surprising me, and turns to face me fully. "*Everything* Volkov said isn't true."

"Reign." I sigh. "I was there. I saw how amazing Wendy is. She's exactly what this production needs in an Odile."

"This production wouldn't exist without you," he says.

He throws the barely smoked cigarette out into the rain and steps closer, inches from me now, causing my breath to hitch.

"I'm not dancing this without you," he says, his tone deathly serious.

"Why?"

He falters, like I've caught him off guard. "Does it matter?"

"Yeah, actually. It does," I reply. "Because surely you know that I can't keep up with you, Reign. I'll end up just another broken partner."

He rears his head back like I've offended him. "Believe me when I say if I wanted to break you, I already would have."

"Exactly! It's so easy to do because we're at two completely different levels. So why are you so set on having me as your partner when you can have someone that's so much better than me?"

Instead of replying, he watches me like I've cracked open something he didn't expect to find, and now he doesn't know what to do with it.

"Forget it," I mutter, stepping back, my voice tight. "Just... forget I said anything."

I turn to go, but his hand wraps around my wrist, gently pulling me back.

"Tell me you won't quit," he says, low.

"What?" I turn to look at him.

His eyes lock on mine, clearer than I've ever seen them. "Don't quit," he says again, softer now. "Promise me you won't."

I don't understand why it matters to him so much to be dancing with me, but I can tell he needs to hear me say it. I can feel it in the space between us, and for once, I don't want to lie, or run, or hide.

"I promise," I whisper.

His hand slips from my wrist, fingers lingering a second longer than they should. It's almost nothing. Almost. But it feels like everything.

"I should go," I say, clearing my throat and stepping back like I've touched something hot. "I'll, uhm... I'll see you in an hour. With Terry."

I turn and walk away, not stopping until I'm back inside, the door shutting behind me, and my pulse still thrumming in my ears.

CHAPTER 12

REIGN

"Angelique, I don't think I've had the pleasure of meeting you yet. My name is Terry Baker and I'm the choreographer for this season's Swan Lake production."

Terry takes Angelique's hand and kisses the back of it. He's a world-renowned choreographer, originally from Australia, and he costs Imperium an exceptional amount of money to keep around. But he's worth every penny, because there hasn't been a single production that he's worked on that hasn't taken my breath away.

He's also my closest friend.

Angelique stiffens the minute he touches her, but she forces a polite smile. "It's a pleasure to meet you, Terry," she says.

"Likewise." He grins, holding her gaze. "I've enjoyed watching your performances over the years."

Angelique's face turns crimson. "You've been to my performances?"

"Oh yes." Terry's eyes slide to mine, a sly smile playing on his lips. "I've practically been to all of them."

Angelique tucks a loose strand of hair behind her ear, and I feel the beginnings of furious jealousy bubbling inside of me, itching to claw its way out and wrap itself around Terry's neck like a noose.

"Why did you want us to meet with you, exactly?"

I can't hide the bite from my tone as I stare at their still-joined hands. Terry looks amused but releases Angelique, winking at me when I lift my gaze to his.

The bastard is playing mind games with me, and he knows I know it.

"I heard through the grapevine that you two have a bit of a chemistry problem?" He gestures between me and Angelique. "Some type of *'underlying trauma with touching'*, as Volkov put it."

I grind my teeth as I hold his gaze. "It sounds like Volkov just doesn't know how to do his job properly, and he's having a hard time accepting that."

"Couldn't agree more," Terry sneers. "But I have to admit, the choreography for this production is boring me."

"Aren't you the one that put it together?" I ask, confused, as I sit down in one of the front row seats.

He pulls himself up onto the edge of the auditorium stage. "I know. Not my best work, but I think the problem is that I tried to stick to the original storyline of Swan Lake a bit too much and now the choreography doesn't feel unique."

I lift a brow, finding that Angelique is mirroring my expression as she stares at him. "What are you proposing, then?"

He grins. "Well, I found your chemistry dilemma inspiring, and it got me thinking...why don't we rewrite Swan Lake? Make it ours."

"What do you mean?" Angelique asks as she takes a seat

next to me, her shoulder brushing against mine and causing a spark of energy to ignite through my entire arm.

I bite down on the inside of my cheek to keep myself from reaching over and dragging her onto my lap just to have her closer, to bask in the tension between us, and to prove a point to Terry.

She's mine.

"In the original storyline, Odile is the villain, and she causes the famous tragic ending where both Siegfried and Odette choose eternal love in death," Terry explains, tapping his clipboard with his pen.

"Right," I affirm.

"Well, what if instead we explore Odile not as a villain, but as a wounded woman reaching for light?"

"You want to turn Swan Lake into a redemptive Odile arc?" I raise a brow.

Terry is known for being an imaginative choreographer, truly one of a kind. But *this*, this is on another plane of existence. And it might just be exactly what my father wants for Imperium.

"It would be a unique approach, one of a kind, especially with us having only one dancer to play both roles," he says, gesturing to Angelique.

"I don't think I understand," she frowns, leaning forward.

"Okay, imagine Odette and Odile as one fractured soul. The curse is not evil magic, but trauma, and the love between Odette and the prince is not just romantic but also healing."

Angelique shifts uncomfortably in her seat but nods in understanding.

"How would that look in terms of the performance?" I ask, my interest piqued now.

"We'd split it up into three acts," Terry says as he draws imaginary lines on his palm that only make sense to him.

"Act One will be *The Split*, where we start with Odette. She's the graceful, delicate, and emotionally raw half. We'll show the audience that she becomes cursed by her trauma, along with everything that she can't process," he continues.

Angelique's brow furrows slightly. "What's the trauma she experiences?"

Terry studies her. "I haven't decided yet. Any ideas?"

She falls silent, picking at a loose thread on her shirt. "What about some sort of assault or betrayal?" She suggests, her voice a little too steady for how loaded the words are.

And instantly, Alec's name flares in my mind like a lit match to gasoline.

Is that what he did to her? Assault her?

My jaw tightens and I can feel my pulse in my teeth now. Every version of what might've happened between them claws through my mind, each darker than the last. I want to be wrong. God, I want to be so fucking wrong. But the way she begged him to stop in her dream, how she won't talk about New York, and how she still flinches when I get too close... it all fits with what I'm thinking. She's not just running from New York. She's running from him.

I study her, this girl who used to burn so brightly, now looking like she's trying to shrink herself out of existence. And all I can think about are the many ways I can make sure Alec never dances again.

No. I'll make sure he never walks again.

Terry taps his chin, staring off into space. "Yes, that's good. I'll see if I can weave something like that into the choreography."

He pauses and writes a quick note before continuing.

"We'll see Odile as the part of Odette that survived by shutting everything down. She channels all the pain and rage that she feels into seduction like it's her armour. She's not trying to deceive the prince, she's just trying to protect what's left of her."

"She's Odette's shadow," Angelique murmurs.

Terry beams. "Exactly. They both want the prince to love them, but he doesn't realize they're the same person. He rejects Odette and her vulnerability, and chooses Odile, thinking she's strong, but that moment fractures her even more."

I sit forward. "So, the tragedy is internal. She's not just heartbroken, she's fragmented?"

"Right," Terry nods. "Then comes Act Two, *The Confrontation*. Odile realizes she isn't her complete self, and she finally sees what she's done by splitting from Odette. It's not power, it's desperation smeared with guilt. She questions herself, and her regret sets in."

Angelique's gaze drops to her lap. I can tell this new version of Swan Lake is affecting her, and my curiosity grows tenfold. I want to know what thoughts are swirling around in her mind right now and what memories are plaguing her.

"She tries to undo it," Terry continues, more softly now, also noticing the change in Angelique and glancing my way for a quick moment, his eyes questioning. "She searches for Odette to try to reconcile. We can throw in a pas de deux here where the two halves meet, and Odile pleads for forgiveness while Odette reaches for her."

"And then Act Three?" I ask.

Terry straightens. "*The Reunion*. The prince returns, and he's changed too. He sees the truth and realizes that he can't love only one version of her. He needs to embrace the whole woman. Odette *and* Odile."

He pauses, then adds, "They dance a pas de trois, and the audience will see the surrender and healing. No death and no tragedy, just redemption. And in the ultimate moment, she rises. Whole. Seen. Loved. Yada yada yada."

The silence between us stretches as Angelique blinks rapidly, her eyes glossy. Her voice is hushed when she finally speaks. "It's not just a ballet."

"No," Terry says, meeting her gaze. "It's a reckoning."

"I like it," I say, sitting up straighter. "But how do we do the pas de deux between Odette and Odile and a pas de trois if Angelique is the one dancing both female roles?"

Terry waves me off. "We have options. We can use projection mapping to show Odile as a shadowed phantom behind Odette for the pas de deux, and if you're up for it, Angelique, we can reimagine the pas de trois as a solo within a duet."

"Meaning?" she asks.

"You'd switch between Odette and Odile live, using detachable costume elements and lighting changes," Terry explains.

"That sounds challenging," I say, glancing at Angelique, but instead of the fear I was expecting to see there, I see determination.

"Let's do it," she says with a finality that sparks excitement in me.

I turn to Terry, giving him my nod of approval, and he grins. "Alright, I'll get to work, and I should have the updated choreography for you by the end of the week."

CHAPTER 13
ANGELIQUE

Lando tugs the hood of his sweatshirt tighter around his curls as we walk toward the studio. The morning air is cool, with a stillness that feels like the rest of the world is still asleep. Dew clings to the hedges, and a faint mist hangs over the estate grounds.

When I woke up this morning, Reign was already gone, but he'd brewed a fresh pot of coffee and left a breakfast plate for me with a sticky note saying *'see you and Lando at the studio'* before leaving.

A small, stupid part of me finds it endearing because in a way, it almost feels like maybe he still cares. But another, louder, part of me wonders why he's like this. Warm one moment, distant the next. Why is he acting like we're still friends? Like we're more than that? Like we never stopped being anything at all? Like he didn't ghost me five years ago?

He never gave me an explanation, or a goodbye, and now he's back in my orbit—making me breakfast, leaving notes, calling in my best friend like he suddenly knows what I need. And the worst part is, a part of me wants to fall right back into him, as if nothing ever happened.

"You're absolutely sure he said he wants me there, too?" Lando asks for the seventh time, glancing sideways at me.

I can't help laughing at how nervous he sounds. "Yes, Lando. He wants you there."

He still looks skeptical. "Are we talking about the same Reign who once told me I'd never be able to do a double tour en l'air because I have *'too much flair and not enough air'?*"

I laugh again, this time louder. "That was twelve years ago, and you landed on your face."

"My flair was ahead of its time," he mutters, but he's smiling now. "But what's the point if we're changing the choreography altogether now?"

"There's still going to be a pas de deux in the new choreo, and I'm still struggling to dance with Reign," I admit. "I haven't let him do a lift yet."

"Why not? What happens when he tries?"

"Images of Alec flash through my mind, and I end up halfway across the studio."

He looks at me with concern. "What if it happens when I try to lift you, too?"

I shrug. "I'm more comfortable with you, so I'm hoping it won't. Otherwise, this entire production is screwed."

Lando laughs nervously. "No pressure then."

We're just about to reach the studio when we both pause at the sound of a soft piano melody drifting out through the partially open door, hauntingly beautiful and full of feeling. The melody winds through the morning fog, wrapping around my ribs until they ache with sadness.

"Do you hear that?" he whispers.

"Let's go look," I reply.

We edge closer to the studio, steps feather-light on the stones. I gently press my fingers against the doorframe, careful not to push it open as we both peer through the narrow glass panel.

Inside, Reign sits at the piano. His eyes are closed, fingers gliding across the keys with little effort. The music pours out of him, and it hits me all at once—this is what he's missing when he dances. This emotion, the way he seems lost in something bigger than himself. He looks...free. And it's at this moment that I realize I've never seen Reign Herrington truly feel before.

"I didn't know he could play like that," Lando whispers, eyes wide.

I shake my head. "I didn't know he could play at all."

The melody slows and softens as Reign's eyes blink open, and in the reflection of the mirrored wall, his eyes find mine, and for a moment, I forget to breathe. When he finishes the last notes, he stands.

"Done spying on me?" he asks, voice carrying easily through the door.

Lando jumps so hard that he yelps and elbows the door, causing it to swing open with a loud creak, revealing us frozen in place, caught eavesdropping.

"Shit," Lando mutters, standing up straighter.

Reign raises an eyebrow. "Subtle, brother."

He deadpans, before his eyes lock on mine again, like he's not quite ready to look away. I break eye contact and attempt to act like my skin isn't prickling from the way he's looking at me. Reign shuts the piano lid with a quiet thud and crosses his arms. He doesn't look mad, just mildly amused in that very Reign way that makes it impossible to tell what he's really thinking.

"You didn't have to wait outside," he says.

"We didn't want to interrupt," I say, stepping into the studio, Lando close behind me. "That was... beautiful."

Surprise and discomfort flicker across his face.

Has no one complimented his playing before?

"I didn't realize you could play so well," Lando adds, sounding almost cautious. "To be honest, I thought you quit after Mum left, but it sounds like you got even better on your own."

Reign's jaw ticks, and his posture shifts uncomfortably. I glance at Lando, who immediately looks like he regrets bringing up their mom.

Reign shrugs, brushing it off. "It helps clear my mind."

I want to ask what it is he's trying to clear his mind of, but we're not close enough anymore for that level of honesty. I step further into the room, walking slowly toward the piano, letting my fingers graze the edge of it, glancing up to find Reign watching me a few steps away.

"What was the piece you were playing?" I ask. "It sounded so sad."

He hesitates. "Something I've been working on."

"You wrote that?" I immediately want to kick myself for sounding so impressed.

Reign nods, then shifts his focus, done with the conversation. "Are you both ready to rehearse?"

Lando claps his hands together and gives me a crooked smile. "Absolutely."

We move toward the centre of the studio to begin a quick warm up. I look back at Reign, the song he played still echoing in my head, and I can't help the overwhelming urge to hear more of the music he's composed.

Lando stretches his arms out with a dramatic sigh, already playing it up like we're about to go on stage at

Covent Garden. It's both hilarious and adorable how excited he is to be here.

"So," he says, glancing between us, unserious, "am I being you or her?"

"You're me," Reign replies, rolling his eyes.

Lando gives a quick bow. "A tall order, but I'll try."

I stifle a giggle as I roll my shoulders and stretch my arms overhead, trying to push through the residual tension. I can still feel Reign watching, and my pulse quickens in response, my breath shallow as heat rises under my skin. I try to focus on Lando, who is doing a grand jeté across the studio and narrating it like an announcer at the Olympics.

"Ten out of ten! Gold medal for sheer theatrical chaos!"

I allow myself to laugh, and for a second, the heaviness lifts.

"Let's start with an adage and then move into a lift," Reign interrupts from his spot by the mirrored wall, and I can't tell if he's annoyed or amused by his brother's theatrics.

"You're no fun," Lando pouts as he steps toward me, already in character, but his eyes are kind.

I step into first position, my muscles still aching from yesterday, but it's different this morning. There's a buzz under my skin that I can't shake, like something's shifted ever since we made the decision to rewrite Swan Lake. This new version feels personal, like it was rewritten specifically for me and my own healing journey.

I exhale slowly as the music begins, letting myself fall into the rhythm. Lando's hands are warm as he takes mine, his grip reassuring. We move through the opening sequence, our turns flowing more naturally than I expected. He's not as technically sharp as Reign, but he listens with his body and gives me room to breathe.

It's easier with Lando. Not easy—but easier. He doesn't push too hard or press too close, he doesn't make my skin prickle like it's waiting for something to go wrong. With him, it feels like I have space. Like I'm allowed to take up space.

We're halfway through the first lift when Reign cuts in. "Angle your wrists—no, softer."

I try to adjust, watching myself in the mirror, but when he steps closer to demonstrate, reaching for my elbow, my body tenses and I flinch on instinct before I can stop myself.

His hand pauses mid-air, then slowly retracts. "I'll talk you through it," he says, voice gentler now. "Your right leg needs to sweep higher on the transition. Let's start again from the arabesque."

I watch him as he returns to leaning against the mirrored wall, arms crossed. His eyes are focused on mine as Lando and I try again, but this time when I move, I feel something spark to life in me; like a nerve waking up after too long asleep.

Lando's hands find my waist again and when he lifts me, I rise steadier. My leg extends with more confidence, the lines of my body cutting clean through the air. I'm weightless, suspended in motion, and I want to believe I can stay there. I want to believe I can trust my body again.

"Better," Reign murmurs, and the word coils around my spine, grounding me as much as the floor when I land again.

The music continues playing and we keep moving, step by step, through the old choreography, but it's different now. Reign isn't correcting every beat anymore. He's watching and making mental notes, and when our eyes meet again, there's heat there. He's studying the way I move, like he's searching for something only he knows how to recognize, and it rattles me in the best way. We finish the run and land the final pose, my breath heavy and my heart louder than the music.

"Good," Reign says after a beat. "Again."

Lando groans. "No praise? No gold star? No break?"

Reign raises a brow. "Do you want praise or perfection?"

Lando mimes shooting himself in the head and slumps dramatically onto the floor. "You sound just like dad. I knew you were always the favourite."

Reign smirks. "No, you were just louder. And you know how much he hated that."

Despite myself, I laugh. It's brief, barely more than a breath, but it surprises me. I catch my reflection in the mirror, noticing how my skin is flushed and how my chest rises and falls. And in that moment, surrounded by the quiet thrum of music and breath and effort, something in me eases. This space, this process—it's feeling like mine again. Like maybe I belong here, even after everything.

After another run through and an almost perfect lift, Lando disappears to grab water, muttering something about needing to *hydrate before he dies*, and he leaves me alone with Reign. The silence stretches heavily between us in the way it always is with him—like there's more being said between the quiet than the words we ever manage out loud. I turn toward the mirror, wiping the sweat from my neck with a towel.

"You're different today," he says. "More relaxed."

I shrug. "Maybe I'm just trying harder not to disappoint you."

His brow lifts just slightly. "I don't want that from you."

I turn around, facing him now. "Then what do you want?"

"I want you to dance like you did before the world broke you. Like you still believe this is your dream."

My chest tightens, the way it always does when someone gets too close to the truth. "I'm trying," I whisper.

"I know."

I look down at my feet, then back up at him, and the air shifts again as his eyes drop for a split second, to the skin of my collarbone, still damp from sweat, and then up to my lips. He doesn't let his gaze linger for long, but I catch it.

Is it possible that Reign Harrington still wants me as much as I want him?

"I should…" I gesture vaguely toward the bench, the water, anywhere else. My throat feels dry all over again.

He steps back just enough to break the moment. "Same time tomorrow."

I nod, but don't turn away yet. "Reign?"

He glances at me. "Yeah?"

"Thanks again for letting Lando step in, and for not pushing too hard."

His eyes soften just a little before he nods in acknowledgement. I grab my bag and turn to leave, feeling his eyes on me again as I leave the studio. But this time, I don't feel exposed; this time, I feel seen.

LANDO IS SITTING ON THE LOW STONE WALL JUST OUTSIDE THE studio, his head tipped back as he chugs from a giant water bottle like he's been stranded in a desert. When he spots me, he lowers it with a dramatic gasp.

"Oh, thank God," he wheezes. "I thought he murdered you and buried your body under the floor."

I huff a laugh and walk toward him, brushing my damp hair off my neck. "He was... restrained."

"Terrifying," Lando nods, standing. "Reign restrained is honestly even more intense than him yelling. He's like a tiger on a leash—very quiet, very golden-eyed, and just waiting to rip someone's throat out."

I roll my eyes. "Charming."

We fall into step, walking the gravel path back toward the guesthouse. The morning air is warming now, sunlight stretching across the garden in lazy slants. My legs ache in that satisfying way ballet always leaves behind, but it's not just the rehearsal that's left me rattled. It's Reign. The way he looked at me. The way it felt to have his attention on me —like I was something he was trying to figure out. I loved every second.

"So," Lando says after a beat, dragging out the word.

I glance at him and see that he's grinning knowingly. "So?" I narrow my eyes.

He shrugs, a little too innocently. "Nothing. Just... wondering how long you two plan on pretending you're not seconds away from combusting in a fit of unresolved sexual tension."

I stop walking. "Lando—"

"Oh, don't Lando me." He halts too, turning to face me with both hands on his hips. "I'm not blind. I know you two fooled around behind my back years ago. There's chemistry between you two," he jabs a finger at me, "he watches you like he's starving and you're the last meal on Earth, and you, you blush every time he so much as looks your way."

"I do not," I scoff.

He cocks his head. "You're literally blushing right now just from the mention of him."

I press my hands to my cheeks feeling the scorching heat for myself.

Damn it.

"It's nothing. We're just figuring out how to work together."

"Uh-huh." Lando lifts a skeptical brow. "And how do you explain the way he looks at you? Or the way you flinched today, and he just backed off? That's not the same Reign that I know."

I bite the inside of my cheek. That moment is still replaying in my mind on a never-ending loop.

"I'm not saying it's a bad thing," Lando says, softer now. "I think you make each other better. But babe... this isn't just artistic chemistry, and you know it."

I look at him, the lump forming in my throat too familiar. "Even if you're right, it's not that simple."

"Because of what happened?" he asks gently, and I nod.

Lando sighs, stepping closer. "I don't know what it's like to carry what you carry, but I know Reign, and I've never seen him like this. He's usually a locked door with a deadbolt. With you... it's like he's trying to open."

That hits something inside me I didn't expect. I glance away, my voice quiet. "I don't know if I'm ready."

"You don't have to be," he says. "But maybe just... try to open your mind to the idea that he could be another safe person in your life."

I exhale slowly, staring out over the lawn. The sun catches on the dew still clinging to the grass and suddenly, everything feels too alive.

"I'm scared," I admit.

Lando nods. "I know."

He bumps his shoulder into mine as we start walking again.

"But just so we're clear," he adds, grinning again. "If this turns into some epic tortured romance where I have to watch my brother pine tragically for you while you pine back in silence, I'm staging an intervention. With snacks and possibly a slideshow."

I snort. "You're the worst."

He flashes me a wink and for the first time in days, I smile without effort.

CHAPTER 14

REIGN

At exactly two in the morning on Saturday, while watching the end of a surf tournament for my favourite surf team, The Saltwater Shredders, my phone pings with an email notification from Terry.

I almost text the bastard and ask why he's still awake but when I open the email, I find several video attachments of the new choreography along with his request that Angelique and I look them over together and come prepared on Monday to rehearse with him and Volkov. Knowing Terry, he's barely slept all week to complete the choreo in time.

Angelique went to bed hours ago, so I forward the email to her inbox so she can take a look in the morning, but minutes later I hear her room door creak open. I glance over my shoulder and see her walking down the hallway in another oversized T-shirt.

"Lord, help me," I mumble, my eyes burning a path along her perfect bare legs. I turn around and hit the mute button just as my favourite surfer, Koa, comes onto the television for a post-race interview.

"I think we're going to need to add a dress code to our rule list," I say with a smirk, turning to face her again, but the words die on my lips when I see her.

Angelique's eyes are vacant and downcast as she slowly walks around the open space, gently bumping into the couch before slowly redirecting herself to avoid it altogether.

"Everything okay, Angel?" I ask, slowly standing from the couch as she nears me.

She doesn't reply, stopping in front of me and staring directly at my chest. My brows pinch together as I watch her, and we stand like that for a few seconds longer before I drift to the side to test something. As predicted, almost instantly she begins walking again.

"Are you sleepwalking?" I mumble, surprised when she stops and turns back around to face me.

Angelique's empty eyes shine with unshed tears, and I feel a protective anger flare up inside me as I take long strides in her direction and pull her into my chest. Her arms slowly wrap around my centre, and she gently lays her head against my torso.

Under different circumstances, I might enjoy how right this feels. Having her in my arms. How perfectly she fits, like a missing puzzle piece finally clicking back into place. How she makes me feel whole in a way I don't quite understand.

But, under these circumstances, I'm more focused on figuring out what's haunting her mind to the point of crying. When I pull back moments later, her cheeks are streaked with tears, but her expression is still void of any emotion.

"I'm going to have to break your rule again," I murmur, my voice low so that I don't startle her awake as I gently turn her around and guide her down the hallway, back to her room.

She moves slowly, eyes still half-lidded. When we reach her room, I steer her toward the bed and help her lie back down. The moment her head touches the pillow, her eyes drift fully closed, and her breathing deepens instantly.

I cover her with the duvet before I sit on the edge of the bed and watch her. Long, dark curls spread messily across the pillow, wild and soft, and her face looks so peaceful now in a way I haven't seen in years.

I allow myself to stay there for a moment, listening to the rhythm of her breath. First night terrors, and now sleepwalking? This isn't normal. Something's not right, and I don't know how to fix it, or if she'd even let me.

My hands tighten into fists on my lap. I want to stay in her room and watch over her as if I can keep her safe from whatever is haunting her, but I leave her room when I'm sure she's back to deep sleeping, softly closing the door behind me and walking back to the couch, ignoring the television completely now.

I turn on my laptop and do a quick internet search, not at all surprised to find that adult sleepwalking can be because of a trauma response. I feel myself begin to spiral, and before I think better of it, I pull out my phone and text Lando.

ME:

Are you awake?

Surprisingly, I don't wait long for his reply.

LANDO:

Woah, so you do remember how to use your phone. Proud of you, brother!

ME:

> Can you meet me outside the gardens?

LANDO:

> Right now?

ME:

> Yes.

LANDO:

> Is everything alright with Angelique?

ME:

> See you in five.

I make it to the bench just outside the gardens in less than three minutes. Lando meets me there shortly after, wearing a long silk robe, and riding boots. I raise my brows, taken aback by his very un-Lando-ish outfit.

"Don't even think about commenting on my outfit right now, Reign," he warns, frowning at me as he takes a seat next to me, arms folded across his chest. "What the hell is going on that you had to meet with me right this very second, in the middle of the night?"

"Was I interrupting something?" I ask, sitting down next to him and leaning forward with my elbows resting on my knees.

"I may have someone over." He crosses his arms and bristles.

"Sorry," I offer. "But I just tucked Angelique back into her bed after she walked around the house."

Lando blanches as he looks at me. "Stop, you're scaring me. This is giving possessed scary movie vibes right now, and I'm already scared enough as it is walking through the halls of our house alone in the middle of the night."

I roll my eyes. "She's not possessed, dumbass. She was sleepwalking."

He lets out a relieved sigh, swiping at the sweat on his forehead. "Oh, thank God. I was ready to call for an exorcism."

"Can you be serious for just one minute?" I snap.

Lando looks at me surprised, but he nods and falls silent, waiting for me to continue.

"I searched up what causes sleepwalking in adults," I admit, sitting straighter now and looking at him. "And one reason listed was trauma."

He averts his eyes right away, confirming my suspicion. *He knows.*

"What happened to her, Lando?"

He tries to play coy. "What are you talking about?"

"She came back to Marlow broken and I can't touch her without her having some type of reaction."

Lando shrugs. "Maybe she's a germaphobe."

"Oh, don't give me that rubbish," I growl.

He makes an exasperated sound, running his hands through his hair, "Look, I wish I could tell you; I really do. But she'd feel so betrayed if I did."

"How am I supposed to help her if I don't even know what the fuck is going on with her?" I growl, closing my eyes and pinching the bridge of my nose to try to calm myself down.

"Why do you even want to help her? You never liked her, anyway."

That catches me off guard. "Who says I never liked her?"

He frowns. "You literally ghosted her for five years."

"That doesn't mean I never liked her."

"Right." Lando scoffs. "So, you're saying you liked her

but just decided she wasn't worth talking to for five years? After she lost pretty much everything and everyone?"

Guilt floods in. "Does she think I ghosted her because I didn't like her?"

He shrugs. "She was hurt, even if she didn't tell me. Aside from me, you were her closest person." After a beat, he turns to look at me. "Why *did* you ghost her?"

I grind my teeth. "It doesn't matter now. Whatever she's going through is getting in the way of this performance," I say instead.

Lando sighs, looking away from me, almost disappointed with my answer. "Well, she has to tell you what happened on her own," he mutters.

"But you know what it is, right?"

He nods, and the silence stretches between us before I speak again.

"On a scale of one to ten, how bad is it?" I brace myself for him to say something like an eight or nine, but what he ends up saying is so much worse.

"Reign," he sighs. "It breaks the scale."

Hours later, Angelique walks out of her room, dressed for the day. She's wearing tight acid wash jeans that make her ass look phenomenal, and a black long-sleeved top. Her hair is half up, half down, pinned back with a clip.

I couldn't sleep at all after my conversation with Lando. I came back to the guesthouse and paced outside her room for over an hour before forcing myself to go to my bed and stare at the ceiling for the rest of the night. As soon as the sun rose high enough to colour the sky, I got ready for the day, and I've been sitting in the living room waiting for her to wake up ever since.

"Good morning," she says, turning the kettle on.

I stare at her, still deciding if I should bring up the sleepwalking, but after remembering how spooked she got when I told her about her screaming in her sleep the other night, I decide against it—for now.

"You look rested." I force a smile.

She pauses and studies my face. "I didn't have another nightmare, did I?" she asks.

"Nah," I say, swallowing down the words I really want to say. "Did you see the email I forwarded you from Terry?"

I stand from the couch and take a seat across from her at the island.

She nods. "I watched some of the videos while getting ready. Are we going to practice the new choreo together today?"

I shake my head. "I was actually thinking we could go on a—" I pause.

A date? Hell no, not using that word.

"A what?" she asks, looking at me with an arched brow as she pours the water from the kettle into a mug, a tea bag floating to the surface.

"A...field trip," I say through gritted teeth, when no other words come to mind.

"A field trip?" Her lips twitch as she watches me. "Okay. Where to?"

"You'll find out when we get there," I say, standing up. "Finish your tea and meet me in the car."

"Okay," she replies, watching me stalk out of the house.

I climb into my car, glaring at the steering wheel. "A fucking field trip, really?" I mutter to myself.

CHAPTER 15

ANGELIQUE

I stare up at the weathered sign of Sugar & Son, the ice cream shop in Marlow that I used to visit with my father before he died. The sun-faded letters, the chipped edges of the hand-painted board... it hasn't changed. Not even a little. It's like the place has been held in time, waiting for me to come back.

My throat tightens, heat pressing behind my eyes as memories rush in—my father's laughter echoing through the small shop, the way he used to pretend to taste test my cone and then steal a bite. I wish he was still here.

"You wanted to go on a trip to Marlow... for ice cream?" I ask, my voice catching slightly as I swallow the knot forming in my throat.

"This is just the first stop." Reign rubs the back of his neck and follows my gaze up to the sign. "We can leave. If you're not up to trying this place out."

"No," I say, too quickly. "No, it's fine. Let's go."

I push open the door before I can change my mind, and a soft chime rings out as we enter, the smell of sugar and waffle cones wrapping around me. It's too much and not

139

enough all at once. My skin prickles with unease at being in such a familiar place after so long.

Reign steps in and stands beside me at the counter, both of us staring up at the hand-written chalk menu. I already know what I want—double chocolate ice cream in a chocolate cone. My usual. My father used to joke that it was the one constant in the universe.

"Do you know what you're getting?" I ask, my voice low, trying to sound casual.

Before he can answer, a man walks out from the back, wiping his hands on a towel. He stops mid-step when he sees me, a flicker of disbelief crossing his features. He blinks hard, then rubs his eyes before blinking again.

"Is that really you, Angelique?" Phil, the shop owner, asks while pulling off his apron and hurrying around the counter.

I brace myself as he reaches for my shoulders and pulls me into a hug before I can step back. My whole body goes rigid. My skin crawling with the contact, the sensation overwhelming and suffocating.

I hate how common touch is—how no one even thinks twice about it. A pat on the back, a hand on your arm, a friendly hug. It feels like a violation now. But to the world, it's just a normal gesture.

I glance at Reign, noticing how he's watching the interaction closely, brow furrowed, posture subtly shifting. When his eyes find mine and he sees the discomfort there, he clears his throat loudly.

Phil steps back immediately, startled. "Sorry," he mumbles, tossing a glance between us before retreating behind the counter and slipping his apron back on. But his gaze keeps drifting to me like he still doesn't believe I'm real.

"What can I get you, sir?" he asks Reign, but Reign looks at me.

"Ladies first," he says, gesturing with his hand.

I step forward. "Uh, I'll have the double—"

"Double chocolate on a chocolate waffle cone?" Phil finishes for me, his smile stretching wider.

I nod, offering a small smile as Reign watches the exchange, his jaw ticking as his eyes jump between us.

"I'll get the cookies and cream," Reign says after a beat. "In a cup."

Phil rings us up, and Reign pays for us both. Then we step aside and watch as Phil scoops our orders, his movements still practiced and fast. I want to ask him how his son is doing, but I can't bring myself to start up a conversation with him today. I wasn't prepared to come to this place, of all places.

He hands Reign his cup first, then turns to me, cone in hand. "I haven't seen you since—" He stops short, the sentence dying on his lips.

Since my father's funeral.

Phil clears his throat. "Well, it's been a while," he says instead. "Are you back in Marlow now?"

I nod. "I just moved back from New York."

A broad grin spreads across his face. "Good. It's nice to see a familiar face again. I hope you'll stop by more often."

I give a polite smile, the kind that doesn't reach my eyes, and glance at Reign again. He catches my silent plea right away and moves to the door, opening it for me.

"Let's go," he says.

I turn back to Phil, offering a quick wave before stepping outside, the cool air hitting my hot skin. The shop door closes behind us, and I exhale slowly, the tightness in my chest loosening just a little.

"You've been here before?" Reign asks after a moment.

I lick my cone, the chocolate familiar and rich, before I nod. "My dad used to bring me almost every week."

Reign doesn't respond and when I look up, I realize he's stopped walking.

I turn back to face him. "What's wrong?"

He's staring at me, his expression unreadable. "That place was special to you and your dad?"

I shrug, suddenly self-conscious. "Yeah. I guess it was."

He looks at me a moment longer, then nods once, a subtle dip of his chin, as he starts walking again, leaving me to catch up.

I look over at him as we walk. "Where are we going now?"

"To watch the swans."

I blink. "The swans?"

He glances sideways. "Swans move the way you need to imitate for the ballet—controlled, but not stiff. I figured watching them might help you get it right."

A few minutes later, we find a quiet patch of grass near the river, tucked slightly away from the walking path. A family with twin toddlers and a golden retriever passes behind us, but otherwise, it's just the soft sounds of water, the rustling of trees, and the slow, graceful drift of white swans gliding across the Thames.

We sit down, the grass cold through my jeans, so I tuck my knees up to my chest and hold my cone with both hands. Reign stretches his legs out in front of him, one ankle crossed over the other, and begins eating his cup of ice cream.

He finishes the whole thing in record time, and when I glance over at him mid-lick, his eyes are tracking my mouth as I swipe my tongue across the side of the cone to keep it from dripping.

He licks his bottom lip once, slow, then his heated gaze jumps up to meet mine, a thousand words behind the way he looks at me, and I freeze, pulse stuttering. The air feels charged between us and I'm positive even the swans have noticed, so I quickly look away and focus on my cone, finishing it in a few fast bites before the tension makes me explode.

He looks back at the water, his voice quiet when he speaks again. "Why don't you like being touched?"

I blink, surprised, and I stare at the grass in front of me as my fingers curl into the fabric of my jeans.

"It just... it feels invasive," I say eventually.

He's quiet for a while before speaking. "But you let Lando touch you."

I glance at him. "That's different."

He says nothing, but I can see the question in his eyes.

"I'm used to him," I explain further. "I know him. We've been around each other forever. He's... safe."

Reign nods once, like he's storing the information away. Then he turns fully toward me, elbows resting on his knees, eyes locked on mine.

"You used to let me touch you." The words leave his mouth with ease, and I feel my mouth drop open slightly.

"I...that..." I'm at a loss for words as my face grows warm. "That was before."

"Before what?"

"Before life happened," I say, dropping his gaze and turning my attention back to the swans. "Before my dad died, before I moved to New York, and before—"

"Before whatever happened in New York, happened," he finishes for me.

I look at him again now, holding his gaze. "Exactly," I reply.

His eyes drop to my mouth for a moment, and then he looks back up at me before nodding.

"I get you don't want to tell me, at least not now, but I hope you remember I was one of the safe people in your life."

"You ghosted me," I say as I stare out at the river, not wanting him to see any of the emotions warring inside of me. "I called and texted you for over a year, and not once did you pick up or reply."

He's quiet now, but I can see from my peripheral that he's staring at me, so I continue.

"We spent every single day together for an entire summer." I laugh to myself at how ridiculously pathetic I sound. "We were almost something, and then suddenly we were nothing."

"Angel..."

"The worst part is that I checked my phone for months. Every single notification that I got, I'd hoped it was from you, but it never was. So, yes, maybe once upon a time I thought you were a safe person, but I realized I was wrong about you when you decided to leave me when I needed you most."

The swans float nearby, one extending its wings out fully, the move smooth and graceful. It raises its wing high enough that my attention snags on the Marlow Bridge behind it instead.

Would I die if I jumped from that high up? Would it hurt or would I be numb to the pain?

I visualize myself standing at the edge, staring down at the swans from that perspective instead, arms held out as I slowly tip forward and—

"Let me make it up to you," he says, cutting into my thoughts.

When I look at him, I can see regret written all over his face. I want to ask him why he did it, why he abandoned me, but maybe now isn't the right time.

"And how do you plan to do that?" I ask instead.

"Let's talk about it over dinner."

CHAPTER 16
REIGN

I button the last cuff of my shirt as I look at myself in the bedroom mirror at the estate mansion. I'm wearing a black suit, no jacket. The lines are sharp, tailored to skim my frame like second skin, just the way I like it.

The suit is new, from Italy, and hand stitched. It cost more than I'd ever admit. I collect suits the way others collect paintings or vinyl. It's the only part of my life I can control down to the millimetre, the only part that never slips from my grasp. And there's no way I could fit my full collection in the guest house closet.

Behind me, Lando is sprawled across the edge of my bed, already dressed for whatever party he has tonight. His shirt is a soft navy, sleeves rolled just enough to show the veins in his forearms. He's been watching me get ready in silence, full of unspoken questions.

"I'm not going to pretend like I'm fully on board with this," he finally says, his tone casual on the surface but laced with warning. "Asking Angelique on a dinner date after you abandoned her."

I adjust my collar, glancing at him through the mirror, keeping my voice even. "It's not a date."

He snorts, leaning back slightly. "You and I both know this is a date. You're just too scared to call it what it is."

I turn away from the mirror, reach for the one of a kind Patek Philippe resting in the transparent case on my dresser, and fasten the strap around my wrist as I speak. "It's not a date," I say again.

He leans forward, elbows resting on his knees, and the air between us thickens. "Listen, Reign, we both know your track record with your previous dance partners doesn't exactly scream... gentle. I just want to make sure you're not setting her up for more pain."

I let that sit between us, unbothered, because he's not wrong and there's no point pretending otherwise. I've burned through too many people to count, pushed them until they cracked just to prove I could. His reservations are valid.

"It's different with her," I say finally.

"Different how?"

I meet his eyes without blinking. "I don't want to break her."

Lando tilts his head, his voice dropping lower. "She's already broken."

I let out a quiet breath, and a small nod of concession. "Then I don't want to break what's left."

"Do you...still have feelings for her?" His gaze narrows, sharp and focused.

The question lands with an almost physical thud between us. My lip curls as I pause and turn toward him with a look of vague disgust. "Don't be daft."

"Would it be such a far-off thing to assume?" he asks, not letting up. "You two have a history and you care about her, that's obvious. More than I've seen you care about anyone in years."

I shoot him a warning glance as I finish adjusting the watch. "Don't start. The only thing I care about is giving the audience the perfect Swan Lake and I can't do that if my partner doesn't trust me."

He sighs like he expected that answer. "Just promise me you won't lead her on."

"I won't lead her on."

Lando holds my gaze a moment longer, reading something in my expression, and whatever he sees must satisfy him because he rises from the bed and smooths out the front of his shirt.

"Alright. That's all I needed to hear."

He walks out of my room, his footsteps fading down the hallway as I turn back to the mirror and give myself one final once-over. The watch clicks closed around my wrist, the sound sharp and definitive, like punctuation at the end of a thought I haven't fully finished.

Dinner with Angelique. What could go wrong?

CHAPTER 17
ANGELIQUE

I hesitate to get up when I hear a knock on my bedroom door. Not because I'm still doing my hair or fumbling with makeup—I've been ready for ten minutes—but there's something about knowing Reign is on the other side, ready to take me to dinner, that causes my heart to lodge in my throat.

I smooth my hands down the front of my dress. It's a simple black number that skims my calves and hugs my body just enough. The long sleeves are a deliberate choice, covering the new round of fresh cuts on my wrist that I gave myself today, and the high neckline gives nothing away. It's the kind of outfit you wear when you don't know where you're going, only that you need to feel safe in your own skin and still look good. I breathe in slowly and open the door.

He's wearing a black dress shirt, sleeves casually rolled just below his elbows, the fabric sleek and clearly expensive, tailored to cling to his frame like it was made with only him in mind. There's a quiet power to the way he wears it, understated but impossible to ignore. It's unfair how elegance looks dangerous on him, how restraint only makes him more tempting.

His gaze rakes over my body slowly, taking his time before returning to my face. And when it does, I swear I feel it all the way down my spine. My body responds to him like gravity, and heat rises in my throat, pooling low in my belly. I force myself to look away before I let him see just how badly I want to touch him.

How badly I want him to touch me.

"Ready?" he asks.

I nod, and he steps aside, motioning for me to follow. We walk out into the warm night, his Porsche parked in front of the house, shining under the moonlight, and when he opens the door for me, I slide in.

He drives fast, cutting the driving time in half. Oxford glows in the dark with golden stone buildings lit from below; old streets dressed up like a movie.

The Folly sits on the edge of the river, its ivy-draped façade soft in the low evening light. Inside are candlelit tables, exposed beams, and linen napkins folded with precision. Reign doesn't pause at the host stand, walking us straight into the dining area. It's only then that I realize we're the only ones here.

He leads me through the dining room without hesitation, down a few steps to a velvet-lined alcove with a view of the river glinting just beyond the window. The space is private and intimate. Moments later, a server appears beside the table and places two heavy menus down.

"Mr. Harrington." He nods at Reign before walking away.

I lift a brow and look at Reign. "Did you book out the whole restaurant or something?"

He doesn't look at me right away, instead flipping the

menu open, fingers gliding down the page, and then he shrugs. "I have some investments in the place and some sway in their business hours."

I blink. Of course the man who showed up in an expensive-looking suit doesn't need a reservation to a fancy restaurant. He can just pay them off to shut down the whole place for the night.

"What do you want?" he asks, nodding to my untouched menu.

I pick it up and scan the page over before deciding on the Fish of the Day. He lifts two fingers and the server from earlier walks up to our table within seconds, a smile plastered on his face.

"One Fish of the Day for the lady," he says, closing his menu. "And I'll have the beef sirloin."

"And to drink?" the server asks.

"Your most expensive bottle," Reign replies, not taking his eyes off mine.

The server nods, taking our menus. "Right away, sir."

Within a few seconds, the server is back with a bottle of wine and pouring it into my glass. I take a small sip to taste, noticing that it's unexpectedly smooth at first, tasting like pears mixed with vanilla, before a citrusy aftertaste kicks in. I drink the whole thing before the server finishes pouring Reign's glass.

Both Reign and the server look at me with surprised expressions, but the server doesn't hesitate to top up my glass before placing the bottle to the side of the table and leaving us. The candlelight flickers against the curve of my wineglass, catching on the sharp angles of Reign's face as he leans back in his seat.

"Why do I have a feeling you plan to fill yourself up with liquid courage tonight?"

I smirk. "Because that's exactly what I'm doing."

I wink at him before picking up my glass and downing the whole thing again. He watches me refill my glass; amusement written across his face.

"Careful, Angel. This particular wine is meant to be savoured slowly. You might not feel it pulling you under, but I can guarantee if you stand up right now, you'll feel the alcohol hit you."

I roll my eyes but listen anyway, setting the glass down with a sigh. He leans back in his seat, one side of his mouth tugging into that maddening, lazy smirk.

"Good girl," he says, voice low and rich. The sound shivers through me, uninvited, heat curling low in my belly. I squeeze my thighs together beneath the table, annoyed at how easy it is for him to undo me.

But I don't let it distract me. "Why didn't you ever pick up when I called?"

His smirk falters as he exhales hard through his nose. "I see we're jumping straight to the point before the food even gets here."

He reaches forward for his glass, swirling it once, then brings it to his nose and slowly inhales the scent before taking a sip. I patiently wait for him to put the glass down, knowing he's just trying to buy himself some time.

"I was busy," he says finally, eyes fixed on the table. "Whenever I was free, it was already the middle of the night for you in New York."

I let out a humourless laugh. "Right. Because time zones are such a bitch when it comes to texting."

His jaw tightens, but he doesn't speak.

"So that's your excuse, then?" I press. "You were *busy*? Too busy for a two-second reply? For a single word?"

"Maybe we should wait for the—"

"No," I snap. "You disappeared, Reign. I went from hearing your voice every day to nothing. Absolute silence from you. Like I didn't even exist anymore. Like everything that happened between us that summer, and all the things we shared meant nothing to you."

He looks at me, desperation and anger blazing behind his blue eyes. "You had your new life. You were doing what you were meant to do, and I didn't want to get in the way."

"That wasn't your choice to make," I fire back. "You don't get to ghost someone who mattered to you and then pretend it was noble."

His expression hardens. "You left me."

"And you let me."

We stare at each other, the air between us taut and trembling. My heart is pounding at an impossible speed, and the wine only adds heat to the fury churning inside me.

"God," I scoff, shoving my chair back. It scrapes against the floor as I stand and wobble slightly from the wine. "If I'd known you were just going to give me half-assed answers instead of owning up to your part in all of this, then I wouldn't have agreed to this dinner."

I reach into my purse, pull out a crisp wad of cash, and toss two-hundred pounds down onto the table.

"For my half," I bite out.

I turn on my heel before he can speak, the buzz making my body sway side to side.

"Fuck," he curses behind me, but I don't look back.

I walk out of the restaurant and into the night, heels cracking against the cobblestone with every step, pulse pounding in my ears. I don't know where I'm going. I just know I'm not staying here, not with him.

I'm halfway down a side street, scanning for a cab, when I hear footsteps. I glance back, thinking it's Reign, and find four drunk men walking toward me instead. They're catcalling at me loudly, words slurring, and some even manage a whistle.

"Where are you going, sweetheart?" One of the guy's sneers. "You dressed like that for us?"

I pivot, hoping to lose them, and realize I've walked into a narrow alley with a brick wall in front of me. When I turn to run out, I find them already standing at the entrance, out of breath, as if they ran to trap me in here. I fumble for the Farbgel Spray in my bag as I back up, trying to keep some distance between me and them.

Two of the guys run at me and when they're close enough, I yank the bottle out of my bag and spray them both in the eyes, revelling when they scream as the dye stains their skin, hands flying up to their eyes as they desperately rub their lids.

The third guy smacks the bottle from my hand and on instinct I kick him hard between the legs with my pointed high heel, not surprised when he lets out a high-pitched squeal, like a pig, before dropping to the ground next to his two friends.

But just as my foot comes back down to the ground, the last guy grabs me by my upper arm and slams me into the brick wall, knocking the air out of my lungs, before he presses a cold blade to my neck.

"Come on," he slurs, breath sour. "We just want a good time with you, sweetheart."

I open my mouth to scream but he applies pressure to the blade, and I feel it cut through my skin, warm blood trickling down my neck. My hands shake, frozen at my sides.

"Let me get a good look at that pretty face," he says, using his dirty hand to push back my curls out of the way.

I spit at him, and he pulls back the hand holding the knife to slap me so hard that the sound echoes through the alley. I'm stunned for a moment, ears ringing and feeling the sting of pain pulse along my cheek.

"I'd rather die," I say, looking at his ugly face. "Than let another man take advantage of my body."

He sneers, looking into my eyes as his knife presses harder against my throat this time. The burn of his blade familiar, but still terrifying.

If this is how I go, then so be it. The world is cruel enough, anyway. What's one less person to fall victim to the tribulations of life?

But he suddenly eases the pressure of the sharp edge against my throat, eyes widening as an arm snakes its way around his neck. A second blade appears—sleek and black —and roughly presses against his cheek. He gasps and jerks back, earning himself a deep cut to his face.

He drops his knife, releasing me, and it clatters to the ground just before Reign slams the guy's head into the brick wall with one smooth, brutal shove. I hear the crack of his skull before he drops to the ground, groaning as blood leaks from his head down his face.

"Oh my God," I whisper, watching as his eyes roll back as he lies on the ground unmoving. "Is he dead?"

Reign pulls out a handkerchief from his pocket and cleans his blade, pure rage reflected on his features. "Not yet."

The other men scramble to their feet, eyes bloodshot and faces stained from the Farbgel Spray. The one I kicked is pressed against the wall, staring at his friend bleeding out on the ground, as he pees himself and bends his body sideways to vomit.

"Mate," one of them shouts. "We've got to get him to the hospital!"

They rush over, pick him up, and run out of the alley screaming for help, not looking back at us once. And it's only when they're gone that I realize how fast my heart is racing. But one look at Reign has it ready to explode right out of my chest.

His angry eyes are silently watching me as he finishes wiping his knife clean, tucking the handkerchief back into his pocket. I don't move from my spot, my back pressing against the cool brick behind me, as he takes two steps toward me and stops just a breath away.

He places one hand on the wall above me, leaning in closer. His scent is intoxicating, and instead of inching away when he places his own knife under my chin, I find myself incredibly turned on. He applies pressure, forcing my face up, and I'm positive he's about to kiss me, but his eyes drift to my throbbing cheek and then down to the fresh cuts on my neck. His jaw pulses as he returns his eyes to mine, eyes flickering down to my lips only momentarily.

"I should've killed him," he growls, his voice deathly low.

The words send a shiver straight down my spine as wild, uncontrollable butterflies detonate in my stomach. My throat tightens as I stare at him, at how angry he is for me. He's breathing hard, his chest rising and falling like he's barely holding himself together. And I know that if I said the word, he'd go finish what he started.

"Why?" I breathe. "Why would you say that? Why did you even—" I swallow hard. "You don't feel anything for me, Reign. You proved that when you disappeared. So why would you take such a risk?"

His eyes narrow as his jaw ticks.

"Do you really think I'd watch someone lay a finger on you and not want to rip them apart?" His voice dangerously low. "Anyone that hurts you doesn't deserve to live."

He lowers the knife, grazing the line of my throat, away from the cuts, with aching tenderness. I exhale sharply, my thighs pressing together, heat flooding my core like a traitor.

God, what's wrong with me? This must be the alcohol, right?

His lips twitch like he's trying not to smirk, gaze locked on mine, watching every flicker of heat that flashes across my face. His hand replaces the knife, warm and grounding against my skin, fingers sliding into the back of my hair, curling tight as he leans in, pressing his forehead to mine. And it hits me that this is the first time someone's touched me like this since Alec, and I haven't flinched. I haven't pulled away or recoiled or frozen. I'm just letting him touch me and letting it feel good.

"Say the word, Angel," he whispers. "Say the word, and I'll make sure no one ever touches you again. Not unless it's me."

I don't say anything, because how do I tell Reign Harrington that yes—being touched repulses me, makes my skin crawl... unless it's *him*? How do I tell him I want his hands everywhere on me? That I want him to take control, to break me, to put me back together? How do I tell Reign Harrington that I want all of him?

But I don't have to, because whatever he sees in my eyes has his mouth crashing into mine with reckless hunger, and I open for him like I've been waiting all my life. Something snaps into place, a feeling of trust, of safety, wrapping around us. I taste blood and desperation, and maybe that should scare me, but it doesn't. It makes me feel alive. *He* makes me feel alive. And for the first time in what feels like forever, I want to feel something other than fear.

CHAPTER 18

REIGN

My hand curls around Angelique's as I lead her out of the alley and toward the restaurant. She's too battered to go back in there, and I don't want any of the staff to make her uncomfortable when they stare. Not to mention, I'm not in the mood to sit down at a table and eat dinner across from her after the kiss we just shared.

I knew the night would likely spiral from the moment she downed her first glass of wine but saving her from a group of drunk bastards in an alleyway and then kissing her on top of that was unexpected.

Gavin, our server from the restaurant, meets us outside with our food bagged to-go. He scans Angelique's red, swollen cheek, along with the cuts on her neck, and his eyes bulge before he turns to look at me.

"Is everything all right, sir?" he asks, glancing at her once more.

"There was a group of men around this area only moments ago that assaulted Ms. Sinclair here. Please send any exterior camera footage you have of the men to the local police station and inform them they're likely at a local hospital."

His eyes go wide again. "Oh, and let them know that two of the men have been sprayed by Farbgel Spray so it should be easy to identify them," I add, sliding him a five-hundred pound tip.

He nods and rushes back inside as I lead Angelique to my car, helping her climb in and buckling her seat belt. My hand intentionally brushes her arm, and when she doesn't flinch away, I nearly groan from the relief.

She takes the bag from me and rests it on her lap while I reach into my pocket and pull out the money that she tossed on the table back in the restaurant.

"Don't insult me by paying on our date." I drop the notes into her lap. "In fact, don't even bring your wallet next time."

"So, this wasn't part of the field trip?" she asks, eyes dropping back to my lips, reminding me of how she tasted in that alley.

I want to take her home and strip her down and worship her until she forgets every man who's ever touched her wrong. I want all of her—but not like this. Not yet. So instead of answering, I close the passenger side door and round the car, sliding into the driver's side bringing the engine to life and pulling out onto the road, driving us back to the house.

I let the low thrum of music from my radio fill the silence between us as I drive, my mind too consumed by thoughts of the alley. *'I'd rather die than let another man take advantage of my body'*, she'd said.

Another.

The times that she'd called me, the texts that she'd sent. Were any of those her attempts at asking for my help? The thought sinks its claws in deep, and I grip the steering wheel hard enough that my knuckles go bone-white the rest of the drive to the estate grounds. I was bitter about her leaving me, but it was really me who left her in the end.

I PARK THE CAR JUST OUTSIDE OF THE GUESTHOUSE AND HELP Angelique climb out, taking the food from her lap.

"Do you want me to reheat your plate for you?" I ask as we step inside, watching as she slips her heels off.

"I'll eat it tomorrow," she murmurs, bending down to pick them up. "I should've listened to you about taking it easy on the drinking. Wine always makes me sleepy."

I nod. "Goodnight, then."

"Goodnight, Reign," she mumbles.

Once Angelique disappears down the hall, I sit at the kitchen island eating my reheated dinner while thinking about the bastards from the alley. I send a quick email to the restaurant to make sure they've filed the report with the police and set my phone down while I wait for a reply. If I ever see them again, I'll fucking kill them with my bare hands for hurting her.

After I clean up my plate, I take a long shower and then make my way to my bedroom while drying my hair with a small towel, but I pause when I find Angelique standing next to my bed, facing me, her eyes unfocused.

"Sleepwalking, again," I mutter, letting my eyes drift over her body as I lean against my door frame, working the towel through my damp hair. "But why my room, Angel?"

My eyes catch on the angry red marks still slashed across her throat from tonight's attack—but then something worse punches the air out of my lungs. My brows knit, and the towel slips from my hand, forgotten as I step toward her, heart slamming against my ribs.

I reach out slowly, careful not to startle her awake, my fingers wrapping gently around her wrist and turning it over. Cuts, dozens of them, litter her arm from her wrist all the way up, disappearing under the sleeve of her shirt. Some thin and faded like pale threads. Others fresh—raw and red, scabbing over in jagged lines.

She's been cutting herself?

No. *No.*

My jaw clenches hard, a bitter taste crawling up the back of my throat. I stare at her arm and a roar of guilt swells in my chest so loud it nearly drowns out my thoughts.

Where the hell was I?

How many of these marks were carved into her because I wasn't there to help her?

I lift her arm higher, bringing her wrist to my lips and press a gentle kiss just above the freshest cut, like my mouth alone could undo the pain it took to make it.

"Angel," I whisper, even though I know she can't hear me like this.

But maybe some part of her does. Maybe that part is why she ended up in my room tonight instead of her own. Maybe she came here because even in her sleep, her subconscious knows I'll keep her safe. Even if it's from herself.

I reach for her other hand and gently guide her to my bed, pulling the covers down and helping her lie against the pillows. She exhales softly as I tuck the blanket around her and I'm careful not to jostle the mattress too much as I slowly ease under the covers behind her.

Her body is turned away from me, curled in tight, like

she's protecting herself even in sleep. I fit myself to her back, leaving just a whisper of space between us, but I want to hold her. God, I want to wrap my arm around her waist, press my hand to her stomach, let her feel that I'm here, and that she's safe.

But I won't touch her, not while she's asleep. Instead, I choose to lie there, close enough that I can feel the heat of her body on mine and the rise and fall of her breathing. My eyes trace the shadows on the ceiling, heart still thundering from what I saw on her wrist.

I should have known. I should have fucking known.

But I've been too wrapped up in my own pain to see hers. Too selfish. Too angry. But not anymore. I don't care what it takes—therapy, patience, time, blood—I'll give it. I'll give her everything I've got left. And if she doesn't have the strength to keep going some days, then I'll carry her. Crawl into her darkness and drag her out, even if it tears me apart. I whisper into the quiet, my lips close enough that the words kiss her hair.

"You're not alone anymore, Angelique. Never again."

CHAPTER 19

ANGELIQUE

I wake up slowly, blinking as the morning light softly bleeds in through the drawn curtains. For the first time in what feels like months, maybe even years, my body feels relaxed and rested. No cold sweat or phantom hands crawling under my skin.

I stretch slightly and then freeze when I look around and realize this isn't my room. The sheets are different, and the bed is much firmer than mine. But it's when the familiar smell of cedarwood and musk floats through the air, that my stomach drops.

I turn slowly, careful not to shift too much, and find Reign asleep behind me. His white-blond hair is a mess across the pillow, his features soft and unguarded as his chest slowly rises and falls. I catch myself staring at the veins on his forearm, his partially open lips, and the line of his jaw.

Why the hell am I in his room, and in his bed?

I peek under the sheets and feel my soul leave my body because I'm only wearing a T-shirt and underwear, my legs bare.

Did I—oh God, did I sleepwalk into his room like some deranged, emotionally unstable creep?

"Oh my God," I mouth, silently cringing as I peel the covers from my body, trying to be as quiet as humanly possible.

I move inch by inch, careful not to wake him, hoping I can disappear back to my room and reclaim whatever scraps of dignity I have left before Reign even notices I was here, but the second I swing a leg over the edge of the bed his arm snakes around my waist and yanks me back against his solid, warm chest.

I go completely still, listening to his steady breathing. I can't tell if he's still sleeping, but I swallow and try again anyway, moving even slower this time as I gently pry his arm from my waist. But the second I shift, he wraps me up again, pulling me flush against him. And that's when I feel the unmistakable press of him, thick and insistent against me as his hips cradle my ass, impossible to ignore.

It sends heat rushing to all the wrong places. Or maybe the right ones. I don't know anymore. He doesn't say a word, but there's nothing accidental about the way his fingers tighten around my middle. We've done this before. That summer when we crossed almost every line and pretended it wouldn't mean anything. But it did, and now it's happening again.

"You're awake, aren't you?" I whisper, my voice breathy.

My heart's thundering like it's trying to escape my ribs, heat crawling up my neck and blooming across my cheeks. I'm flushed, wound tight, and way too aware of how good this feels, even though it shouldn't be happening.

A lazy, amused chuckle vibrates through his chest, sleepy and dangerous in the way it makes my stomach flutter. He buries his face in my hair and inhales deeply, and I swear every nerve ending in my body ignites.

"Were you trying to take advantage of little ol' me while I was asleep, Angel?" Reign mumbles.

My cheeks erupt with heat. "Absolutely not!" I hiss. "I was trying to leave but you're the one who wouldn't let me go."

He pulls back just enough for me to turn and look at him over my shoulder, and when I do, he's smirking.

"Right," he says, dragging out the word.

He buries his face in my hair again, pulling me even closer. I bite down on a gasp, my thighs pressing together instinctively. Every inch of my body feels overheated and traitorous.

"Did you know you snore?" he mumbles after a few silent minutes.

My jaw drops. "I do not."

Reign chuckles. "You do."

"You're such a liar," I mutter.

He laughs and rolls onto his back, tugging me so that I roll with him, landing half on his chest. I should move. I should definitely move. But instead, I let my head settle there, and I listen to the steady beat of his heart under my ear.

His fingers stroke my back lazily, and I bask in the feeling of having someone touch me without it causing memories I wish I could forget to resurface, without my body flinching on its own.

I missed this. I missed him.

He reaches for my wrist and gently lifts it up, holding it between us so that my cuts are on full display. My stomach sinks and I instinctively try to pull away, but he holds on tighter.

"Does it make you feel good when you cut?" he asks, his thumb stroking one of my scars.

My throat tightens as I consider how to answer him. I don't want to lie, not to him, so I choose not to say anything at all.

He turns his head, eyes finding mine again. "The knife," he says, carefully. "Last night, when I held it under your chin you leaned into it instead of flinching away."

I feel the heat rush back into my face, but this time it's a slow burn that coils lower in my stomach.

"It turned you on, right?"

Shame and desire war inside me, spiralling into each other, feeding off each other. I want to run, but I also want to stay.

"I don't know what's wrong with me," I whisper.

"There's nothing wrong with you," he says firmly, his thumb strokes coming to a stop. "Pain can be a release."

I look away and close my eyes. "It just... it helps me take back control."

"Because it was taken from you?"

I don't answer when I realize that I've already said too much. Reign shifts, letting go of my wrist and cupping my jaw instead, tilting my face back up to his. When I meet his eyes, there's no disgust there, or pity, just understanding.

"There's nothing wrong with having a pain kink, Angel," he says quietly. "And there's nothing wrong with wanting to feel in control of your body."

He gently brushes his thumb across my cheek, then over my bottom lip, dragging it down softly.

"You don't have to hurt yourself in secret, and you don't have to punish yourself, either. If pain helps, then let's figure out a safe way to use it."

I tense slightly, but I don't pull away. "You're saying you'd... help me with that?"

"If you let me." His voice stays steady, and he lets the words hang in the space between us.

"What the actual fuck is going on here?" Lando says from behind me, interrupting the moment.

I shriek, startled, and curl my body into Reign instinctively. He tightens his grip on me as he looks over my head to find Lando standing in the doorway, wide-eyed and breathing like he just sprinted across the estate.

"Oh, it's you."

Reign drops his head back onto his pillow and I turn around to face Lando, Reign's arm still wrapped around my middle. His eyes bounce between me and Reign, and the fact that I'm tucked against his chest like this is completely normal for us.

"Lando—"

"Oh my God, Angelique," he gasps, interrupting me. "Are you naked under there?"

"What?" I shriek, glancing down at the bare part of my leg that's sticking out from under the sheets. "Of course not!"

"Lando," Reign says calmly. "Close the door and wait for us in the living room."

"Absolutely not." He storms further into the room. "I leave for one night, and I come back to see that my best friend has answered none of my texts from last night. So of course I call her, and of course she doesn't answer a single time, which sends me into a panic."

"I'm so sorry, I was—"

"So, what do I do?" Lando continues, cutting me off again. "I race over here and instead of finding her fast asleep in her own bed, she's wrapped up in bed with my brother, half-naked."

Lando is livid, and he's staring down Reign like he's ready for a fist fight.

"I was sleepwalking," I blurt. "And I woke up here instead of in my bed."

I try to pull away from Reign, but he just tightens his grip again, keeping my back pressed against him as he continues to stare down his brother.

Lando returns the glare, just as threatening. "And let me guess, brother, you thought cuddling her to sleep was the solution? I thought I told you not to lead her on."

"I didn't touch her until a few minutes ago," Reign replies, his tone calm. "She walked in here all on her own."

"That's not the point. You could have just brought her back to her room, like last time. But you tucked her in right next to you instead. Why doesn't that surprise me?"

Like last time?

Reign's jaw tightens. "And what exactly does that mean?"

"It means I know you. You see someone vulnerable, and you jump at the chance to break them."

"It wasn't like that, Lando," I say, forcing my voice to stay steady.

His chest rises and falls with shallow breaths. "Wasn't it though? You two snuck around behind my back all summer before you moved, and what happened after you left?"

Reign loosens his grip on me slightly as he focuses on every word that Lando is saying now.

"He broke you," Lando shouts. "Just like he does to everyone who gets too close. And now you're about to throw yourself into another mess as if it's not the same mistake that already nearly destroyed you once. Don't act surprised when it ends the same way."

The room goes silent as I stare at Lando, my heart pounding loudly in my ears, and my breath caught in my throat. I've never had him speak to me like this before, but he's right, isn't he? I'm just opening myself up to more heartbreak, like I haven't had enough of it.

"I think it's time for you to leave," Reign says behind me, his voice deathly calm.

My skin erupts in goosebumps just from the sound, and Lando's eyes widen before he turns and walks out, the front door slamming shut behind him. I sit in silence with my back to Reign, unsure how to face him after what Lando just said.

The bed creaks as he readjusts himself behind me, the headboard tapping against the wall when he leans back on it.

He lets out a deep, frustrated sigh. "Can you turn around, please?"

I swallow back my nerves and hesitations, turning around to face him, the blanket slipping off and exposing my bare thighs even more. His eyes catch on my skin, but he forces them back up to my face.

"I want to talk about how I ghosted you," he says, holding out his hand for me to take. "For real this time."

Tightness forms in my throat as, second by second, the pain I endured when he vanished on me floods back in. I take his hand and let him pull me onto his lap, my palms resting on his shoulders and his on my hips.

"Why did you do it?" I whisper, unable to look into his eyes for fear he'd see too much.

He lets out a heavy breath, opening and closing his mouth like he's struggling to find the words. Then, he tilts his head back against the headboard and finds my eyes.

"I thought I was doing what was best for you," he says carefully. "I thought if you had nothing to come back to in Marlow, you'd focus on the amazing opportunity in front of you in New York and live out your dreams."

His answer isn't enough, it will never be enough. So, I ask the one question that I've asked myself almost every day for the last five years.

"Why was it so easy for you to let me go?"

And just like that, I see all the pain he's been hiding behind the mask. He's looking at me like I've just ripped his heart out with that one question.

"It was the hardest thing I've ever done," he whispers, voice cracking.

"Was it though?" I laugh, a watery sound. "You never once gave in, not even one."

He reaches up and carefully wipes away my tears with a pained expression. "I did. You just never knew about it."

I frown. "What do you mean?"

He opens his mouth to answer, but his phone vibrates obnoxiously on the nightstand. We both look over and see a picture of Terry's face lighting up the screen.

"Answer it."

He reaches over and picks up the call, putting Terry on speaker.

"Hey," he says, pushing a loose curl behind my ear, his eyes never leaving mine.

"Are you and Angelique up for an impromptu rehearsal session right now, without Volkov breathing down your necks?" Terry asks.

Reign looks at me, lifting a brow in question. I nod, attempting to climb off him so I can go get ready, but he clamps a hand down on my thigh, stopping me from escaping.

"Yeah, give us an hour. We haven't got out of bed yet."

There's a pause on the other line before Terry speaks again. "We?" he asks slowly. "Is Angelique in bed with you?"

I look at Reign, my eyes wide, and wave frantically for him to end the call. He can't hold back his chuckle as he watches me.

"She is, isn't she?" Terry asks, and I can hear the smile in his voice.

"Goodbye, Terry," Reign says before hanging up and grinning at my flustered state.

His smile slowly fades as he runs a thumb along my cheek. "We'll continue this conversation later?"

I nod as his arms wrap around me and hold me close. I can't say I fully trust Reign again. I mean, I trust him not to physically hurt me, but I think in the back of my mind there will always be a voice warning me he might break my heart if I'm not careful.

But maybe that's a good thing. Maybe it's what I need to keep myself safe.

CHAPTER 20

REIGN

The drive to Imperium takes longer than usual. I keep the speed low, letting the world blur past us because there's something sacred about being together in the quiet with Angelique, like we're both trying to memorize this feeling before it slips away again. In a perfect world, that wouldn't be something we'd have to worry about. But in this world, we've both hurt each other enough to create some scars and doubt.

Terry is sitting on the stone steps outside when we pull in, with a cigarette pinched between his fingers. He grins when he sees us, flicking the butt to the ground, and gives me a knowing wink before tipping his head to Angelique.

"I want to try one of the duet scenes today," he says when we reach the steps, standing and dusting off his jeans. "There's a turn in the middle section that isn't flowing right, so I'll need to see it on you two before Volkov rips me a new one tomorrow."

Angelique lets out a dry laugh as we head toward the doors. "Don't worry, Terry. If the pas de deux falls apart, I'm pretty sure I'll be the one he tears into first."

Over my dead body.

"You'd be surprised," he mutters, holding the door open with a mock bow. "That man lives to be disappointed."

The studio is quiet when we step inside, except for the dull hum of the overhead lights and the echo of our foot-steps on the polished floor. The curtains are drawn back, exposing the stage. Terry beelines to the soundboard, perching himself on the stool and twisting a cable between his fingers, and Angelique walks ahead of me, her curls bouncing slightly with each step. I trail behind slowly, my eyes never leaving her.

We both climb onto the stage, changing out of our sweats, and begin stretching. My eyes catch on the slope of her back, the soft fabric of her leotard clinging to her like second skin, the way the thin straps dig into her shoulders, the arch of her spine as she folds over her legs, the curve of her hip pressing into the floor. My body reacts before my brain can shame it into obedience, blood rushing low, heat curling deep in my gut.

I glance away, jaw tightening.

Focus, Reign. It's a rehearsal, not foreplay.

But it doesn't help that she glances up right then, brushing her curls back with a flick of her wrist, and it makes me want to cross the stage, drag her into my arms, and make us both forget why we're here. Instead, I turn my face toward the stage wings, blow out a slow breath, and adjust myself discreetly.

"You alright?" she asks, unaware of the war she's started in my head.

"I'm fine," I lie, and drop into a deep lunge, hoping the stretch will hurt enough to ground me.

Terry doesn't notice, or if he does, he's pretending not to. He fiddles with his laptop for a few more minutes before he pulls up the rehearsal track for the pas de deux. The first few bars spill through the speakers and Terry claps his hands once.

"Alright, children. Ready?"

I nod. "Let's do it."

We move to centre and Angelique steps into position just as the music begins. My hands find her waist, lifting her easily as she extends into an arabesque. We move together like breath and shadow, her body anticipating mine, and mine steadying hers. I circle her slowly, hand outstretched, and she places her palm in mine.

We hit each mark fluidly and when I lower her to the floor, she doesn't break eye contact. Her lips are parted slightly, chest rising and falling. I wonder if she feels it too —that tether between us pulling tighter.

Terry's voice cuts in after a few seconds. "That turn is still looking sticky. Try shifting your weight a little earlier, Angelique." He stands, brushing off his joggers. "Actually, let me try. I want to see if it's your spacing or Reign's timing."

He starts walking toward her. "No." The word comes out before I think it through.

Terry raises a brow, blinking innocently. "You sure? Sometimes a second body helps."

"I said no," I say, my voice flat.

I don't want anyone else touching her. I don't care if it's for the sake of the choreography or a goddamn Nobel Peace Prize.

She's mine.

He lifts his hands in mock surrender. "Alright, Harrington. Keep your tutu on."

He turns back to the soundboard, restarting the track before taking a seat and gesturing for us to try again, but I spot the grin he's trying to hide and when he winks, I realize he's poking at me, and he knows it's working.

The rehearsal with Terry runs until just before dinnertime. Angelique and I are both exhausted when we finish, but we also feel more confident with our onstage connection, especially once we perfect the turn issue Terry was struggling with. It's improved enough that Volkov might just lay off the bullshit tomorrow.

"Lando just texted me," Angelique announces as we finish packing up our things to leave. "He's inviting us all to a new lounge that opened in town. You too, Terry."

Terry looks up from his laptop, surprised. "Sure. If Reign's going, I'll tag along too."

Do I want to go to a lounge? Not really. But if Angelique is going, then so am I, because I can't risk a repeat of what happened in the alley yesterday.

"Sure, let's just stop off at the house first so we can shower and change."

She nods in agreement.

"I'll follow your car," Terry says, holding the door open for us again as we leave.

"Whatever," I mutter, intentionally bumping his shoulder hard as I pass him, and I hear his playful chuckle in response.

"So, you're telling me you two have been living together all this time?" Terry asks from the backseat of my car. "And you never told me?"

We'd stopped off at the guesthouse to shower and change, and I let Terry come in because Angelique felt bad about him waiting for us outside. Somehow that turned into him leaving his car behind and hitching a ride with us into town, all in the name of easier parking.

"It was part of my hiring agreement with Reign," Angelique says, tossing me a pointed look as I steer us toward the lounge.

Terry lets out a low whistle, then leans forward until his chin nearly rests on my shoulder, eyes wide with mock shock. "Reign. You sick motherfucker."

"Shut up," I mutter, eyes fixed on the road. "I did it so that we could speed up the chemistry bonding."

"Oh, sure," Terry says, sitting back and grinning at me through the rearview mirror. "Whatever you say."

Angelique's laugh bubbles out of her, and I can't stop the smile that tugs at my lips. I sneak a look before I can stop myself and she's looking out the window, the corner of her mouth still lifted, shifting something inside my chest. I've heard that laugh before, back when things were easier, but now... now it hits differently. I keep my eyes on the road, jaw tight, heart doing something I don't want to admit to.

It's not love. I can't call it that and I don't deserve to. But it's something that sits in my chest and aches when she smiles at someone else. It's something that calms when she looks at me like I'm still worth something. It's wanting her to find herself again—even if I'm not part of the ending. It's staying close enough to catch her if she falls, but far enough to pretend I'm not already falling too.

And fuck me—I think I am.

When we reach the inner town, I park the car on the side of the road just outside of the lounge and we get out. It doesn't take long for us to find Lando inside, along with three others—Willow, Alfie, and Max.

Lando stands up quickly when he spots us, and I watch

as he rushes to Angelique and apologizes for the things he said in the morning when he found us in bed together. But I don't get the same apology from him. Instead, he shoots me an angry frown before guiding Angelique to the seat next to him.

"What the fuck was that about?" Terry whispers next to me.

"Long story," I say under my breath, taking a seat at the head of the rectangular table.

The table is scattered with small plates—crispy duck bao, tuna tartare, rosemary fries, and olives soaking in oil and garlic.

Angelique reaches for a shrimp skewer, and I watch the way her lips part slightly as she takes a bite. Lando leans in to say something to her, and she nods, expression soft. The table conversation turns to Swan Lake once the food settles in as Max brings up lighting cues. Willow rants about quick changes, and Alfie throws in a joke about someone nearly getting kicked in the face at the last techniques class. Angelique laughs again, and I can't help noticing that she's glowing here. She's looser around these people, like she's finally remembering how to breathe again.

I don't realize I'm watching her until Terry leans in and says, "You gonna eat that, or just stare at her the rest of the night?"

I flick a piece of bread at him.

"Alright," Alfie announces, pushing his plate away. "I'm bored with being well-behaved. I vote we play a game."

"No," Lando groans.

"Yes," Willow says at the same time.

"Truth or Dare," Alfie says, grinning like a devil. "But with house rules. If you pick truth, you still take a shot, and none of that pass bullshit. If you're in, you're all in."

Angelique tilts her head, smirking. "And dare?"

"No shot," Alfie shrugs. "But if you back out, you do two shots and answer a truth anyway."

"I like it," Terry says, flagging down a server. "Let's get a couple of rounds of tequila."

"Tequila?" I echo, raising a brow.

"You scared, Harrington?" he teases.

I glance toward Angelique, who's already holding up two fingers for the server—ordering for both of us. She catches my look, her mouth curving up. Dangerous and beautiful.

Shit.

"Not in the slightest."

CHAPTER 21
ANGELIQUE

It's been years since I last played Truth or Dare, and I'm pretty sure the last time was with these same people—minus Reign and Terry. We're all a little older now, but the electrifying energy is still the same.

Willow starts the game off with a smirk. "Alfie," she says sweetly, "Truth or dare?"

He leans back, eyes glittering with the challenge. "Dare."

"I dare you to make out with Max," she says without missing a beat.

The table bursts into laughter when Max groans, dragging a hand down his face. "Of course you would."

"Just close your eyes and think of England, mate," Alfie says, already leaning in.

Max sighs. "Let's get this over with."

Alfie grabs him by the collar and pulls him in for a noisy, exaggerated kiss that lasts just long enough to make the entire group lose it. Willow's cackling, Lando nearly chokes on his drink, and even Reign lets out a soft exhale that might've been a laugh.

"Alright, alright," Max says, flipping us off as he wipes his mouth with the back of his hand. "Angelique. Truth or dare?"

I lift a brow, already bracing for something diabolical. "Dare."

He grins. "I dare you to feed Reign one of your truffle fries without breaking eye contact."

The table breaks into obnoxious cheering. I throw Max a look—*traitor*—but reach for a fry anyway, heart thudding. When I turn to Reign, he's already watching me, blue eyes lit with dangerous curiosity, mouth tilted in the slightest challenge.

I lean forward slightly. "Open."

His lips part slowly as I place the fry between them, and just as he leans in to take it, his tongue drags across the pad of my finger before he bites down, causing my breath to catch and stomach to flip. The moment lasts less than a second, but it's enough to make my face burn.

Oh. Shit.

The table whoops and bangs on the wood like we're at a rowdy pub instead of a posh lounge. I sit back and try to play it cool.

"Your turn."

Reign doesn't look away from me. "Terry."

Terry smirks. "Dare."

"I dare you to show the table your last saved selfie."

Terry groans. "You bastard."

But he still unlocks his phone and passes it around. I lean over to look as it makes the rounds. It's a shirtless mirror picture, with a bright green face mask smeared across his cheeks, and I can't stop laughing.

Max wheezes. "Why do you look like the Hulk in the middle of a thirst trap?"

Lando takes the phone next and whistles. "Honestly? You're kind of hot. We love a man with a skincare routine."

Terry smirks. "Thank you. I exfoliate for the gays and the gods."

Then, without missing a beat, he rubs a hand along his beard and gives Lando a once-over, slow and obvious. His tongue pokes out a little, almost thoughtful. "You'd be surprised what else I'm good at."

Lando blinks, surprised, and I giggle as he turns a light shade of pink. When the phone makes it back to Terry, he lifts a brow and turns to Reign.

"Alright, Harrington. Truth or dare?"

I look at Reign when he doesn't answer right away. His jaw tightens a little, eyes narrowing just slightly like he's trying to weigh the safest option. Then his eyes find mine and he holds my gaze as he answers.

"Truth."

Terry doesn't hesitate. "Where was the last place you flew to?"

His eyes slide back to Terry, and based on the innocent grin Terry shoots back, I know this question is something Reign doesn't want to answer. He reaches for his tequila shot, clearing his throat.

"New York."

The sound of the table fades, everything muffled under the ringing in my ears, and he throws back the tequila before anyone can react. The burn of it ripples across his throat, and something in me unravels.

"What?" I breathe, staring at him.

Terry jumps in casually. "That's right!" He snaps his fingers. "I was with you on that trip, wasn't I?" He turns to me. "That was the last time I saw your performance."

I turn back to Reign, blood rushing in my ears. "You were in New York?"

He's quiet for a long moment before he gives me a slow nod.

"Did you watch me perform, too?"

Another nod. I sink slowly back into my chair as I stare at him. My back touches the seat, but I feel nothing except for the pressure building in my chest. He was there, and I never knew. I never saw him in the audience, never got a text. Nothing.

The words Terry had said to me days ago echo in my head.

"You've been to my performances?"

"I've practically been to all of them."

I turn toward Terry now. He looks a little drunk, eyes glassy, but not completely out of it.

"How many times did you two come to New York together?"

"Angel," Reign says in a low warning.

Terry waves a hand like he doesn't even hear him. "Oh, I lost count. We went down every few months over the last five years."

Five years.

My breath catches. That's the entire time I was gone. The whole time he ghosted me. The whole time I thought he didn't care.

"And each time... you came to see me perform?" My voice is quieter now, but shaky.

Terry nods. "Every damn time."

I can't stop staring at Reign, and he doesn't look away as he watches me come apart, my throat tightening. The burn behind my eyes is sharp, but I blink it back. He didn't speak to me, but he watched me. Repeatedly. Even when I didn't know he was still there...he was.

What the hell do I do with that?

"Let's go," Reign says, grumpily, standing from the table and looking at me, Terry, and Lando. "We have rehearsal in the morning with Volkov, and I don't want anyone puking on me because they're hungover."

"I'm not even that drunk," I pout, but I stand up, pulling Lando with me.

"Nuh-uh, no way am I getting in your car," Lando says, holding up a finger in Reign's face, moving it side to side. "I saw you take those tequila shots, and I don't ride with intoxicated drivers."

Reign slowly pushes Lando's hand away from his face and pins him with an annoyed look. "I called us a cab."

"Oh," Lando says, pulling his hand back. "Forgot those existed."

"I'll need to crash at your place when we get there," Terry says, standing up and stumbling to the side before he throws his hands out to steady himself. "There's no way I'll be able to drive myself home."

"You can stay in the main house with me," Lando offers.

Terry tuts before smirking at Lando. "Nuh-uh, twinkle toes. I don't sleep with coworkers, no matter how good looking they are."

Lando turns a deep scarlet but keeps his mouth closed as we make our way out of the lounge, waving goodbye to the others, and jump into the cab. Terry takes the seat next to the driver, and I sit squished between Lando and Reign.

Twenty minutes later, we reach the estate and after

saying a quick goodnight to us, Lando makes his way toward the main house.

"Terry, you can sleep in my room," Reign says, walking toward the guesthouse and unlocking the door.

"Mate, I know we're best friends and all," Terry says, walking in after Reign as I follow closely behind. "But I am not sleeping next to you."

Reign turns around and narrows his eyes at him. "You can have my room because I'm sleeping on the couch."

"Aww," Terry says, placing a hand on Reign's shoulder. "Such a gentleman."

And without another word, he throws a hand up over his shoulder, waving goodnight as he walks down the hall and into Reign's room, leaving us alone by the front door.

"Are you sure you'll be okay on the couch?" I ask as I slide off my shoes.

Reign smirks, crossing his arms over his chest and leaning against the wall. "Is this your way of inviting me into your bed?"

I don't answer as I slowly rise. Do I want him in my bed? I mean, I did sleep next to him last night, and apparently, I'm okay with his hands on me now, too. But I know that if I have him in my bed, things might get heated, and I don't think I'm ready to be touched like that. Not yet. Not to mention, we still need to have a conversation about him ghosting me.

And silently keeping tabs on me in New York too.

He clears his throat when I don't answer. "I'll be fine," he says, pushing himself off the wall and walking over to the couch to set up a spot for himself. "Get some sleep."

I nod. "Goodnight, Reign."

CHAPTER 22

ANGELIQUE

"**R**eign!"

I blink awake and find myself standing in Reign's bedroom, a flashlight shining at my face. I squint at the brightness and use my hands to block the light as I hear the rush of footsteps behind me, and a second later the bedroom light clicks on.

Terry is sitting in Reign's bed, shirtless, holding his phone up with the flashlight feature on and staring at me with his mouth ajar.

"Mate," he breathes, looking over my shoulder at Reign. "I swear she just walked in here on her own, all possessed looking."

Fuck.

"Terry, I'm so sorry," I say quickly, taking a step back and bumping straight into Reign's chest.

"She sleepwalks," Reign says, placing his hands on my shoulders. "Close the door, Terry."

He quietly steers me back to my room and gently helps me back into bed.

"That was extremely embarrassing," I mutter into my

hands. "He's probably so freaked out."

"Nah, don't worry about it," Reign reassures me, tucking a loose curl behind my ear. "He was more worried I'd beat the shit out of him if I found you two together."

"Funny," I say dryly, lowering my hands to my lap and looking at him now.

"I'm not joking."

I tug the blanket higher, curling my fingers into it when I realize he means it. My heart skips, then pounds, a confused flutter of heat. I should feel uneasy, but I don't. I feel... protected. Wanted, in a way that makes my chest ache. But instead of acknowledging it, I deflect.

"I don't get why I've been sleepwalking."

"The last time you did, it was after you drank all that wine at the restaurant," he says. "And tonight, you had a few drinks, too."

"You think the alcohol is triggering it?"

"It's possible that it's *one* of your triggers," he says, standing up. "But don't think of that for now. Try to get some more sleep."

I nod and give him a grateful smile as he walks out of my room, turning off the light and closing the door behind him. He's right though, the times that I've sleepwalked were nights that I drank to the point of being drunk. I think back to the morning after Lando's party when I woke up on the couch with no memory of falling asleep there. I had drunk champagne that night too. If alcohol is the reason, then I need to cut it out completely. I can't keep doing this.

MY PHONE ALARM VIBRATES ON MY NIGHTSTAND, DRAGGING ME out of my sleep. I look at the time and see it's ten past six in the morning, which means it's time to get ready for what I hope is a good day at Imperium. But seeing as it's a day I'll be spending rehearsing under Volkov's eye, I can't imagine it'll be much better than last time.

I grab my clothes from the dresser and open my bedroom door so that I can get to the bathroom for a quick shower, but my soul almost leaves the earth when a body tumbles into my room as the door swings open. Reign hits my floor with a thud and his brows furrow in pain before he opens his eyes and looks up at me.

"Oh my god," I breathe, staring down at him. "Are you okay?"

He lets out a heavy sigh as he sits up, rubbing the back of his head. "Yeah, just fine."

"Were you sleeping against my door?"

He nods. "Just wanted to make sure I could steer you back to bed in case you tried to sleepwalk again."

"Oh," I whisper.

My heart thuds fast in my chest as I take in what he just said. Reign gave up the comfort of the couch to sit guard outside my room door and stop me in case I tried to sleep-walk again.

He stands up and brushes off his clothes. "I'm going to go wake up Terry," he says, walking out of my room without a glance back.

I step out into the hall and watch as he bangs on his bedroom door before barging in. "Time to get up, dickhead."

~

VOLKOV SITS ON A CHAIR IN THE CORNER OF STUDIO B, EYES GLUED to me as I do warmup stretches next to Lando.

"I swear he has something against me," I whisper to Lando.

But he doesn't answer, eyes tracking Terry, who's whispering to Reign as he stretches in front of him across the room from us. Wendy is in her own little corner, sitting on the floor and folded forward in a deep stretch, music from her earbuds blasting.

"Do you think Terry is bisexual?" Lando whispers, oblivious to the fact that he ignored me.

"One thousand percent." I nod. "He was definitely flirting with you last night."

"He was, wasn't he?" Lando's lips curve up into a smirk. "Too bad he doesn't mess around with coworkers."

"Oh, please," I scoff. "If there's anyone that can get him to break that rule, it's you."

Lando turns his smirk to me. "Thanks bestie, I love the confidence."

"Enough stretching," Volkov shouts from his corner, causing me and Lando to jump. "We begin."

Terry mumbles under his breath, something about how that was his call to make, not Volkov's, and comes to stand in the centre of the room.

"Alrighty folks, as you know, we made some changes to the choreography of Swan Lake," Terry says, clapping his hands once.

Volkov doesn't even look up from his notebook. "Hopefully, changes that make sense. Last version makes Odette look like she fall asleep mid dance."

Wendy snorts and Terry, unbothered, grins. "Thank you for that glowing endorsement, Volkov. I will quote you on the posters."

"That would require posters to be worth reading," Volkov mutters.

Terry ignores him. "Right. As I was saying, Lando, Wendy, Angelique, and Reign—today we'll be rehearsing the first pas de deux between Seigfried and Odette. We'll be focusing on the characters' emotions and connection."

I swipe my palms on my tights, my stomach twisting in knots as I glance at Volkov, who's watching me again.

"We'll start with the leads." Terry looks between us, a knowing glint in his eyes. "Positions?"

Reign moves behind me, his hand brushing lightly against my lower back as he takes his place. It's just a casual touch, but I feel it everywhere.

"Eyes on each other," Terry says. "You're not just dancing. You're communicating. Every movement needs to say something. Feel something. Ready?"

Volkov leans forward in his chair, a predator watching prey, and the music starts. My arms rise slowly, trembling just enough to show the effort it takes. Odette isn't strong, not in this version. She's barely holding herself together. Everything she offers is fragile and haunted. Already slipping through her own fingers.

Just like me.

Reign steps forward as I turn. His hands hover before they touch me—one at my waist, the other cradling my elbow. I let myself lean into him, the weight of my body sagging slightly as if Odette is trusting him more than she should. I let my head fall against his chest, chest rising and falling with effort.

When he lifts me, I don't reach for the air—I collapse upward. My legs extend, but the fight is gone from them because this lift isn't supposed to show power, it's supposed to show surrender.

He lowers me gently, breath brushing my ear, and a shiver runs down my spine. It shouldn't make me feel this way. I should be letting the sorrow seep into my limbs and hollow me out. But it's impossible around him. The warmth of his breath lingers, curling low in my stomach and my chest tightens, awareness blooming between my thighs in a slow, traitorous pulse.

When he kneels and offers his hand, I take it, and the duet ends with me in his arms, forehead resting against his. Our chests rise and fall as the last note fades, and I don't realize I'm trembling until I feel his hand press firmer against my back, grounding me.

Volkov leans back in his chair, arms crossed. For once, his expression is unreadable.

Finally, he grunts. "Hmph."

Terry blinks. "Well?"

Volkov waves his pen. "Better. Much better."

Reign's grip loosens, but he doesn't step away. I slowly pull back from him, my skin buzzing everywhere we touched.

Lando beams. "That was beautiful."

But before I can respond, Wendy scoffs from across the studio. "Please," she says, standing. "Anyone could do better than that. She barely moves. It's not hard to look sad."

The air in the room shifts and my spine stiffens, but Wendy doesn't stop there.

"She's not even trying. She's got limp wrists and is constantly seeking pity points. If she wasn't Reign's little damage control project, she wouldn't even be cast."

I flinch, like she slapped me, my breath sticking in my chest.

Damage control project? What is she talking about?

Lando steps forward, jaw tight. "Wendy. That's enough."

She ignores him. "I'm just saying what everyone's thinking. We're all walking on eggshells around her. God forbid, we critique her, right? Because if we do, she might cry, or quit, or—"

"Wendy!" Lando snaps.

Still, she barrels forward, venom curling her lip. "She's not even good. She's *fragile*. And that's not artistry, it's dead weight."

"Get out," Reign says, voice low.

Wendy blinks. "What?" she says, laughing like she misheard him.

"I said get out." He holds her gaze until her face twists in disbelief and fury, before her eyes snap to me, full of loathing.

"You don't deserve him," she spits. "You don't deserve any of this. Everyone's just pretending that you're something special."

The words hit harder than I expect, and I don't even realize I'm holding my breath until it shakes in my chest. Wendy turns on her heel and storms out, the studio doors slamming behind her and the silence hangs, heavy and brittle.

Terry clears his throat awkwardly. "I think... that's enough practice for the day."

Lando brushes my arm as he heads out, giving me an apologetic look. I nod once, not trusting my voice.

Reign stays behind, exhaling slowly before he finally speaks. "Up for another field trip?"

I look at him and force a smile. "Sure. Why not?"

He holds my gaze for a beat longer, like he knows I'm faking it, but he nods and leads the way.

CHAPTER 23

REIGN

I keep the car ride into town quiet on purpose, giving Angelique space to decompress from the shitshow that Wendy just caused at rehearsal, because I can tell she's spiralling from everything that was said. When we reach town, I park on the side of the street and we get out, quietly making our way toward the river.

Angelique wraps her arms around herself as we walk, still quiet, and I can feel the tension rolling off her in waves. She stops near the edge of the water, eyes fixed on the swans, as I step up beside her, careful not to get too close.

"You know why we're here, right?" I ask, keeping my voice low.

She glances at me briefly, then looks back at the water. "More swan watching?"

"Nope." I shake my head. "Trust falls."

She raises an eyebrow. "You're joking."

I shake my head again, a small smile tugging at my mouth. "Not joking."

She side-eyes me, skeptical. "What does falling backwards into your arms have to do with ballet?"

"Everything," I say, turning to face her fully. "Trust is the foundation of every partnership. You might not flinch when I touch you anymore, but I still felt you bracing like you expected to be dropped."

She's quiet for a moment, looking back out at the swans. One dips its head beneath the surface, then emerges, droplets trailing down its long neck.

"So, you want me to fall into your arms repeatedly, until I fully trust that you'll catch me?" she asks, a dry note in her voice.

"Yup."

Her face scrunches like she wants to roll her eyes but doesn't have the energy. "You're serious?"

"I'm always serious," I say, starting toward a levelled spot in the grass. I hear her sigh behind me, and then her footsteps follow.

I stop and gesture for her to stand with her back to me. "Feet shoulder-width apart. Arms loose at your sides."

She stares ahead. "If you drop me—"

"I won't."

She breathes out, her shoulders tense like she's bracing for pain, and she begins to fall but doesn't go far—barely leans, really—before catching herself and stepping forward.

She glances back. "I just—I thought I heard something."

She looks like she's ready to run, but I pretend like I don't notice. "Try again."

This time, she leans further, and I catch her easily. Her body is warm and soft in my arms for just a second before she pulls away, fast, and I let her go.

"What's wrong?"

She clears her throat. "I don't know." She rubs her palms down her thighs. "I feel stupid."

"Don't," I say. "In the pas de deux, you need to fall into me like that. Vulnerability isn't just emotion, it's physical, too. It lives in the way you move; in the tension you hold."

Her gaze flicks to mine. "Is this your way of calling me a terrible partner?"

I hold her stare. "No. It's my way of saying I want to be a better one. But I can't do that if you don't let me fully in."

Her throat moves as she swallows, and her eyes drop to the grass, then back to the water again. "I'm trying."

"I know." I step forward, just enough that she can feel me there. "One more?"

She nods slowly before she closes her eyes, takes a deep breath, and falls. I catch her and hold on a little longer than I should, but she doesn't pull away this time.

"Again?" I whisper, and she nods.

We do it over and over until her body stops locking up mid-fall. Until her breath doesn't hitch every time I catch her. Until she lets her weight drop into mine without resistance. But the last time, when I hold her a second too long, she finally speaks.

"What did Wendy mean earlier?" Her voice is quiet. "When she called me your damage control project?"

I let out a slow breath, jaw tensing because I knew that line would stick with her. Of course it would.

I nod toward the nearby bench under the old willow tree. "Come sit."

She follows without a word, and we settle into the quiet. She sits perched at the edge; her hands tucked under her thighs like she's trying to ground herself. I stare out at the river as I try to find the right words.

"It was last year," I say finally. "The last time I danced."

She doesn't move, but I feel her eyes on me.

"My partner, Elira—we were performing a piece from Manon when she slipped during a lift and tore her ACL in front of a full house."

Angelique winces. "Oh my God, that's horrible."

"Yeah. It wasn't my fault, technically, but the press didn't care. They made it sound like I threw her across the stage."

She's silent for a beat. "Is she okay now?"

"She recovered physically, but she left the company and went back to Berlin. After that, people started walking out. Sponsors, a few long-time dancers, even stage crew. There were whispers about Imperium being unsafe. About nepotism and favouritism. All the shit people love to throw around when there's blood in the water."

Angelique frowns. "So, your dad—"

"Wants something different this season," I finish for her. "Something that reminds people why we matter. And I get it, I do. But none of this," — I motion between us — "none of this is damage control to me."

Her lips part slightly, but no words come out.

"I didn't agree to dance again for press, or ticket sales, or redemption. I came back because of you." I pause, holding her gaze. "I saw you dancing the day my father offered you the part, and I couldn't look away. You made something I wasn't sure I enjoyed anymore feel like art."

She blinks fast, and I watch the words land.

I lean forward, elbows on my knees. "So no, you're not some PR stunt. You're the only reason I want to be on that damn stage again. That's why I refuse to dance without you."

Faint colour rises to her cheeks, and she looks away. I sit back, letting the moment settle because I don't need her to say anything, if she understands. But something's still caught in my chest, a weight I've been dragging around for too long. I glance at her—at the girl who's spent every moment trying to pretend she's fine even though she's not, and I'm no better. If I want her to trust me enough to let me in, maybe I need to start with the truth I haven't told her.

I shift on the bench, pressing my palms together. "There's something I should've said before now."

I don't look at her when I speak—I stare at the water, because it's easier than watching her face fall.

"When you left for New York," I begin, "I shut down. I didn't reply to your calls. Your messages. All those late-night voicemails."

Her breath hitches, but I keep going.

"I told myself it was better this way. That you needed space. That if I answered, I might've dragged you back into something you'd outgrown. I convinced myself I was protecting you." My throat burns. "But that wasn't the truth. Not really."

The wind picks up, and a swan lifts its wings in the distance, arching slowly and gracefully. I watch it as I keep speaking.

"I didn't answer because I thought you were just another person leaving me. And if you were going to go, I didn't want to be the one left waiting."

Her hands go still in her lap. "Reign—"

I shake my head, because I'm not done. "I've been abandoned enough times to know what it feels like when someone's already halfway gone. So, I did what I always do—I cut the cord before it could snap. But that didn't make it hurt any less, and as much as I told myself it was for the best... I couldn't stay away."

"And that's when you flew to New York?" her voice is quiet and shaky.

I nod. "I flew to New York with Terry every few months, and I sat at the back of the theatre and watched you dance," I admit, my voice low. "I missed you so fucking much. It made me sick."

"I missed you too, Reign," she whispers, eyes shining with unshed tears.

I shift toward her, barely brushing her knee with mine, but it's enough to crack something wide open inside of me.

Fuck. I love her.

I don't know why it took me this long to admit it. I fell in love with her before she ever got on that plane, maybe even before she knew what the pain of losing a parent felt like. And even now, knowing she doesn't feel the same, I'd still choose this. Choose *her.*

I'd take every sharp edge, every fucking wound she carries and press them to my chest just to keep her close. She could tear me apart, and I honestly think I'd thank her for it. Because this love...it's not soft or safe. It'll ruin me, I can see that coming, but I'm already in the wreckage, crawling toward her like I don't know how to stop. Like I never wanted to.

"I'm in love with you, Angel." The words hang in the air between us, too raw to take back when I realize I said them out loud.

Angelique recoils slightly, a flicker of panic in her eyes. "You're delusional," she breathes.

I huff a laugh, nodding. "Probably."

She turns away, but I don't let her get too far. I reach up and tuck a loose curl behind her ear, knuckles grazing her cheek.

"But I think you're scared."

She whips her gaze back to mine. "Scared of what?"

"Of how I make you feel."

She opens her mouth, but nothing comes out, so I keep going.

"Because you don't want to feel anything," I murmur, my hand lingering near her face. "Because if you let yourself feel, you might not survive it."

CHAPTER 24

ANGELIQUE

The aisles of Turn the Page, Marlow's well-worn second-hand bookstore, still smells like old books and cracked leather. Lando and I used to come here on Friday nights—his excuse to sneak off to the back of the historical fiction aisle with whichever boyfriend he was seeing, while I wandered toward the poetry section, pretending not to hear their muffled laughter between the shelves.

I run my fingers over the cracked leather spines, not really reading the titles. I'm too aware of Reign behind me. He used to pick us up from here after he got his license, and it was always something I'd look forward to. Those stolen minutes with him in the car, steeped in my teenage longing and the impossible crush I never quite shook.

But today, I'm not looking forward to the drive back to the estate. Not after what he said.

I'm in love with you, Angel.

His words echo through my mind, looping over and over, and I don't know how to stop. I hadn't expected him to say it. Not now, not ever. We made an agreement years ago that whatever was happening between us was physical and temporary. We were just two people using each other to feel a little less alone.

So, when did it stop being just that? When did loving each other become the truth?

"This was always your favourite, wasn't it?"

I turn to the sound of Reign's voice and find him holding up a worn, thin copy of Love Poems by Pablo Neruda. The cover is faded, and the pages are yellowed with time—just like I remember. He flips through it slowly, fingers lingering on each page as if he's searching for something. Then he stops, clears his throat, and reads out loud.

"I love you without knowing how, or when, or from where. I love you straightforwardly, without complexities or pride..." He trails off, eyes fixed on the words for a moment too long.

When he finally looks up, the intensity in his gaze steals the air from my lungs and my heart kicks into a faster rhythm, my skin tingling with awareness. He wants me to continue.

"So I love you because I know no other way..." I finish softly, unable to look away from him.

His eyes darken with desire before he snaps the book shut and tucks it under his arm.

"Are you buying that?" I ask, arching a brow while I try to steady myself.

He nods, lips lifting into a faint smirk. "I think it's about time I figured out why this Pablo Neruda guy had your heart when you were a freshman."

I roll my eyes and turn away quickly, hiding the flush that creeps up my neck. I hadn't expected him to remember the poet I used to obsess over—especially not my favourite poem. Back then, he barely noticed me. He always had a different girl on his arm, someone effortlessly beautiful, while I was just Lando's quiet best friend. But maybe he was paying attention all along.

I drift through the aisles for a few more minutes, pretending to browse, but the air between us feels different now, charged and buzzing, like something unspoken is pushing to the surface. Finally, I glance over my shoulder.

"Can you play for me?"

Reign stops mid-step, brows lifting in quiet surprise. "The piano?"

I nod, my voice hesitant. "Yeah."

He studies me for a beat, as if trying to decide whether or not I'm serious. I hold his gaze, swallowing the nerves rising in my throat. I haven't been able to stop thinking about that melody Lando and I overheard him playing. It was beautiful in the way only sadness can be, and I want more.

"Okay," he says, after a long pause. "Let's go."

"Wait, like right now?" I ask as I follow him.

Reign is already moving toward the front of the store, pulling out his wallet. "I like playing at night, so yeah, why not tonight?"

I stay quiet as he pays for the book, heart thudding. After he checks out, he opens the door for me, his hand brushing my back lightly as I step out into the cool evening air. We walk side by side toward his car, and once we reach it, he opens the passenger door for me and waits until I'm buckled in before closing it gently and getting in on the driver's side.

By the time we reach the estate, the sky has deepened into velvet blue, stars just beginning to peek through the fading light. Reign parks the car and steps out, and I trail behind him. Without a word, he reaches over and takes my hand. His fingers are warm and sure against mine, sending a wave of energy up my arm.

I glance up at him and he's already looking down at me with that familiar crooked smile. I roll my eyes, but I don't pull away. He tugs me gently down the winding path, gravel giving way to stone as we approach the studio. He opens the door, stepping aside to let me in first before he follows right after, turning on the light and then dimming the room to a comfortable brightness before walking over to the piano.

"Sit with me," he says, as he slides onto the bench and pats the spot next to him.

I hesitate, then walk over and sit down. "Don't you need your sheet music or something?"

He shakes his head before tapping his temple. "Every song I've ever composed lives in here."

He lifts the key cover up, gently running his fingers along the keys, and then looks at me with an expression that's a bit more serious now.

"Do you want me to play the song you heard me playing the other day?"

I nod, sitting up straighter. "Please."

He turns back to the keys and gently places his fingers on them before he begins playing. His fingers move at a precise speed and fluidity that I know took years of practice to achieve, the same sad melody filling the studio space. But I'm not watching the keys, I'm watching Reign.

His eyes are closed, brows slightly furrowed, and his mouth is soft with emotion. He leans into the sound as if the music is pulling something out of him that he can't say with words. It's beautiful to watch and heartbreaking to listen to.

After a moment, he speaks, voice low and steady. "I

started writing this after I saw you dancing in the studio that day." He opens his eyes, looking at me. "It's called *How She Breathes.*"

My breath catches as I hold his gaze. "You wrote this... inspired by me?"

He nods. "This was what I heard in my head while I watched you dance."

My throat feels tight as I look away, realizing Reign really has been watching me a lot closer than I'd realized. He saw something broken and aching just from the way I danced that day and turned it into this...this breathtaking thing.

He keeps playing, and I rise slowly to my feet, walking to the centre of the studio and sliding my sneakers off. He slows his playing slightly as he watches me, but when I begin dancing, the same dance that he saw that day, he readjusts the tempo, matching my pace with instinctive precision.

Dancing to his music feels like nothing I've ever experienced and without even meaning to, I shift into Terry's new choreography—the revised Odette sequence—the one that aches in all the same places I do. When the last notes fade into silence, I turn to him, breathless.

"Why do you keep your music so private?"

Reign pauses, fingertips still resting on the keys. Then he leans back slightly, loosely resting his clasped hands on his lap.

"I'm the firstborn Herrington," he shrugs. "My father expects me to take over Imperium one day. There's no room for my music in that world."

My brow furrows. "I don't agree. Your music could be in our world. It should be. This piece belongs in Swan Lake."

He lets out a dry chuckle, but there's no humour in it. "My father would never allow that."

"Then screw what your father allows," I snap, crossing my arms. "You said it yourself—Imperium will be yours one day. So, make it into something that feels like yours. Something you want to come back to."

He looks up at me, something fierce lighting behind his eyes.

Then, without a word, he lifts a single finger and crooks it at me—calling me forward. The gesture sends a shiver down my spine, but I go to him anyway, stopping just in front of the bench.

He places his hands gently on my hips, his gaze roaming my face.

"When did you become so fiery, Angel?"

I roll my eyes, though a small smile tugs at my lips. "Maybe I always was. You just didn't notice."

He closes his eyes and presses his forehead to my stomach, causing something to lurch inside me.

"I'll talk to him," he says into the fabric of my shirt.

"And Terry," I add, lowering my voice into a pout.

He laughs—this time, warm and real. "And Terry," he agrees.

AFTER A HOT SHOWER BACK AT THE GUESTHOUSE, I WRAP MYSELF in my robe and climb into bed, grabbing my phone off the nightstand. Two texts from Lando wait for me.

LANDO:

I swear to God I'm getting Wendy's bitch ass cut from this production.

Who does she think she is!?

ME:

You're sweet. But don't worry about her, she's not worth it.

LANDO:

Not worth it? Babe. She called you dead weight. I almost threw hands.

Ballet hands.

With jazz fingers. 🖐️ ✨

ME:

Not jazz fingers 🙉

LANDO:

Deadass. I was ready to pirouette straight into a lawsuit.

Anywayyyy… where'd you vanish to after rehearsal?

ME:

Reign wanted to try some trust-building exercise. Said it might help with vulnerability for the duet scenes.

LANDO:

Okay but like…was it a professional trust fall or a "fall into my arms, baby girl" trust fall?

ME:

🙂

LANDO:

I knew it. You two are gonna kill me with this slow-burn nonsense.

ME:

It's not like that.

LANDO:

Sure it's not.

And I'm the Sugar Plum Fairy. 🧚

ME:

Goodnight, Lando.

LANDO:

Fine, be mysterious. But if you two elope before opening night, I expect a seat at the head table.

ME:

Goodniiiiiight. 🤍

LANDO:

Night, Swan Queen. Don't let your trust fall into the wrong arms. 😉

I'm smiling as I go to set my phone back on the night-stand to charge, but it vibrates again in my hand—Reign's name lighting up the screen.

REIGN OF TERROR:

Why did Lando just text me asking if I, and I quote, "caught you like it was a scene from Dirty Dancing"?

I laugh, breath catching in my throat as I sink deeper beneath the covers.

ME:

I mean... you kinda did.

Minus the retro halter top.

REIGN OF TERROR:

Pity.

You'd look good in one.

ME:

You're insufferable.

REIGN OF TERROR:

And you're deflecting.

But it's fine.

I can wait.

ME:

Wait for what?

REIGN OF TERROR:

For you to stop pretending that whatever
you feel for me isn't real.

My fingers freeze above the screen and the breath leaves
my body before I even realize I was holding it. His words cut
straight through me—true in a way I don't know how to
face. I stare at the message a little too long before I finally
respond.

ME:

Goodnight, Reign.

REIGN OF TERROR:

Goodnight, Angel.

CHAPTER 25

REIGN

"Let's skip Imperium today," I mutter, tearing a piece of toast apart with my fingers instead of eating it.

Across from me, Angelique lifts her mug to her lips, watching me over the rim. "What about rehearsals?"

I shrug, jaw tight. "We'll rehearse at the estate studio. I'm not in the mood to growl at people all day."

But that's just the surface excuse, the digestible one, because the truth is I'm not in the mood to watch her slip out of my reach again. Ever since the night I played for her, we haven't had more than a few damn minutes alone with each other. If we're not locked in rehearsal from sunrise until our bodies are too sore to keep going, she's out with Lando and their friends—dinners, drives, late-night laughter that doesn't include me. And when she finally gets back, it's like she evaporates straight to bed. She's so close and I still feel starved.

She snorts and sets her mug down with a clink. "I'm beginning to think you growl for attention."

I tilt my head. "That wasn't a no."

Her lips twitch as she eyes me for a beat, weighing

whatever's simmering beneath the suggestion, and then she finally nods. "Alright. Let's try it."

The tension in my chest loosens just enough to let a grin pull at my mouth. I wolf down the last of my breakfast and follow her out, matching her pace as we cut through the garden path toward the studio. Morning mist still clings to the hedges and the world feels quiet; ours. She types out a text to Lando letting him know she won't be at Imperium today, so I pull out my phone to text Terry.

ME:

Are you free for a drink today?

TERRY:

Yeah mate, after rehearsal?

ME:

I won't be in, and neither will Angelique, but I'll come pick you up later

TERRY:

Volkov is going to skin you alive.

See you later.

"Lando's throwing another party tonight," she says, still half-focused on her screen.

I sigh. "He throws one every time my father leaves town."

She looks up at me, brows pinched. "Charlie's gone?"

"Off to London. Finalizing details for the gala."

"The gala?" she repeats, blinking.

Right. She wasn't here last season.

"It's a fundraiser. Before every major production, my father hosts an event to get investors drunk while we perform a preview, wine them, flatter them, and then take their money."

She frowns, curious now. "I thought you guys were self-funded."

"We are, but investors are leverage. Their names carry weight, and their money comes with influence. It's more than cash; it's connections and prestige. It gets eyes on Imperium and gets big name dancers talking. They'll want to come to us instead of the other way around."

She nods slowly, then glances sideways. "What kind of preview?"

"We usually do a short number. Just a taste of the production. This year?" I pause. "Probably you and me."

She stops walking. "What?"

I stop too, facing her. The morning is so quiet I can hear the wind pushing through the trees. "It won't be anything crazy, just enough to show them what we're building."

"When is it?"

"Probably in a month. I'll know more once my father is back," I reply, reaching out for her hand and tugging her gently until she walks again. "Worried about getting stage fright?"

She huffs a nervous laugh. "Something like that."

But I don't miss the way her other hand creeps to her sleeve, tugging it down, or the way she bites her lip nervously. I wonder if this is what she was like in New York —on edge before every show—or if this is new.

When we reach the studio, the cold hits us first. I flick on the lights, flooding the space with sterile fluorescence, then head to the back wall to start the heater. The space hums to life, but it'll take a while to chase the chill from the air.

We don't talk. We just start stretching, side by side, both of us buried in our own heads. I watch the way her spine arches into each bend, the soft curve of her neck when she tilts her head back, the way her thighs tremble ever so slightly when she deepens a stretch. She's so focused, so serious, so beautifully unaware of the chaos she wakes in me just by existing.

She's wearing a black leotard and her ballet skirt, but it's her bare legs that undo me—smooth skin exposed beneath slouched leg warmers and pointe shoes. I'm hard before I even realize it, strung tight with the need I've been trying to ignore.

When our warmup ends, we launch into the new choreography—Odile's seduction of the prince. It's the piece she's been struggling with the most. Not because of the technique, Angelique is too well-trained for that. It's the intimacy; the hunger written into the steps.

The performance requires her to reach into a darker part of herself, and I can see how it pulls something painful to the surface for her. Every time we run it, I see the same thing happen—goosebumps prickling down her arms, her breathing tightening, her body tensing against the implied desire in the movements.

We try it again, but she falters halfway through again. Her gaze drops, jaw clenched, chest rising and falling too fast. She looks frustrated to the point of tears, so I step forward, not touching her yet.

"Let's slow it down," I murmur. "I want you to feel what Odile feels."

Her eyes study mine, uncertain and vulnerable, but she nods. Carefully, I reach for her, sliding my hand across her stomach in a smooth, gliding motion. My fingertips barely press into her leotard, just enough for her to feel it. Her breath hitches, but she doesn't flinch or pull away.

Small victory.

"Again," I say.

We move together, and something shifts. Slowly, like she's unzipping a piece of herself that's been locked inside, her body loosens, and her hips start to move with intention. Her gaze lifts to mine in the mirror—and *fuck.*

Her lashes lower slightly, framing those wide, dark eyes, and something hungry flickers behind them. A quiet, wicked promise only I'm meant to read. Her mouth softens, just enough to make me imagine how it would part if I touched her, kissed her, slipped my fingers behind the fabric of her leotard.

She pushes back on me during a turn, her ass grazing my hip with a heat that snaps the air between us. A low sound claws up my throat before I can stop it. I lean in, breath brushing her ear.

"If you're going to press into me like that," I murmur, "at least pretend it's part of the choreography."

Her arms shiver—tiny bumps rising along her skin like a wave. She closes her eyes and draws in a deep and steady breath, like she's grounding herself. But I can feel her heart pounding against me, frantic and uneven, and it tells me everything. She wants this—wants *me*—but she's scared, too, and I know I've cracked open a place she's kept locked away.

She pulls away, just slightly, and says, "From the top?"

Her voice is soft, almost fragile, but there's a shift beneath it. Hunger tangled with hesitation. Like she's standing at the edge of something dark and doesn't know if it'll swallow her whole or set her free. Either way, I'll be right beside her, every step of the way.

We run it again, and again. Each time, she gives a little more. Her movements are deliberate now, like she's embodying Odile's danger and seduction. It's beautiful, and it's killing me. But I know that it's not just technique holding her back. It's permission. She hasn't given herself any. So, I decide to take a risk and see if she'll give it to me.

As we pass the mirror again, I pivot her body to face it. She stumbles slightly but recovers, her wide eyes locking with mine in the glass.

"Watch yourself," I murmur behind her. "Odile knows exactly what she looks like. What she's doing to him."

I settle my hands on her hips and guide her through the next part of the sequence—fingers gliding over her waist, then up her ribcage. The music is still playing low in the background, but I barely hear it. I'm locked on her. Every breath and every muscle twitch. Every inch she lets me touch.

"Trust me, Angel," I say softly. "Let go. I promise I won't hurt you."

And she does. She moves differently now, bending into the steps, pressing her hips back against me in the turn again, but this time, she doesn't stop, she lets her body do the speaking. Her gaze jumps up to the mirror, and she sees me behind her. How close I am, and how I'm looking at her like I might lose my goddamn mind.

When I step forward and press my chest to her back, she surprises me by staying. I slide one hand up her stomach again and her breath stutters, but she leans into it.

Beautiful, I think. *Fucking beautiful.*

My other hand comes to rest gently on her jaw, tilting her face just enough for me to see her mouth. The air around us thickens while every inch of her body is pressed against mine, and when I dip my head to kiss her, she doesn't hesitate to turn around.

Our lips meet slowly—testing, tasting, but not tentative, because it's a kiss full of everything we've been holding back. I slide my hand into her hair and tilt her head to deepen it. Her lips part in response, and her breath hitches when my tongue grazes hers. Her fingers clutch at my forearm, then drift down to my hip, anchoring us together.

I walk her forward until she's pressed against the mirror, and her back arches as I kiss her harder. My hips press into hers, and *God,* the way she moves with me—creating friction like her body's starving for contact—is maddening. Her breath comes fast against my mouth as we move together in a rhythm that's no longer dance, no longer anything choreographed—just us, burning slowly. But then Angelique stiffens, and her hands shoot up between us, pressing to my chest.

"I can't," she whispers.

I freeze, my chest heaving, heart pounding. "Okay," I breathe, forehead dropping to hers. I close my eyes, trying to steady myself and not ruin this bit of progress we've made, but I want to know what's stopping her. "Is it because you're still upset about me ghosting you?"

Her fingers tremble slightly where they rest, and she shakes her head. "Something... bad happened to me," she says, voice tight. "In a studio. I don't want to talk about it."

My gut twists, a dangerous rage simmering beneath the surface—but not at her. At whoever did this. And something tells me it's Alec.

I'll kill him, I swear to myself.

"You don't have to," I say softly, lips barely brushing hers.

She exhales like it's the first real breath she's taken in minutes, and her hand slides away from my chest. I take a step back, letting the air settle around us again, and she blinks up at me, cheeks flushed, and lips swollen. I reach for her, fixing the strap of her leotard that slipped down, brushing her shoulder with an appreciation I can't hide.

She lets out a shaky little laugh. "You gonna kiss me again or put me to work?"

I smirk faintly. "Both."

I step back, giving her space, letting the moment settle into something safe.

"Alright," I say, nodding toward the mirror. "Let's run it again."

CHAPTER 26
REIGN

The bar Terry picked out smells like cheap beer, and someone's leftover fries. We sit near the back, where the lighting's low and the noise from the front doesn't reach us. My beer's cold, untouched. His is halfway gone, but he's been talking more than drinking.

"Mate," Terry says, shaking his head and laughing. "Volkov nearly strangled me today. Strangled. Like full-on 'what do you mean they are not coming today?' with the accent getting thicker by the second."

I smirk, tapping the side of my bottle, letting the condensation soak into my fingers. "What'd you tell him?"

"I told him you were off helping your father plan the gala," he says, raising a brow. "And Angelique was... also helping."

I give him a look. Everyone at imperium knows my father takes full control of gala planning. In all the years I've worked there, he's never had me help him with it. And he most certainly would not have Angelique helping, too.

He raises his hands in mock innocence. "I didn't say

what kind of help. Anyway, Lando handled the rehearsal like a professional, Reign. That guy's unreal. Even with Wendy raging all over the studio because you weren't there, he just tuned her out and danced."

"He's good," I say quietly, still tapping the bottle.

"No, he's better than good." Terry leans in, eyes serious now. "I've been thinking about it. Why the hell hasn't Lando ever had a lead role before? I know he's done small, featured stuff here and there, but he's got the skill, presence, and the work ethic. Everything."

The bottle in my hand sweats and I track the bead of water running down its neck.

"My father always said Lando didn't like the attention," I murmur after a long pause. "That he preferred supporting roles because leads made him uncomfortable."

Terry scoffs. "That doesn't sound like Lando."

No. It doesn't. It never really did.

I keep my gaze fixed on the table; brow furrowed as something cold twists in my chest. I think about the way Lando laughs when the spotlight is on him at parties, how he owns a room without even trying, dancing like he's on fire.

I wonder if my father never gave him the lead because he thought it would scandalize or stain the company's precious legacy somehow. It's no secret he hasn't been supportive of Lando's sexuality. I make a mental note to talk to them both about this. I won't watch from the sidelines anymore.

"Anyway," Terry says, taking another swig. "We should let Lando take more leads in future productions. He's ready."

I nod slowly. "Yeah. Good idea."

There's a lull in the conversation as he nurses what's left of his beer. I rarely talk much—Terry's used to filling the silence—but tonight I need to say something.

"I've been composing," I say, taking a quick swig from my bottle.

His eyes jump up. "Composing what?"

"Music," I reply, fingers tightening around the bottle. "Mostly piano pieces, some full scores. It started small, but now it's... something I do when I'm not dancing...something I'm considering doing instead of dancing."

Terry stares at me for a beat, then breaks into a grin. "Seriously?"

I nod.

"That's fucking sick," he says. "You gonna let me hear something?"

"Yeah," I say, then hesitate. "Terry, I want my music in our Swan Lake production."

His eyes go wide. "Wait, what?"

"I'm serious," I say. "I've rewritten a few scenes. Just alternative themes—variations on Tchaikovsky's structure. I think it could give the production something different."

Terry blinks, then slowly a wicked grin spreads across his face.

"No fucking way," he says. "Reign Harrington going rogue on a classic? You have to show me."

"I will," I say. "Tomorrow."

He looks like he's about to explode. "Mate, this could be insane. A modernized Swan Lake with your music? Angelique dancing to you? That's got revolutionary written all over it."

I'm about to say something else when my phone vibrates. I flip it over and see a text from Angelique. It's a photo of Lando in the middle of a crowd, champagne being poured down his entire face, grinning.

ANGEL:

Your brother has started a riot.

I exhale a laugh through my nose and rise, grabbing my leather jacket off the back of the chair.

"There's a party we have to get to."

Terry grins like he's just been called into battle. "Lando's?"

"Where else?"

He chugs the rest of his beer, wipes his mouth with the back of his hand, then stands, pulling on his jacket.

"Let's go," he says.

THE PARTY IS ALREADY UNHINGED BY THE TIME WE GET THERE. THE first floor is packed wall-to-wall—music blasting, bodies swaying, laughter echoing off the floorboards and up the staircase. The air reeks of expensive cologne, sweat, and spilled liquor. Champagne fizzes in cups and onto the floor. Someone's already dancing on the goddamn coffee table.

Terry steps in beside me and immediately whistles. "Jesus. He really threw one tonight."

I spot Lando first, his shirt half-unbuttoned, curls damp from champagne, arms thrown around two people I don't recognize as he grinds against someone else entirely. He's glowing. Completely in his element.

When his gaze finds us across the room, he lights up like he's just won the lottery.

"Teeerrrrryyyyy!" he screams, waving a hand and completely ignoring me.

Terry groans. "Oh my."

Lando sprints across the room, wrapping himself around Terry with zero hesitation. "You came!" he squeals, breath sweet with alcohol. "You're here! You didn't tell me you were coming!"

Terry fumbles to steady him. "You're drunk."

"I'm celebrating," Lando corrects, poking Terry's chest. "We killed rehearsal today. That deserves a fucking parade."

"You're hot when you're this chaotic," Terry mumbles under his breath.

I shiver like someone poured cold water down my spine.

"Please," I mutter. "Don't say shit like that about my brother around me."

Terry smirks. "What? Can't picture him getting railed?"

"I said don't."

Terry just grins wider and holds up his hands in surrender, wandering off toward the kitchen with Lando. I scan the room again until I find Angelique standing near the window, one hand curled around a bottle of water, curls falling loose down her back, cheeks slightly flushed from the warmth and noise. Her dress is black and long, stopping loosely mid-shin, low in the back.

But she's not alone. There's a tall, tattooed, tanned guy standing a little too close, wearing a smug grin. His body's angled toward her, leaning in when he talks, like everything he's saying is some kind of secret. She's not smiling, but she's not walking away either.

I know that look. She's being polite.

But he's laying it on thick, and it makes my jaw twitch. I can feel it rising inside me—the possessiveness that doesn't care if I'm being irrational or dramatic. All I know is that guy does not know who he's standing next to and he sure as fuck doesn't get to look at her like that.

I thread through the bodies and noise, ignoring the way some random girl grabs my arm and slurs my name. I yank my hand free, keeping my eyes locked on Angelique, and when I reach her, I don't introduce myself or make small talk.

I grab her by the waist, pull her in tight, and my mouth crashes against hers, deep and consuming as my tongue slides against hers like I've been starving for it. Her open bottle tilts dangerously in her hand, and I feel her breath stutter against my lips. Her hand finds my chest, fingers clutching the fabric, anchoring herself as she kisses me back.

By the time I pull away, her lips are parted, her breathing shallow, her eyes glazed with heat. I look past her, straight at the guy who was talking to her. He's still standing here, watching us with an amused smirk. Like he knows I'm jealous, knows I couldn't take it, knows I had to mark her in front of him just to sleep tonight. And he's right.

I tighten my grip on Angelique's waist and stare him down until he finally shrugs and turns away, disappearing into the crowd. Only then do I exhale and let myself look at her again.

"Where were you?" Angelique asks, still a little breathless from the kiss.

"Terry and I were at the bar," I murmur. "I was pitching him my music... for the production."

She pulls back just enough to see my face, her eyes going wide. "Seriously?"

A slow warmth spreads through my chest, filling all the

empty, cracked places. It's the way she says it, like she's proud. Like she believes in me, no hesitation.

I nod once, unable to stop the small smile tugging at my lips. "Yeah."

She smiles back, and it's so genuine it almost knocks the air out of me. I lean in and press a quick kiss to her lips, just a soft, affirming touch, but we pull apart almost instantly when cold liquid splashes across her shoulder and chest.

She gasps, flinching, and I feel her body jerk in my arms. I look up to find Wendy standing in front of us, holding an empty cup, smug as hell.

"Oops," she says, with zero fucking sincerity.

My eyes drop back to Angelique. Champagne clings to her skin and soaks into the fabric of her dress. Her jaw tightens, and her fists clench as her shoulders tremble.

She's pissed.

Lando's across the room one second and beside us the next. He takes one look at Angelique and doesn't hesitate. "Come on, gorgeous, let's clean you up before you commit a crime."

He glares at Wendy over his shoulder. "Maybe go fuck yourself with that drink next time."

Angelique lets him lead her away, still trembling. And I instantly feel rage as I turn back to Wendy.

"What the fuck is your problem?" I ask, my voice low and dark.

She scoffs, trying to toss her hair like this is some kind of joke. "My problem?" she snaps. "She crept her way in, stole everything, and you just let her."

I stare at her coldly, trying to calm my anger back to a manageable level.

"She doesn't deserve it," Wendy spits. "And you're too blind to see she's just playing you. You think she wants you? She's using you to get her career back, and the minute she's succeeded, she's going to leave you."

My blood hums and my hands flex at my sides. The old me would have believed that. Believed that I'm not worthy enough for Angelique to want to stay with me, for me. But not the new me. The new me won't let her slip away again. I take a step forward, close enough that Wendy takes one back.

"Listen carefully," I say, voice deadly serious. "Stay the fuck away from Angelique. This is your last fucking warning."

She opens her mouth, but I'm not done.

"Piss her off again, and you don't just lose the understudy role. You lose Imperium. All of it."

Wendy's face drains of color when she finally understands I'm not bluffing.

Her voice is small. "I understand."

"Good," I say. "Now get the fuck out of my house."

She doesn't even try to argue as she grabs her clutch and disappears into the crowd. Angelique returns a few minutes later, wearing one of Lando's oversized shirts. Her damp curls are tied up messily and there's a tight line around her mouth. She looks tired.

"I think I'm just going to call it a night," she says, rubbing the back of her neck. "I feel gross and sticky and—yeah. Not in a party mood."

"I'll come with you," I say instantly.

She nods, grateful, and I scan the room for Lando and Terry, but they've vanished into the chaos. We slip out the back door and into the cool night air, walking side by side through the gardens to get to the path that leads to the guest house.

I haven't taken this way to the guesthouse in years and I'm almost surprised when I see the maintained pool come into view. Memories rush back of seventeen-year-old me shoving sixteen-year-old Angelique into the water just to annoy her.

She walks past it without noticing, but I don't. I turn, grab her around the waist and, in one fluid motion, lift her into my arms.

"Reign! what the hell are you doing—" she shrieks, but it's too late.

I toss her and she screams as she hits the water with a splash so loud it echoes through the courtyard. She surfaces, loose curls plastered to her face, eyes wide with shock.

"Are you insane?!" she yells, wiping water from her eyes.

I chuckle, tugging my shirt off over my head, noticing how her gaze catches on my chest. She quietly watches me as she treads water and her eyes travel down my chest, over my stomach, lingering on the ridges.

I take a step forward, toss the shirt to the ground, and dive in. The water surrounds me, cold and perfect, and I swim under, reaching her in a few easy strokes, before I rise slowly, surfacing just in front of her. She's treading water, her back brushing the edge of the pool, and I'm so close now I can feel the ripples from her body touch mine.

I look down at her mouth, then drag my eyes lower, catching the way her soaked, oversized shirt floats around her. Beneath it, I glimpse the pale fabric of her underwear and my skin buzzes. Even though the pool is cool, I feel hot now.

"Sorry for throwing you in. I just figured you wanted the stickiness off," I say.

I'm not sorry at all.

I reach for her, fingers sliding beneath the water until I find the waistband of her underwear. It's delicate as it clings to her hips. I tug hard enough to pull her body toward mine, and she lets out a breathy gasp.

"I could've just taken a shower at the guesthouse," she murmurs. But there's no conviction in her voice. Only heat and want.

"Mmm," I hum against her neck.

My mouth finds the soft skin just beneath her jaw and I kiss her there, slow and open-mouthed, letting her feel every ounce of restraint I'm not using.

Her breath catches again when my hand slides into her underwear. She's warm despite the water, my fingers finding her clit, and I work it in slow, tight circles. She clings to my shoulders, legs struggling to float, but I hold her there—one hand planted against the pool wall, the other worshipping her beneath the surface.

"A shower wouldn't be as fun as this," I murmur into her skin, lips brushing her collarbone.

She closes her eyes and lets her head fall back, hair dripping into the water, chest rising and falling in stuttered, desperate breaths.

I slide two fingers inside her and she moans, her hands digging into my shoulders now, hips rocking forward instinctively as I move in and out, deep and slow. She clenches around me with each thrust, each soft gasp swallowed by the night.

"You're so fucking beautiful like this," I whisper.

Her cheeks flush rose-red. Whether from my praise or

from the orgasm building behind her eyes, I'm not sure. Her thighs tremble and her lips part wider. She's close.

I lean forward to kiss her, and she moans into my mouth just as she tips over the edge. I feel her pulse around my fingers, her entire body tightening, breaking, falling apart in my hands.

"Oh my god, what is going on here?"

Lando's voice cuts through the air like a knife.

Angelique gasps and hides her face in my neck, mortified. I slide my fingers out of her slowly, carefully, then wrap one arm around her waist to shield her as I turn my head. Lando stands poolside, hands on his hips, eyes wide with mock horror. Terry's next to him and his zipper is down.

I blink and lift a brow. "Zip's down, Ter."

Terry glances down, mutters "shit," and quickly zips it up.

Next to him, Lando instinctively wipes the corners of his mouth then freezes mid-motion like he just realized what he's doing.

"Oh my god," he groans, face twisting in embarrassment. "We'll be talking about this later, Sinclair!"

He grabs Terry's hand and yanks him back toward the house, muttering curses the whole way as they vanish into the dark.

Angelique groans into my neck. "I can never show my face again."

I tighten my hold on her, fingers splayed protectively over her lower back. "Then you'll just have to stay home with me."

She huffs a laugh, warm against my skin, and I feel the tension start to melt from her shoulders.

"Home," she murmurs, like she's testing the word on her tongue.

I press a kiss to her temple, lingering there. "Yeah. With me."

She doesn't reply right away, but the way she settles into me—quiet, safe, a little shaky but still here—says enough.

Whatever this is, we're in it now.

Together.

CHAPTER 27
ANGELIQUE

We're still damp from the pool when we get to the guest house, my curls dripping water down my back, while the hem of the shirt I borrowed from Lando sticks to my thighs. Every step leaves a faint trail of water on the floor, but none of that matters because the second the front door clicks shut behind us, Reign's on me.

Lips crashing against mine, hands in my hair, teeth catching my bottom lip as I gasp into his mouth. I don't know who reaches for who first. All I know is that we're both hungry—wild with it—and the second his tongue touches mine, my knees almost give out.

He backs me into the wall, our bodies slamming together, soaked fabric and flushed skin colliding in the dark. My fingers tug at his shirt, dragging it over his head as he kisses me like he's afraid I'll disappear.

We stumble down the hallway, tearing at each other's clothes and flinging the damp material behind us. He mouths at my throat as we move, then he grips my waist, spinning me into another wall. I whimper when his thigh slips between mine, pressing up where I need him most. He grinds there once—slow and deep—and I bite down on his shoulder.

By the time we reach his bedroom door, I'm panting. Almost naked and completely undone. Reign pauses with his hands on my waist, his chest rising and falling like he's struggling to keep himself tethered. He leans in, brushing his lips over my cheek.

"Angel," he murmurs, his voice lower than I've ever heard it. "Do you want to try it tonight?"

I blink, breath catching. "Try what?"

His fingers gently trail up my sides.

"The knife," he says quietly. "Only if you're ready to test out your pain kink."

I go completely still, because being naked with him is already terrifying enough. He hasn't seen all of me yet, the worst of me. The places where I've carved reminders into my skin. The raw, ruined parts. The ones Alec made me feel like I'd never reclaim.

But this isn't Alec, this is Reign.

When I look up, his expression isn't lusty or pushy, it's patient, focused on me. He's giving me the choice. And maybe... just maybe... letting him all the way in—scars and all—might help me take back something that was stolen.

So, I nod, slowly. "Yes."

He exhales, eyes searching mine for any sign of hesitation. "Tell me to stop anytime. Do you understand?"

"I will," I whisper.

Because I want this. Not because I enjoy pain for the sake of it—but because I want to feel something that belongs to me. Something no one took. Something I can control. And right now, I want Reign to be the one to give it to me.

He kisses me once, then leads me into the room. I watch as he disappears into the closet for a moment, and when he comes back, his expression has shifted. His body language is different now—more in control.

He sets the knife on the nightstand, and I stare at it. It's a beautiful black steel, the edge gleaming even in the low light of Reign's bedroom. It looks dangerous in a way that makes my blood heat and my thighs clench in anticipation. Reign turns to me and runs his fingers down my bare arms.

"Lie back for me," he whispers.

I climb onto the bed, heart pounding, and sink into the pillows.

He undresses me the rest of the way—slowly, with worship—kissing along every inch of new skin he uncovers. His hands move with care, but his eyes never stray. He sees the faint white lines that slash across my ribs, and the pale, ridged scars on the insides of my thighs. He doesn't flinch or ask questions. He just kisses me softly, everywhere.

"Thank you for letting me see you," he whispers into the space between my breasts.

Then he picks up the knife. It's cool to the touch when the flat side of the blade drags along my collarbone. My breath hitches, but not in fear, *in want*. His eyes stay on mine as he glides the blade lower, pressing the blunt edge to the dip between my ribs, then down the curve of my waist, teasing me.

He watches my reactions carefully. "Tell me if it's too much," he says again, voice husky.

He leans forward, kissing the inside of my thigh, just above one of my oldest scars. He whispers something I can't quite make out and when he rises, he shifts the knife in his hand and slices a shallow line along my hip, just below the bone. My body jerks from the sheer electric shock of it. The pain is immediate, bright, and weirdly beautiful.

I gasp, and then I moan. My legs fall open instinctively, like my body knows exactly what it wants before I do.

Reign's eyes flash. "You like that?" he asks softly, voice full of awe and heat.

"Yes," I breathe. "Fuck, yes."

He leans down and presses a kiss just above the fresh cut, then goes lower. He doesn't give me time to recover before he slides his fingers between my legs and touches me like he owns me. Like he's trying to worship and ruin me at once.

The sting of the cut lingers, making every other sensation sharper. My body is on fire, so keyed up that I cry out when his thumb grazes my clit. My hips roll up against his hand, shameless now, and greedy.

"I love how you respond to this," he mutters, dragging his tongue along the line of my stomach while his fingers move inside me, slow and deep. "So fucking perfect."

He curls them just right, and I writhe beneath him. The pain on my hip pulses with every heartbeat, amplifying the pleasure until it's all one overwhelming current.

"You're so beautiful when I hurt you like this," he whispers against my skin.

My eyes flutter shut and my head tilts back as my mouth falls open around a breathless moan. And when he kisses me, I taste my own desperation on his tongue.

It doesn't take long before I come with a cry, my body spasming around his fingers, my hand gripping his wrist as if to anchor myself while the world fractures. This feeling is *mine.*

When I collapse back against the pillows, trembling, he slowly presses soft kisses to my throat, my cheeks, my forehead and then he sets the knife aside with care and lowers his body over mine.

"You okay?" he murmurs.

I nod, still catching my breath.

"More than okay," I whisper.

I feel powerful.

He brushes the hair from my eyes and kisses my lips again—this time slow and soft. We lie tangled together in his bed, skin damp and warm, the scent of sweat and chlorine still lingering in the air between us. His arm is slung around my waist, our legs woven together beneath the sheets. My body aches in the best way.

I finally feel entirely mine. But also, his.

After a while, Reign tilts his head and murmurs, "We should shower together. Save warm water."

I lift a brow. "You live on an estate with endless amounts of hot water."

He smirks. "I'm trying to be environmentally conscious." I roll my eyes but let him pull me from the bed.

The bathroom mirrors fog up from the steam within minutes of Reign turning on the hot water. I step in first and he follows. He grabs a bottle of soap and lathers it between his palms, then gently starts running his hands over my body.

It doesn't feel sexual though, it feels healing. He washes every part of me like I'm something sacred, not something ruined. And when he moves behind me to shampoo my hair, my eyes flutter closed. His fingers massage my scalp with firm, patient strokes, and I let myself lean into him, my back against his chest, the sound of the water drowning everything else out.

He rinses my hair and works in the conditioner next, gently running his fingers through my curls, detangling them with care. When he finishes rinsing that out, I turn to him, pouring soap onto my hands now. My hands move across his chest, his abs, and down the V of his hips.

I watch his body respond to me, the tension tightening his jaw and the hunger flaring in his eyes. When I wrap my fingers around his cock, he's already half-hard, and by the time I stroke, he's groaning.

I rinse the soap off him, watching the way the water rushes over the muscles that tense beneath my hands, and then I sink to my knees. His breath hitches, his head tilting slightly like he's not sure he's seeing this right.

"Fuck," he breathes, one hand sliding up to rest on the back of his neck as the water beats down on his back. "Angel…"

I look up at him through wet lashes. His cock is thick and flushed, and when I wrap my mouth around him, his hips jerk forward slightly.

"Jesus," he groans. "I've thought about your lips around my cock since the summer we spent together. I can't tell you how many nights I lost sleep over it."

I moan softly at his words and take him deeper. As deep as I can. His head falls back against the tile, a sharp sound catching in his throat as I work him with my mouth—slow and hungry, full of intent. I flatten my tongue, tighten my lips, and suck harder as he unravels above me.

His hands find the back of my head, but he doesn't push, he just holds me, anchoring himself as I take him over and over, greedy for every sound, every moan, every twitch of his hips. When he finally explodes, it's with a loud groan that echoes off the walls. I swallow it all, every drop, keeping my eyes on him the whole time.

When Reign finally opens his eyes, his gaze locks on mine and the look in them makes my stomach twist in a way that has nothing to do with arousal and everything to do with danger. He reaches down and runs his thumb across my bottom lip, slow and gentle.

"Fucking perfect," he murmurs.

There's love in his eyes, and it should scare me. I should pull back and maybe even run, but I feel like something inside me that's been frozen for years is thawing. Reign helps me gently to my feet and grabs a towel before wrapping me up in it carefully. He wraps a second towel around my hair, and then he wraps one around his own waist and steps back. I study him in the silence that follows, the water still running behind us, the air thick with steam and affection. And as I stand there, dripping and breathless, I wonder—

Is falling for him even possible after everything I've survived? Or have I already fallen... without even realizing it?

CHAPTER 28
ANGELIQUE

I wake to the soft drag of slow gentle fingertips against my skin, like a caress. I keep my eyes closed, not ready to break the spell. The room is warm, and the blankets are tangled around my bare legs, my cheek pressed into one of Reign's pillows.

His fingers are moving across my back, drawing shapes I can't see. I concentrate, trying to make out what he's drawing, when I realize he's spelling something.

i-l-o-v-e-y-o-u.

I suck in a tiny breath, and his hand stills, like he's waiting for me to shift. I do a tiny wiggle, my way of telling him to keep going.

"Good morning, Angel," Reign murmurs.

He presses a soft kiss to the top of my head, and I finally turn to face him, eyes still heavy with sleep. His blond hair is messy, his blue eyes softer than I've ever seen them. His hand moves again, but this time he just draws slow circles on my back.

I smile faintly, still not speaking as I watch him. Then I feel him twitch against my leg, and I remember we're both completely naked. I wiggle my ass, teasing him as he smirks.

"Dangerous game you're playing," he murmurs.

His fingers trail down my spine, light as air, then over the swell of my ass. My breath hitches when he grazes my folds. One slow stroke, then another, and I'm already wet. A soft moan slips from my lips as his fingers circle my clit, gentle but skilled.

But before I can sink fully into it, he moves, kissing his way down my spine until he's between my legs. He props up my hips, spreading me with one strong hand, and then his tongue is on every inch of me.

He licks into me with slow, filthy strokes, teasing and devouring in equal measure. He doesn't just taste me—he worships me. Like this is his religion. His prayer. His offering. His tongue sweeps higher, licking softly over my asshole.

I moan, shocked and undone, my fingers clutching at the sheets as heat pulses through me in dizzy waves. He eats me like he owns me, and I come hard. Again, and again, and again. My body barely recovering from one orgasm before the next crashes over me.

By the time he pulls back, I'm barely coherent, trembling and dripping. He rises behind me, and I feel the thick weight of his cock rub against my entrance.

A memory of Alec flashes through my mind, and I freeze. The pain he made me feel, the pressure of his body on me, losing control. I squeeze my eyes shut and almost scream for him to stop, feeling like I'm back on that studio floor, but then Reign speaks.

"You're so good for me," he murmurs against my back. "I've got you, angel. You're safe."

Reign's voice grounds me, bringing me back to the

present. His hands are slow, steady, loving. It's like he knows I need to hear those words. Like he knows I need to be reminded that I'm safe now, that no one can hurt me.

"You don't have to do anything you don't want to," he breathes, his cock nudging gently at my entrance. "But if you let me in... I'll make you forget anyone else ever touched you."

I let out a breath. How could he possibly know that? How could he know that's all I want? To forget the hands that touched me before. I chew on my lip and nod. He pushes in, inch by inch, slow enough for me to adjust. His hands never stop moving, brushing along my sides, stroking my thighs. His lips finding my shoulder and gently kissing me.

"You're doing so good for me," he murmurs against my skin. "Let me take care of you."

I feel every fucking stretch as he fills me from behind, one steady push at a time. My muscles tremble from the sheer pressure of him sliding deeper, deeper, until he bottoms out inside me. He stays buried and unmoving, and then the pressure is gone, replaced by heat, the fullness of him, and...pleasure.

I nod again, panting. My body's pulsing around him, adjusting to his size. His hand comes around my waist, fingers dipping down to stroke my clit again, slow circles that make my hips roll back against him.

He groans. "That's it, ride me."

And I do. I rock back into him, feeling the drag of his cock pulling almost all the way out before he thrusts back in, harder this time. The wet slap of our bodies meeting echoes in the quiet room. He sets a rhythm, and every thrust makes my body jolt forward. Every time he drives in, I feel him hit that spot that makes me see stars.

"You feel how tight you are around me?" he growls. "So fucking perfect."

I whimper, arching my back, my ass pushing into him as he grips my hips tighter and starts to really fuck me. Long, hard strokes. He fucks me like he's been waiting forever for this.

"Look at you," he pants. "Taking all of me. Fuck, Angel… I'll never get over how good you feel."

His chest presses into my back now, skin hot against mine, his arm sliding under my body to pull me tighter against him. One of his hands fists in my hair, tugging my head to the side so he can kiss my neck, bite my shoulder, devour me.

I'm soaking wet—slick and messy—loud with it. And I love it. He shifts his angle slightly and hits the spot that makes me cry out, my legs shaking as he keeps grinding into it, over and over.

"Are you going to come for me again?" he murmurs, biting my earlobe. "Come on, Angel. I want to feel you squeeze me while I fuck you."

And that's all it takes for me to fall apart, moaning his name. I come hard, my body convulsing as he fucks me through it, never slowing down, letting me ride every wave until I'm trembling, overstimulated, and wrecked. He groans, the sound almost feral now, and his thrusts become rougher and sloppier.

"Fuck, you're perfect," he growls, grinding against me as he chases his release. "You were made for me."

And then he shudders, burying himself deep one last time as he explodes inside me, moaning into my shoulder, his hips twitching with every final pulse. For a long moment, we just breathe, our bodies tangled and sweat cooling on our skin. The smell of sex thick in the air.

He slowly pulls out, kisses the back of my shoulder, and rolls to his side, one arm looping around my waist, holding me close.

"Still with me?" he murmurs against my neck.

"Yeah," I whisper. "More than I've been in a long time."

And it's true, because with him by my side, loving me like this...I finally feel like I belong to myself again.

I HOVER BESIDE REIGN NEAR THE BACK OF THE CHEMIST, ARMS folded tightly across my chest, my hoodie zipped to my chin like I'm trying to disappear inside it. This was my idea—technically—but now that we're here, I want the floor to swallow me whole. The hush of pharmacy counters and the faint clink of bottles feel more real than any hospital. Reign leads me straight to the pharmacist's hatch, and the pharmacist looks up from filling a prescription.

"How can I help?" she asks, professional but kind.

"Plan B, please. She needs it today," Reign answers for me.

"Of course. If you'd just come through here, I'll ask a few questions to make sure it's right."

She gestures to a small consultation room behind the counter, and I follow her through, barely registering the pharmacist asking about timing, weight, current meds, but within minutes I'm holding a box of Plan B.

"Take it as soon as possible. It can work up to five days after but sooner is better."

Reign takes the box from me with no hesitation, or shame, or awkwardness, and he slips it into the little blue basket he's holding as if he's tossing in a bottle of water.

I follow him down a narrow aisle lined with blister packs and skincare bottles, tugging my sleeves over my hands like that might somehow make this less awkward. My insides feel scrambled, like I'm trying to settle into my skin again and it's not quite fitting the same way it did this morning.

Without saying a word, he grabs a box of condoms off the shelf and sets it into the basket. Then he glances back at me, smirks, and picks up a second box, too.

I raise a brow. "That's optimistic."

"That's restraint," he says, calmly. "Optimism would've been a third box."

I blush so hard I'm pretty sure my face is actively combusting. "Reign."

He leans in, lips brushing my ear, voice dropping into that dangerous place between teasing and thoughtful. "I'm never forgetting again, Angel. But just in case..."

He pulls back with a wink, tosses the second box into the basket, and keeps walking. I groan and follow as we drift into the snack aisle next. It's quiet, just the distant beep of a till and the occasional hum of footsteps on the tile.

"You should pick some things," he says.

I blink. "What things?"

"Comfort food. Salty, sweet, whatever helps. You might feel like shit later. Cramping, nausea. Mood swings. I googled it."

"You googled it?"

He nods once. "Of course I did. I'm not letting you go through this alone," he says, eyes on the shelves now. "Not for a second."

My chest pulls tight at the honesty in his voice. At how

simple he makes it sound, like protecting me is as easy as breathing for him. I turn toward the aisle and start picking things I recognize from old, bad days—plain crackers, salted popcorn, dark chocolate, mint tea, a bottle of Lucozade. Reign adds a box of mac and cheese, a giant bag of crisps, and a box of ginger biscuits to the basket without comment.

At the till, I glance down at the Plan B box nestled between our mess of snacks and feel a dull ache of reality twist in my stomach. I can't tuck away everything that's happened between Reign and I into a dark corner and pretend it doesn't matter. Sooner or later, I'll have to admit to myself, and to him, how much I care about this. About us.

Reign's hand brushes mine, knuckles skimming carefully. "You okay?" he asks, voice barely audible.

"Yeah," I whisper.

But he studies me for a beat longer, like he's trying to see if I'm lying to myself. Then he turns back to the cashier and pays.

Outside, the sky is painted in deep purples and steel greys as Reign opens the passenger door for me. He waits until I'm in, then walks around and slides into the driver's seat, the bag of snacks resting between us.

"I'm putting on Pride and Prejudice when we get back," he says, starting the engine.

I glance over at him. "You remember my favourite movie?"

His jaw flexes. "I remember everything that matters."

I squint my eyes at him. "I bet you don't remember which version of Pride and Prejudice is my favourite."

He gives me a look like I've insulted his intelligence. "The 2005 version with Keira Knightley."

My eyebrows raise in surprise, and he scoffs in response. "I've been paying attention," he mutters as he backs out of the parking lot and begins the drive home.

My throat tightens just a little as I smile. "I guess you have."

He reaches over and runs his thumb along the inside of my wrist, like a grounding wire. Like he's reminding himself I'm real, and that I'm here, and I'm his. As we drive through the darkening streets toward home, I realize something that hits deeper than panic or afterglow or consequence.

Reign doesn't just want me. He claims me—quietly and completely—and I've never felt safer.

WHEN WE GET BACK TO THE ESTATE, HE KILLS THE ENGINE, GRABS the bag, and comes around to open my door like always. But this time, when I step out, he doesn't let go of my hand. The minute we're inside, I head straight to the kitchen and get a glass of water while Reign sets the bag down on the counter, unpacks everything, and places the Plan B packet down in front of me. I take the pill while he watches me swallow, and then he nods once like it settles something in him.

"Come on," he murmurs, already walking toward the bathroom. "Bath's next."

He starts the water and pours a lavender-scented bubble bath into the tub, testing the temperature with his hand before stepping back. His gaze rakes over my naked body once, slow and appreciative, and then he leaves the room without a word.

I soak for a while, letting the warmth work into my

bones. My thighs ache faintly, and my lower stomach feels a little off as I rest my head against the back of the tub and close my eyes, breathing in the steam, letting my muscles uncoil one at a time.

Before I step out of the tub, my eye catches on the razor I've used on my wrists. I stare at it for a moment, realizing I don't have the overwhelming urge to cut anymore, as if being with Reign has satisfied that voice in my head that begs for the self-inflicted pain.

I step out of the tub and find a towel along with one of his hoodies and a pair of my underwear waiting for me on the sink. After drying off, I change into the clothes and walk barefoot into the living room.

The lights are low, and Reign has rearranged the couch with blankets and pillows. A mug of tea waits for me on the coffee table too, still steaming. He's in the kitchen, putting popcorn in a bowl when he glances up and sees me. I watch as his eyes rake over my bare legs, but he looks away with restraint and crosses the room, placing the popcorn down, and gently tugging me toward the couch.

Reign settles in first, back against the cushions, legs spread slightly. Then he pulls me between them, guiding me to sit against his chest like he already knows I need to be held, and I let myself sink into him.

"You're warm," I murmur.

His arms curl around my middle, protective and solid, and then the TV turns on. The opening piano notes of Pride and Prejudice drift through the room and my chest squeezes. We stay like that—wrapped in blankets, our bodies pressed close, as Elizabeth Bennet walks alone through the fields.

Halfway through the film, Reign slides his hand under

my hoodie, resting flat against my lower stomach, and his other arm tightens around my waist, drawing me closer. The pain never comes, but regardless, for the first time in a long, long time, I feel taken care of.

CHAPTER 29
ANGELIQUE

It's just me and Reign in the studio today. Most of the company is out preparing for tonight's gala. The mirrors stretch around us, and the floor creaks gently under our movements. The only other sound comes from the faint music looping from the speakers.

Ever since we slept together, I can't stop thinking about him, his mouth on me, the sounds he makes when he's close, and the way he looks at me when he thinks I'm not watching. Every time he touches me now, even in rehearsal, it lights a fire low in my belly. Even now, as he places a hand on my waist to guide me into a turn, I need to bite down on my lip to stay focused.

"Again," Reign says, oblivious to the effect he's having on me.

We move through the sequence, the same one from the estate studio weeks ago. I think of that day often and of how far I let it go. I wanted Reign's body on me, even through my fear, but I had to stop it when I started seeing images of Alec pop up in my head.

I'm tired of letting Alec take up space that he doesn't deserve. I'm tired of him owning places that should be mine. My body, my art, and my memories. This space belongs to me. To *us*.

We reach the last movement of the sequence and Reign steps back slightly to reset. But I don't move. Instead, I turn to face him, breathing hard as I step into his space, and he goes still.

"Angel," he murmurs.

I reach for his shirt and fist the fabric. "Don't talk. Just… let me."

Reign's eyes darken instantly, jaw ticking, but he nods. I stretch up onto my toes and kiss him, softly at first, but the moment his mouth opens beneath mine, something hungry and desperate cracks wide open inside me.

He groans against my lips, and I press closer, rolling my hips forward until I feel him—hard, hot, and just as wrecked as I am. His hands slide to my lower back, gripping me tight as I move against him. I gasp into his mouth, overwhelmed by the friction, the pressure, the want. It hits me like a wave, crashing into my ribs and making my legs shake.

We stumble backward, my spine brushing the mirror, and his body cages mine in. His mouth finds my neck, kissing and biting gently, his breath ragged. I grind against him, moaning when he presses back, and as the studio dissolves, all I see is him.

His breath hitches. "Angel…"

"I want to," I whisper. "Here, with you. I don't want him to have this place."

His fingers flex against me, but he doesn't move.

"Please," I beg, and Reign kisses me hard, his hand

sliding up beneath my ballet skirt, fingertips brushing over my leotard, causing me to shudder with need.

"Fuck, baby," he groans against my mouth. "You're already shaking."

I choke on a moan. "Don't stop," I breathe.

He hooks his fingers into the side of my leotard and underwear, sliding them aside to bare my pussy to him. I cry out when he sinks two fingers inside, the stretch sweet and perfect. My hips roll, desperate for more, for everything. He thrusts slowly at first, deep, curling just right. Then faster, setting a rhythm that has my knees nearly buckling.

My hand slams against the mirror, the other clutching his shoulder. The obscene sound of his fingers moving inside me fills the room, mixing with my moans.

"You like that?" he growls. "You want to come for me right here, where anyone could walk in?"

I nod frantically, unable to speak, breath ragged. His thumb circles my clit, and I shatter, my body jerking as pleasure snaps through every nerve while I fall apart in his hands. He groans, holding me steady as I cry out his name, trembling against the mirror. He doesn't stop until I'm spent, slumped against him, breathless.

"No one else gets to touch you like this but me," he whispers, kissing my temple softly. "And I want this to be what you remember when you're in the studio, not anything else. Just this. Us."

I nod, still shaking, tears pricking but not falling. I won't cry. Not this time. This time, I'm proud. He fixes my leotard and reties my skirt with care before helping me stand steady.

"Thank you," I whisper, pressing my forehead to his chest.

He kisses the top of my head. "You don't have to thank me. I should be thanking you"

And just like that, something in the air shifts. My body and the way I see studios no longer belongs to Alec, or fear. It's mine again.

I'M BAREFOOT IN THE UPSTAIRS DRESSING ROOM OF IMPERIUM, standing in nothing but my strapless bodice and nude dance tights, arms raised as Lando tugs the zipper of my gown up with a dramatic sigh.

"I still don't understand how you managed to get through a ten-hour rehearsal without murdering someone," he mutters. "You're practically glowing."

"I'm just trying to survive the night," I say, voice tight with nerves. "And this corset might kill me first."

Lando gives the zipper one last tug, then smooths the back of the gown with an appreciative touch. "Well, if you're gonna go out, at least you'll look celestial doing it."

I glance at myself in the mirror and my breath stutters. The dress is breathtaking. Ivory satin and sheer mesh, fitted through the waist and flaring into layers of delicate tulle shaped like feathers—tiny, shimmering wisps cascading down to the floor. It hugs my body like it was made for me, the sweetheart neckline dusted in fine pearls. A gift from Reign.

Lando walks over to the vanity and retrieves my mask. "It's time," he says, handing it to me.

It's white and gold with soft feathers fanning outward from the eyes like wings. As soon as I place it on, Lando gasps.

"You look like a goddess," he murmurs.

I turn to him, taking in his outfit, a black tux that fits him like a glove, the lines sharp and clean. His mask is deep purple with jet-black feathers, dramatic and bold.

"You're one to talk," I tell him, smoothing a wrinkle from his lapel. "You look like the hot villain in a gothic opera."

"Stop, you're going to make me blush," he deadpans, then leans in with a mischievous gleam in his eye. "Want to know what Wendy's wearing?"

I raise a brow. "Tell me."

He makes a face. "A puffy black feather dress."

I blink. "So... she's the Black Swan?"

"More rooster than swan, if you ask me."

I bite back a laugh as I roll my eyes in response.

He takes my hand. "Ready?"

"No," I whisper. "But let's get this over with."

We walk through the candlelit hallway, and I hear a live symphony rising from downstairs—violins and soft percussion. At the top of the grand staircase, Lando stops and faces me.

"Make an entrance," he says with a wink. "And don't trip. But if you do, at least fall beautifully and pretend it was intentional."

I laugh under my breath. "Thanks."

He kisses my cheek and runs down the stairs first, leaving me to take a steadying breath. I begin to descend and the moment my pointe shoe touches the first stair, I feel the room sway, but I push forward. As the guests come into view below, heads turn and voices hush, eyes on me.

The train of my gown swishes behind me, feathers swaying, and the chandelier light catches the pearls at my neckline and the mask over my face. I move slowly, as graceful as I can manage, as if I'm not shaking inside.

My eyes catch on Reign at the bottom of the stairs. He's dressed in a custom-tailored black suit with white gold embroidery stitched into the lapels, just like swan wings, matching my dress. His mask is a simple matte black, sculpted perfectly to his face, but it doesn't hide his blue eyes piercing through the crowd and locked on me.

The moment I meet his gaze, a wave of calm rolls over me and the nerves vanish. As if the chaos of the night, the pressure, the weight of this role and all it symbolizes for Imperium, for me... none of it matters. Not while he's looking at me like I'm the only person in the room.

As I take the final step, the soft tap of my shoe's echoes against the marble, and Reign steps forward, taking my hand without a word, fingers threading through mine, his touch is warm and grounding as his eyes roam over me slowly—neck to waist to the tips of my shoes—and when he meets my gaze again, it's like the rest of the world disappears.

"You're going to ruin every man in this room who thought they were going to get your attention tonight," he murmurs.

Heat blooms up my neck. "Reign—"

His smirk curves slowly. "Don't blush now. I haven't even gotten to the part about what I want to do to you later."

I let out a breathy laugh, cheeks burning behind my mask. He lifts my hand to his lips and presses an indulgent kiss to the back of it. Then, with his other hand, he passes me a champagne flute, the crystal glass already fizzing with gold.

"For the nerves," he says. "And to celebrate how goddamn lucky I am."

I take it with a grateful nod, the bubbles tickling my lips

as I sip. He keeps hold of my hand and guides me into the crowd. Wherever Reign walks, people part for him, and I follow. He stops in front of a small group—three men and a woman in cocktail masks, all laughing behind flutes of champagne. The moment we step into their circle, the air shifts and their attention locks on him, and then on me.

"Ah," one of them says. "The elusive Mr. Harrington. You've been keeping out of sight for quite some time."

"I've been working hard behind the scenes," Reign says smoothly, before sliding his hand around my waist. "May I introduce Angelique Sinclair—our Odette and Odile. The soul of Swan Lake."

Their eyes snap to me, glittering with curiosity.

"She's even more stunning in person," the woman murmurs.

"The one from New York?" one man asks.

Reign's voice turns darkly proud. "She's the best principal I've ever shared a stage with."

The praise makes my spine straighten. I smile politely, but my heart thuds against my ribs. Reign's thumb rubs a slow, grounding circle against the small of my back. His body angled toward mine, protective without being obvious.

"She's the reason this entire production exists," he adds, eyes never leaving mine.

I barely have time to respond before the lights dim slightly, drawing everyone's attention toward the stage where the orchestra plays.

"Ladies and gentlemen," Charlie's unmistakable voice echoes across the marble and crystal space. "Thank you for joining us tonight to support Imperium's upcoming season. It's an honour to host you all at our annual gala—and tonight, we have a rare gift."

My heart pounds uncontrollably with nerves, but Reign gently presses his palm against my back, and my heart calms a fraction.

"Before Swan Lake graces our stage this Summer, we invite you to witness a small preview—a duet between our Swan Queen and her Prince Siegfried, choreographed by our very own Terry Baker, and accompanied by a special musical composition."

He pauses, blinking down at his speech cards that his assistant must have written, based on the shocked expression he has as he looks up, eyes connecting with Reign's from across the room.

"Written by my son...Reign Harrington."

The crowd reacts instantly in soft gasps, murmurs of surprise, and a few turned heads in our direction. I turn to look at him, but Reign just lifts his chin slightly, expression unreadable beneath the mask.

He turns to face me. "Ready, Angel?" he asks quietly.

I nod and take his hand, my fingers sliding into his like they were meant to fit there. The centre of the room has been cleared, a polished circle of floor surrounded by the onlookers. We stand in our starting positions, and there's a long pause as the orchestra's instruments raise and still.

I take a deep breath and as I exhale, the first note blooms, melancholy and tender, the piano lead aching. The string instruments follow, slow and mournful. It's not Tchaikovsky's, or anyone else's. It's Reign's masterpiece. I glance at him as we move, but he's already watching me.

Terry's choreography is devastatingly intimate and I'm aware of everything—the crowd, the lights, the eyes fixed on us—and my body hums. I feel myself tightening inside, heat pooling low as I melt into the performance and into Reign. The music rises, and everything falls away, leaving only him. His mouth just inches from mine, and his breath hot against my cheek.

His eyes lower to mine and I see the exact moment he realizes how turned on I am. The slight parting of his lips and the surprised look in his eyes before his gaze deepens, turning molten and hungry. He tightens his hold on me just slightly, and my pulse stutters in answer.

I let the choreography melt into instinct, the music carrying me to the places I never let myself feel in New York. And when he lowers me into the final dip, our faces barely an inch apart, no one makes a sound.

I stare into Reign's eyes, certain now that I love him more than anything, and his eyes soften, almost like he can hear the thoughts in my mind. Applause erupts, crashing against the quiet we left behind.

The applause is still echoing as we bow to the crowd, but as we straighten, something changes. Reign's hand stiffens slightly against mine, and his head turns toward the crowd, eyes locking onto something, or someone, just beyond where I can see.

I glance up at him, confused by his stillness, but he doesn't say a word for a moment. His jaw clenches, and his expression reminds me of the night those drunk men tried to corner me in the alley. It gives me goosebumps as I look around, fully expecting one of them to be here. When he finally turns back to me, his voice is quiet and way too calm for how he looks.

"I need to check on something," he says. "I'll be back."

And then he's gone—walking off without another word. A chill rushes over my skin as I step back into the crowd of people, disoriented, still trying to catch my breath when Charlie appears beside me.

"There she is," he says, clapping with a proud smile. "That was magnificent, Angelique. Absolutely unforgettable."

"Thank you," I manage, my eyes still scanning the crowd, looking for Reign. Hoping he'll come back through the haze of bodies.

"There's someone I want you to meet," Charlie continues. "He's a guest of mine tonight. He'll be joining Imperium next season. I think you'll be delighted—you two know each other."

I turn toward him absently and my entire body goes cold when I see the man standing beside him.

"Hey, Pigeon," Alec says, and my lungs forget how to function.

I blink, but I can't move as I stare back at him, my legs frozen and my vision beginning to blur at the edges. The sound of his voice cuts through me like a dull, rusted knife —one that's already been buried there once before.

He's here, standing right in front of me, and he's smiling like what he did to me never happened. I taste bile rushing up my throat.

"I—" My voice catches. "Excuse me." I turn and run, and I don't look back.

I don't even know where I'm going, all I know is that I need to get out of Imperium, and away from Alec. My pointe shoes tap furiously down the front steps of the estate until I hit gravel, the stones uncomfortable under my shoes, causing me to stumble. I internally curse myself for not bringing a change of shoes to this stupid gala.

I gasp in a full breath of air, but it's not enough. Nothing is enough. I hit my knees at the bottom of the steps and vomit. It burns up my throat, violent and ugly, and my eyes water from the force of it, mascara bleeding down my cheeks.

"Well, that wasn't the reunion I imagined," Alec says from behind me, voice casual like we're old friends.

My blood turns to ice as I wipe my mouth with the back of my hand and slowly force myself to stand.

CHAPTER 30

REIGN

I stand outside of Imperium, half-shielded behind a marble column. Behind me, Wendy shifts, her heels pressing softly on the stone. She's holding her phone up, quietly recording everything, just like I told her to. She owes Angelique after the shit she pulled. It was this or get kicked out of Imperium for good.

Angelique wipes her mouth with the back of her hand and pushes herself to her feet. Her back is still to Alec, shoulders trembling, and she doesn't know we're here. She doesn't know I've been watching her like a hawk since the second she ran from the ballroom.

My father mentioned Alec's name a few days ago—some bullshit about a surprise guest. I didn't think the bastard would show, but the moment I saw him in the crowd after our performance, I knew.

I knew he'd come for her.

I knew I'd finally get the chance to burn him to the fucking ground.

"Beautiful performance tonight," Alec says, his tone

easy. "You dance better than your understudy at Big Apple ever could. So much emotion."

Angelique turns to face him now, and he takes a step closer while she instinctively takes one back. I can see the fear in how her body trembles before him and it makes me clench my hands into fists, wanting to run out there and beat the shit out of him already.

"I was heartbroken when I heard you left the company," he goes on. "You had this spark. A true star quality."

"Stay away from me," she hisses, voice shaking, but Alec keeps walking forward.

He rips off his mask and tosses it to the gravel, and I see the twisted, hungry expression on his face as he stares at her before lunging forward and grabbing her arm.

"You look fucking sexy in that dress," he growls, inches from her face. "Reign doesn't deserve to dance next to what's mine."

His eyes narrow as he stares at her, his teeth bared. "Did you let him fuck you, too?" he spits.

She jerks her arm, trying to get away, but he tightens his grip, and she screams, a panicked sound that makes my whole body go still.

"I never let you fuck me," she snarls, shaking. "Now let me go!"

He shoves her backward, causing her to fall onto the gravel path with a cry that rips me in two, and time stops, my vision going black at the edges, as I watch him unbuckle his belt and pull his dick out.

"Still trying to tell me what to do," he seethes. "Looks like you need another lesson in shutting your fucking mouth."

Another lesson, the words echo in my head.

"Film everything," I hiss at Wendy, sprinting towards them.

I reach them within seconds, the rage in my chest burning hotter than anything I've ever felt. Angelique's on the ground, trying to crawl backward, her hands shaking too hard to push herself up. Her eyes meet mine for a split second and I swear, she's never looked more scared.

My fist connects with the side of Alec's face in a sickening crunch before he even realizes I'm there. He staggers sideways and hits the ground hard, spitting blood. Angelique scrambles to the edge of the path, hands over her mouth, but I don't stop. I climb over him and start swinging.

"You think you can touch her?"

Crack.

"You think this is a game?"

Crack.

"You should be dead, you fucking coward."

His nose breaks beneath my knuckles, blood spattering across my arm and tux, but I don't give a fuck. I want him to feel the way he made her feel; powerless and small. But Angelique's cries reach me again, somewhere in the fog.

"Reign—Reign, stop, please—" Her voice cracks on the last word, and that's the only thing that makes me pause.

My hands are shaking, covered in blood, and my chest heaves as I stare down at Alec. He's barely conscious, gasping, his face an unrecognizable mess of crimson and bruises. I grab him by the collar and haul him upright so that he's facing Wendy as she films him, pressing my forearm into his throat until he gags. He tries to look away, but I shake him hard.

"No," I growl. "You don't get to look away now."

Alec's eyes flutter. He's dazed, dizzy, somewhere between pain and panic, but not far enough gone.

"You think I'm just going to beat the shit out of you and walk away?" I whisper, low and lethal. "No. You're going to confess to what you did. You're going to say it out loud, or I swear to God, I'll rip your fucking face off."

His throat works under my arm, and I ease the pressure just enough for him to speak. He coughs, wheezing, blood bubbling at the edge of his mouth.

"I—I don't know what you want—"

I slam him back down against the gravel and his head cracks hard against the stone.

"Wrong answer."

"Reign—" Angelique's voice breaks behind me. I can hear her fear, feel her pain.

I grit my teeth and lean close to Alec's ear. "Tell the camera what you did to her, and I'll make sure your death is quick."

His lip trembles. "I—I didn't—"

I jab my fist into his ribs, hard and sharp, causing him to gasp.

"What did you do to her?" I shout.

I slam my hand down on his chest, hard enough to make his eyes roll. His breath comes out in broken bursts.

"The bitch deserved it," he spits, voice wet and raspy. "She wanted to act like she was running shit, like she was running *me*."

"Keep going," I snarl, shoving him again. "Say it. All of it."

"I took her right there on the studio floor." Alec laughs, the sound wet and breathy. "I didn't know she was a fucking virgin, though, but I guess that made it even better."

Wendy sucks in a breath. "You raped her?" she asks, voice shaking.

His eyes dart toward Angelique as his mouth twitches into a sick, bloody grin. "She said no, and I didn't stop. Call it what you want."

My blood runs cold as rage detonates inside me. Blinding rage. And in a split second, blood smears across his cheekbone, dripping into the gravel, and I hear Wendy gasp, shifting her angle but never stopping the recording.

Good. Let the world see what I do to men who touch what's mine.

My knuckles are raw now, but I only stop when I feel her hand—small, shaking—on my shoulder.

"Reign," she whispers, and suddenly I'm breathing again.

The red fades just enough for me to look back at her. She's kneeling in the gravel, mascara streaked down her cheeks, hair wild, her dress torn at the shoulder, and her lips are trembling. I rise off Alec slowly and go to her, my body still tense with fury. I reach for the arm he grabbed, and when I see the bruises already forming, my throat closes.

"He'll never hurt you again," I whisper. "I swear to you."

Angelique nods, a tear sliding down her cheek as she lifts my raw knuckles up between us, placing a gentle kiss on them, getting blood on her lips.

"What the fuck is going on here?" I hear the familiar sound of my father's voice behind me.

He storms toward us, eyes wild. His gaze jumps from Alec's limp body to my split knuckles before finally landing on Angelique and taking in her dishevelled state. He looks back at me, furious.

"Reign," he says, voice raised. "What did you do?"

"He deserved everything," I say, chuckling through my rage. "And more."

His jaw ticks and he turns toward Angelique, eyes narrowing like he's trying to piece something together. "What happened?"

"He hurt me," she whispers. "Again."

"Again?" He blinks.

"He raped me at the Big Apple Ballet Company," she says after a pause, finding her voice now. "I told my mother, hoping she'd help, but she pulled me out to protect him, the money his parents donated, and the company."

My father's entire face goes still, and so does mine as I look at her.

Her own mother didn't protect her?

My rage reignites and I vow to myself I'll find a way to make her mom suffer for not choosing her daughter over a company. Over money. Over a man.

"I've spent months trying to pretend it didn't happen," she continues, voice shaking. "But it did. And tonight, if it wasn't for Reign, he was going to rape me again."

Wendy steps forward, lifting her phone. "I recorded the whole thing."

Charlie stares at Alec, who's still wheezing on the ground, blood leaking from his mouth.

"This can't be real," he mutters, rubbing his hand down his face. "I invited this man here. I thought you'd be so happy to see him. I didn't know that he—" his voice cracks.

"No one did," she says, softly.

My father's silence stretches before he looks at me. "Get her out of here," he says, his voice dangerously low. "Take her home. I'll deal with this."

I don't move. "You mean—?"

Is my father capable of killing?

"I'm calling the police," he says, pulling his phone from his jacket. "There will be legal action. This won't be swept under the rug the way it was at The Big Apple Ballet. Not this time."

He swipes his phone screen and begins dialling the emergency line.

"Ms. Wu, please stay with me. I'm sure the police will want to see your video recording," he says to Wendy, before looking at Angelique again, his face twisted with regret and guilt. "I'm sorry, Angelique. I promised your father the day you were born that I'd protect you like you were my own. I should have asked if you were okay with me inviting him."

"It's okay," she says, but her voice breaks on the last word, and we all know it's not.

I take her hand and lead her to where my car is parked, leaving Alec on the ground with my father and Wendy. But I know this isn't the last time I'll be seeing him. Because the next time I see him, I won't have anyone around to stop me from finishing him.

CHAPTER 31

ANGELIQUE

The world blurs around me on the ride home as I sit in silence beside Reign, numb and exhausted, barely aware of the road winding through the trees, or of the shadows chasing us in the rearview mirror.

My dress sticks uncomfortably to my skin, stiff with sweat, and my hands won't stop shaking as I hold on to Reign. But I can't feel it. I can't feel anything. My mind is far away, floating somewhere above the car, above the estate, above all of this.

When we pull up to the house, Reign parks the car but doesn't move. Instead, he turns in his seat and silently stares at me, like he's afraid I'll shatter if he says the wrong thing.

"I'm fine," I whisper.

I see the way his eyes narrow for a second at the lie, but eventually he nods. "Come on," he says softly. "Let's go inside."

He helps me out of his car, but he doesn't touch me the whole time, choosing to hover close instead, and it's exactly what I was afraid of. Now that he knows what Alec did to me, I'm just another girl with baggage and a body deemed damaged goods.

I walk beside him up the stone steps and through the front door, pointe shoes in hand. My skin is buzzing, like I've been peeled open and left out in the cold. Inside, everything looks the same, but nothing feels familiar. I hold his gaze, knowing he has questions, but I don't think I have any answers for him tonight, so I look away.

"I just... I need a shower," I say, forcing my voice to stay even. "I need to... get him off me."

Reign studies me, eyes flickering over every inch of me like he's reading between the lines, but he doesn't ask questions. He nods once and lets me go.

The door closes behind me with a soft click, and the lock slides into place with a finality that makes my chest tighten before I fall apart. I press my back against the door and sink to the floor, my legs folding under me like I've been hollowed out.

The sob breaks before I can stop it, torn straight from my lungs. I bury my face in my hands and curl into myself, shoulders shaking as I cry into the silence. I try to be quiet —No. I *have* to be quiet, because Reign is right outside, and I don't want him to hear this part. I don't want him to see me like this. Not this version of me.

I reach for the shower knobs with trembling hands and turn the water on, twisting it all the way to hot. Steam fills the space, curling around the mirror, the air quickly becoming thick and suffocating.

I strip out of my dress slowly, letting it slide off my shoulders and puddle at my feet. The corset is next, then my bra and underwear. Piece by piece, until I'm left bare, every inch of me feeling wrong.

I step into the stream, and the heat bites at my skin,

scalding. I close my eyes and stand there for a long moment, letting it burn, but it's not enough. I reach for my loofah, pour body wash into the mesh, and scrub hard.

I scrub my chest, my stomach, and my arms. I scrub the bruises forming on my upper arm, where Alec grabbed me, until the skin goes raw and pink. I scrub until the pain overtakes the memory. Until the sensation of him—his hand and his voice—is buried beneath the sting of friction and heat. But it still doesn't work. No matter how hard I scrub, he's still there.

My skin burns as my eyes blur, and I toss the loofah to the side, spotting the razor on the ledge as I do. I stare at it, blinking through the fog, heart thudding quietly in my ears, and then reach for it without a second thought.

My fingers wrap around it, and there's a strange calm that settles over me, like I'm sliding underwater. The steam clings to my skin as I sit down in the bottom of the shower, water pouring over my back, and draw my legs up against my chest. My fingers tremble as I press the blade to my wrist and draw it across slowly, revelling in the sharp, immediate, pain.

The cut blooms red almost instantly, a thick line that's far too deep, yet somehow not deep enough. I feel a release as the blood flows, like I've finally done something right. Like I've found the pressure valve and opened it just enough to breathe. I watch the water wash the blood away, pink spirals circling the drain.

Maybe they'd be better off without me. Maybe I'm just too much. Reign...Lando...Everyone. Maybe the weight I carry is too much for them and for me. Maybe I'm the problem that never goes away. Maybe this world doesn't need me in it anymore. And maybe, just maybe... I don't want to do this anymore.

With a trembling hand, I press the blade to my skin again and the pain is worse this time, but I keep going because anything is better than this ache inside me. Anything is better than feeling like I don't belong in my body.

Anything is better than being me.

I WRAP MY ROBE AROUND MYSELF, CINCHING IT LOOSELY AT MY waist. My curls are soaked, clinging to my face and neck, water dripping steadily down the curve of my spine, and my skin is raw, stinging from where I scrubbed too hard, but I don't really feel it. I feel little of anything except the weight on my wrist, and the warmth of blood.

It drips steadily from beneath the sleeve, down my hand, leaving small red trails across the tile as I walk. I watch them but don't register them. They don't look like mine.

I open the bathroom door, and my eyes connect with Reign's. He's leaning against the opposite wall, one foot propped casually behind him, hands deep in his pockets like he's been standing there forever. He doesn't speak as he lifts his eyes to mine, searching, and then they drop to my hand.

His body shifts before he pushes off the wall and walks toward me, his expression unreadable. He doesn't ask for permission as he takes my hand gently in his, fingers steady despite the blood, and pulls the sleeve back.

I look down, finally. The cuts are deeper than I thought, red glistening across the edge of the robe, the blood trailing down in lazy arcs. It should hurt, but it doesn't. Nothing does. Reign's brow furrows as he studies it. Then, without a word, he leads me back into the bathroom, never letting go of my hand.

He kneels in front of the vanity and pulls out a white first aid kit, flipping it open calmly, his hands moving like this is muscle memory to him. He pulls out gauze, antiseptic, steri-strips, and tape.

"Are you trying to kill yourself?" he asks quietly, but he doesn't look at me as he works, wiping the blood from my skin with practiced care, the antiseptic burning.

I don't answer. He squeezes my wrist gently, pressing the skin around the cut together with two fingers, applying the steri-strip to keep it closed.

"You didn't cut deep enough to do that," he murmurs. "If that was your aim."

I stay silent as the blood pools on the cotton pad in his hand. He changes it right away as I sit on the closed toilet lid, wrapped in my robe, hair dripping onto my shoulders.

He sighs deep and heavy, frustration clinging to the edges of it. "I'm removing everything sharp from the house as soon as you're in bed," he says.

And when I still say nothing, his jaw tightens. Then, slowly, he sinks down to the floor, landing hard on his ass, legs bent, arms draped over his knees. For the first time since I opened the door, he looks up at me. His eyes are tired and bloodshot. But there's a quiet, pleading desperation.

"Please talk to me, Angel."

The nickname makes something crack inside my chest. I don't respond right away, but he stays right there, waiting. Like he always does.

"Angel," he says again, softer this time. He closes his eyes for a second, jaw flexing like he's trying to keep it together.

"I feel like I'm disappearing," I finally say, my voice

cracking around the truth. "Like I'm made of glass and grief and everything hurts to touch."

He pushes up onto his knees and reaches for me, his hands settling on either side of my face. His thumbs brush beneath my eyes, and I don't even realize I'm crying until he does it again.

"You're still here," he whispers. "And I will keep holding onto you until you believe that, too."

CHAPTER 32
REIGN

Angelique looks half alive as she sits on the toilet lid, soaked, bloody, and hollow-eyed, wrapped in a robe that clings to her damp skin. Her curls hang in dripping strands around her face, and she doesn't blink or speak as she sits there, barely breathing, eyes red-rimmed from all her crying.

I stay on the bathroom floor, arms braced on her knees, staring up at her, waiting for a sign of life or crack in the ice. Anything. But there's nothing except for the silence, and the low thrum of water still dripping from the shower head, along with the raw ache building steadily in my chest. She's here in front of me, but I don't think I've ever seen her so far away.

The cuts she gave herself scare me. They're not deep enough to kill her. The razor she used can't go that far, but the intention behind it...that's what turns my stomach. She meant for it to end something. If not her life, then the part of her that's still fighting to stay in it, and I don't know how to fix it, or how to fix her. All I know is that I can't leave her like this.

After a few more minutes, I push off the floor and stand, reaching out and taking her good hand in mine, relieved when she doesn't resist. She lets me lead her down the hall, and when we reach her bedroom, I pull back the duvet and help her climb in.

She moves like a marionette, like her soul isn't fully inside her body anymore. I crawl in beside her and wrap my arm around her waist, pulling her to my chest. We lie there for a long time in the dark, our bodies pressed together, the only sound the wind through the trees outside and the occasional creak of the house settling.

She gasps suddenly, and then the sobs come, hard, fast, and uncontrollable. Her whole body shakes as she clings to me like she's drowning, and I'm the only thing keeping her afloat. Her fingers fist into my shirt, and her face burrows into my chest while I silently hold her.

I bury my face in her hair, breathing her in, anchoring myself in the warmth of her body even as she comes undone in my arms. I'd give anything to take it from her—this memory eating her alive from the inside out. She cries for a long time before the sobs slow, and I notice how her grip loosens and her breathing evens out in small, shaky exhales.

My sweet girl cried herself to sleep.

I stay there, curled around her, wide awake in the dark, heart splintered from the inside out. I stare at the ceiling, but all I can see is her face and the way it looked tonight. It was like someone lit a match and blew the last piece of her away. But I want her back. I want her laughing again, and dancing like the world belongs to her, tearing through it with that beauty that made me fall in love with her in the first place. I want her alive, not just breathing, and I'll burn this world to the ground before I let it take another piece of her.

I slowly untangle myself from her, careful not to wake her, then slip out of the room. For the next hour, I scour the house in silence, pulling open drawers, rummaging through cabinets, searching every dark corner for anything sharp enough to harm her. Razors. Scissors. Blades. Even the broken piece I found of the mug I broke. I toss them into a bin—every last one—then carry it to my closet and shove it onto the highest shelf, out of sight, and out of reach.

I hear a thud come from Angelique's room and I run down the hall, swinging her door open to find her phone dropped on her bedroom floor as she climbs out of bed, her robe trailing behind her.

"Angel?" I whisper, moving to the side as she approaches, her bare feet moving across the wooden floor without a sound.

When she walks out into the hall, passing me, that's when I see her half-lidded eyes and blank expression.

She's sleepwalking.

I'm not surprised though. It's been some time since she last did it, but I'd expected that it might happen the second I gave her the champagne glass earlier, and I was certain it'd happen after everything with Alec.

I follow her as she turns into my room and slides into the bed, pulling the blanket over herself like it's the most natural thing in the world. Like that's where she belongs. I stand there for a second, staring, before I cross the room and slide in next to her. Her body finds mine instinctively, curling into my side. I watch her for a long time, wondering why, when her subconscious needs safety, it always brings her here.

To me.

I rest my hand lightly over her waist, fingers brushing the soft fabric of her robe, and close my eyes. Whatever she needs, she can have all of it, as long as she keeps choosing to stay.

~

It's early when I wake up, and for a moment I forget the night before. I forget Alec, the blood, the bruises, the sound of Angelique's sobs ripping through me like shrapnel. But when I remember, I look down, relieved to see she's still here, tucked beneath my arm with her cheek pressed to my chest, breathing even and slow.

The sunlight beams golden against the warm brown of her complexion, brightening the curve of her shoulder where her robe falls open. My chest tightens as I watch her, reaching up and sliding a curl from her cheek, careful not to wake her.

But a small breath escapes her lips as she shifts, her lashes fluttering against her skin. Her eyes open slowly, and she blinks up at me for a long moment, like she's not sure if I'm real, and then her gaze softens.

"Hey," I whisper, noting how swollen her eyes are.

"Hi," she whispers back.

I lean in slowly, brushing my lips against hers.

Are you still here, Angel?

Angelique answers by kissing me back, her hand finding my chest, fingers curling over the fabric of my shirt like she needs to feel the beat of my heart beneath her palm. I tilt her chin and kiss her again, deeper this time, and she parts her lips, letting me in.

Her body presses closer, soft and hungry, and my hand drifts to her waist, sliding beneath the edge of her robe. Her skin is warm and sensitive from the shower last night, and when my fingers graze the small of her back, she exhales a shaky breath, like she's still relearning how to feel.

We move together slowly, limbs tangling, mouths meeting in slow, reverent kisses. I peel the robe from her shoulders, letting it fall away as I kiss a line down her neck, pausing when I feel her heartbeat flutter beneath my mouth. I need her to remember what it feels like to be cared for, to be loved by me. I want her to feel everything. Every brush of my hands. Every breath. Every way I worship her.

I reach toward the nightstand without fully leaving her, never breaking contact for more than a second. She watches me as I open the drawer and pull out the condom box, the foil packet glinting under the low light.

I tear it open with my teeth, push my boxers down, and roll the condom on with one hand. Her gaze drops briefly, then jumps back up to my face, cheeks flushing. I settle between her thighs again and my hands frame her face, thumbs grazing her jaw as our mouths mold together again and again until the kiss deepens, her tongue brushing mine in a gentle stroke that makes my control splinter.

My cock is already hard; heavy with need—thick and pulsing at the base, the head sensitive, aching. Every second not inside her is excruciating, and yet, I force myself to move slowly, to take care, because this isn't about release. It's about her.

It's about us.

I guide myself to her entrance, rubbing the head of my cock against her slick pussy, and she gasps softly, her hips tilting up to meet me. She's so fucking ready for me as I press in, inch by inch, the heat of her wrapping around me so tight it punches the air out of my lungs.

"Fuck," I grit, eyes falling shut for a second. She's so

warm and so wet. I can feel every flutter of her body as she stretches around me, her cunt gripping me like she doesn't want to let me go.

She moans, breath hitching as I push deeper, and her fingers claw into my shoulders like she needs me buried inside her to feel whole again. I bottom out slowly, holding there for a moment, my forehead pressed to hers.

She's everything.

Moving inside her is slow torture—perfect torture. Her walls tighten with every thrust, and I'm thick inside her, stretching her open in a way that makes her tremble beneath me. Her legs lock around my waist, pulling me in deeper, and I feel it down to my spine—this raw, aching need.

We find an unhurried rhythm, my hips rolling deep and purposeful, and I swear I feel her shiver every time I drag across that perfect spot inside her. When I hear my name slip past her lips in a soft moan, I lose it.

I kiss her, again and again, our mouths brushing between breaths. My cock drives into her slowly and powerfully, like a promise I'm carving into her skin.

"I've got you," I whisper, lips brushing her temple. "I'm right here."

She whimpers when she comes, her body clenching around me, her face tucked into my neck. I feel her break apart beneath me, unraveling in my arms, and I let go right after—groaning low in my throat, thrusting once, twice more before I still, buried deep as I come hard inside her.

We don't move for a long time as our breathing evens out. She draws lazy patterns down my back, and I keep one hand cradling the back of her head, the other stroking her hip in soothing circles.

Words feel useless right now, so I say nothing. They'd

only dilute the truth of what's already been spoken between our bodies. She doesn't have to tell me out loud that she loves me, but I feel it now. She hasn't said it, maybe because she's scared to after everything, but I know she does. So, I hold her tighter, anchoring us both in the silence, where nothing needs to be said to mean everything.

ANGELIQUE IS CURLED UP ON THE COUCH, WRAPPED IN A BLANKET with her knees tucked tight to her chest. Some trashy dating show plays low on the TV, bright lights flickering across her blank face, but I can tell she's not really watching.

I've tried everything. I made her breakfast this morning, played piano for her after lunch, kissed her hair, her shoulder, her fingers, anywhere I could reach, just to remind her she still means everything to me. But she only ever gives me these faint brief nods—ghosts of what she used to be.

My phone buzzes in my pocket, and when I pull it out, my stomach tightens.

DETECTIVE POWELL:

> He's being released tonight. On a plane back to JFK by morning. Charges aren't sticking here—not for what happened in New York. UK can't touch it.

I stare at the screen for a second too long, then I look at her. Angelique doesn't notice. She's still sitting there, barely blinking, her hand clenching and unclenching under the blanket like even her body doesn't know what to do with itself anymore, so I unlock my phone and fire off a quick text to Lando.

ME:

> Need you at the guesthouse now. Stay with her. Don't ask questions.

His reply comes seconds later.

LANDO:

> On my way.

I tuck the phone away, eyes still locked on her, but she doesn't look at me. I walk over and press a kiss to her temple, smoothing my hand over her curls.

"I'll be right back," I murmur.

She nods slowly, but I know she didn't really hear me.

As I grab my coat and head for the door, my hands are already curling into fists. Because tonight, I'm not coming back until I finish what I should've done the first fucking time.

CHAPTER 33
REIGN

I wait across the street from the police station, tucked into the shadow between two buildings, hood up, black baseball cap low over my eyes. My head is down, and my hands are in the pockets of my coat. I've been standing here for forty-two minutes while the cold crept in, but I don't feel it. All I feel is the steady pulse behind my eyes, like a countdown.

Angelique's safe back at the guesthouse. Lando's with her, thank fuck, and he's good at distracting. My phone buzzes in my palm and when I glance at the screen and see Terry's name blinking up at me, I answer it.

"What?" I growl.

"What's the verdict?" he asks, unfazed by my grouchiness. "You think she'll be ready?"

"Too early to say," I mutter, eyes still on the front doors. "She's been through hell. She can barely get through the day without shutting down, let alone stand in front of an audience."

There's a pause.

"Yeah," he says finally. "Makes sense. I'll hold rehearsals

and shuffle the order to give her a few more days to breathe."

"Give her a week," I correct. "I'll have a better answer by then."

"Alright." Another pause. "Are you okay?"

The doors of the station slide open, and Alec strolls out wearing a smug fucking smile, his nose bandaged after I broke it last night. I grind my teeth; guess I'll just have to break it some more until he can't fucking smile at all. He walks easily, not even a limp to show for what happened outside of Imperium.

Time to change that.

I hang up on Terry without another word and watch as Alec crosses the street. According to detective Powell, because the rape happened in the U.S., British police couldn't touch him on that. All they could do was charge him for public indecency and attempted sexual assault. Wendy's video got him in the door, but not in the cell. And even that was reduced to a warning.

A warning. That's all he got for all the pain he's caused.

The justice system is a joke, so here I am, about to give him my version of a warning. As much as I want to kill the bastard, that would be too easy. I want him alive for what I'm about to do. And I'll be sure he feels it every single day for the rest of his life. Because after tonight, Alec will never dance again.

It's the least he deserves after everything he put my Angel through.

I slip out of the shadows and follow him as he turns off the main road, heading down a narrow pedestrian path between two buildings—construction fencing on one side, graffiti-covered brick on the other. It's quiet and empty; no witnesses to see what I'm about to do.

Stupid bastard.

He doesn't hear me until I'm right behind him. "Hey, dickface."

He turns, just in time to see my fist slam into his nose. The hit sends him staggering back, sunglasses flying off his head, blood spurting from his nose as he catches himself on the wall, crying out in pain.

His eyes find mine and go round when he realizes it's me. "Reign!?"

Another punch—harder—this one to the gut. He doubles over with a grunt, wheezing, so I grab him by the collar and slam him into the brick wall behind him, his head cracking against it.

"Didn't think I'd let you just walk away, did you?" I hiss.

His eyes go wide. "Reign—Reign buddy, don't—fuck, you don't want to do this—"

"I do," I admit, unable to hold back the laugh that bubbles out of me. "I've wanted to since the day I heard her scream your name in her sleep, begging you to stop."

I let go just long enough for him to scramble back, and then I kick his leg out from under him. He crumples to the ground, hands out in front of him.

"Please," he whimpers, voice cracking. "Please, man—"

I don't stop as I lift my foot and bring it down on his knee. The crack is immediate and his scream echoes down the alley, high and shrill. He rolls to his side, clutching his leg, sobbing, and I crouch beside him, grab his collar again, and force him to look at me.

"One more," I growl. "To match the other."

I stand and stomp down on the other knee, closing my eyes to the delicious sound of his scream, more desperate now. I don't feel guilty, only cold and vicious clarity. He'll struggle to ever walk right again, and he most definitely will never dance again.

He'll never think about touching someone like her again. Because now, every time he looks at his own fucking legs, he'll remember me. I stare down at him, broken and wailing on the concrete, and then I pull my hood up, turn, and walk away without a word.

BY THE TIME I GET BACK TO THE GUESTHOUSE, THE MOON'S HIGH, and my fists are stiff with dried blood. I quietly slip through the front door, wanting to wash off before Angelique sees me like this. The glow from the TV bathes the living room in soft blue, and I spot her curled up on the couch asleep in a nest of blankets, her curls wild across the cushion.

Lando's at the other end of the couch, nursing a glass of wine, his legs stretched out. He glances over his shoulder when he hears me and when his eyes drop to my bloodied hands, he lowers his drink. He stands up and walks over to me, his eyes never leaving the blood crusted across my knuckles, looking up at me when he comes to a stop.

"Please tell me that's Alec's."

I nod once. "He won't be dancing again."

Probably won't be walking right either.

Cold satisfaction flashes in his eyes as his jaw clenches. "Good. I'm glad one of us could avenge her." He glances back at Angelique, his expression softening. "She didn't want to eat anything today. I'm worried about her."

I follow his gaze to where she lies asleep on the couch, her lips slightly parted.

"She's not herself," Lando says quietly, rubbing his arm. "I feel like we're losing her."

The knot in my throat pulls tight as I step further into the room, closer to the couch, watching her chest rise and fall. She looks at peace, but I know it's not real. As soon as she wakes up and the memories come crashing down, she'll go back to self-destruction mode, but I'm determined to save her from it.

"I'll take care of her," I say, but under all my determination is fear because I've taken revenge, but I haven't saved her yet. And that's what terrifies me most.

I head down the hall, leaving Lando behind in the blue-tinted dark. The door to the bathroom clicks shut behind me, and I turn on the water, letting it run hot while I peel off my coat and shirt. Dried blood cracks along my knuckles as I flex them under the faucet, watching Alec's remnants swirl pink down the drain. My skin is raw and split in places, but the sting doesn't bother me. Not really.

I brace my hands on the edge of the sink, my head bowed, steam curling up into my lungs until it hurts to breathe. The man in the mirror doesn't look like me anymore. He looks like he hasn't slept in days, and that's because I haven't. Not since she started slipping through my fingers again. I press my forehead to the cool mirror and close my eyes.

You protected her. That's what matters.

That's the voice I've been clinging to—the one that sounds like reason. But underneath it is the other voice, the one I try to drown out every time I look at her and see nothing looking back, the one whispering what I don't want to admit.

You're losing her.

And this time, if she goes... she's not coming back. Not like last time—when she left for New York and I found excuses to be in the city just to check in on her. Not like when I watched her from the shadows, convincing myself I didn't love her because it hurt too much to want someone who wasn't mine.

No. This time, she wouldn't just leave the country, she'd leave this world, and if I lose her... I won't come back from that either.

~

ANGELIQUE IS STILL ASLEEP WHEN I RETURN TO THE LIVING ROOM, the flicker of the TV playing across her skin. Lando's at the door, dressed to leave, and when he spots me, he gives me a quick wave before walking out.

I kneel next to her, careful not to wake her, and watch for a while. Her lashes flutter now and then, like she's dreaming—hopefully about something good. Her hand is tucked under her cheek, and I reach for it carefully, brushing my fingers over hers.

The guilt comes next, because I wish I'd killed him. Not for me, but for the peace I want to put back inside her. But if I'd done that, I'd be risking prison and never seeing her again, and I don't think I can survive in a world without Angelique next to me.

I lower my head and kiss her bandaged wrist, causing her to stir but not wake.

"I'm still here," I whisper into her skin. "And I'm not going anywhere. Not until you find your way back."

Her fingers curl tighter around mine, the tiniest squeeze —instinctive but still unconscious—and it wrecks me. I let out a shaky breath and rise slowly, careful not to wake her. Then I bend down and slide one arm beneath her knees, the other around her back, curling her up against my chest. She rests her head against me like she belongs there, because she does, and maybe that's the only thing I know for sure anymore.

Her curls brush my chin as I carry her down the hall, her body warm and weightless in my arms. I press my face into her hair and breathe her in, grounding myself in the scent of her before pushing open her bedroom door with my foot, crossing the room in the dark, and laying her gently onto the mattress. She makes a soft noise, brows twitching, but doesn't wake. I slide in next to her, pulling the blankets up, and curl my body around hers, tucking her into my chest.

My arm loops around her waist, pressing her back into me, and for the first time in days, the storm inside me goes quiet. When I close my eyes, I fall asleep fast, because holding her like this is the only thing that still makes sense.

CHAPTER 34
ANGELIQUE

The house is quiet this morning, too quiet. Reign left for a board meeting at Imperium, claiming he'd only be gone a few hours, and Lando conveniently showed up at the door with only two coffees and a bag of pastries just as Reign was leaving.

It's obvious that they're tag-teaming, not that I don't appreciate it, but it's exhausting having people watch me like I'm fragile. Like they're just waiting for me to shatter. And sure, maybe I am on the verge of breaking apart completely, but I don't need them constantly reminding me about it.

I curl up on the couch, wrapping my blanket around myself like a cocoon, ignoring the fact that I'm wearing the same oversized sweatshirt and shorts I slept in for the last two nights. The news flickers across the screen, but I barely pay attention.

Out back, I hear Lando's voice as he paces near the French doors, his phone to his ear, laughing softly.

"If you want me to come down there and show you how good I can—"

He stops speaking and then laughs again shortly after, low and warm. "You'd better clear your schedule for the entire weekend then, babe."

I blink.

I shouldn't be listening to this.

I pull the blanket tighter and sink into the couch cushions, letting the muffle of the TV drown him out, but when my phone vibrates, I sit up and glance at the coffee table. My screen lights up with a name I haven't seen since the day she sat across from me in her office at Big Apple—Mom.

For a moment, I just sit there and stare at the call, my skin turning icy cold. I should ignore it, and block the number, but my thumb betrays me, sliding across the screen to answer.

I lift the phone to my ear. "...Hello?"

"Well, are you happy now?" Her voice is clipped, the tone of someone who is clearly pissed off with me.

"What?"

"You got what you wanted, didn't you?" she snaps. "Alec's a goddamn cripple now. Can't even stand without help. He'll be lucky to walk in a straight line again, but he'll never be able to dance."

My heart lurches as my throat tightens. "What are you talking about?"

She lets out a bitter laugh. "Oh, don't play dumb, Angelique. You know damn well what your little boyfriend did. He shattered both his kneecaps and left him in a fucking puddle of blood outside a police station," she shouts. "His parents were my biggest donors. You just cost me my job."

The breath leaves my lungs like a sucker punch. "He—

Reign did that for me?" I whisper, barely able to form the words.

"God, you're pathetic." Her voice curdles with disgust. "You act like you're this poor little victim, but all you do is leave ruin in your wake. You always have."

My voice shakes. "What are you even talking about? Alec *raped* me. I did nothing wrong."

"Well, now he's broken, and so is your future if you keep pushing this lawsuit nonsense. Alec told me you're considering it, so let me give you some free advice, darling —don't."

My mouth opens, but no words come out. Reign has been talking to me about pressing charges for the rape, now that I have video evidence of Alec admitting to it, but we both know it will be a long process to go through, and with Alec's parents' money it might not even work out the way we hope.

"Go ahead. Embarrass yourself in court," she continues. "Drag Reign down with you, too. Do you really think his father's just going to stand by? You think Charlie Harrington is going to let his golden son date a trauma case who invites scandal into his company?"

Tears prick the backs of my eyes as I stay quiet, not wanting to give her the satisfaction of knowing her words are getting to me.

"Don't be stupid, Angelique," she finishes. "Alec will go after Reign for what he did to him if you so much as think about going ahead with this legal battle. Back off, or you'll both lose everything."

The line goes dead, and I sit there, frozen. I can't hear anything except the ringing in my ears and the echo of her voice hacking through my chest like a dull blade.

Reign did that for me. He beat Alec so bad he may never

walk again, and now my mother's threatening his future. All because of me. My hand falls into my lap, the phone slipping from my fingers and hitting the carpet with a dull thud.

My choices are simple. Let Alec get away with raping me and protect Reign or go after Alec and bring Reign down with me. Either way, I lose. I stare at the wall for another minute or two as I feel like I'm slowly sinking into something cold and empty until something in me snaps.

I need out of this fucking war I never asked to fight.

I push up from the couch, moving through the room on autopilot. My limbs feel heavy, but I force them forward, quietly looking over my shoulder to the French doors where Lando is still outside, laughing under his breath as he paces the patio with his phone pressed to his ear.

"If you think your choreography's hot now, wait 'til you see what I do with it naked," he murmurs.

He doesn't notice me as I head straight for my bedroom and close the door behind me. I rip off my shirt, fingers trembling, and scan the room for anything sharp, anything at all, but Reign's already cleared every drawer and every shelf.

Except...

My gaze snaps to the candle flickering on my nightstand. I lunge for it and snatch the silver lighter from beside it. It shakes in my grip as I click it a couple times, then hold the small flame up to my bare ribs. The heat makes me flinch, but I keep it there, right against my skin, because I need the burn. I need something that hurts worse than this.

But my hands shake too hard, and I can't hold it steady, the flame lighting out.

"God fucking damnit," I say through clenched teeth as I try again, desperate now.

The bedroom door swings open and the lighter slips from my fingers, clattering to the floor, as my eyes fly up to find Reign standing in the doorway, chest heaving, eyes wide and frantic. There's mud on his boots like he just ran across the whole property. His eyes land on the lighter, then my bare ribs—pink and reddened—and his whole face drains of colour.

"Fuck," he breathes, storming into the room.

He grabs the lighter and slips it into his pocket without a word, then turns to me. His hands tremble as he gently cups my waist, eyes scanning the spot where I tried to burn myself.

"You didn't..." His voice is barely audible.

I shake my head, chest tight. "But I tried."

He exhales like he's been holding his breath for hours, and wraps both arms around me, pulling me into his chest. I sink into him, letting him hold me there, a comforting calm taking over. Heavy footsteps echo down the hallway as Lando appears in the doorway, the phone still in his hand.

"Is she—" He freezes when he sees the scene.

"I called you at least thirty times," Reign growls.

"Shit. I'm sorry. I—I didn't hear anything. I thought she was napping. I was on the phone with Terry and—"

Reign doesn't look up. "Get out."

Lando goes still. "Reign—"

"I said get out!" he roars, voice ragged, breaking on the edges.

Lando flinches but doesn't argue as he backs out of the doorway, eyes wide, and disappears down the hall without another word. I hear the front door shut, leaving just me and Reign together again.

"I can't lose you," he whispers. "Not again. Not like this."

And something about those words—so soft and so gutted—makes me want to crumble. His arms tighten around me, holding me so close that I feel the tremor in his chest, and that's when I realize he's scared. Not just angry, or furious. He's fucking terrified.

His lips graze the tops of my head. "You need to talk to someone," he says, his voice cautious.

My chest tightens. "What do you mean?" I ask.

"A therapist," he murmurs. "Just someone you can talk to. Someone who knows how to help. Someone that's not... me."

That last part feels like a slap, and I feel my throat tighten.

Someone that's not me.

That's what he really means. I'm too much and he's tired because loving me is a burden he never signed up for. I pull away from him like I've been burned—worse than I almost burned myself. His hands falling from my body like dead weight.

I take a step back, heart pounding now for a different reason entirely. "Wow," I breathe. "Okay."

He frowns, like he's confused by the shift. "Angel—"

"No, I get it," I cut in, voice shaky. "You've been doing damage control ever since the gala. You beat Alec to a pulp, you take care of me, you carry me to bed every night, and now you're over it. I'm too broken, right? Too much to hold on to."

His jaw tightens. "That's not what I said—"

"But it's what you meant." My voice breaks. "You want someone else to deal with this version of me because you can't keep cleaning up after me."

"That's not fair."

"No, what's not fair is pretending like you're okay watching me fall apart and then asking me to offload my pain to someone else because you're tired."

"I'm not tired of you," he snaps. "I'm scared of losing you."

I stare at him, trembling, as he exhales hard, dragging a hand through his hair. "You think I don't want to be enough for you? That I haven't fucking tried? I would bleed for you. I *have* bled for you. But watching you destroy yourself, not being able to stop it, not knowing how? That's killing me, Angel."

"Well, Reign," I say, my voice cracking as I whisper. "It's the only thing I'm good at, so maybe you shouldn't watch."

He blinks, hurt flashing in his eyes, but I turn my back on him anyway and walk out of the house.

CHAPTER 35

REIGN

I stand in the middle of her room, her scent still hanging in the air even after she walked out. My chest feels tight, my lungs barely working as her last words ricochet in my head like stray bullets.

'Maybe you shouldn't watch', as if she doesn't know I'd die before I ever looked away.

I drag both hands through my hair before I hear the telltale sound of rain hitting the roof. The front door is wide open when I bolt outside, and through the downpour, I spot her silhouette as she stalks down the path toward the gardens, arms crossed over her chest, shoulders hunched.

"Angelique." My voice is rough, torn open, but she doesn't turn around.

I catch up to her fast, boots slamming through puddles, and grab her upper arm. She tries to pull away, but I tug her gently into my chest and wrap my arms around her like a fucking vice.

"I'm not letting you walk away from me," I shout through the loudness of the rain. "Not again."

"Let me go," she chokes out, her voice soaked in tears. "Please, Reign, just let me—"

"No." I hold her tighter, one hand cradling the back of her head. "You're hurting, and I get it. But if pain is the only thing that makes you feel alive right now... then let me be a part of it. Let me help you do it safely, like before. Don't go through it alone."

She looks up at me—eyes red-rimmed, soaked lashes clinging together, rain dripping down her cheeks like tears —and I crash my mouth against hers. She gasps into the kiss, startled, but then she kisses me back just as desperately, clutching my soaked shirt in both fists.

The rain is pouring between us, our lips sliding and clashing, and there's nothing delicate about it. It's everything we've been holding in and holding back, spilling out all at once. And when I finally pull back, we're both breathless.

I press my forehead to hers and whisper, "You don't have to be okay right now, but I'm not going anywhere."

Her lips part, and her breath catches like she wasn't expecting that I hadn't given up on her yet. Silence stretches between us until finally she gives me a single nod.

My hands are still shaking as I slide my fingers through hers and turn us around, leading her back toward the house where I can take care of her properly.

We barely make it through the front door before I press her against it, hands braced on either side of her head, trying to get a grip on the storm inside me. Her chest rises and falls rapidly, her lips parted, eyes already glazed with that familiar pull—equal parts fear and need.

"You sure you want this?" I ask, voice low, guttural.

She nods, then swallows. "I need to feel something that isn't... this."

I lead her down the hall, letting the tension climb between us with every step. Once we're in my bedroom, I close the door behind us and turn the lock, settling something feral inside me. This is our space. No one gets in, and no one touches her but me.

She stands near the foot of the bed, her wet shirt clinging to her frame, rain dripping from her curls. I take off my coat, toss it aside, and reach into the drawer for my knife. The blade glints under the low lamplight as I flip it open.

She shudders when I kneel between her legs. "Sit," I say.

She obeys, hands gripping the edge of the bed as I take my time running my hands up her thighs, feeling the tremble in her skin. Her eyes never leave mine as I inch her shirt up slowly and kiss her bare stomach, soft and warm, then lift her arm—the one she cuts—and press my lips to the healed scars, causing her to shudder again.

"I missed this," I murmur against her skin. "All of you. Even the broken parts."

I look up at her then, and she's already breathless. Her eyes are dark, lips parted, and her pupils are blown wide with arousal and vulnerability. And fuck... she's never looked more beautiful.

"Do you trust me?" I ask.

She nods without hesitation, and I bring the blade to her inner thigh, just above her knee, and press the cool metal flat against her skin. She gasps in anticipation, excitement flashing across her features.

Slowly, I tilt the blade and make a shallow cut. She gasps, her head tipping back, thighs twitching against my sides. Her hands fist the sheets, her whole body arching toward the sensation. My tongue traces the skin beside the blood. Close enough that she moans from it.

"Again," she whispers, voice strangled.

I drift higher, lifting her shirt to reveal the side of her hip—the faint scar from last time still visible. I press a kiss there and then slice a new line an inch above it. Her breath comes harder now, her thighs clenching around me as her hips jerk forward.

"You're beautiful like this," I whisper. "Bleeding just for me. Giving me your pain."

Tears form in her eyes, but they don't fall. I kiss each thigh, the space between the cuts, the soft flesh that trembles beneath me. And when I rise over her, she lies back on the bed, hair wild against the pillow, lips parted, dazed and wanting. I straddle her gently, blade in hand, and pull her shirt up to expose her ribs.

"This one..." My voice is low, almost a growl. "This one's for the version of you that thinks no one would stay."

She moans as I cut a shallow line under her ribs. She releases a broken sob, and a gasp fused together before she grabs at my shoulders, lips trembling.

"I can't breathe," she whispers.

"You're safe." I drop the blade onto the nightstand. "You're mine."

Her hands find my face, pulling me down, and our foreheads touch.

"I love you," she whispers, barely audible. "I'm in love with you, Reign."

Time stops and everything inside me goes still as I pull back, just enough to see her face. Her eyes are wet, so full of fear, yet so full of trust.

"Say it again."

"I love you."

My mouth crashes into hers and I kiss her like I've been starving. She melts under me, lips desperate, her hands clawing at my back. I kiss her until she's gasping again, and this time it's not from the knife, it's from need. I slide down, pull her shorts off, and roll on a condom before I bury myself between her legs like it's the only place I'll ever belong.

When I take her, it's not gentle. Her back arches as I slam into her, hands gripping her thighs to keep her spread wide and open for me, her heels digging into the small of my back. I'm deep—so fucking deep—and she takes all of it, over and over, like she's starved for it. Like a good girl. Her breath hitches, gasps tearing from her throat as I fuck her into the mattress hard enough to make it creak.

Her body is fire under mine, damp from the rain still, flushed from head to toe, her hair fanned across the pillows like a crown. Her mouth is parted, moaning my name, and I can't take my eyes off her.

Her breasts move with every hard thrust, flushed and perfect, like they were made to fit in my hands, and her nails rake down my back, like she's desperate to anchor herself to something—someone—before she completely falls apart. She lets out a sob when I drive into that perfect spot, the one that makes her legs shake and her fingers claw at the sheets like she's unraveling right beneath me.

"You feel that?" I growl against her throat, thrusting deeper and rougher. "That's mine. You're fucking mine."

Angelique cries out, nodding, barely able to breathe. "Yes—Reign—fuck—yes."

I shift, hook her knees over my shoulders and drive into her harder, pounding her into the mattress until the headboard slams against the wall. She screams loudly as her body spasms beneath me, clenching around my cock, eyes rolling back as her orgasm hits her.

But I don't let up. I fuck her through it, making her take

every second until her moans turn into desperate little whimpers, tears slipping from the corners of her eyes as her thighs twitch uncontrollably. When I finally slow down, it's not because I'm spent. It's because I want to feel her fall apart again, slowly this time.

I pull out and flip her, dragging her onto all fours and ripping off her soaked shirt. Her shaking arms barely hold her up, but she lifts her head and looks back at me with wet lashes and parted lips. And fuck, I nearly come from just that. I push back inside, and her mouth falls open in a silent cry, forehead pressing to the sheets as I roll my hips into her, deep and slow now, punishing in a different way.

"You feel what you do to me?" I murmur, one hand gripping her waist, the other sliding up her spine to wrap around her throat. "You feel how fucking perfect you are like this?"

She whimpers, and her walls flutter again.

I lean forward, lips brushing her ear. "You ruin me, Angel. Every time."

And when the pressure finally snaps and I spill into her with a strangled moan, hips jerking, muscles locking tight, I stay buried. I hold her there, breathing ragged, chest pressed to her back, her hair stuck to our skin.

We collapse together, limbs tangled, hearts racing like war drums. I kiss her temple, slowly, then her cheek, and finally her jaw.

"I love you too, Angel. I always have," I whisper against her flushed skin.

HER BREATH IS STILL HITCHING SOFTLY AS SHE LIES CURLED INTO my side, her body slick with sweat, flushed and trembling. I stroke her curls back from her face, watching her chest rise and fall with every shallow inhale.

She said she loved me. She finally said it.

I press a kiss to her temple and slowly slip out of bed. Her lashes flutter, but she doesn't stir, murmuring my name under her breath.

"I'll be right back," I whisper, and she settles again.

In the bathroom, I remove the condom and toss it in the garbage bin before I run warm water into a basin, gather antiseptic, and fresh cotton pads, carrying it all back into the bedroom. Angelique watches me from the bed now, eyes open but still a little dazed.

"Are they bad?" she asks softly, her voice raspy.

"No," I murmur as I set everything on the nightstand and kneel beside her. "But I'm still going to clean them."

She nods and shifts so I can reach the cut on her inner thigh first. I dip the cotton into the warm water and clean the dried blood from her skin, careful not to touch the cut too directly yet. She hisses when I bring the antiseptic close, but I pause, pressing a kiss to the inside of her knee.

"Breathe through it," I whisper.

She nods again, bracing herself while I work slowly. I speak barely above a whisper the entire time, murmuring things she doesn't need to respond to.

"You did so good tonight."

"You're stronger than you know."

"I'm proud of you."

When I reach the last one—the one below her ribs—I pause and let my hand rest lightly against her side. I kiss the skin beside it, and she exhales shakily.

"I needed that," she whispers.

"I know." I look up at her, meeting her gaze as I press

the gauze gently to the last cut. "I'll give you what you need every time. No matter what it looks like."

Her lip trembles, but she doesn't cry. "I thought you'd get tired of me," she admits.

"I thought you'd leave me," I say back. "Turns out, we were both fucking wrong."

When I've finished cleaning her wounds, I tuck the covers around her and climb in beside her, wrapping my arms around her waist and pulling her close. She rests her head against my chest, right over my heart.

"You love me?" I murmur, just to hear it again.

She nods against my skin. "I love you."

My hand finds hers under the blankets, and we lace our fingers together.

"Then I'll fight like hell to make sure you're here to say it again tomorrow."

CHAPTER 36

ANGELIQUE

The cemetery is quieter than I remember, colder too. I step off the bus and wrap my coat tighter around me as I make my way down the familiar path, my fingers tucked into my sleeves. My boots sink into the wet ground, the sound loud in the hush of early morning as the clouds hang low and grey above, like even the sky's mourning this day.

Five years ago, today, my dad passed away, and this is where I buried him. I told Reign and Lando that I needed to do this alone and that I'd meet them at Imperium later for rehearsal, but as I round the bend that leads to the two old oak trees where my father's buried, I freeze in place.

I catch a flash of white-blond hair, the unmistakable broad shoulders, the way his long black coat flutters slightly in the wind. I step behind the nearest tree, peering out from behind the trunk, heart thudding as I watch Reign. He's standing motionless in front of the headstone, a small bouquet of marigolds in his hand—my father's favourite. The sight punches the breath from my lungs.

"Hi again, Elijah," he murmurs. "It's been a while."

The wind shifts, rustling the branches overhead as I try to keep my breathing steady.

"I don't really know if this is as weird for you as it is for me," he continues. "I don't think I've ever spoken to you about your daughter whenever I've visited you here." He pauses. "But she... she's everything to me."

My breath catches, my hand curling against the tree bark.

"I know you probably already know that. Wherever you are. I just wanted to say..." He clears his throat. "She's hurting. A lot. But I'll take care of her. I'll do whatever it takes to get her through this. I swear."

He's quiet for a long moment, then he glances down at the bouquet in his hand and kneels, laying the flowers down carefully. His fingers brush the edge of the tag before he lets go. Then he stands and steps back, looking at the grave one last time.

"Thank you... for her."

He turns and walks away, his coat whipping behind him in the wind, and I wait until he's fully out of sight before stepping out from behind the tree, my legs trembling beneath me, and my eyes burning.

I make my way forward and stop between the two oaks, staring down at the well-kept headstone.

Elijah Sinclair

Loving Father. Devoted Dancer. Gone too soon.

My eyes catch on the bouquet Reign rested at the base of the stone. My dad always said Marigolds looked like tiny suns and refused to let my mom plant any other flower in the garden. Even after they divorced, that was the only plant he made sure stayed alive in that garden.

I blink slowly, staring down at the careful arrangement. A simple black ribbon is tied around the stems, but my eyes catch on the handwriting scratched into the small white tag attached to the ribbon. I bend down and hold the tag up so I can read it.

For the man who left me the most important piece of himself.

—R.

I swallow around the lump rising in my throat as I sink to my knees in front of the stone, the cold from the ground seeping into my bones. A gust of wind pushes through the trees above, making the branches creak like they're grieving too. I place my hand on the top of the headstone, grounding myself.

"Hi, Daddy," I whisper. "Happy death day. That sounds wrong, doesn't it?" I let out a breath that's half a laugh, half a sob. "I don't know what else to call it."

I run my fingers over the grooves of his name, blinking back tears as the wind lifts my curls from my face.

"I didn't think anyone else would come," I whisper. "But... you've already had a visitor this year."

I sit with him in silence for a while, letting the quiet hold me, then, slowly, the words come.

"Things are... bad. I don't even know how to explain it all. I don't even know who I am anymore. Some days I wake up and feel okay for an hour or two, and then other days, like today, I wonder what the point of all of this even is."

My eyes sting, but I don't wipe the tears away.

"I miss you. I miss you more now than ever. And I hate that you're not here to tell me what to do. I don't know how to make the hurt stop." My voice breaks on the last word. "I don't know how to breathe without feeling like I'm suffocating on everything that was done to me."

I reach down and touch the ribbon Reign left, my hand trembling.

"Reign's been amazing. And Lando too. They're both trying so hard to keep me together, but I can't keep leaning on them like this. I can see how scared they are, how much I'm breaking them just by existing."

Tears fall, warm against the cold air.

"My mother doesn't even believe me," I whisper. "She called me to scream at me. To defend my abuser. To tell me I was ruining everything." I laugh bitterly. "How can the one person who's supposed to love me the most... not love me at all?"

I clutch my coat tighter, like I can hold myself together with just fabric.

"I'm so tired, Dad. I'm trying, I really am. But I feel like I'm losing the will to live. And I know that sounds dramatic and maybe it is—but I can't stop thinking about what happened. I can't stop feeling like I'm broken in ways that can't ever be fixed."

The wind picks up again, and I curl forward, resting my forehead against the cold stone, pretending it's him as I try to stay warm.

"I love Reign," I whisper. "God, I love him so much, and I know he'd fall apart if I ever left him. But sometimes... sometimes it feels like I'm already gone. And I don't know how to come back. He doesn't deserve that."

The silence that follows isn't comforting, it's heavy.

"I wish you were here," I whisper. "Because maybe if you were, I wouldn't feel so goddamn alone."

A sob slips through my throat as I sit up straight now, wiping the tears from my cheeks.

"I guess I just came to say goodbye," I whisper again. "And see you soon."

I lay down my bouquet of peonies next to Reign's arrangement, and kiss the headstone before I stand and walk away without looking back. I don't take the same path I came in on either, because I'm not going home.

CHAPTER 37

REIGN

Angelique is an hour late to rehearsals. She should have been here hours ago. She promised she'd come straight here after the cemetery, and she left to go there early this morning. It's dark outside while I pace the rehearsal corridor at Imperium, ignoring the stage crew trying to get my attention, my pulse pounding harder.

She promised she'd be here. She's the whole reason we're even having this rehearsal today because she said she wanted to run the pas de trois one last time before opening night, and I believed her. I needed to believe her.

"Hey, have you seen Angelique?" I ask one of the corps dancers.

She shakes her head. "No. Not since yesterday."

I spin around, eyes scanning the hallway just in time to see Lando sprinting toward me, his face drained of all colour.

"Reign——" he chokes out, waving his phone in the air. "She sent me something. I think it's a goodbye text."

My stomach drops so violently, I stagger. He shoves the

screen at me, but I don't even read the words because the fact that it ends with *'I'm sorry'* tells me enough.

"Fuck," I whisper. "No, no, no."

I dig into my duffel bag with shaking hands, pulling out my phone and unlocking it. There's a missed call from her and a voicemail. My pulse stutters as I press play and lift the phone to my ear, holding my breath as her voice crackles to life.

"Hey..."

There's a long pause and I can hear her shaky and uneven breathing.

"I don't even know what I'm supposed to say. I—I just needed to say thank you. For everything. For loving me. For staying. For fighting for me when I didn't think I was worth it."

Her voice breaks, and when she speaks again, it's barely more than a whisper.

"You made me feel safe... wanted... even when I couldn't stand myself. But I can't do this anymore, Reign. I'm so tired. I feel like I'm dragging you down with me, and I can't be the reason you hurt anymore."

Another pause as she lets out a soft sob.

"I love you. God, I love you so much it hurts. But I need the pain to stop. I just... I'm sorry. Please don't hate me."

The message cuts off with the sound of her crying and my vision goes red.

"Fuck!" I roar, my voice tearing out of me like a wounded animal, echoing through the rehearsal studio as my phone clatters to the floor.

"Where would she go?" Lando panics beside me. "Where would she—shit, do you think she's at the guesthouse?"

"Call the estate security," I growl, already dragging him toward the back exit.

We burst through the doors into the pouring rain outside, and I don't wait for him to buckle in before I slam the car into reverse and peel out of the Imperium lot, gravel spitting beneath the tires.

Lando's still trying to breathe through the panic. "Come on, come on..." he mutters into the phone. "Yes, hi, this is Lando Harrington. Can you check if Angelique Sinclair is at the guesthouse right now? It's an emergency."

There's a pause on the other line that feels like an eternity before Lando looks at me with wide, terror-stricken eyes.

"She never came back after this morning," he whispers.

I floor it, feeling the panic rising tenfold.

"Where the fuck is she, Reign?" Lando demands, twisting in his seat. "Think. Where would she go? Do you think she's still at her father's grave? The bridge? The station—"

My fingers tighten on the wheel as my chest constricts. I don't know how I didn't think of it sooner.

The bridge.

Marlow Bridge. Her dad's favourite spot. The bridge that overlooks the spots we sat at, re-building our trust and our love. Where the water runs high and fast and cold. My blood turns to ice as I think back to all the times we sat near it, and every single time she'd just stare off at the bridge without a word.

"She's at the bridge," I whisper.

"What?"

I whip the car around the corner so fast we nearly lose traction. "She's at the fucking bridge. Call 999!"

Lando fumbles for his phone, hands shaking. "I'm calling—I'm calling—"

We fly through town like hell's chasing us, every red

light, and every slow pedestrian a fucking obstacle. I don't stop though, not until we hit the narrow lane that runs parallel to the Thames.

"She says they're dispatching someone," Lando says, his voice thin with panic. "But they said ten minutes, maybe more."

"We don't have ten fucking minutes," I snap, my heart about to split open in my chest.

And then I see her silhouette on the ledge, her arms out slightly, and as we get closer, I can see that her eyes are closed, like she's finally at peace.

Lando gasps beside me. "Oh, God—"

But I'm already out the door.

"Angelique!" I scream, bolting toward her. "Don't you dare!"

She jolts, eyes snapping open as her body stiffens. She turns slightly, wind and rain whipping her curls across her face.

"Don't you dare make me live in a world without you," I yell, my voice shattering. "I already barely survive in mine."

Her lips part, trembling. "You'll be better off without me, Reign," she says, voice shaking. "I'm just the supplementary pages of your life story. You'll find someone that's good for you. That isn't so hard to love or understand. Someone who isn't so broken."

I let out a sound halfway between a laugh and a sob as I stumble forward and fall to my knees on the concrete, drenched from the rain, hands shaking.

"You could never be the supplementary pages, Angelique," I breathe. "You're the whole plot."

She stares at me for a long time, rain running down her cheeks like tears, and then smiles softly.

"You know..." she says quietly, turning her gaze back to

the water. "I think that's the first time you've ever said my name."

Lightning flashes somewhere in the distance and she startles, wobbling on the ledge while my lungs seize.

"Angel," I beg. "Come back to me. Please baby, come back to me."

I barely hear Lando's footsteps pounding the pavement behind me over the roaring blood in my ears, but then his voice cuts through the night like a fucking blade.

"If you jump," he shouts, "I swear to God, Angelique, I'll seance you every fucking night and make sure you never have a peaceful afterlife."

The sheer desperation in his tone guts me. She turns sharply toward him, startled, her eyes wide and wet and full of disbelief.

"You weren't supposed to be here," she cries. "Neither of you were supposed to find me here."

Lando's already walking toward her, recklessly, because fear has torn through every ounce of caution, and I'm too torn up to stop him.

"You're stronger than this!" he yells.

"No, I'm not!" Her voice sounds so raw it barely resembles her; it comes out like a wail instead of a shout. "I'm weak in here!" she screams, jabbing both fingers into her temples.

"I can't cope with what I went through. I can't cope with the fact that my mom doesn't care, and that everything else in the world matters more than me in her eyes." She's sobbing harder now, shoulders shaking violently, and I'm so scared she'll fall over the edge without even meaning to.

She gasps out the next words like they're choking her. "I

can't cope with the fact that just existing puts Reign in danger."

My heart… my fucking heart splinters in my chest, because I've known she was hurting. I've seen it and I've held her through it. But this? This depth? This darkness that's convinced her she's not just broken, but dangerous to love? That, I didn't know.

Lando doesn't back down though. His voice cracks, but his eyes stay locked on hers.

"Wanting love from the people who are supposed to give it freely doesn't make you weak!" He lets out a wild, bitter laugh and throws his hands up. "If you're going to trust anyone on that, trust me! My own fucking father doesn't love me, my mom left me, and my brother only started talking to me again because of you!"

I turn to him, guilt punching straight through me.

His gaze cuts to mine. "Don't even try to deny it," he growls.

And fuck, he's right. I don't have the energy to argue because he's absolutely right. I've spent years shutting Lando out, and I let my silence mean something it never should've. I made him feel invisible in the one place he should've always felt safe. My throat works around words I don't know how to say. Sorry doesn't feel like enough. Nothing does.

Lando looks back at her now, everything in him softening except his voice. "You are the only constant in my life, Angelique."

He takes a slow step forward, rain dripping from his lashes, voice trembling now. "Please don't do this." He keeps going until he's reached the ledge, holding his hand out for her to take. "Please," he whispers. "Please don't abandon me too. Not you."

The rain's falling harder now, soaking all three of us but I can't move. I can't speak. My heart is in my throat, suffocating me, while I pray she reaches back. She doesn't move for what feels like hours but then she suddenly looks straight at me.

"Please, Angel..." I whisper. "Baby, please."

I hold my breath as she stares at me like I'm her final tether, and when she finally takes Lando's hand I let out a strangled breath, sitting back on my heels, watching while Lando grips her tight and eases her down.

The second her feet hit the ground, he pulls her into his chest, wrapping his arms around her like he'll never let go again, and she buries her face in his shoulder and sobs. I lower my head, gasping, hands gripping my own thighs, the relief so big it rips me apart. Because we were one second away from losing her.

One second.

The cold wind whips around us as the rain lets up, but all I hear is the echo of her voice saying she's weak... that we'd be better off without her. I stand up, moving slowly, and take one step at a time until I'm right beside them. Lando glances at me over her head and nods, his eyes red-rimmed and soaked with tears. I don't think I've ever seen him cry like this.

"Come here," I whisper.

Angelique lifts her head, her curls tangled and wet, face blotchy, but her eyes find mine like they always do. She hesitates, fingers still clinging to Lando's jacket. Then, finally, she lets go and stumbles into me and I catch her instantly.

My arms wrap around her tighter than I mean to. I'm scared if I let go, she'll vanish, like this is still a nightmare I haven't woken up from. She sinks into my chest, and I kiss her temple, holding her like my life depends on it.

"I'm sorry," she whispers, barely audible.

"Don't," I murmur. "Don't apologize for hurting."

She shakes her head, crying harder now. "I didn't want you to see me like this."

"Then you don't know me at all," I whisper, pulling back enough to look at her. "Because I'd rather see you broken than buried."

Her lips tremble, and her eyes spill over again. I brush her cheeks with both thumbs, wiping the tears away, though they keep coming. That's fine. I'll wipe away every single one for as long as it takes.

"You want to die," I say quietly, "but I need you to live."

She closes her eyes.

"I need you to wake up next to me and fight with me. To rehearse with me and to fucking laugh again. And I know that's a tall fucking order right now, Angel... but I'm not going anywhere."

My voice cracks.

"I'm not leaving you. So please, don't leave me. Don't give up."

She opens her eyes again, the guilt in them pulling at my heart, and I take her hand, kissing her knuckles. "Let's go home."

She nods against me, and I glance at Lando, who's wiping his face like he's trying to get it together.

"You coming?" I ask as the sound of sirens in the distance grows closer.

He lets out a shaky breath and nods. "Yeah."

I lead Angelique back toward the car, one arm tight around her, her head resting against my shoulder. Every step we take away from that ledge feels like a small miracle, but I know this isn't over. Tonight was the warning shot, and I'm not letting the next one be fatal. If I have to stand between her and the dark every fucking day—I will. Even if it kills me.

~

ANGELIQUE SITS CURLED IN THE PASSENGER SEAT BESIDE ME, HER knees pulled up to her chest beneath Lando's oversized hoodie that he passed to her from his duffel bag. She has said little since we left the bridge. Her head leans against the window, eyes unfocused, watching the streetlights flicker past as we wind back toward the estate.

The silence in the car isn't tense, but exhausted. Lando's quiet in the back seat too, just letting her breathe. But when we pull into the long drive and the car finally rolls to a stop in front of the guesthouse, I kill the engine and glance over at her. She's still staring out the window like she's not here. Like she never really came back down from that ledge. I rest my hand on hers and she blinks slowly, turning toward me.

"You don't have to say anything," I murmur, keeping my voice low. "But I want to ask you something. Just one thing."

She nods, barely, and I give her hand a gentle squeeze. "Would you consider talking to someone?"

Her brows crease and I hold my breath, but she doesn't pull away or lash out like last time.

"Not because we're tired of you," I say, my voice rough. "And not because we can't handle you. But because we're not professionals, Angel. We're just two broken idiots trying to patch up our favourite person with duct tape and a bit of panic."

She huffs a breath. It's not a laugh exactly, but it's close.

Lando rests his chin on the back of the seat. "You scared the fuck out of me tonight," he says gently. "And if there's even the smallest chance something might help... even a little... would you try?"

Her eyes jump between us, filled with pride and shame, fear and exhaustion, before she nods slowly.

"Okay," she whispers, her voice hoarse. "I'll try."

Relief barrels through me so fast I almost sag in my seat. Lando makes a choked sound behind me, like he's holding back a sob of his own.

"Thank you," I say gently.

She turns her face away again, but not before I see the shine in her eyes. And this time, I know it's not because she wants to give up. It's because, for the first time in a long time, she might be ready to fight for herself.

The guesthouse is silent when we step inside, except for the wind pressing against the windows. I lock the door behind us, switch off the porch light, and keep her hand in mine as we move through the hallway in the dark while Lando takes himself to the couch.

"Come on," I murmur, leading her into the bathroom. "Let me help."

She nods once, too tired to argue while I turn the shower on and let the steam fill the space. She undresses behind me, and when I turn around, she steps into the spray, eyes closed, arms wrapped around herself.

I strip off my clothes and join her, allowing her to lean into me like she needs my hands to stay upright. I wash her hair gently, my fingers combing through the wet curls as her forehead rests against my shoulder. She breathes in slow, steady pulls while I press a kiss to the crown of her head.

"I've got you," I whisper. And I do. For as long as she needs me. For as long as she'll let me.

When we step out, I dry her off carefully with the softest towel I can find, dressing her in one of my long black shirts and a pair of boxers. She looks impossibly small in them, and I bite back the urge to call her cute. I carry her to my bed and tuck her in as her eyes drift closed from the kind of exhaustion that's more mental than physical.

I sit on the edge of the bed and watch her breathing, count the rise and fall of her chest, memorize the lines of her face in the shadows. Minutes pass. Then hours. I lie beside her eventually, but I don't sleep. I keep my eyes on her, one hand resting lightly against her stomach just to feel the rhythm of her breath.

The fear never leaves, not completely, because I've seen how fast the light can leave her eyes. How quick the shift from "okay" to "gone" can come. So, I stay awake all night, listening to the storm outside while watching the girl I love sleep in the bed that I'd tear the world apart to keep her in, and pray to a God I don't believe in that when the sun rises, she's still here.

Still choosing to stay.

CHAPTER 38
ANGELIQUE

I wake with a headache that feels like someone took a mallet to my skull. My eyes are stinging when I open them, swollen from crying, and for a while I lie there, staring at the ceiling, letting the ache settle behind my eyes.

Yesterday replays in fragments in my head. I'd woken up on my dad's death anniversary with an overwhelming feeling of giving up. I just couldn't imagine a world where life got better for me and I desperately just wanted all the pain to end. I might not have woken up at all today if Reign and Lando hadn't come for me.

A quiet voice breaks through my morning fog. "Good morning."

I turn my head slowly and find Reign sitting on a chair in the corner of the room. His eyes are bloodshot, and his hair a mess. He looks like he's been dragged through hell and back.

"Good morning," I whisper, sitting up slowly. Shame rolls through me while I tuck the surrounding blankets tighter, suddenly aware of how small and pathetic I probably look. "Did you sleep?"

He doesn't answer, instead giving me a tired, lopsided smile. The kind that makes my chest ache. I lower my gaze and fidget with the edge of the blanket, tugging a thread loose between my fingers.

"How are you feeling?" he asks, leaning forward to rest his elbows on his knees as he watches me.

I shrug one shoulder, keeping my eyes down. "Ridiculous? Stupid? Embarrassed? You name it, I'm probably feeling it."

The bed shifts as he takes a seat beside me, his hand reaching for mine. His thumb slowly brushes over my knuckles, grounding me.

"There's nothing to feel embarrassed or stupid about," he says gently. "You just need some help right now, and it's understandable. You've been through more than most." He pauses. "Are you still open to speaking with someone?"

My throat tightens and I don't answer right away, letting my gaze drift across the room. There's a part of me that still wants to run and hide. To pretend that if I just sleep long enough, I'll wake up in a version of my life that doesn't hurt.

But I remember the fear in Reign's voice last night, and the way Lando's hand shook when he reached for me. I can't put them through something like that again. And maybe... maybe this is what trying looks like. It's not pretty or poetic, but it's still a beginning.

I finally nod and Reign lets out a quiet breath that he was holding in this whole time, nodding back, a small smile tugging at the corner of his mouth in relief.

"Okay then," he says. "Let's get ready. Your first appointment is in an hour."

〜

THE CAR RIDE IS QUIET, AND I SIT WITH MY HANDS IN MY LAP, fingers twisted together, trying to breathe like I'm not unraveling from the inside out. I can feel Reign glancing over to me every so often from the driver's seat in that protective way he always does—without pressure, but with every ounce of presence.

He hasn't let me out of his sight, not since yesterday, and even now I can feel the tether between us stretching across the console, anchoring me.

"Still doing okay?" he asks.

I nod. "Yeah."

It's a lie, because I don't feel okay. I feel like I'm walking into something I won't be able to walk back out of. Like once I sit down and say it all out loud, I won't be able to shove it back into the locked box I've kept it in. They'll label me insane, send me off to some sterile white psych ward for the rest of my life, and feed me pills that will only make me worse.

I pick at a hangnail. "What if I go in there and don't talk?"

Reign glances over briefly, then back at the road. "Then you don't talk. You sit, and you breathe. That's enough for the first time."

I let out a small, dry laugh. "You sound like you've done this before."

I mean it as a throwaway comment, but when I look over at him, he isn't smiling. He doesn't say anything right away either, and the silence makes my chest tighten.

"Wait," I murmur. "Have you?"

He nods once. "Yeah. After my mom left, my dad put Lando and me in therapy. We were both so angry and I think he didn't know what else to do."

A lump rises in my throat. "Did it help?"

Reign's jaw shifts slightly as he considers. "It helped Lando," he says after a beat. "It helped me, too... just not right away. I didn't want help back then. I didn't want to be fixed. I just wanted my mom back."

I press my fingers together tightly in my lap. I know what that kind of longing feels like. The kind that coils around your ribs and squeezes until you can't breathe. Wanting a parent who's gone—whether they chose to leave or just couldn't stay—it leaves a scar.

A silence falls between us until I whisper, "What if they ask me what happened?"

"They'll wait until you're ready to answer." He pauses. "You get to set the pace, Angel."

The way he says that makes me feel like for once, I'm not at the mercy of what's been done to me. I stare out the window noticing how peaceful Marlow looks this morning.

"By the way..." He clears his throat. "I asked my dad to push opening night by two weeks."

My head snaps toward him, eyes wide. "What?"

"There were other reasons," he says quickly. "The crew needed time to rework lighting, and a few costumes weren't ready. But I also told him you needed space, after everything that happened."

The air shifts in my lungs, expanding and tightening at once. I was planning to step down from my role as Swan Queen and let Wendy have it. I don't want to let Imperium and Reign's family down, but I know that if I went out there and performed right now, I'd ruin the whole thing.

"Was he mad?" I ask.

He shrugs, eyes still on the road. "No. But even if he was, it wasn't up for discussion."

I look down at my lap again, twisting my fingers. "Thank you," I whisper.

"You don't have to thank me. I'd push the whole goddamn world back if it gave you time to breathe."

WE PULL INTO THE TINY PRIVATE PARKING LOT OF THE WELLNESS clinic. The building is old stone and glass, with a slate sign at the front that says Briar Hill Therapy Centre. My stomach lurches as I stare up at it, and my heart picks up speed.

Reign parks the car and turns to look at me, one arm resting on the wheel. "You don't have to go in alone."

"I know," I whisper.

But the truth is, this is the one thing that I do need to do alone. The one thing that I need to face to get better. I reach for the door handle but pause when I feel his hand slip into mine.

"I just want you to know that you're brave for coming," he says. "Even if you don't feel it yet."

His words settle in my chest, warm and heavy. "Will you wait for me?" I ask, my voice small.

He gives my hand a gentle squeeze. "Always."

SOFT UPBEAT MUSIC PLAYS IN THE WAITING ROOM AS A WOMAN behind the desk gives me a kind smile when I check in, but I don't really register what she says as I hyper focus on the muted colours of the walls that feel like they're closing in on me.

I take a seat by the window and watch Reign through the glass. He's leaning against the hood of his car, smoking a cigarette, eyes on the entrance like a sentry. Moments later, the therapist, a tall woman with wavy dark hair and warm brown eyes, comes to the door and calls my name, giving me a warm smile. I return the smile and stand up, my legs feeling like they belong to someone else, and follow her into the office as she closes the door behind me.

Her office is nothing like I expected. Soft sunlight pours in through sheer curtains onto pale walls painted in warm ivory, and a plush cream rug that stretches across the floor. The scent of eucalyptus floats out of a diffuser, and a few leafy plants line the windowsill.

The couch is soft, upholstered in a buttery beige fabric that instantly hugs my body when I sit down. There are no cold desks or ticking clocks. Her office feels almost...inviting. Nothing like the sterile white walls and furniture I'd envisioned.

The therapist sits across from me in a matching armchair. She's elegant, her wavy brown hair pulled back in a loose knot, and her warm, kind eyes meet mine without judgment. I'm surprised to see that she doesn't have a notepad or clipboard. She's just sitting there looking like she's ready to jump into casual conversation with me.

"I'm Talia," she says gently. "It's really nice to meet you, Angelique."

I give her a small nod, fingers curling into the hem of my sleeves as I sink further into the couch.

She tilts her head slightly, her voice low and steady. "I hear you've been having a tough time?"

My breath catches in my throat and the tears well instantly. It's like that single sentence unlocked something deep in me I've been trying to keep buried, and before I can stop myself, I'm crying.

I tell her about everything. The rape, New York, my mother, the cutting, the lighter, the bridge. Every fragmented, shameful piece I've been carrying, and she listens intently the whole time, like she's holding every word in her hands because she knows how heavy they are.

And at some point, I realize she's crying too. Her fingers brush under one eye and she offers a small, tearful smile. And weirdly... that helps. It helps to not be the only one falling apart for once. We sit in silence for a long while when I finish, the tissues in my lap damp and crumpled. My head aches from crying, but for the first time in days—maybe weeks—my chest doesn't feel so full it might crack open.

Talia leans forward, resting her hands on her knees. "You're carrying so much," she says, voice still warm but tinged with sorrow. "And I want to help you carry it. One piece at a time."

I nod slowly, the lump in my throat too thick for words. She smiles again, and something about it feels like an anchor. She rises, walks to her desk, and returns with a slim leather notebook and an elastic band holding them out to me.

"When the urge comes," she says, gesturing to my wrist, "try using the elastic band first."

I take it from her, slide it over my wrist, then glance up at her face before pulling the band back. It snaps sharply against my skin and the sting is brief—nowhere near the pain I've inflicted on myself before—but it's sudden enough that it might snap me out of a spiral.

"And then I'd like you to write," she continues, tapping the notebook. "Anything you're feeling or can't say out loud."

"Why?" I ask.

"Because it helps us track what's triggering you. Once we know, we can work on creating boundaries around those moments. We're aiming for protection, not punishment."

I stare down at the notebook, fingertips brushing over its worn leather cover.

"But Angelique," she adds gently, "if things ever feel too much, I want you to call me. I'm always available for emergency sessions. Anytime. Day or night."

I look up at her, and my mouth trembles into a shaky smile. She means it—I can feel that she does. She reaches over, wraps her fingers around mine in a quiet squeeze, then glances at the clock.

I follow her gaze, surprised to see the hour has already passed. "Reign booked you in everyday for the next two weeks. After that, we'll see what pace feels right to you."

My eyes widen a little, but I shouldn't be surprised because of course that's something he'd do.

I clear my throat, my voice still shaky. "Are you... going to put me on meds?"

Talia doesn't hesitate as she leans back in her chair and shakes her head gently. "No. Not unless you decide you want to explore that route later on. But right now? I think you can do this without medication."

I blink. "Really?"

"You're not broken, Angelique. You've experienced trauma. Deep, life-altering trauma. But everything you've shared with me, I believe you're strong enough to do the work without medication... if that's what you want."

I sit with that for a moment, letting the weight of her words settle over me. It's strange how quickly her confidence in me wedges itself into the cracks I didn't even realize were still gaping open. I nod slowly again, eyes burning, but this time for a different reason. Relief, maybe.

"Tomorrow, if you're up for it, I'd like us to talk about your mother. Not just what she's done, but how it's shaped the way you see yourself, the way you love, and the way you hurt."

Just the mention of my mom makes my throat tighten, but I nod again, firmer this time. "Okay."

Talia gives me one last soft smile, then rises from her chair and walks over to the door, holding it open for me. I gather my things slowly, the weight of everything still in my bones, but feeling just a little lighter than when I walked in.

When I step outside, Reign is still leaning against the hood of his car. He straightens immediately when he sees me, tossing his keys from one hand to the other.

"How'd it go?" he asks, nervously.

I don't answer right away while I walk up to him and wrap my arms around his waist, pressing my face into his chest and breathing in his calming scent.

"You okay?" he mumbles into my hair.

"Yeah," I murmur. "I think I will be."

CHAPTER 39

ANGELIQUE

It's strange how much can change in just seven days. A week ago, I stood on Marlow Bridge with the tips of my toes hanging over the ledge and my heart barely beating. I'd already said my goodbyes and decided there was nothing left for me here.

But now I'm slowly healing, clinging to life, learning how to breathe all over again. It's not perfect, because I still have my moments where I cry randomly, and I still wake up from nightmares soaked in sweat, but I don't feel like I'm drowning anymore. I feel like I've surfaced, even if it's just enough to catch my breath.

That's what daily sessions of therapy for the past seven days has done. Every one of them hard and terrifying but also giving me a little more clarity. And today, for the first time in a long time, I feel something I haven't felt in ages— hope.

I stare at the email glowing on my laptop screen, my fingers hovering over the trackpad. The name of the lawyer Charlie found for me sits in bold at the top. She's one of the best in New York, known for her ruthless cross-examinations and her refusal to let abusers get away with just a slap on the wrist.

"She's confident we can win," I whisper out loud, more to myself than anyone else.

Reign is beside me, close enough that I can feel the warmth of his thigh against mine while he scans the same email. He hasn't gone far from me this entire week, and sometimes I catch him watching me like I might vanish if he blinks too long. If this had been a few days ago, maybe I would've, but right now I'm too angry. I want justice.

"Charlie really came through," I murmur, scrolling down to the draft of the legal complaint already being put together.

The attorney isn't just building a case against Alec. She's pursuing legal action against my mother and the company as well, citing gross negligence, failure to provide a safe working environment, wrongful termination in retaliation for reporting misconduct, and willful retention of an employee with a documented history of predatory behaviour.

"He always does," Reign says quietly.

I nod, then lean back into the cushions, exhaling slowly.

"Do you still feel good about going forward with this?" he asks gently.

I glance at him. "Yeah. It's time."

His hand finds mine, lacing our fingers together. "Then we go all the way."

He's already pulled together everything he could find on Alec, and Charlie helped me draft the full affidavit. Reign was even able to get his father to hire a private investigator to dig into Alec's past, his finances, travel, every relationship he's ever had. It's not just about me anymore. This entire case is for every girl Alec's hurt and left in the dark.

Reign's thumb brushes against mine. "The PI found one girl who filed a sexual misconduct complaint against him at a summer intensive five years ago. It got buried, but she's willing to talk."

I sit up straighter. "Seriously?"

He nods. "She says watching what you're doing gives her courage."

My throat tightens. "Do you think there'll be more?"

He hesitates, then shifts a little closer. "The PI thinks he might've found a second victim. A girl from The Big Apple Company three years ago. She suddenly quit mid-season, no warning, never said why, but he tracked her down and she's agreed to talk."

Three years ago? I was still at the company three years ago. It's the same year I became a principal dancer, which must mean the girl he's talking about is Simone, Alec's partner before me.

My stomach twists. "Is she okay?"

"She's guarded," he admits. "She said she's not sure if she'll go public, but she doesn't want to stay silent anymore. She asked for your affidavit because she wants to read your words before she decides.

"Send it to her," I whisper. "She deserves to know she's not alone."

Reign nods. "I already did."

I stare at the laptop screen as it turns black in front of us and imagine the ripple effect this will have. One truth bringing about another. All it takes is one voice to break the silence and I've spent too long being afraid of what speaking up would do to me and to those I care about, but now, I realize I should've been afraid of what staying silent was doing all along.

It wasn't just eating me alive; it was letting him keep

everything he took, but not anymore. I push off the couch and stand, stretching my arms over my head as I take a long, shaky breath. Reign watches me, waiting.

"I want to meet her," I say. "If she comes forward, I want to be there. I want her to see my face. I want her to know what I didn't know back then."

"That you survive," he says.

I nod, eyes stinging again. "Yeah. That you survive, and that surviving doesn't mean staying quiet."

He stands too, pulling me into him. His chin rests on the top of my head, and I close my eyes against his chest, letting myself soak in the safety of him for a moment longer. I know what's ahead won't be easy. Lawsuits, headlines, cross-examinations, being dragged through the mud by Alec's legal team—everything my mother warned me about. But for the first time, I don't feel like running. I feel like standing my ground.

"I'm proud of you," he whispers. "So, fucking proud."

I squeeze my eyes shut and press my face deeper into his shirt, letting that settle in my bones. His pride and my own.

We stay like that for a while, arms wrapped around each other in the quiet of the living room, the weight of everything finally beginning to shift. Not gone—but redistributed. Lighter.

And then, when I pull back and meet his gaze, there's a fire in my voice I haven't heard in myself in far too long.

"Let's take him down."

Reign's lips curve into a half smirk. "Oh, we will."

CHAPTER 40

REIGN

My father's office at Imperium hasn't changed in years. It still smells like old varnish and espresso, and it still has that same mahogany furniture, and heavy curtains that are pulled halfway shut.

I sit in the leather chair across from his massive desk, hands clasped on my lap. Lando's beside me, perched on the armrest. He's wearing a cropped sweater—bright cherry red, clashing with the heavy mahogany furniture—but it suits him.

Our father is standing behind his desk, reading over a thick packet of renovation notes. His silver pen scratches occasionally on the paper, but his eyes don't lift to meet mine. I take this time to really look at him and notice how much I look like him. We have the same bone structure and white-blond hair, though his is shot through with silver now. His eyes are darker than mine—steel instead of ice. I clear my throat, and he finally glances up.

"We need to talk."

His brow lifts. "If this is about Wendy's last-minute costume changes, I already approved it."

"It's not about that."

Lando shifts beside me, sensing the tension pulling at my shoulders.

My father narrows his eyes. "Then what is it?"

I inhale slowly. "I've decided."

His face tightens just a fraction. "Go on."

I meet his gaze. "Opening night will be my last performance."

Lando's head snaps toward me. "Wait, what?"

I keep my eyes on our father. "I'm stepping back from dancing. For good."

Silence drops into the room like a guillotine.

My father straightens behind the desk. "This is a joke."

"It's not."

"You're not even twenty-six. Do you know how many dancers would kill to have your body, your training, your stage presence—"

"And I've given this company everything," I interrupt. "My time, my body, hell even my sanity. But I'm not in love with the stage anymore, and I won't keep performing just to preserve your legacy."

Lando blinks, stunned into silence. My father looks like he's about to explode.

"You want to just... what? Walk away?"

"No." I lean forward, resting my elbows on my knees. "I still want to run Imperium, but not as a principal dancer."

He glares. "Then what the hell do you want to do?"

"Compose. I want to build something more with Imperium, create from the other side of the curtain. My heart's not in the spotlight anymore."

He scoffs. "You think I built this company on heart?"

I give a bitter laugh. "No. You built it on control."

His jaw clenches. "So, you're done dancing, fine. But running this company is a different beast entirely."

"I know, that's why I'm not doing it alone." Lando's head turns to me slowly. "I want to run Imperium with Lando."

He stills like I've knocked the air from his lungs, and our father's expression shifts from cold to contemptuous in a blink.

"That's not an option."

"Why not?"

He tosses the renovation packet onto the desk. "You already know why."

"Say it."

"You want me to say it?" His lip curls. "Because he's gay. Because he doesn't understand the depth of the work or the discipline that goes into it. He doesn't have the instincts."

Lando whistles. "You got all that just from who I fuck?"

My father's eyes cut to him. "Watch your tone."

I stand abruptly, the chair legs scraping back.

"That's bullshit and you know it. Lando's been here every damn day. Working hard and training even harder. He's never once let Imperium down."

"He doesn't have the image," my father snaps. "You do."

"And you only ever cared about that, but image isn't enough anymore. The future of this company depends on people who understand artistry and empathy."

Lando stands now too, his face pale, hands clenched at his sides.

"I'm not asking for your blessing," I say. "I'm telling you the plan. Lando will take over the lead next to Angelique after opening night. And when it's time, he'll become co-owner next to me, as my equal. I'll continue building Imperium with him, but if you can't get behind that—if you won't even try to see his worth—then I don't want any part of Imperium."

My father's eyes narrow. "You would throw this all away. Just like your mother."

I flinch at the mention of her, but I push through. "I'm not walking away from this family," I hiss. "But I'm not living a life I don't enjoy anymore, either."

And then I turn and walk out. The hallway is cold as my boots hit the marble.

"Reign!" Lando's voice breaks through behind me and I stop.

He catches up, standing in front of me like he's not sure if he wants to cry or scream.

"You didn't have to do that."

I exhale, slow. "Yeah, I did."

He swallows. "I've never heard anyone stand up to him like that. Not for me."

"I should've done it a long time ago."

"Why didn't you?"

I run a hand through my hair. "Because every time I looked at you, I saw Mom."

His face falls.

"You look like her," I admit. "You have her eyes, her hair, her laugh. It hurt being around you after she left, because you reminded me of the version of the family we used to have, and then Angelique left too, and hearing you talk about her and her accomplishments in New York, I just couldn't do it."

Lando blinks fast, trying to hold the tears in. "Reign..."

"I was angry," I say. "At her, and at you. Honestly, I was angry at everything, but none of that was your fault, and I'm sorry. I'm sorry for the distance I kept and for making you feel like I'd abandoned you, too."

He nods slowly, his eyes glassy. "You really think I'm ready to help run Imperium?"

"I think you're the heart of this place," I say. "The one person who never gave up on it, or on me."

He lets out a shaky breath. Then he lunges forward and wraps his arms around me.

"Let's rebuild it," He murmurs. "The right way. Together."

For the first time since we were boys, it feels like we're on the same side again.

I hear the faintest sound of a throat clearing behind us and when I turn around, I find my father standing there. He's no longer the looming figure behind his desk. Just a man in a dark wool coat, his hands buried in the pockets of his slacks, his silver hair slightly tousled like he's run his fingers through it one too many times.

"Reign," he says, voice lower than usual, almost... tentative. "May I have a word?"

Lando's shoulders tense, but he gives mine a quick squeeze before stepping away. I nod silently and wait as my father walks toward me. He stops in front of me but says nothing at first—studying my face instead. Then he looks past me, down the hallway, like he's gathering his words from somewhere far off.

"I overheard what you just said to Lando," he says finally. "And I think I was too hard on you."

I blink, surprised into silence, because of all the things I expected, that wasn't one of them.

"I thought... after your mother left, if I gave you a goal—something tangible, something with discipline and focus—you wouldn't fall apart the way I did."

He exhales through his nose, not quite a laugh. "You were always so damn still when you were little. Observant and easy to overlook, but hard to forget, and I didn't know what else to do with all that quiet hurt in you. Lando had therapy, and he flourished in it. But you..." His eyes slide to mine. "You didn't want help. You just wanted answers I couldn't give you. So, I gave you Imperium instead."

I'm stunned into silence. I don't know what to do with this man—this version of my father. One who admits regret, and who sees me. He nods toward the corridor behind us and starts walking and I fall into step beside him, hands in my coat pockets.

"Tell me about your compositions," he says.

I glance over at him. "What?"

"I heard the piece you composed for the gala," he says. "During the pas de deux you and Angelique danced to. I was shocked," he continues. "It was... beautiful...layered, and sophisticated. Alive, even."

I slow a little. "You actually liked it?"

"I didn't just like it. I was... proud." He stops walking, and I do too. He looks at me. "I know I haven't said that much over the years, but I am. And not just for the dancing. For the way you see things and the way you're able to translate emotion into sound. That's rare, Reign."

My chest tightens, but I nod once, too caught off guard to say anything more.

He looks down, clears his throat again, like emotion sits awkward in his throat. "If composing is where your heart is now, then it's where you should be."

It's not everything. It doesn't erase the years of pressure, of silence, of trying to shape myself into something worthy. But it's a beginning.

"Thanks," I say, my voice quiet but real.

He gives me a small nod. "I still think you're insane for stepping away from the stage." A flash of his old fire glints in his eyes. "But then again, maybe you're just braver than I was."

I chuckle. "Yeah, maybe."

He bumps his shoulder against mine. "I think it's time I apologize to Lando now."

He starts walking again, towards the direction that Lando ran off to, leaving me standing there in the middle of Imperium's halls feeling, for the first time, like my choices don't have to be acts of rebellion.

They can just be mine.

CHAPTER 41
ANGELIQUE

The dressing room light buzzes with electricity, my nerves twisting my stomach into knots. It's opening night and somehow, I made it. I sit at my mirror, dabbing a soft peach blush onto my cheeks, watching the colour bloom across my skin. I've already done my base and liner, but my lips feel dry, so I reach for my balm and press it on with trembling fingers.

Everyone around me is in a state of chaos—laughing too loud, adjusting leotards, fixing buns, spraying hair—but I stay quiet, cocooned in my little corner, trying to block out the noise and steady my breathing.

My leotard's mostly on, the sheer mesh overlay unzipped in the back and bunched around my hips. I'm still barefoot, my pointe shoes beside me—ribbons freshly sewn, toe boxes softened just enough. My thighs are covered in faint marks, but I don't feel the need to hide them tonight. I've stopped apologizing for what helped me survive.

Tonight needs to mean something.

I'm brushing on mascara when I catch the reflection of

a tall frame, dark hair pulled into a high bun, brows slightly furrowed behind me, and I freeze.

Wendy hovers awkwardly, like she's not sure whether to stay or run. Our eyes meet in the mirror, and for a second neither of us says anything. She opens her mouth, then closes it, then crosses her arms like she's trying to hold herself together.

"I just—" Her voice cracks a little. "I have something I want to say."

I turn slightly; mascara wand paused midair. "Okay."

She looks at me, then down at the floor, then back up, gathering the nerve. "I've been awful to you, and I know that. I was... jealous, and pissed off, and I felt like I had something to prove. So, I created this story in my head where you were the problem."

The word hangs there between us, heavier than I expected.

"I shouldn't have said all the horrible things I did," she adds, quieter this time. "None of it was true, and I'm sorry."

I set the mascara down gently on the vanity and stand up, offering her a small smile as I extend my hand to her. She hesitates, then reaches out, but pauses when her eyes catch on my forearm where my mesh sleeve has slipped up slightly. Her eyes land on the scars, some faded while others are still pink and healing. She flinches, just a little, like it finally clicks for her that I'm not just drama or trauma. I'm a person who's been trying to survive.

I keep my voice gentle as her gaze lifts to mine again. "I appreciate the apology. And... I wanted to thank you for what you did at the gala."

"I didn't do it for you," she says quickly, her voice defensive even now.

I laugh softly. "I know."

Her cheeks flush a deep pink, and she immediately glances away like she hates that she's blushing. "I should, um... go finish my makeup."

I nod. "Okay."

She spins on her heel and all but scurries off, mumbling something under her breath. I watch her disappear into the row of mirrors and I half-smile, shaking my head as I sit back down and glance at my reflection again. For the first time in a while, I don't hate the girl looking back at me.

BACKSTAGE IS HUMMING WITH A TENSION THAT COILS IN MY GUT and makes my lungs feel too tight. The lights are low behind the curtains, and the stage crew moves in the shadows, quiet and focused. I stand just out of view of the stage, my hand locked tightly with Lando's, both our eyes shut as we take one last second to ground ourselves.

"Say it," he whispers.

I nod, swallowing around the knot in my throat.

"We are ready."

"We are powerful."

"We are art."

"And we're going to fucking destroy this stage," he finishes fiercely.

We exhale together, squeezing each other's hands once more. It's a ritual we used to do back in school before every big performance. Back when we had dreams bigger than our fears. I take a deep, steadying breath, but pause when I feel a presence beside us.

"Seriously?" Lando mutters, and I open my eyes to find Reign standing next to us, dressed in his costume.

His platinum hair is slicked back, and that signature

smirk—the one that makes my stomach dip—is already tugging at his lips. My breath catches embarrassingly loud in my throat and his smirk grows because he knows exactly what he's doing.

Lando doesn't even pretend to be mad. He just rolls his eyes with a smirk of his own. "All it took was two seconds, and you're already melting."

"I'm not melting," I mutter under my breath, though my skin's already flushing.

"Right," he deadpans.

His gaze shifts and lights up when he sees Terry across the stage, waving at him. "Got to go," Lando says, giving my hand a final squeeze. "Be amazing out there."

"I'll try."

And then he's gone, striding off toward Terry, leaving me alone with Reign and my suddenly stuttering pulse. Reign steps forward slowly, like he has all the time in the world. His eyes sweep down my body, his expression darkening just slightly when they land on my costume, on the bruises blooming from rehearsal, the ones he kissed just last night.

He lifts a hand to my face, brushing his knuckles down my cheek, and then—without warning—his lips are on mine. He kisses me like there's no one else around, like this moment matters just as much as the one we're about to perform. His mouth moves against mine with the kind of focus that makes my knees feel like liquid, and when he finally pulls back, I'm breathless, my skin buzzing like it's been charged.

"Ready for a performance of a lifetime?" he murmurs, still cupping my cheek.

I nod, voice barely above a whisper. "With you by my side, I'm ready for anything."

The stage manager signals us with a soft clap and a thumbs-up, and just like that, we step into the wings together.

~

THE THEATRE IS SILENT AND PITCH BLACK, EXCEPT FOR THE FAINT outlines of the set. My feet rest in fifth position, my arms held high, spine lifted like a string is pulling me from the stars. I keep my breathing measured as I stare into the blackness, eyes adjusting slowly. I can hear my heartbeat in my ears and the tremble in my limbs.

I glance across the stage, knowing Reign is there, and he lifts his head just enough to meet my eyes and wink, making my stomach flutter even now—on one of the most important nights of my life. I huff out a breath, barely a smile, and then I watch him look away, bowing his head just as the first chord of his composition begins.

The lights blink on, and we start. Terry's choreography pulses in my muscles, and each step, each turn, feels like a confession. I dance to the story of grief, of betrayal, of pain buried so deep I nearly drowned in it, like Odette. But I also tell the story of love, of being held, of being seen, and of healing.

Reign's hand touches my waist, and I don't flinch. He lifts me and I rise, feeling more alive than I've felt in years because in his arms, I'm not broken. I'm free. For a few perfect seconds, I'm flying, like I used to when I was little, leaping through the living room in my socks while my dad clapped along to Tchaikovsky, telling me I'd be a principal dancer someday.

When he sets me down, I spin into him, letting my head fall against his chest for a beat before we separate again, dancing like our souls are tied together. And maybe they always have been.

The music builds, and I close my eyes as my body bends and glides and soars. I think of my father, watching from wherever he is, and I think of the little girl he used to twirl around the garden, the one who believed she could fly just because he told her she could.

And I think of Reign, and Lando. Of the boy who kissed my scars like they were sacred and the best friend who never let go of my hand, even when I was ready to let go of everything else. The final crescendo builds like thunder and I push through the last movement with everything I have. Reign lifts me once more and I soar—arms out, eyes to the heavens—before he lowers me gently to the ground as the last note fades.

Applause erupts, loud and fierce. It crashes over me like a wave, and I blink hard against the tears rising in my eyes. Reign's hand slides into mine and squeezes. I turn to him, and he's already looking at me like I'm the most breath-taking thing he's ever seen.

"You did it," he whispers.

My chest heaves, tears trailing down my cheeks. I look at him—the man who helped stitch every broken piece back together. The one who never walked away and who taught me how to fly.

"No," I say. "We did."

EPILOGUE
ANGELIQUE

The city is quiet today. Maybe it's just the early hour or the weight in my chest muting everything. I stand in front of the mirror inside our New York hotel room, smoothing down the front of my slate-grey pantsuit. The fabric's soft and expensive, but inside I feel like the seams of me are barely holding.

Two years. That's how long it's been since I saw my mother. Since I saw Alec. Since I stood on a bridge and thought there was nothing left for me. And now, here I am, on the other side of survival.

"You look gorgeous."

I blink, meeting Reign's gaze in the mirror. He's buttoning his jacket, a deep navy tailored within an inch of his life. His platinum hair is neatly styled, his Patek watch catching the light as he adjusts it. He's calm and composed, as usual. He walks up behind me and wraps his arms around my waist, planting a kiss on the back of my head.

"You always do," he murmurs.

I offer him a weak smile, but the moment I do, my lip trembles. Reign turns me to face him without hesitation, arms caging me in with a kind of devotion I never get used to. I let my forehead fall against his chest, and he holds me tight.

"We should go get matching tattoos after this," he says suddenly, voice teasing. "To celebrate."

I laugh through the nerves, the sound watery. "You make it sound like winning's a sure thing."

He pulls back just enough to meet my eyes, his gaze unwavering. "You're winning, Angel. Because if you don't..." His jaw flexes. "I'll burn this city to the ground."

I snort, wiping under my eyes. "You're ridiculous."

He grins. "And you love me."

"I do," I whisper.

THE COURTROOM IS COLD. WHITE WALLS, POLISHED WOOD, murmured tension stretching through every bench and corner. Alec sits in a wheelchair next to his lawyer, chin high but skin pale, and my mother is beside him, not a hair out of place. She doesn't look at me, not once, but I don't care.

My attorney, Cassandra Vale, stands in front of the court. Her tone is composed as her closing statement echoes through the silence.

"Your Honour, this case is not just about misconduct— it is about willful silence. Her partner and senior, Alec Fontaine, subjected Angelique Sinclair, a professional dancer, to manipulation and sexual coercion."

She pauses and stares at Alec with disgust before turning her attention to my mother.

"When she came forward, not only was she ignored— she was fired. Marginalized. Treated as a liability. The Big

Apple Ballet Company had knowledge of Alec Fontaine's prior complaints and still kept him on payroll. Analise Sinclair, my client's own mother and a Director at the company, actively discouraged her from pursuing legal action and instead protected the perpetrator."

Cassandra returns to facing the judge as she continues.

"We are not asking for sympathy. We are demanding accountability. For negligence. For wrongful termination. For aiding and abetting abuse in a professional environment. For the irreparable harm inflicted on a young woman's life. The time for silence is over."

She sits beside me without a word, placing her hand over mine and giving me a small squeeze. The judge flips through his documents, lips pressed in a firm line as he carefully examines some reports.

While we wait, I feel a gentle tug on my ponytail. I turn around and find Reign watching me with a tiny smirk and it grounds me.

"All rise."

I turn back around and stand, my heart pounding so fast I think I might pass out any second.

"In the matter of Angelique Sinclair versus Alec Fontaine, Analise Sinclair, and The Big Apple Ballet Company..."

I hold my breath as I stare at the judge.

"...this court finds Alec Fontaine guilty of rape in the first degree. He is hereby sentenced to twenty-five years in prison and will be registered as a sex offender. Mr. Fontaine is ordered to pay a criminal fine of five thousand dollars to the state, as well as any restitution Ms. Angelique Sinclair may require, including costs related to therapy."

I close my eyes for a second, my knees nearly buckling.

"Upon the completion of his sentence, he will be

permanently barred from working in the dance industry in any capacity."

I did it, I think to myself.

"... Analise Sinclair is found guilty of obstruction of justice in the first degree, a Class D felony, and is hereby sentenced to seven years in state prison."

For the first time since I can remember, my mother's mask cracks—just for a second.

"...The Big Apple Ballet Company is found liable for wrongful termination, gross negligence, and institutional failure to protect its employees. The court orders the company to pay one-million dollars in civil damages to the victim, covering lost wages, therapy, and emotional suffering. An additional $250,000 in punitive damages is awarded. Furthermore, the company is mandated to implement comprehensive reforms to its internal policies, staff training, and reporting procedures."

I turn and meet Reign's eyes, and in them, I see all the things that matter—love, pride, relief, but most of all, safety.

He pulls me into his arms right there in the aisle, and I whisper against his chest, "Let's go get that tattoo."

He laughs softly. "Wings?"

I nod. "Wings."

He gives me the smallest, surest smile, and I feel my body exhale in a way it hasn't in years.

As the judge's gavel strikes, the bailiffs move in. Alec is cuffed and wheeled past me, his jaw clenched, his eyes black with rage. He stares me down with a look that once would've chilled me to the bone, but I don't flinch or look away. I smirk, and disbelief shifts in his face. His power is gone, and he knows it.

My mother follows next, wrists shackled and expression blank, like she's still trying to understand how it all slipped through her fingers. I don't offer her a look, because I don't owe her one.

Cassandra leans over and squeezes my hand. "You did beautifully," she whispers. "It's over now."

I nod, but I don't stand until I feel Reign slide in next to me, the worn floor creaking softly under his polished shoes. His tie is a little loosened now, hair a little messy, like he's been running a hand through it all morning. In his arms is a bouquet of ballerina-pink peonies, my favourite flowers, the kind my father used to bring home when I was little.

I stare at them for a second, then up at him. "You remembered," I breathe.

He nods. "I remember everything," he reminds me. "You bloomed, Angelique. Even after everything."

My throat thickens as he presses the bouquet into my arms and leans forward, brushing his lips against my forehead. When he pulls back, he keeps his eyes on mine.

"You ready?" he asks quietly.

"Yeah," I whisper. "I'm ready."

Acknowledgments

To my readers, thank you. Whether this is your first book of mine or one of many, your support means more than words can express.

To my ARC readers, thank you for showing up with enthusiasm and open hearts. Your early reviews, encouragement, and love for these characters gave me the strength to hit publish.

To my incredible alpha reader and co-editor, Chelsea Braga, thank you for your sharp eye, your honesty, and your belief in this story. You pushed me to make it stronger in all the right places, and I'm endlessly grateful.

To every single friend who stood by me during the darkest chapters of my life, thank you. You held me when I couldn't hold myself. Your presence, your love, and your light mirrored the way Lando stood by Angelique when she needed someone the most. You know who you are. I love you. Always.

And lastly, to my husband—my love, my anchor, my wings. Thank you for being the one to teach me how to fly again. For never letting my trauma clip my spirit. For reminding me that my dreams are still mine to chase. This book—and every one after—exists because of you.

About the Author

Tanisha Headley is a Canadian romance author whose stories—whether light or dark—always centre broken characters learning to feel whole again. Whether she's writing small town slow burns or twisted, emotional roller-coasters, her books explore healing, identity, and the kind of love that wrecks and rebuilds you.

When she's not crafting characters who feel too real to be fictional, Tanisha is drinking too much tea, listening to moody playlists, or daydreaming about the next story that won't leave her alone. More often than not, though, she's climbing mountains (literally), dancing in the kitchen, or making memories with her husband and kids—the best parts of her real-life love story.

For more on Tanisha Headley, visit tanishaheadley.com

ALSO BY TANISHA HEADLEY

<u>SALTWATER SPRINGS SERIES</u>

Beyond the Break

Below the Barrel

<u>STANDALONES</u>

Teach Me to Fly